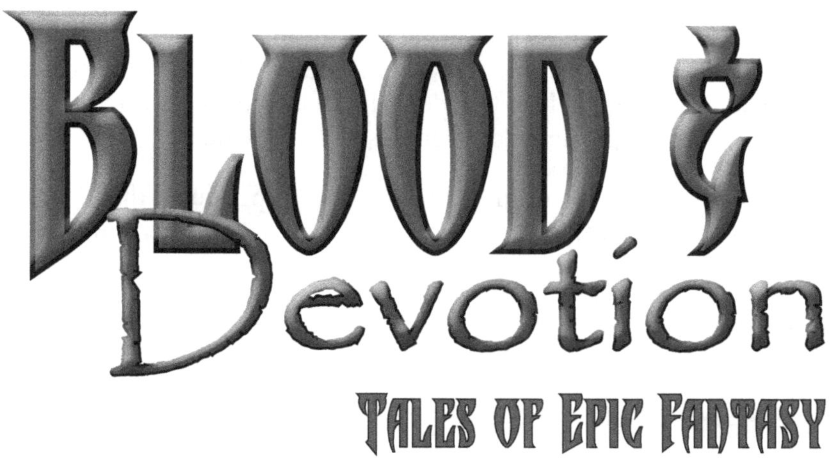

Edited by

W. H. Horner

Illustrated by

Nicole Cardiff

Wilmington, Delaware

Fantasist Enterprises
PO Box 9381
Wilmington, DE 19809
www.FEBooks.net

Designed by W. H. Horner Editorial & Design

Blood & Devotion: Tales of Epic Fantasy

ISBN 13: 978-1-934571-02-6
ISBN 10: 1-934571-02-4

First printing: January 2010

10 9 8 7 6 5 4 3 2 1

This book is available for wholesale through the publisher and through Ingram Book Group. It can be ordered for retail at most booksellers, both online and off, and is available from the publisher's website.

Fantasist Enterprises grants a discount on the purchase of three or more copies of single titles.

For further details, please send an e-mail to payments@fantasistent.com, or write to the publisher at the address above, care of "Bulk Orders."

Please interact with us on the following websites:

The FE Forum:
http://www.fantasistent.com/FORUM/

FaceBook:
http://www.facebook.com/FantasistEnt

MySpace:
http://www.myspace.com/fantasist

Twitter:
http://twitter.com/fantasistent

For my wife,
with all of my devotion.
—W.H.H.

Contents

FOREWORD

David B. Coe

I'll be honest with you. I don't understand how accomplished authors of short fiction do what they do.

I'm a novelist. In fact, I'm a novelist who specializes in multi-book projects. Extended story arcs, we call them. That's a fancy way of saying that authors like me take several hundred thousand words to tell a tale. We build worlds, develop a pantheon of characters, weave together several different narrative strands. Such writing is fun. It has its place in the market. It pays a few bills.

But when I encounter a well-structured, well-written short story—much less an entire collection of them, like this volume you're holding in your hand—I am humbled. I can build a world and make you care about its people in half a million words. The authors listed in the table of contents of *Blood and Devotion*, have accomplished the same thing in a fraction of that total. Don't underestimate the skill such a task demands.

Think of a novel as one of those towers of amethyst crystals that one sees in a mall nature shop or mineral store. It's huge, it sparkles; looking at it, one can't help but be impressed. But if a novel is such a tower, then a short story is a single crystal. It doesn't need to be part of the larger piece; it shines on its own. It's small, but multifaceted; simple, but brilliant and captivating.

Each of the tales in this anthology is a gem: sharply drawn, polished, a blend of beauty and power. And yet, like the crystals in that amethyst tower, they share certain attributes. These are tales of love and betrayal, of mythology and magic, of politics and war. To open this volume is to step into rich, complex worlds, to encounter living breathing characters, to be caught up in tales of, yes, blood and devotion. From the intriguing opening lines of Jay Lakes' "The Daughters of Desire," to the stunning climax of "Magic's Choice," by R. W. Day, this book will entertain and surprise you. It will make you think, and it will leave you hungry for more.

When I published my first novel back in 1997, fantasy was all about big, Chihuahua-crushing books in multi-book series. (Yes, "Chihuahua-crushing" is an industry term, and it strikes me as suitably self-explanatory. . . .) At the same time, there were any number of markets for short fiction, many of them popularly sold magazines.

My, how times have changed. Economy is the watchword now in genre fiction. Shelf space in bookstores is at a premium and publishers are trying to keep down production costs. As a result books are getting shorter. For most authors, the two hundred thousand word novel has gone the way of the Frodo—uh, Dodo. Over the same period, too many short fiction venues have vanished, leaving writers of shorter work with a narrowed marketplace, and devotees of short stories with fewer places in which to find them.

If this strikes you as inherently contradictory, that's because it is. While novels are becoming leaner, more concise, the medium that exemplifies these admirable qualities is vanishing. It's long been expected that young authors would cut their professional teeth on short fiction before writing their novels. Not all writers start this way—I didn't—but it is the common progression. This is why it's so important that we continue to nurture the short story market. And this is why it's so heartening to see an anthology of this quality at this particular time in the market's evolution. Fantasy needs short fiction to remain vibrant, to explore innovative narrative concepts, and to introduce readers to the next crop of writing stars. In a sense, you're holding the future of fantasy in your hands.

Themed anthologies like this one offer readers and writers alike a wonderful opportunity to explore different interpretations of words like "devotion," to delve creatively into the meaning of "magic" and "blood" and "treachery." For Aliette de Bodard ("Eye of the Destroyer") and Jay Lake, these themes led to stories of love and lust, ancient religions and the ways in which powerful gods turn ordinary people to their purposes.

In several of these stories, magic itself is the source of treachery. Such is the case with James Maxey's "Greatshadow," Peter Andrew Smith's "The Perils of Twilight" and Ian McHugh's "The Gifts of Avalae." In others—notably "Hammer Song," by K. L. Van der Veer, and "The Treachery of Stone," by William Jones—magic provides a backdrop to the interplay of human emotions with the themes of devotion and treachery. Finally, we have two stories—Gerard Houarner's "In the Light of Dying Fires" and R. W. Day's "Magic's Choice"—that explore the anthology's themes through the stark violence of the battlefield.

Throughout the book, as we step from story to story, watching the familiar themes of fealty and magic cast and recast, we sense another creative hand at work. These authors have done their part to thrill and delight. But it is the editor, William Horner, who has found them for us and gathered them into a single volume. An editor's touch in such a project is subtle, but unmistakable. We read one story and are impressed. We read a second and realize that we're in for a fun ride. And soon we come to expect that each story will satisfy. That's trust and an editor has to earn it. Horner has given us an excellent collection, and I, for one, will look forward to whatever he offers us in the future.

I can say the same about the authors represented here. A few of them I knew personally prior to reading *Blood and Devotion*. Others I knew only by reputation, and still others I'd never heard of before. I'm familiar with all of them now, and I will be looking for their next tales.

But I'm getting ahead of myself. You've yet to read this. Enough from me. You hold in your hand a volume filled with wonders—worlds to be explored, characters to be loved and hated, magic and legends and plot twists to be savored. Dive in!

—David B. Coe

The Daughters of Desire

Jay Lake

Brass apes raced through the streets of the great port city of Copper Downs, making an unholy noise of metal hammering on stone. They knuckled along with the peculiar rolling gait of their fleshly prototypes, pressure vessels shrieking as their mechanical controllers clattered through lengthy instructions punched into rolls of eelskin. Every few blocks an ape would go awry and charge into the cheering crowds to hammer itself to shards against a wall. Souvenir hunters carried away the pieces while the civic-minded cared for the wounded and tended the dead. Most people just continued to watch the races.

"By the flames, the sheer simple waste of it," Firesetter said as he watched from his rented balcony above. "So much energy, so much life, for what?"

A large man with dark hair and skin almost as red as his name, he had been created several centuries past to labor forever in service. Like the brass apes, he was a made thing. Nowadays, he traveled as a wizard, complete with the traditional kilt and ogreskin vest. Folk expected strangeness from a man who appeared so strange. Firesetter boasted sufficient skill to demonstrate his claimed profession, but his true mission was darker and deeper, hidden along with the caul of his true power.

"There's less here than meets the eye," Fantail said. A water sprite long since out of her element, Fantail was his full-time partner and sometime lover. Also Firesetter's keeper, courtesy of their distant masters in the Saffron Tower. Whatever else she was, Fantail was a supernatural beauty when she chose to display her true self, though she walked the world in the guise of a plain and natural woman. "They stage these spectacles to hide the rot at the heart of their *civitas*."

"Maybe." Firesetter let loose a rumbling sigh. "Wondrous creations made just to be broken again do not impress me. These folk of the Stone Coast invest their energies badly." A thick-muscled red arm swept wide to include the view of Copper Downs from their rooms. "The poor outnumber the rats in these streets, they are infested with monsters and gods, and their governance isn't worth hot piss."

"Wars. There have been wars."

"You'd think the locals could rebuild from those, at least. Have they no pride?"

Their view extended south toward the harbor across a quarter of high-walled compounds, some almost as large as palaces. Before the fall of the last Duke of Copper Downs, these had been the trading houses of the great factors of the Stone Coast—men, and a few women, who controlled monopolies in courtesans, artists, slaves, spices, gems, or sometimes goods more alien and obscure than those.

Though the harbor remained crowded, the city had fallen on hard times. Some of the compounds were simply burned-out shells where people, animals or worse skulked in the shadows. Many more were in disrepair, holes visible in the roofs, courtyards filled with figs and hollies gone wild from lack of tending. Others bristled with armed men watching the walls lest the race crowds surge from their appointed places.

At the edge of their view to the east of the Factors' Quarter lay the Temple Quarter. There were broken domes there as well, showing signs of riot and flame. Firesetter and Fantail had been warned on entering the city not to venture into the Temple Quarter after dark unless they fancied a divine revelation of a most personal and potentially fatal sort. That, of course, had stimulated his curiosity. He'd been interested in nothing else for two days until someone had told him of the ape races.

West, toward the other edge of their view, the land sloped up from the harbor. There was the old city wall, now clustered with little reed homes like birds' nests. Each remaining tower wore a cap of wooden balconies and verandas. Shops and houses surrounded the wall on both sides, the so-called New Districts, before petering out to orchards and croplands that rose to the Scantrock Hills. At least the New Districts seemed to have escaped the fires and god-terrors that plagued the older parts of town.

All in all, it was an uninspiring view.

The apes had passed below them. The crowd surged behind, trailing off into small streams and knots of people being herded forward by the city guard.

"This is a failed place." The brass apes depressed Firesetter. "I wish to move on."

"Our work here is not done."

"Our work here is not even *begun.* Nonetheless, I am tired of Copper Downs."

"And I am sure Copper Downs will soon be tired of you." Fantail touched Firesetter's cheek fondly. "You are a great, bumbling fool at times, but there is no one else I would rather spend my years with."

He reached for her with a sex gleam in his eye, but she danced away light as the sprite she had once been. "I am not in season for you now. Go down to the streets and hire a woman or three."

Firesetter's face collapsed into a bathetic frown. "They would not be my sweet little Fantail."

Fantail snorted. "Any woman can fan her tail for an hour or two to *your* satisfaction. I swear you were crafted from a goat."

"I am a man," Firesetter said. His manner of coming into the world had been a subject of sore feelings for decades.

"Of course you are. That's why you need a woman."

"I need to be shut of this wretched place," he growled. "Maybe then you'll come back to my bed."

"Maybe." She patted his butt. "Now go. Find some likely bowl in which to dip your wick. I must see to the details of our business here."

Down in the Bile Bucket on Nailsmith Street, Firesetter found himself a pair of sisters short on cash and shorter on moral sensibilities. One was petite and lithe, not unlike Fantail, though with brown hair to Fantail's silver. The other was colored much like her sister but taller, which meant Firesetter could exchange the kiss of bliss with her without bending his neck too far. He'd find ways to deal with the short one, he told himself. The difference in height had never seemed to trouble him with Fantail.

They drank together a while after striking their bargain. Firesetter had found over the years that this sometimes made his hired women feel less cheapened and more at their ease. Often enough they were drawn to his enormous size, curious to see if his manhood was as large and red as the rest of him. In that his creators had not failed him, nor had his penis failed the many women Firesetter had met in his journeys. The offers of men he gently declined.

"We haven't had such a one in Copper Downs since grand-dam's time, have we?" the short sister said to her tall sib. Firesetter thought her name was Solis. Her voice chirped like a morning wren. The sound was sweet at first hearing, but he suspected it would be irritating within an hour. Luckily Firesetter had other plans for Solis's mouth.

"No." Laris, the tall one, shook her head and stared speculatively at Firesetter.

"Such a what?" he asked. It seemed expected of him.

"A Red Man."

Firesetter's thoughts froze in their tracks. His pleasant warmth and burgeoning erection fled. The caul of his power descended upon him, and he felt poised on the edge of combat. Every noise was magnified so that the crackle of the fire was a holocaust, the clink of clay mugs a rockslide, the laughter of the corner table gamblers the war cry of a legion. His vision blurred slightly as objects and people around him acquired hard, glittering edges, each motion like a flare in the night. The fingers of his right hand spasmed for a sword that lay back in their rented rooms. His left drew a knife from his boot without any particular thought.

"What Red Men?" Firesetter tried to keep the power from his voice but both women shrank away.

"No-nothing," Solis said.

Laris set his coins back on the table. "You are not for us, sir."

He stabbed the knife three fingers deep into the tabletop. It quivered like a lute string. "*What* Red Men?"

Laris stood, tugging at her sister's arm. "We will go now, while there are witnesses." She put an odd emphasis on that last word. "Drink away your troubles, foreigner, but leave the women of Copper Downs alone." She glanced at Solis. "We will go offer ourselves at the Temple of Marya."

Firesetter pushed back the power, though he knew what that would bring. Under the table his fists clenched and unclenched so hard he threatened to cut open his own palms. "Ladies," he said, his voice descending into a low growl. "You cannot go to the Temple Quarter at night. Even I know this."

Solis still sat, staring at Firesetter as a bird stares at a snake. Laris tugged at her arm. "Come, sister, while he retains some sense."

"My sense is returned." Firesetter's voice was almost normal, though he was glad they could not see his hands. "For my part I release you from our bargain. Keep the coins. I have more." He summoned his courage. "I only beg this one favor of you. Please tell me of the Red Men."

Outside the caul of his power, those last words brought a stabbing ache to Firesetter's skull. Just as he had known they would.

Laris sat, one hand hovering near the money. Solis still hadn't moved. "I knew a man once," the taller sister said, "one of my first clients back when my breasts were just strawberry buds. He would take ill sometimes even as he cried out while topping me. His eyes rolled in his head and his limbs shook like trees in the wind. One of Marya's Mothers told me there was a demon in that man's head. She said I need not fear it because it ate only his soul. Do you have such a private demon in your head?"

"More . . ." The ache in his skull grew deeper. "More of a spell than a demon." His masters had ensured that Firesetter could not know his own beginnings, binding pain to his power in one looping spell. He ground out words between clenched teeth. "But much the . . . the . . . same."

"Red Men," Solis said. She appeared rapt.

"Do not say those words again, please," Firesetter managed. "Not now at least."

Laris swept the coins away then took Firesetter by the arm. He rose to follow. Solis tried once to pull the dagger out of the table, but it was set too deep for her strength, so she reached for Firesetter's other arm to help her sister walk him home.

Morning brought a drowsy half sleep to Firesetter in the pleasant light of their tower room. It also brought Fantail. She looked disgusted.

He opened his eyes further. "They were just women," he pleaded. "You sent me out for them." He had pleasant memories of the kiss of bliss in twos and threes, not to mention dipping his wick in every bowl two women had to offer.

They *had* liked his wick. With that thought, he realized Laris and Solis were gone.

"Look at yourself." Fantail picked up a brass tray and handed it to him.

Firesetter held the tray so that he could see his reflection. Two runes were written large upon his chest, and two handprints set above and below the runes. All of it done in blood.

"I am not hurt!"

"Of course not, you great oaf. That is women's magic. They drew blood from within themselves. Probably after being stabbed by that great huge prick of yours!"

He looked down at his genitals. He definitely needed to wash. Last night Firesetter had thought the cries were pleasure. They'd certainly wanted more, with enthusiasm far beyond the pretenses that the fee should have bought him.

Had they wanted blood? That *was* a pleasure for some folks.

"And that blood is mixed with your seed, no doubt," Fantail said tartly.

Firesetter couldn't help but chuckle. "Oh, and for sure." He stopped laughing at the look on her face. "What do these runes mean? How have they magicked me?"

She studied his chest a while. "I do not know their cult, but my guess is that they intend to draw you to their temple."

"The Temple of Marya."

"Ah." Fantail met his eyes. "They will set you on some task they believe suited to your mighty strength."

"And the Saffron Tower?"

"Marya is the sister-goddess we are here to send home."

He shrugged. "Kill the goddess, kill her magic."

Fantail's eyes clouded with worry. "Let us hope it is so simple. I suggest you wash yourself well before we go about our errands."

The Fathers' Tale

Long ago, the world was a garden and each race of being and kind of creature grew in neat little rows tended by the gods. Father Sunbones walked each day among them and remarked upon the health of the crop. Mother Mooneyes came by night to prune the shoots and claim the harvest.

Desire, their third daughter, was allowed to play among the fish-trees and the bird-vines, but forbidden the rows of anything that had fur or hair. "Your nature will wake them out of time," Mother Mooneyes said as they feasted in the Blue Hall of the Sky. "Stay rather with the cold waterbreathers and the thoughtless fliers who will not feel your pull."

"It is not fair," Desire complained in the manner of children everywhere.

"Nothing is fair," rumbled Father Sunbones. "We are lucky if we merely find order in this world, let alone fairness. Your brother Tide complains of being denied the fish-trees for himself. He whines constantly of fairness as he walks among the trellises where the souled ones grow."

It was the souled ones Desire wished to sport among, those with two arms and two legs and thatches of forbidden, lovely, unruly hair. Though their eyes were not yet open and their souls had not yet flowered, she imagined embracing one then another, pressing her lips to theirs, touching their bodies with hers, until she hung like they from their trellises to voice her lust to her cousins the stars.

"I know your thoughts," whispered her brother Time. "Later, I will help you."

"It is always 'later' with you," Desire hissed. "I want what I want."

"My power is in passage, not fulfillment." Her brother smiled a tiny smile of promise. "Take me for what you will."

Desire could not keep her thoughts from the men in all their colors, and the ogres and fey and sprites and all their close-kinned kind, so she sought Time in his observatory tower at that part of the day where Father Sunbones and Mother Mooneyes exchanged their pleasantries in the privacy of the horizon's blanket.

"What is this help you offer me?"

Time smiled again, the promise in his face a little larger. "Lie with me, for the fulfillment of my dreams, and I will grant you time to lie in the garden with the souled ones."

"Lie with you?" Desire laughed. "You are a stripling boy with a hollow chest and eyes as dark as Uncle Ocean's dreams." She touched her generous breasts through her shift, lifting them toward Time in mockery. "Why would I share my bounty with you?"

Time smiled again. The promise had become great. "Because Desire will always be subject to Time. Absent in an infant, unformed in a child, raging in a youth, unfulfilled in an elder. My grant of time to you will return a hundredfold in the world that is to come when Father and Mother awaken the garden."

So Desire lifted her shift above her head and showed her body to her brother Time. She was the perfection of woman, hair every color, eyes flashing so bright they were no color at all, lips as full and rich as the lily between her legs, skin smooth as a new-ripened peach. And though Time was hollow-chested and pale, and his manhood not so great, he could hold himself at stiff readiness forever if he chose—the power of his name—and so he rode his sister long into the night, until her cries of pleasure became pleas for release. For even Desire can pale of her appetites.

Eventually Time spent the last of his seed upon her breasts. He rose, tore a strip from the nail of his least left finger and pressed it into his sister's shivering hand. "Take this into the garden with you. Keep it close to your person at all times, and the time you need will be yours there."

Desire was so tired and sore that she shuddered to imagine another penis coming near her body. But she burned to put Time's promise to the test. Gathering her shift over one arm, for she ached too much to reach up and draw it onto her body, Desire limped slowly into the garden.

She smelled so of sex and fulfillment that even the cold fishes in their trees stirred at her passing. Birds thrashed on their vines, hungry for her flesh or just the hard salty scents on her breath. When Desire walked among the furred animals they strained and bellowed as they were disturbed within their dreams.

But when she came to the trellises where hung the fathers and mothers of all the souled races, their eyes flickered open pair by pair. Penises rose erect, nipples sprang from firm breasts, tongues crossed lips. Every being in that garden smelled her, wanted her, lusted for her.

In her soreness and fatigue, Desire took fright and fled to the Hall of the Blue Sky. She dropped her shift and Time's nail paring in the garden as she ran. Later when Father Sunbones came to check his crops he found the souled ones awake and the animals disturbed. He also discovered the evidence of Desire's passage and Time's complicity.

"The damage is done," Father Sunbones told Mother Mooneyes. "Our children have awakened the souled ones. The newcomers will go into the world with their spirits unformed." He wept golden tears that seared the soil.

Mother Mooneyes peeked out from the daylit heavens. "Perhaps that is well enough. Each can find his own path. Each can grow his own soul fit to suit who he is."

"But so many will be lost. Heartless, vicious, cruel."

"You name more of our children, Father. Not every child is Loyalty or Truth. Let the souled ones have their world."

Father Sunbones listened to the counsel of his wife. He threw open the gates of the garden, plucked all that they had grown there, and herded his charges into the world. The fish fell into the rivers, lakes, and oceans. The birds took wing into the spring sky of a new world. Animals bellowed and fled across the land. And the souled ones took themselves to those places that suited each best and began to make towns and farms and tell each other stories of the hot dreams that invaded their long nights' sleep.

Then Father Sunbones went to Time's observatory tower and cursed his son's disloyalty. Ever more Time's strength wanes with the year so that he passes all the pains of a life between each winter solstice. This is his punishment for lying with his sister Desire.

Then Father Sunbones went to the Hall of the Blue Sky and banished Desire to her chambers for a year and day, so that she might not come out until her brother's curse had fulfilled its first round and she could learn what had been done to him.

But Desire had quickened with Time's seed. While she stayed hidden in her chambers she gave birth to a torrent of sisters, one for each little animalcule that her brother had spent within her womb. She fed the daughters from the seed that still lay upon her breasts, so that they drank milk of both man and woman. These thousands of sisters became the goddesses of women and spread out into the world in the aid of midwives and mothers and sapphists and prostitutes and girl children everywhere.

Ever after, the gods of men made it their business to send these sisters home to Father Sunbones whenever and however they could, though it is a terrible and difficult thing to kill a goddess. The gods who were most passionate about this errand each gave a scrap of themselves to a holy order that raised the Saffron Tower in dedication to restoring the purity of souls and righting the wrongs of Desire.

Firesetter and Fantail visited the Dockmarket. Despite the name, it was in fact one of the great marts of Copper Downs. People there sold far more than shipped trade goods and fresh-caught fish.

They walked among thatched stalls that sold fittings for wagons, monkeys trained to thievery or prostitution, great gourds from far inland rumored to have magical properties, bags of raw wool, the mummified heads of clowns, brass fragments from the previous day's ape races, and much, much more.

Firesetter bought himself a string of spiced sausages and ate them one by one as they walked. The taste masked the reek of rotten fish and moldy straw that seemed to be the smell of markets everywhere. Fantail as usual declined to eat in public, but rather satisfied herself by examining the finer junk they passed—debris of times past, jewelry brought up from shipwrecks or deep diggings, and so forth.

"What do we seek?" Firesetter asked between mouthfuls of greasy pork.

"An audience." She turned over a fragment of what might have once been a metal bowl. "You will be easier for them to find out here." Smiling, Fantail set the bowl down and moved on.

He smacked his way through another link. The spices were hot but varied, and Firesetter found himself wondering exactly what pepper had been used. His chest still itched where he had washed off the runes, as if there were some sympathetic magic there echoing the scratch of the sisters' nails. "We could just go to the temple and demand admission."

"Has that *ever* worked?" She snorted. "You tried that in Parmayat. Remember?"

The Lady Goddess of Parmayat had taken exception to Firesetter's direct approach. Strong as he was, he'd survived, but several streets had burned out in the resulting fires. The two goddess-hunters had been chased out of Parmayat at spearpoint, unsuccessful in their mission.

"I guess I would do better to go in with other things on my mind."

"Like those two women last night. Just keeping thinking of tits. They'll find you. And they'll never suspect a thing."

Firesetter shifted his pace uncomfortably. He had told Fantail nothing of the onset of his power the previous evening. When Solis had mentioned Red Men—

His line of thought was interrupted by a stabbing pain in his skull.

"I am not alone in the world," Firesetter muttered, then dwelled on his memories of sharing Laris's breasts with Solis, then sharing Solis's breasts with Laris, then having both sisters suckle at his own muscled chest. The thought brought a smile to his face and purged the burgeoning ache in his skull. It quickened his groin, too, but Firesetter just adjusted his kilt and enjoyed the sensation.

A traitor voice inside his head whispered, *You are a man, not a made thing.*

Some hours later they still haunted the Dockmarket. The streets and paths had become slick with the refuse of the day. The crowds changed, too, the poorer folk coming out for the picked-over food and goods, hoping for a bargain price or at least a less vigorous chase after theft. Even the vendors had changed. The jewelers and gem cutters were gone with the wealthy morning trade, while toymakers and swordsellers had taken their place.

"Look at this," Firesetter said. He stood at a toy booth while a short distance away Fantail tested throwing knives with such verve and accuracy that several had stopped to lay bets on her casts of the blade.

"I am busy," she called.

"I mean it." Firesetter held a child's model of a castle. It was something around which wooden horses or painted lead men might rally to drive off a kitten or a troop of mice. That in itself did not interest him. Rather, the toy castle was a strange construction, with a rounded wall and single tower that curved impossibly like some great horn thrust up to the skies. It was painted yellow to boot.

Fantail stepped up beside him. "The Saffron Tower." Her voice was quiet.

"What a strange coincidence," he said.

"Hardly." She took the model from him. "Toymaker," Fantail snapped. "Why did you make this castle?"

The old man behind the booth was pale-skinned with scars of a long-ago plague, clad in some nobleman's cast-off burgundy velvet. He shrugged. "It came as part of a lot from a jobber in the New Districts. Some things I order, some things he just sends me in hopes I will order more. That is a new item. One silver obol, just for you."

She passed the old man a coin without comment, which surprised the toy vendor, then tugged Firesetter away.

"Was that wise?" he asked. "Everyone haggles. The old fellow is sure to remember us. I could go back and kill him."

"This toy was set there for us."

"Ah," Firesetter said with satisfaction. "That signal we were expecting from Marya."

Fantail whirled. Anger danced in her eyes. "What does their little whore goddess know of the Saffron Tower? This is more likely a message from farther away. From *home*."

Firesetter's sense of rebellion rippled once more into action. "'Home.' Were you born in the Saffron Tower?"

"Of course not! You know—" She stopped and stared.

"Then the Saffron Tower is not 'home.'" *Home is where the sisters' Red Men are*, Firesetter told the demon that once again invaded his head. *I am not a made thing*. The pain stabbed deeper. *I am not alone*.

Laris stepped between them, slipped her hands into the crooks of each one's arm. "I invite you strangers to walk with me a while."

The three of them approached the god-haunted Temple Quarter at dusk along Divas Street, arms still linked as they walked in silence. This did not seem the place for questions. Besides, Firesetter felt a brown study settling in amid the aftermath of his most recent bout against the pain of freedom. At an intersection with a grand boulevard leading into the quarter, a sour-faced city guardsman dipped his pike at Laris.

"Don't be going deeper than your lady's house tonight, ma'am," he muttered to her, ignoring Firesetter and Fantail. "Old Blackblood's priests been killing dogs and horses all day to keep 'imself quiet. Word is t'ain't working."

"Thank you, Settle." Laris's smile for the guardsman stirred envy in Firesetter's heart.

Then she led them along the deserted boulevard. It was strewn with the debris that came with abandonment. A single lane was swept clear by the passage of what looked to have been light foot and cart traffic. That more than anything told Firesetter what was becoming of the gods of Copper Downs. "Temple treasuries getting a bit thin?"

Laris's grip tightened on his arm and she increased her pace. "A moment. Please."

His chest itched even more, right where he'd washed the runes off. Firesetter wished he'd brought his sword and damn the peace bond they'd paid on entering the city. He wished many things. Few enough of them ever came true.

Three buildings within the Temple Quarter, counting from the left, Laris stepped into an alley. She still drew Firesetter and Fantail after her. He followed, feeling the tingle of the caul of his power.

Laris laid her hand on Firesetter's wrist. "And we are here."

"Here" was not much. A narrow door in a blank wall of glazed brick. In the last of the day's failing light, Firesetter could see the pale streaks of pigeon shit. Generations' worth. It was an old wall.

The door promised little more than the wall had. Thick planks of some foreign hardwood, it had seen the attentions of both axe and flame at various times in the past. There was no latch or lock, but the door swung open even as they stopped before it.

"The Temple of Marya," Laris said. "It would be good for us to go in now."

The whole situation smacked of hurried danger. Under most circumstances he would have walked—or fought—his way out. But Fantail seemed unperturbed. She hadn't met Firesetter's eye since Laris found them at the Dockmarket, but he put that down to feminine jealousy.

I am here to send a sister-goddess home, Firesetter thought. *What do I have to fear from entering her house?*

Everything, said the rebel voice inside his head.

Still he crossed the threshold. Someone inside would know of the Red Men.

Past the door was a room which had once been a kitchen, presumably in service of a much larger establishment. Three great fireplaces lined the outside wall by the alley. Though a squad of bowmen could have waited within each of them, only one, a small cook fire, had any flame at all. Several kettles hung on hobs and a table pulled onto the apron of the hearth held a variety of vegetables in various stages of being chopped. Judging by the gleam of candles, glass, and silver, the other two fireplaces had been made into altars, though Firesetter could mark few details in the interior gloom. It all smelled of garlic and unwashed bedding.

The rest of the kitchen had been made over into a dormitory of sorts, mixed with a counting house. Sleeping pallets lined the floor. Small desks were set in rows where the bread tables would once have stood. Even the sinks had been given over to stacks of scrolls and bound volumes.

No one was present.

Laris smiled. "Evening is when Marya's acolytes offer their most fervent devotions. Out on the streets. Her temple is always empty at this hour."

"Surely all the whores of the city are not priestesses here?"

"Of course not. Scarcely one in ten even makes offerings to Marya. Most work too hard at paying their panderers to spare coin for spirit."

Fantail almost spat her next words. "This temple is nothing more than an institution of pandering."

"Hardly." Laris reached out to touch Fantail gently, taking her hand. "You know better than this. Our acolytes' earnings mingle before the hearth to buy food and shelter for all. From the mingling they each take what they need. Women are free here, free of men's lusts and their narrow purses alike. Which is more than most goodwives or serving maids could say. Or even the daughters of noble houses."

"All women are born fricatrices," Firesetter said. "Some grow into it, some grow away from it. Some take their price with their marriage vows, others a day at a time."

"A blunt philosophy," Laris said, "and both unkind and untrue in the bargain, but perhaps you've taken my point."

"Perhaps he's an oaf who's forgotten his purpose," Fantail snapped.

Firesetter tired of the discussion. His vision had begun once more to glitter. The caul of his power was coming on. That meant the goddess must be near. He opened the knucklebone buttons of his vest and scratched his chest. "Why did you call me here?"

Laris drew herself up to height. Behind her, candles flared on the altars. "Did you not have business with the goddess Marya?"

His body shivered. The small sounds of the kitchen took on an extra sharpness. "Yes."

"And so she has business with you." Laris's eyes glittered to match the candles. "The Lady Goddess of Parmayat has spread the tale of her attackers wide."

Damnation, Firesetter thought. The goddess Marya was definitely settling into this woman he'd bedded the night before. Through her divine patron, Laris knew much of what he and Fantail were about. This would not be a simple deicide, where priestesses were left behind to cover their loss with louder prayers to empty altars.

Would he have to exterminate all of Marya's followers in Copper Downs? He doubted that was possible.

"Have you no words?" Laris demanded.

"There has been a great wrong," Fantail said. "Mistakes were made at the beginning of time, mistakes that bore fruit in the form of your goddess and a thousand of her sibs."

"You may follow those words, but you do not believe them, little sister." Laris's eyes narrowed as she studied Fantail. "I see water in your blood. This is none of your affair at all, sprite."

Fantail's knife was in her hand. "I am bound to what I am bound."

That was enough for Firesetter. He drew deep into his power. The flames rumbled within his soul. His fingertips and ears warmed with their energy. He would strike Laris and her goddess where they stood, then raze the temple.

"You are wrongly bound as well, Red Man," Laris said.

Vision rainbow-bright, ears so sharply painful they seemed to bleed, he clenched tight the flames within. "I am alone in the world." Fantail winced, but did not gainsay him. "I am a made thing."

"Words," the priestess said. "No more true of you than of the sprite."

Hot red sparks crackled from Firesetter's fingertips. "Tell me different."

Laris's smile was bitter. "You are of a kind as much as the sprite or myself. Your folk used to trade in this port. They voyaged in black ships with a fire-altar on the aft castle deck. Their sails were red with a black flame dyed large in the center. *They* were large." She glanced at his groin. "Grandmother Desire walked in the garden of the souled ones. Mother Marya was taught the list as were her sisters. There are even Daughters of Desire among the Red Men. Would you slay your grandmother, Firesetter?"

He wanted to believe. Badly. Desperately. It was an ache within his bones. The fire still crackled. Outside the glimmer of his power, Firesetter could hear the demon screaming for him to look away, close his ears. But he had never met a Red Man. Never seen or heard of one before coming to Copper Downs.

"I . . . am . . . *made.*" He tore the words from his mouth, knowing them for lies even as he spoke. They had been beaten into him in his long-ago youth in the Saffron Tower. They must have been lies. Who beats the truth into a child?

"Selistan," Laris whispered. "To the south across the Storm Sea. Where

the sun burns closer to the eyes of men and the very plants are hot. There are lakes of fire in that place which are home to the Red Men."

"Lies," Fantail shrieked, spinning a kick into Laris's knee even as her knife slashed for the priestess's neck.

Firesetter felt the power bloom within him.

The Mothers' Tale

Once, when the world was new, Mother Mooneyes ruled the skies. Father Sunbones had not yet woken to his place at her right hand as consort, but rather slept endlessly on a bed of burning sand beneath her ivory-walled halls. Mother Mooneyes sometimes went to him when she rested from her labors in the heavens. Even in his sleep she could draw forth Father Sunbones' seed to make her children.

Mother Mooneyes' favored daughter was Desire. Desire was possessed of a beauty which challenged even that of her mother. Desire's hair was the gold of summer wheat and the brown of autumn leaves and the black of winter ice and the palest rose blush of spring all at once. Her skin shone with the luster of starlight and the richness of cream. Her lips were more sweet than honey with the heady fullness of wine. Every portion of Desire mirrored the perfection of the morning of the world.

Now it happened that Mother Mooneyes kept a garden in the lands around her ivory halls. This garden held all the promise of the world to come ripening on vine and root and tree. To the east, cattle lowed and snuffled within their cradles of soil. Other beasts of the field were clustered around them, each with its own stalk and stem. To the north were the cold creatures and those on the wing, that partake of the world without fur or fang or thinking. To the south were the hot animals, those that would hunt and feast on the flesh of others once they stalked beneath the bright regard of Father Sunbones.

Mother Mooneyes knew that to harvest the garden she would have to wake her consort. Like all men, Father Sunbones would take counsel from his loins as much as his thoughts. She held that dread day in abeyance as long as possible.

In the west of the garden was the plot where the souled ones grew. Each lay at sleeping ease upon a bed of soft leaves. Each was watered and cleaned by a sweet spring. These were Mother Mooneyes' special care, that the world would be populous and happy. There were men there in all their colors and shapes, aelfkin and dwerrowkin, nixie, pixie and sprite, giant and troll—all the manifold imaginings of Mother Mooneyes' busy hands in the long shadows of the morning of the world.

Just as men had their sibs, so did Mother Mooneyes' children. Desire sported with Love and Understanding, the twins Truth and Mercy, Justice, Obedience, and all her sisters. Outside their windows along the lawns of the ivory halls, their brothers wrestled and fought and hunted each other with arrows tipped with sky-iron.

Watching the boys at their play, Desire had formed a lust for her brother Time. He was a likely lad, robust with all the years of the world on his broad shoulders. One day when Mother Mooneyes was about her travels in the heavens, Desire invited Time into her chambers.

"Brother, come, I have a game to show you," she said as they met upon the western steps. Desire licked her lips so that Time might not mistake her intent.

"Is it a manly game?" he asked, for while men are ruled by their loins, those loins have two tiny brains each no larger than an olive and thus do not think well.

Desire touched her breast and smiled. "The manliest of all." Surely he could not mistake her intent.

"Then I shall invite my brothers!" Time declared. He turned to spread the word.

Desire grasped his arm and pulled him close, and set her other hand upon his sex. "A private game of man and woman," she whispered in his ear.

At last Time came to understand what she wanted of him. He followed Desire to her chambers, but was so eager in his lust that he pushed aside both her shift and her needs with a sweep of his hand and spent himself in moments of careless thrusting. She cast him from her chamber with hard words, chasing her brother out to western steps. There he fled laughing.

Desire's breasts were heavy with need, and her loins were hot with the quick touch of her brother Time. She took herself into the west of the garden where the souled ones were couched in their rest and there she lay with them one by one, male and female alike, to slake her lusts. Each smiled in her sleep as she quickened her sex. Each murmured his thanks and slipped into the pleasant dreams of lust to which we all are heir.

Finally Desire returned to the ivory halls. Though filled with seed and the scent of all the souled ones of the garden, her loins still quivered. She went beneath the earth to her father's bed of burning sand and there took the guise of her mother. Desire rode him harder than any mortal man could bear, making her use of his godly strength, so that Father Sunbones woke fully in the midst of their coupling. Thinking he saw his wife, Father Sunbones drew Desire closer and made her body his toy in all the ways that a woman can be used.

Mother Mooneyes came home to find much moaning in the west end of the garden, and giggling among her sons. She stalked quickly into her house where Father Sunbones' radiance already painted the walls with dawn's orange glow. She found Desire coupled with Father Sunbones and in her wrath banished her daughter to her chambers for a year and day. Then Mother Mooneyes lay with Father Sunbones herself, to see if she could coax him back to sleep.

It was too late. Desire had woken the world. Men stirred in their lust and Father Sunbones rose from his bed aflame with heat and leapt to the skies. Much that is ill in this world comes from those early awakenings, but perhaps the good also. Desire's daughters were born to her in her chambers, some for each of the races of the souled ones. She taught them all she knew—the lists of who had grown in the garden, the names and powers of her brothers and sisters, the constancy of Mother Mooneyes in her unvarying cycles—and sent them into the world to watch over the women of the souled races whom she had mistakenly betrayed in her innocent lust.

Ever after the goddesses of women made it their business to shelter females from the predations of men and turn male lusts to their advantage. The marriage bond when wrought well can bind a man to woman's bed. A coin spent for an hour's fancy can at the least sap his anger away. The choice to lie only in the company of other women is another comfort and safety. Always these goddesses watch their shoulders, for there is ever an angry man or his god at the window. And so the temples of women have thick walls and heavy doors.

Flames shot from Firesetter's hands to engulf Laris. Fantail's knife caught the fire in a spray of molten steel. The sprite shrieked as she dropped the weapon, water pouring from her skin like rain from a gravid cloud.

Laris laughed through the blaze, stepping out of the flames as someone larger, more brilliant—the goddess Marya.

This was what he had trained for. Endlessly.

Firesetter flexed his hands and matched her step, leaning into the goddess so he could throttle her back to where she belonged.

Red Man, Red Man, Red Man, said the rebel voice in his head even as his grip closed upon Marya's neck.

She smiled.

Lakes of fire across the sea.

Fantail's torrents flashed to steam, clouding their little battle so that the flames flickered with eerie reflections. The kitchen-temple was a vision of a world of fire.

His hands paused in their work.

You are a man born, not made. They lied.

The powers of the Saffron Tower would spindle his guts and send him walking to his death if he betrayed them. Firesetter was sure of it. But the ghostly traces of the blood runes on his chest smoked with the scent of truth. His fingers still set firm on the goddess's throat and still she smiled.

"Stay your hands, Firesetter," said another voice. It was all the melodies of birdsong and sweet flowing water and the crisp rustle of grass.

He looked around.

Solis stood in an inner doorway, but she was not Solis. Just as Marya rode Laris into the world, so Desire had ridden Solis. The goddess was every color and size of woman, and none. She was hard-muscled and man-rough while also soft and open. She was a raging torrent of contradiction, every lust and want and liking he had ever felt in his life.

She was the mother of every goddess he had slain in his centuries of wandering.

"Grandmother," Fantail whispered. She shimmered at the edge of his vision, having gone completely into her sprite self, farther than he had ever known her to do. He saw only dancing wave and rippling water poured into the shape of a woman.

Then Fantail stepped forward and the illusion cleared. She was soaking wet, her clothing smoldering, but she was just his sweet Fantail.

He dropped his hands from Laris-Marya's neck and faced Solis-Desire. This was a goddess of such power she could take mastery of him with no more than the crook of her finger. She was another order of divine from the woman-goddesses he had hunted down the long years. The same stiff sense that had always rebelled against the Saffron Tower surged again now. "Grandmother, I will not beg your forgiveness for what I have done."

Desire smiled, which wounded him even more than her anger would have. "Forgiveness would not restore my daughters."

Fantail crouched on the floor between Firesetter and Desire with her arms spread wide. "*I* will beg forgiveness of you."

He wanted to say "no" for her, to call out, but for once in his life Firesetter held his tongue.

"I refuse." Desire kept her gaze on Firesetter, not even looking at the sprite.

Fantail wept.

The goddess raised her hands and Firesetter saw that she meant to make an end to them both. He had no doubt the death she gave him would be pleasurable, even exquisite. But he wished to live.

Even if he escaped, the Saffron Tower would have him killed. He'd learned of the Red Men of Selistan's fire lakes. He'd seen Desire's face. Despite the preaching of his masters, he now knew the goddess had done no wrong to the world. Whatever she did, it was correct. That was her nature.

And they had lied to him. About everything.

"I choose neither forgiveness nor mercy," Firesetter said as Desire gathered power to her fingers.

The goddess paused in her killing chore. "And you shall receive neither. Yet tell me Red Man, what choice do you believe remains to you now?"

"I choose to meet you on your ground." Firesetter slipped free the knucklebones that bound shut his ogreskin vest. The traces of Laris's blood-runes smoldered upon his chest though he felt no pain. "I choose to offer you what you took unbidden in the garden at the morning of the world." He dropped his kilt, touched his massive red penis, which already swelled. "I will buy your love with a coin and spend my seed upon you. If your lusts are slaked when I am finished, then we are done with one another. I will hunt your daughters no more."

"And if I am not yet slaked?" The goddess's smile was girlish and wicked at the same time.

Firesetter shrugged. "That is yours to decide." He reached down to his kilt, drew a silver obol from his pouch, and stepped forward to meet Desire with the coin between his fingers. She drew off her shift and opened up her arms to him.

Sex with the goddess was more demanding than any fight he'd ever had. Her appetites were deeper, her every muscle stronger than the swords of his enemies. Firesetter kissed lips that burned like the heart of the sun, suckled on breasts from which rivers flowed to choke him, knelt between legs that could have been the very pillars of the sky.

When Desire took the rhythm of their dance away from him, Firesetter was no more than a puppet to her whims. She whipped him bloody, rode him hard, ground him into the stones of the temple floor, until the fires that were his power erupted of their own accord to blow the walls to ash. The goddess mocked him and raised him up at the same time so that he became his own sacrifice.

When the hours of her pleasure were complete, he was spent like the bones after a feast while she smiled with stars in her teeth. In their mockery of lovers' drowse, Desire took the little yellow castle toy from his scattered things and turned it in her hand.

"These goddess-haters bind you with long chains, Red Man," she said.

Firesetter just groaned. He felt withered.

"I give you this gift." Desire closed her hand over the toy, grinding it to dust. "Their chains are riven. You are free."

Even as he heard her words, Firesetter felt the demon flee his head, shrieking into the farthest east of treachery and ruin. He closed his eyes to breathe the smoky, salty scent of freedom.

Firesetter blinked himself awake as water violently soaked his head. Fantail stood over him with an empty bucket. He felt dizzy and sick.

There were stars above him and the air reeked of smoke.

"You'd better get moving. Something that smells of dead whale is shambling around in the street."

Firesetter sat up. He had been lying in a smoldering ruin. Walls were blown down around him. Scorched roof beams crisscrossed one another, though he seemed to be in a cleared circle. It looked like one of his fires had been set.

"Gods, I had . . ." He was unable to continue. The memory was too much.

"Yes, you did."

Fantail seemed unlikely to comment further, so he accepted her help in getting up. Every muscle of his body was sore.

"She must have let me fall." It had been years since he'd felt such bruising.

"You flew. Now let's go."

He realized he was naked. "Where are my clothes?"

She laughed. It was like listening to a running stream. He'd never heard such clear joy in Fantail's voice. "Back in our rooms is the best you're going to do. Here," she added, handing him a meat cleaver with a half-burned handle. "You're going to need this."

Firesetter took the makeshift weapon. "For the dead whale in the street?"

"I doubt it's anything half so pleasant or simple."

It wasn't.

The next morning he curled in bed with Fantail and looked across the city at the New Districts. The bustle of life and commerce was much more interesting than he recalled.

"Copper Downs is not such a bad place," Firesetter said.

Fantail tossed the covers free. "Don't get used to it."

Oddly, though they were nude together, he couldn't remember making love to Fantail the previous night. There had been a nasty fight in a darkened street with something quite a bit taller and fatter than it had any business being, some demonspawn following the spoor of divine distress. He did remember that pretty well. Especially the stench, which had been the creature's most offensive weapon.

Before that . . . Firesetter smiled, though he couldn't quite get a handle on exactly what had happened. It had been like setting fire to the sun. His time with the goddess was something bigger than he could fit in his head.

And he was free. That memory found him with a jolt. "She broke the bindings," he said. "Desire, I mean."

"I know." Fantail skipped around the room, gathering clothing and weapons with a speed that spoke of ambush rather than a lazy morning's lying in. "Now we're in more trouble than we've managed before. The Saffron Tower's already got agents after us."

There was a rhythmic clanging out in the street. Firesetter jumped to his feet and ran to the balcony. Three of the brass apes approached at speed, their gait thrown off by the great hammers each carried.

He was pretty sure he knew where the apes were heading.

"You're right," he said. "Time to go." Firesetter quickly donned his second-best kilt from the traveling chest at the foot of the bed. Then he tore the peace bond from his sword.

As they clattered down the stairs, Firesetter called over his shoulder, "I suggest a trip to Selistan."

"Selistan?" Fantail said. "It's hot there."

They burst out into the street.

"I know. I like it hot," he shouted, stepping under the wild hammer blow of the first brass ape to stab at its joints.

Hammer Song

K. L. Van der Veer

The runes on the blade glowed silver-white, and with each blow of the hammer, the light intensified. Amren hummed, his deep voice filling in the melody around the rhythm suggested by hammer and anvil, calling the runes into being. The hammer rose and fell. Power coursed through Amren's being and pulsed down his arm. With a final, resounding ring, the runes flared a brilliant white-gold, then faded to mere grey lines on the blade—scars marking the severing of creation from creator. Amren drew a deep breath and let the last strains of the crafting wash through him, leaving behind a warm peace. Just a little magic was all anything needed to strengthen it, to make it special. This sword possessed a little bit more. It lacked but a name. He traced a finger over the runes, letting the subtle tingle of craft focus his thoughts—

"Papa! Papa!"

Amren looked up and blinked away the fog of the magic-weld. Esyllt stood in the doorway of the smithy, finally heeding his warnings about hot metal and stray magic. Her lower lip was clenched tight between her teeth, but she bounced in excitement. Her short tunic and knee-breecs bore the dark battle scars of a tumble in the mud. In one grubby hand, she wielded a forked stick. Amren shook his head. She had been catching snakes again. At some point, weren't little girls supposed to despise dirt and wiggly things? He wiped sweat from his eyes with the back of a hand no cleaner than his daughter's and smiled.

"Papa—" Esyllt pushed back her tousle of golden hair. "A knight—in front—his shield's brokened and he felled off his horse! Mama said fetch you!"

Amren's peace drained away, replaced by a chill knot. He snatched the longsword off the anvil, hefted it for a moment in one massive hand, then ran out the smithy door. "Esyllt, stay here." A knight? Had the border skirmishes between Iserterre and Pandour flared up again? The Kophalen Hills had always been disputed territory, from King's Pass all the way to the sea. But then, that was just a pretext for the animosity between Iserterre and the Lyfeian Sovereignty.

Amren rounded the front porch and ran past the flower garden where Catrien had been working that morning. A barded, grey warhorse stood in the middle of the dirt track that led to their house. Two score yards past the horse, a knight in full plate armor lay unmoving against the great oak by the lane. Catrien knelt in front of him, head bent forward. Her long golden hair cascaded down over her arms, and her delicate hands, swathed in a misty amber light, rested on the knight's breastplate.

Amren slowed. He was built for swinging things, not running, and he was already breathing hard. Besides, he didn't want to startle Cat while she was deep in her healing. The mist snaked its way around the fallen man's body in long, glowing streamers. Wherever it encountered a gap or joint in the armor, it seemed to wriggle beneath the steel. Soon, golden light radiated from every opening.

"See, Papa!" whispered a small voice at Amren's side as he reached the horse. "It's a knight! Just like the one I dreameded about . . . in the fire with Mama . . ."

"Esyllt, I thought I told you to stay in the smithy."

Esyllt nodded, still staring at the knight. "He looks hurted, but Mama will fix it."

Amren took up the reins of the horse and handed them to Esyllt. "Here. Take his horse back to the house and tie it to the porch . . . and stay there." He walked slowly toward Cat and the knight. Esyllt followed, horse in tow.

The knight's shield lay face down in the grass a few yards away. Amren knelt, resting the sword against his shoulder, and lifted the shield out of the dirt. He turned it over and brushed it off. It was dented and gouged, and some of the lacquer was blistered and peeling as if it had been in a fire, but the markings were plain enough—two arms, hands closed into fists, armored and interlaced on a black field—men of the Iron Hill, an unaligned border territory to the north. But a pair of white wings flanked the arms. Those belonged to an order of knights far to the east called the Sons of Dawn. They called themselves paladins and were rumored to be Sidhehana, fey blood. Their own blazon was simply a pair of white wings, but a resident paladin often took the coat-of-arms of his host and added the wings. Apparently, the Iron Hill was not so unaligned, anymore.

The glow around the knight faded and Catrien slumped. Amren dropped the sword and shield and rushed to her side. She lay on the ground, shivering despite the day's warmth. Healing always drew the heat out of her. He knelt and gently scooped her onto his lap. Her skin was icy, but her face reflected only peace.

"Cat?"

No response.

Amren stroked her cheek. "Catrien?"

Catrien opened her eyes and smiled. "I'll be fine," she whispered, though she closed her eyes again. "He was sorely wounded. I wasn't sure I could save him."

For the first time, Amren took note of the extent of the punishment inflicted on the man's armor. It was scored and battered, and the left side was scorched—like his shield. His visor remained in place, hiding his face.

With a rattle of steel, the paladin lurched forward. Amren fell backward, rolling to shield Catrien with his body. The paladin scrambled to his knees. His hand went first to the empty loop on his belt, likely where an axe or mace once hung, then to his chest and head, as if surprised to find everything whole. Relaxing somewhat, he cautiously lifted his visor and looked around. "What has happened? Where am I?" He appeared young, but his voice had a composed, confident quality that suggested experience.

"You are at the forge of Amren d'Kort," Amren said, climbing to his feet and helping Catrien up. "Just north of the village of Coane."

Relief washed over the paladin's face. "I know that name. Some of the ironwork and arms in the Iron Hill bear your mark. I'm still in the Hills, then."

"Yes. My wife has healed you of your wounds."

"Then she wields powerful magic, for I was swiftly departing this life. Mi'lady, I thank you for its timely return and praise the Light for its gift to you."

Catrien shook her head. "No thanks are necessary, sir. We don't take sides in the Hills, and my gift has no value if it is not shared. In truth, I have but mended the worst of your injuries. You are not yet hale and should rest. We have room, and I'll be starting supper soon. . . ."

Amren pursed his lips. "Sir, I don't mean to. . . . Are there more knights behind you, Pandourian militia or Iserterrian shields?"

"Amren!" Catrien swatted his arm.

The paladin held up his hand. "Your husband is right to be concerned," he said, climbing unsteadily to his feet. "I am alone . . . now . . . but the

Lyfeians will most likely be seeking me. You have done enough, and it will serve us all best if I speak no further to you and take my leave now. You can tell anyone who inquires that you saw but a lone knight from the Iron Hill." He climbed stiffly into the saddle and exchanged a broad grin for the reins handed up by a beaming Esyllt.

Amren picked up his sword and returned the paladin's shield. An air of calm purpose seemed to radiate from the knight as he settled the battered shield on his arm, and again the blazon with the white wings caught Amren's eye. Maybe the knight was Sidhehana, maybe not, but he had already demonstrated a kindness beyond many in the Hills. Amren held out the sword. "Here, sir," he said. "Take this. It isn't quite finished, but it may see you safely home."

The paladin looked as if he were about to refuse but then took the sword and studied the blade. He cast an appraising eye on Amren. "Thank you, sir. It just may at that. Your service will be remembered when next I visit Iserterre's heart." He slid the blade through his belt, then clucked to his horse and set off down the lane at an easy pace towards the woods.

Amren watched him ride away. So, the Iron Hill hosted a paladin, and the paladins were also friendly with Iserterre. The pretense of a border dispute would soon dissolve. Iserterre clearly was not going to join the Lyfeian Sovereignty or submit to the guidance of the church. The Sovereignty would view that as a challenge to their faith, which they could not let stand. Not for the first time, Amren wondered if life under the Sovereignty would be all that bad. He had visited cities in Pandour and Lecarra, and, for the most part, both kingdoms seemed free to govern themselves as long as they pledged first loyalty to the Holy Rite. He wasn't particularly anxious to join them, but peace in the Kophalen Hills had always been about walking the knife's edge, and the Iron Hill may have just sent all of them over it.

The nameless paladin hadn't ridden thirty yards when a squad of six armored knights wearing the black and white raiment of the Lyfeians cantered out from beneath the shadow of the wood at the end of the lane. An ivory-robed domini rode in their midst. Both the Lyfeians and the paladin paused for a moment; then, the paladin drew Amren's sword and charged.

Four of the Lyfeian knights moved to protect the domini. The other two spurred their mounts forward and lowered their lances. The paladin swept aside the lance on his right with the sword and rolled his left shoulder back, letting the lance on his left slide off his battered shield. His pivot brought his sword forward, and he drove the point into the breastplate of the knight to the left. Fire flared from the tip and the breastplate split. As the Lyfeian toppled backward off his horse, the paladin yanked the blade free and galloped straight toward the domini.

The other knights rushed forward, but the domini raised his hand. The daylight seemed to dim. Amren blinked, trying to clear his vision. Beside him, Catrien staggered and put a hand to her head. There was a bright flash, and a gout of white fire arced from the domini's hand. Amren's eyes stung, and the air burned in his throat and lungs. The fire struck the paladin in the chest. He tumbled from his saddle and lay unmoving in the dusty lane, smoke curling up from his armor.

The domini rode to the fallen Lyfeian and dismounted. He was tall, almost as tall as Amren, but older and balding. The other knights reined up beside him as he knelt and held a hand out over the still form. A white light spread out from his palm and enveloped the knight, growing in intensity until Amren had to squint and shield his eyes with his hands. When it faded, nothing had changed. The fallen Lyfeian did not stir or draw breath. The domini shook his head and rose. He walked to the smoldering paladin and picked up the blade Amren had forged. He studied it for a moment, then looked to Amren and Catrien. His pale blue eyes were hard and cold.

"Go inside," Amren whispered. "Take Esyllt with you."

Catrien grabbed Esyllt's hand and turned.

"Hold!" the domini called. Two of the knights spurred their mounts forward, swinging around between Catrien and the house. The other knights drew up in a circle around them. Amren pulled his wife and daughter close, folding his great arms around them both.

The domini led his horse forward and stopped several yards away from them, holding the sword. "You will tell me what you know of that Iron Hill knight," he said softly. "When last I saw him, he had not the strength to fight." He held up the sword. "Nor did he bear such a weapon."

"We know nothing," Amren said, "not even his name. He rode in wounded not half an hour ago and collapsed by that tree. My wife is a healer. She mended his wounds as best she could, and he took his leave."

"And this?" The domini held up the sword.

What had he been thinking, offering the knight that sword? Amren searched for safe words, but he'd already taken too long in answering. No lie would pass now. He sighed. "I made it. I'm a smith."

The domini's brows rose. "Oh! And quite the smith too." He ran his fingers over the runes on the blade, then looked at the knights around them. "This," he said, "is why we cannot allow magic to run wild in the hedges beyond the Sovereignty! Magic is a holy gift, but the uninitiated are not discerning in its use! Would that we had more sway in these lands. There is talent here that would benefit all, could it be brought into our fold." The domini rubbed a hand over his balding head and stared, first at Amren, then Cat, as if looking for something. "At least we can bind their magic to the service of the Light to keep them from doing further harm. I will administer the crae'ath." He put the sword down and held out his hands to Catrien. "Mi'lady, you first."

Catrien shook her head, trembling.

Even outside of the Sovereignty, most people had heard of the crae'ath. The dominii strictly controlled the use of magic. When it was wielded to the detriment of others, the guilty faced two options, death or the crae'ath—an oath bound by magic that restricted or prevented the use of magic. "No!" Amren said. "She bears no ill toward the Sovereignty! She sought only to help a wounded man."

"I understand," the domini said, "which is why this is necessary. It will help her not to make such mistakes again." He beckoned to the knights. "Bring her."

Two knights dismounted and approached, warily eyeing Amren who was half again their size, even in armor. When they reached for Cat, Amren turned, shielding her and Esyllt with his body.

"My good smith," the domini said, not unkindly, but he waved a hand and two more knights dismounted and stepped around in front of Amren. "Don't make this difficult."

"Wait!" Catrien shouted. "Don't hurt him! I'll take the oath." She turned to face Amren and whispered, "It'll be okay. We'll take the oath, they'll go, and we'll live in peace." She touched Amren's cheek as she backed away and knelt before the domini.

Amren picked up Esyllt. "Is there going to be more fire, now?" she whispered.

"No," Amren said. "She just has to make a promise not to hurt any of these men or their friends." Esyllt buried her head in his shoulder.

The domini placed his hands on either side of Cat's head. "*Ande litha tante vira.*" His hands began to glow. "What you swear, shall be bound to your life. You shall not use your healer's magic to restore any but those loyal to Lyfaye *and* the Sovereignty."

"No . . ." Amren whispered.

"No!" Catrien said. "I can't do that!" Tears streamed down her face.

"Yes," the domini said, "you can, and you must. Your life depends upon it."

"I can't." Catrien wept into her hands. "I can't." Suddenly, she looked up at the domini, tears gone. The air around her seemed to sparkle with golden motes of crystalline light. They twinkled and danced as they swirled together, forming a golden cloak around her.

Amren's heart pounded. What was she doing? Then, his eyes began to burn, like when the domini—"No! Cat!" he screamed, setting Esyllt down and taking a step forward.

Cat turned toward Amren, trembling. Green light shone behind her eyes. *I love you*, she mouthed. The golden sparkles spiraled into the air and vanished as green flame erupted from her skin.

"Caaaaat!" Amren put Esyllt down and rushed forward, but she was gone. Only a trace of grey-black ash remained where she had knelt. He fell to his knees and put his hand to the still-warm ground. Tears welled in his eyes. "Cat . . ."

"Now," the domini said, "*you* will take the crae'ath."

Amren looked up, tears blurring his vision. The two knights on either side of the domini must have read the rage in his face for they stepped in front of him. Amren growled and rushed forward. He slammed a fist into the breastplate of the knight on his left, denting the steel and knocking the man to the ground. The other knight reached for his sword. Amren grabbed him before the blade cleared the scabbard and heaved him off his feet. The knight crashed to the ground in a sprawl of armored limbs.

A lance tip swung in front of Amren. He grabbed the shaft and yanked. The knight tumbled from the saddle. Amren swung the butt end of the lance around with both hands and knocked another knight from his feet. The wood shaft splintered. He shifted his grip on the remains of the lance and lunged at the domini. Before he could strike, a jolt like thunder slammed through him, throwing him to the ground.

Amren gasped for air. Each breath seared his lungs. He opened his eyes, but saw only flashes of light. When at last his vision cleared and he could breathe again, he struggled to his hands and knees. The domini hadn't moved. The knights had regained their feet and stood with swords in hand but well back from Amren.

"I understand your pain," the domini said, his cold eyes anything but understanding, "but it was her own fault. Once the crae'ath is begun, it must be completed. By seeking to use her magic, your lady recanted, and Lyfaye judged her. It is your turn."

Amren shook his head.

The domini nodded toward the house. Amren turned. A knight held Esyllt with a dagger at her throat.

"You will," the domini said, "or your daughter will die."

Amren knelt.

"*Ande litha tante vira.*" The domini's hands glowed. "What you swear, shall be bound to your life. You shall forge no weapon against the Sovereignty, bear no blade against it, nor take the life of a defender of the Holy Rite. Swear it."

Amren simply stared straight ahead. He could crush the domini's throat before he could summon his magic . . . he was sure of it. But Esyllt was too far away. . . .

"Swear it!"

"I swear."

"*Sinun sana oni tanta.*" There was a bright flash of light and Amren felt as if a door had closed somewhere inside.

The domini stepped back. "You have made a wise choice, smith." He picked up the longsword Amren had forged, turning it so the light played across the runes. "It would have been a shame to lose you. You do good work. We shall call on you, again." He motioned to the Lyfeian knights and they mounted up. "You may keep the Iron Hill horse for your loss." He swung into his saddle and, with the remaining knights, rode down the lane and into the trees.

Amren sat and stared at the ashes. A cold numbness crawled through him. She was gone. She had been tending her garden . . . now she was gone. He put his head in his hands. They completed each other. How could she just be gone?

He heard a sniff behind him and turned. Esyllt stood, tears in her eyes, staring at where her mother had knelt. She looked so much like Cat. Amren climbed to his feet and gathered her up. "Let's take you inside," he said, "then I'll. . . . Let's just get you inside."

He took Esyllt inside and sent her to wash up and find some clean clothes—something to keep her busy—then went out to the shop to look for something to put Cat's ashes in. He couldn't just leave them on the ground. If he could just find something—a box or . . . something.

He saw a hammer lying on the large anvil and picked it up. They'd be back. He tapped the hammer on the anvil. It voiced a discordant clang. And he'd be forging weapons for Cat's murderers. . . . He turned and flung the hammer against the wall, fighting new tears. And they would keep coming back. . . . He picked up the smaller anvil and heaved it into the tool rack. It went down with a loud clatter. Until he'd used his craft to make enough magical swords for their whole damn army. . . . Sobs wracked Amren as he grabbed a sledge and pounded his workbench into splinters.

A splash of color caught his eye, and he paused mid-swing. Over the workbench hung a burgundy silk pouch. Dropping the sledge, he reached out and took it down. Carefully, gently, he opened it. It held dried rose petals. Cat had brought him some roses from her garden once in an attempt to introduce some color to the sooty shop. Then she'd made him the pouch saying that he could only have dried flowers—his shop wasn't fit for live ones. He clutched it tight and smiled in spite of himself.

"Papa?"

Amren turned. Esyllt stood in the door with a doll Cat had made from some clothes Esyllt had outgrown.

"You brokeded everything."

Amren wiped a tear from his eye and knelt. Esyllt shuffled over. "Papa . . . is a little angry," he said, then noticing the worry etched on Esyllt's face added, "at those men."

Esyllt nodded.

Amren brushed a stray lock of hair out of her eyes. The Lyfeians would keep coming back. There would be no peace here . . . for him or his daughter. "Esyllt, go back inside and get your things together. We're going on a journey, tomorrow."

"Where we goin'?"

"Avidan. In Iserterre . . ."

King Belimawr sat on his throne with the scorched and battered shield across his lap and scratched his thick, black beard. Though large and powerfully built, Belimawr was somehow not overbearing, and his eyes held a vibrant sparkle that had immediately made Amren comfortable telling him everything. When they'd arrived in Avidan, Amren had had no real plan. He'd loaded his wagon with enough tools that he could probably find work as a smith, if it came to it, but he had no sooner presented the shield to a soldier wearing the lion blazon of Iserterre than he found himself ushered before the king himself.

"I do not suppose," the king said at last, "that you know what has befallen the Iron Hill?"

"No, sire," Amren said. "We only saw the one knight. He gave us neither his name nor an accounting of what led him to us, and we did not dare venture near the Iron Hill when we left, not after . . . " Feeling his voice break, he paused. To his relief, the king waved away the rest of his response.

Belimawr laid the shield on the floor beside his throne. "So, they have set the dominii on us, at last. I was wondering how long our friendship with the Sidhehana would go unrewarded. The Lyfeians would sooner destroy them for a rumored taint of magic than determine if that rumor holds any truth. And to think they both serve Lyfaye." He heaved a great sigh. "I am very sorry for your loss, Master Amren. You will be well rewarded for bringing me this news, though I know I cannot replace what has been taken from you. You may also find it some comfort to know that Iserterre will not bind itself to the Sovereignty's Holy Rite. . . ."

Holy Rite, indeed. Amren felt the anger rising again. That and a deep sadness had seemed to be the extent of his emotions these last several days. The Lyfeians' oath was living torture, worse than death, for some. The image of Cat kneeling before the domini flashed unbidden in sharp clarity, long golden hair flowing off her shoulders. People were *alive*, but she had been life itself. He touched the silk pouch that hung around his neck. It held the rose petals and the little he had been able to gather of Cat's ashes. This couldn't be the end. "Begging your pardon, sire," he said. "I didn't come here seeking a reward. The peace the Sovereignty offers is the peace of the grave, for the spirit if not the body. They must not cross the Hills. I would offer my services to Iserterre."

"Indeed!" Belimawr's laughter boomed through the hall. "I apologize, my good smith. I do not mean to make light of you. You are a bold man, but by your own telling, you are bound by more than words to forge nothing that can be used to strike at the Lyfeians. Nor can you wield a sword against them. Besides, I already have a mastersmith." Nonetheless, the king leaned forward, furrowing his brow. "What exactly would I do with you?"

"I would try, my liege. We are far from the Sovereignty here. Perhaps the crae'ath is not so strong. I am a good magic welder. At the least, I am a good smith."

Belimawr lifted a sword from where it hung on the throne. He drew the blade. Light shimmered down its length, and Amren thought he saw the dull lines of runework. The king stretched out his hand, extending the hilt towards Amren.

"What do you think of this?"

He was being tested. Without even touching the sword, Amren could tell the blade was finely wrought. But the runes had been etched too deeply, probably made as a guide for the magic instead of growing from it. He took the sword, and his hand tingled slightly, confirming the modest power suggested by the runes. And there was something else, something he'd never felt when handling another magic welder's work. Its essence was that of a background melody. He concentrated on it, hearing it in his mind but trying not to hum aloud. His own craft stirred in response, and he reached out with it gently. In a rush, the sword's magic opened to him as if he had forged it himself. The blade was stronger than a normal sword and, when in motion, would feel lighter to the bearer. He even felt the nature of the magic weld, not really weaker than his own, but more rigid, constrained, bound around the runes rather than knitted with the steel. And . . . Caniad. Its name was Caniad.

"Mastersmith?"

Amren started. Sweat ran down his forehead. "It's fine craftsmanship, sire," he said, turning the blade over in his hands, "but the magic is not as well rooted as it could be. The strength and speed of the blade are certainly great assets, but if—" Amren saw Belimawr's frown and realized that he was not only criticizing the king's sword but saying far more about it than he should know just from handling it. "I'm sorry, my liege," he said as he handed the sword back. "I was just thinking out loud. It is a fine weapon."

The king slid the sword into the sheath and hung it back on the throne. "You obviously believe it could be better. But you are observant and forthright with what you think. Those two traits in combination are rare." Belimawr leaned back and tapped his fingertips together before him. After a moment, he brought his fists down on the arms of the throne. "Very well. Eimon!" he bellowed.

A wiry young man stepped out from among those gathered at the side of the throne.

"This is Eimon, my seneschal. Eimon, find this man and his daughter lodging and then take the good smith to Moren's forge." Belimawr's eyes narrowed as he studied Amren. "Let's see what you can do."

Eimon led Amren and Esyllt to the ring of large houses encircling the hill on which the castle stood. "Dahme Rhiain Torguardan. Her husband was Sir Kelyn Torguardan," Eimon said as they walked, "a knight banneret from the Circene Mountains in the northwest. He died holding King's Pass against the northern tribes nearly a score of winters ago. For a while,

Dahme Torguardan continued to maintain and defend their keep, until her son came of age to succeed his father. By that time, she'd had enough of the border marches and. . . ."

Amren tried to pay attention, but his thoughts drifted back to his experience with the king's sword. Anyone with the craft could sense a magic weld, but that should have been it, just a sense that magic was present. Could the rest be a side effect of the crae'ath? He couldn't believe that the dominii would like having people running around who could read the nature of any magic they encountered. But if it wasn't the crae'ath, then what was it?

They crossed a stream that flowed down from the hill, and Eimon turned up a stone walk flanked by flower gardens that Cat would have been proud to call her own. The walkway led to a generous, two-story manse of stone and rough-hewn timbers. Wrought iron vines framed the tall, narrow windows, but not a hint of rust showed. The house was apparently as well cared for as the gardens. The seneschal walked straight to the ironbound, oak door and knocked. An older, but still handsome, woman answered.

"Dahme Torguardan," Eimon said, leaning forward in a slight bow, "I bring you two guests of the king in need of lodging. Master Amren d'Kort and his daughter, Esyllt. I need to get Amren over to Moren's, but I thought perhaps the little lady could visit with you now." Eimon leaned forward and whispered something to the dahme.

She looked at Esyllt and a sadness flitted across her eyes. Then she smiled and knelt. "Esyllt, is it?"

Esyllt nodded.

"Come in, dear. Moren's is no place for a proper lady. Would you like to see my garden?"

Esyllt looked up at Amren. He reached out and tousled her hair. "Go ahead. I'll be back by dinner."

She smiled and took the hand offered by the dahme.

"Thank you," Amren said. "I. . . . It's. . . . We're grateful. Thank you."

"It is my pleasure, Master Amren. My home has been wanting for guests." She made a shoeing gesture with her free hand. "You go do what you need to. We'll be just fine." She turned and led Esyllt inside.

As the door to the manse closed, Amren turned and followed Eimon back out to the road. Eimon guided him down through the city proper to the artisan quarter. Overall, Avidan seemed better kept than most cities. The broad streets were busy but clean. Both the stone-cobbled main avenues and the hard-packed dirt side streets looked to be well maintained.

All the shop fronts they passed were neat and orderly with signs and shutters painted not too long ago. Their route paralleled the stream, and even it remained reasonably clear and fresh as it ran through the city.

"Here we are," Eimon said, pointing. "Just up ahead there."

Amren stopped and gaped in awe at the smithy—two long stories of stone built next to the stream. A millrace diverted water that turned two undershot water wheels. The ring of hammers on anvils, at least half a dozen, cut through the noise of the street.

"Our smithy and armory are combined," Eimon said. "Master Moren runs the whole works. He's a hard man to please and a bit gruff, but he knows metal—iron, steel, gold, copper. He'll grumble and complain, but he'll see you are set up with what you need."

One of the large doors was chocked open to let in the breeze, and they stepped inside. No fewer than a score of men worked in the shop—some working the forges, others shaping plates for armor, still more filing, grinding, and polishing, or shaping the wood or leather needed to finish a piece. The water wheels pumped the bellows to two large forges, and secondary gearing suggested they also raised the giant tilt-hammers that hung over massive anvils. Several smaller forges, numerous small anvils, and even a small oven were scattered among the workbenches and racks of tools. Amren had never seen the like. One man, older than the rest and shorter, with a shaved head and a short, dark beard, hustled between forges, gesturing wildly and cursing. His temper appeared to match his height.

"That's Moren," Eimon said.

Amren nodded grimly.

When Moren glanced their way, Eimon beckoned to him. The mastersmith swore and stomped over, a scowl fixed on his face. He was still several paces away when a familiar wave of craft rolled over Amren. This was the forger of the king's sword. He shouldn't know that, shouldn't feel anything from Moren at all, and yet it was as clear to Amren as if he had witnessed the forging himself. But if Moren sensed anything similar, he gave no sign.

"Mastersmith Moren," Eimon said, "this is Mastersmith Amren. His Majesty would like you to give him some space to work for a few days."

Moren's scowl deepened. "Does it look like I have any extra space? If I had space, I'd hire a real smith instead of these ungrateful apprentices that have been foisted on me by parents who have given up any hope of shaking talent of any other sort out of them."

Eimon pointed to an empty forge. "No one's using that one."

"I'm using that one . . . if I can ever get these ungifted bastards to learn how to treat steel. You'd think they were beating a snake with a rock!"

"Master Amren is a magic welder," Eimon said, undaunted. "His wife was slain by a domini, and he was made to take the crae'ath. He wants to see if he can still forge a weapon to strike at them."

Moren looked hard at Amren. "Magic welder, eh? Don't much like the Lyfeians? Maybe we can work something out." He scratched his beard. "I don't have to give him room and board, do I?"

"No. He's staying at Dahme Torguardan's manse with his daughter."

"Well then, maybe you can use that forge over there . . ." Moren nodded toward the one Eimon had pointed out. ". . . and any of the tools. I apparently can't leave these louts unattended for a minute, anyway." As if to prove his point, one of the apprentices dropped an iron as he took it out of the fire. "Gryn!" Moren shouted as he stomped off. "What the blazes are you doin' boy! You have to hold onto it! Drop it and you lose the heat! Or you burn the place down! Damn, boy! With a grip like that it's a wonder you don't starve to death for dropping yer food!"

Eimon sighed. "That's about all the welcome you'll get. I suggest you just get started. If you need anything else, send someone to fetch me. I'll see that your things are brought over to Dahme Torguardan's."

Amren nodded and walked hesitantly over to the forge. He wished he had thought to bring a few of his own tools, but he could get them later. He stuck a long iron suitable for a sword blank in the fire and looked over the rack of hammers, hefting first one, then another. An older, short-handled, cross peen felt right in his hand. He set it on the anvil and began to pump the bellows.

As the iron heated, he watched Moren stomp around the shop, yelling and waving his arms. He'd never felt craft in another person before, and Moren hadn't seemed to notice anything. It had to be the crae'ath. There was no other explanation. Something must have gone wrong. He just hoped it meant he could wield his own magic.

After a few minutes, he drew the glowing iron out of the fire and slid it onto the anvil. He tapped his hammer on the anvil a couple of times, finding a rhythm, and reached for his craft. Immediately, an unfamiliar tightness closed around his chest. Pushing the discomfort aside, he raised the hammer. Magic surged through his arm as the weld took shape in his mind. The hammer struck the tip of the glowing iron. There was a bright flash, and Amren was thrown backwards to the ground. Fire seared his chest and ripped the breath from his lungs. He rolled to his hands and knees gasping for air. He looked up and shook his head. The anvil had cracked and the iron burned white on the floor, hissing and spitting sparks. He sat back on the floor and put his head in his hands. The shop was silent.

"What the blazes!" Moren's stomps followed his voice. "What'd you do, lad? I've never seen anyone channel that kind of craft! Look at that anvil!"

"I'm sorry," Amren said. "I'll buy you a new anvil . . . or work it off. It doesn't seem the bond of the crae'ath diminishes with distance."

Moren chewed on his lip, his fire apparently stolen with Amren's offer to replace the anvil. "Well enough, then," he said, though he still looked uncomfortable. A clang behind the mastersmith ended the awkward moment, and Moren turned, swearing before he even saw the cause.

Amren hauled himself up. He picked up the hissing metal with a pair of tongs and dropped it into an iron water bucket. Steam boiled up as he stuck another iron in the fire and reached for his hammer. So much for the crae'ath being flawed. He had been able to draw on his craft when he'd studied Belimawr's sword, but then he hadn't been using it in a manner contradictory to his oath, either.

Throughout the rest of the afternoon he tried making normal blades with similar, if much less destructive, results—the metal would burn and the pain in his chest would force him to cease his efforts before he could rough out the shape of a sword. He tried making a knife, telling himself it might only be used for hunting, but the crae'ath knew the lie.

With each failure, the need to prove himself grew. It wasn't that he cared what Moren and the other smiths thought. He needed to know for himself whether he could ever work magic through the rhythm of the hammer again. At last, he turned his attention away from weapons and simply concentrated on the craft. He succeeded in making a pen-annular brooch that was attuned to magic and would glow in its presence. It was a small victory, but it eased his heart somewhat. Moren examined his work and grunted before turning to yell at one of the apprentices. Amren took that as high praise.

By the time he dragged himself back to Dahme Torguardan's, it was getting dark. Uncertain of whether he should just walk in, he knocked at the door. A young man—a servant, Amren guessed—opened it, and the smell of roast fowl, potatoes, and baked apples wafted out. Amren's stomach growled, reminding him he hadn't eaten since before meeting the king. The servant showed Amren through a large dining hall where a long, polished table sat empty, to a smaller, cozier room where a simple but sturdy table was set for three. Esyllt was already sitting and Dahme Torguardan was fussing with a wildflower arrangement on the table.

The dahme looked up and smiled. "Here he is now," she said, "good as his word."

"Dahme Torguardan, you don't—"

"Oh, don't be so formal. It's Rhiain. Eimon's a good lad but he makes too much of titles, ranks, and lineage . . . just Rhiain."

"Yes, ma'am," Amren said, "but you don't have to go to all the trouble with supper. Esyllt and I can manage. You've put yourself out enough with the room, and—"

"Nonsense. It's been a long time since I've been able to set a proper table, and besides, I have servants to help. I was about to have Esyllt go ahead and eat, so you're just in time, although . . ." Rhiain paused and looked him over, frowning.

Amren followed her gaze. His hands and arms were streaked with soot, and his clothes were stained and still damp with sweat. "Umm. I think I'd like to change first."

Seemingly satisfied, Rhiain took a carafe from a servant and began filling the mugs, herself. "Eimon came by again with your things. Your wagon and tools are in the carriage house. The rest is upstairs, second door on the left. If you want to wash up first, there's a cistern out back." She gestured toward the kitchen.

Amren nodded and stepped through the kitchen and out into the back yard. A stone walk led through a well-tended garden, mostly flowers that he couldn't name and a few fruit trees. He did recognize the rose bush that climbed up the cistern just outside the door. He reached out and touched one silky, red petal. Sometimes the smallest thing made it feel like Cat was still there. He picked up the copper basin leaning against the cistern and dipped out water that was warm from the afternoon sun. As he washed off the grime of the forge, the many failures and lone success of the day crept back into his mind. He had to find a way to strike at the Sovereignty. They could not take Cat and not pay. And Esyllt was not going to grow up with dominii looking over her shoulder. He could still weld magic; he would just have to find a way to make a weapon that wasn't a weapon. After two changes of water, he felt he was clean enough to put on some fresh clothes and return to the table.

"Eimon explained everything," Rhiain said as he sat down. "I'm sorry about . . . well, I wanted to say I was sorry. How did things go at Moren's?"

"Thank you," Amren said, then sighed and shook his head. "Not nearly as well as I had hoped. I can't forge weapons because I want them used against the Sovereignty." Then he smiled. "I did manage to break and burn enough steel with magic that most of the apprentices assumed I must have great power and began calling me master."

"That must have pleased Moren immensely."

"I don't know that I would be able to tell."

Rhiain laughed, and Amren found himself laughing with her.

"Papa?" Esyllt asked.

"Yes?"

"Is magic alive?"

"Not exactly, sweety. Life is. . . . Well, magic is. . . . They're different. Why?"

Esyllt shrugged. "Mama always said they're the same, and . . ." She pushed a piece of potato around on her plate. Amren waited quietly for her to continue. This was the first time she had spoken of her mother since she died, and he didn't want to push her. ". . . and I had a dream . . . that Mama was golden light and that she wasn't really hurted and that she could see us and that maybe magic was alive."

Amren considered how Cat had always been able to shape and strengthen life. Not only could she heal, but she had kept an amazing garden. For her it had been as if life were magic. Perhaps it was. After all, where did life come from? How did the tree grow out of the seed? How did an infant grow in the mother's womb? Where was that life before the moment it manifested in this world? Even the magic in the steel he forged came through him. Then there was the crae'ath and its bond between magic and life. Maybe the golden light when Cat died hadn't been failed magic as the domini had said. Maybe she had defeated him and freed a part of herself. "Perhaps it is at that," he said finally.

Esyllt nodded. "Papa?"

"Yes?"

"I miss Mama."

"So do I." Amren reached over and tousled her head. "But I think maybe she's still looking after us, don't you?"

Esyllt nodded. Then her eyes turned suddenly hard. "Are you gonna stop the bad magic so that no one else gets hurted?"

Amren froze, fork hovering over his plate. It couldn't be that easy, could it? Almost on its own, the fork picked up a piece of meat and carried it to his mouth. He chewed, swallowed, but his thoughts were no longer on food. He had been so focused on striking at the Sovereignty—on what had been taken from him—that he hadn't thought much about the ability that was left to him. He had been able to make that brooch, after all.

Amren rushed through the rest of dinner, not even tasting the food, and pushed his chair back. "I think I have an idea. Da—umm . . . Rhiain, do you mind keeping an eye on Esyllt a little longer?"

"Oh, dear me, no!" Rhiain reached over and patted Esyllt's arm. "We'll be fine, won't we dear?"

Esyllt nodded.

"You go do what you have to do."

"Thank you. I'll likely be late." He kissed Esyllt on her head and rushed out the door into the darkness.

He almost ran to Moren's. A light shone from the open door, and the ring of a single hammer on an anvil floated out into the night. Inside, one of the junior smiths, a tall, sandy-haired boy—Huw, if he remembered right—was still working, most likely at something Moren had told him he needed more practice on. He glanced up as Amren entered.

"Good evening, Master Amren."

"Good evening, Huw. Where's the steel plate for the armor?"

"In the back, sir." Huw set down his hammer and dipped a rough-shaped blade in the quenching barrel. "I'll get you a piece. Want me to start up another forge, too?"

"No. I'll share yours if you don't mind. I don't want to heat up another forge for what I need to do. And just fetch me a small bit of scrap for now. I don't want to wreck any of the good stuff."

Huw returned quickly with a small piece of steel plate large enough for a vambrace. "Another idea, sir?"

"I think so." Amren hadn't noticed before, but the faintest hint of craft radiated from the junior smith.

Huw set the plate on the anvil and edged back.

"Don't worry, Huw. I don't think I'll break anything this time. At worst, I expect nothing to happen at all."

The junior smith looked doubtful, but stepped a little closer. "What are you going to try?"

Amren picked up a piece of charcoal and contemplated the steel. "I can't forge weapons. The crae'ath prevents me from making anything that

I believe will be used to harm the Sovereignty." He laid his left forearm on the steel and sketched the outline of a vambrace, then began cutting it out with the heavy shears. "But it doesn't prevent me from making something to protect the knights of Iserterre. I intend to make armor that will stand up to the magical fire of the domini."

"But sir, it won't . . . I mean, Master Moren says you can't forge magic that strong into armor. It won't stick."

"I know. I've tried before, and you're right. Armor doesn't lend itself to powerful magic welds. Part of the difficulty is that, unlike a sword, there are many pieces, and all of them have to work together to be effective. The magic has to . . . line up, but I'll worry about that later. The main problem is that the bulk of the hot work is done at the oven or mill where the blooms of iron are pounded into the large plates that Master Moren buys. Shaping the plates into armor is a mix of hot forging and cold hammering to give it the final shape." He slid the rough, flat shape into the fire and raked glowing coals over it. "There isn't much time to really work the magic into its core. And strong magic tends to burn the thin plate in the making or bleed away later."

Huw reflexively moved to work the bellows. "What if you worked the bloom straight from the oven and built the magic into the big plate?"

"That won't work." Amren walked over to the tool rack and rummaged through the hammers. "While the heat aids in binding the magic, a great part of the magic is in the shaping of the piece itself. Once I make a square plate, the magic is bound to that shape. If I cut it and reshape it, then the power bound into that original form is lost. It's like a warrior who loses an arm on the battlefield. If he lives, he won't ever be the same again." He picked out a medium-weight raising hammer, a smaller planishing hammer, and a rounded planishing stake and headed back to the forge. "But I'm not going to try and work the ward itself directly into the armor. Have you ever seen a healer work her magic?"

"Once," Huw said, "when one of the tilt hammers fell on an apprentice. She got the bleeding to stop, and mended his arm. He's still able to swing a hammer."

"Well, healers know how to shape life force, and I think that maybe life is a form of magic. If that is so, then we all carry at least some magic within us. Healers know how to touch it directly. Others, like Master Moren and myself, tap into it differently. Most people, like soldiers and knights, don't think about it at all. If I'm right, then I'm going to make armor that does that for them."

When Huw didn't offer any further comment, Amren glanced over and received a doubtful frown.

"Just wait . . . you'll see. Unless I'm wrong, that is."

Amren handed the stake to Huw, then set the planishing hammer aside, but within easy reach, and hefted the raising hammer. He tapped it on the anvil, imagining the feel of the plate, and sought the proper rhythm. He would have to have it down before he touched the metal. When hammering a shape out of an ingot or bar stock, he could feel out the steel and the magic at the same time, making minor adjustments as necessary. With this, the work was not so much in hammering a form out of the metal, but simply giving shape to the cut piece. He had to know exactly where he was going to place every blow to fix the magic in the steel.

He began by thinking about Cat and her healing and the peace that settled over her when she worked. He remembered how he had felt when she held him or lay next to him, wrapping him in her own living magic and strengthening his. He tapped out a gentle rhythm, and his craft responded immediately.

Next, he focused on the domini fire, how it cut through the air and shredded life—not just the body, but the life force, the spirit. He felt the rhythm of its destruction. The hammer rang harshly, discordantly, on the anvil, and his eyes burned and watered. This is what the armor would counter—the disruption of life.

He guided his thoughts back to Cat but pictured her in danger, surrounding herself with golden light. The rhythm softened, but took on a counterpoint that had an edge.

He slid the glowing plate out of the fire and onto the anvil, letting the rhythm guide the hammer as he gently built the curve. Weaving his craft with the delicate work took far more concentration than usual, but after several heatings, a thin tracing of a rune darkened on the surface. He began to hum a melody that completed the rhythm and switched hammers. Huw quickly dropped the planishing stake into the hole on the anvil. As Amren smoothed the surface of the steel and rolled the edges, the rune began to glow silver-white. With a final tap of the hammer, it flared white-gold.

Amren stepped back and blinked away the magic fog. He was soaked with sweat even though the physical work hadn't been that hard. Beside him, he heard a groan.

"It almost worked," Huw said.

"What?" Amren looked down at the vambrace. The rune faded to black and then vanished. What happened? He'd felt the weld take. With a pair of tongs, he picked up the hot bracer. The faintest tingle of magic coursed up his arm, and he smiled. "Just a moment." He dunked the bracer in the quenching barrel, swirling it to remove the last of the heat, then laid it back on the anvil. "Now, put it on."

"What? Me?"

"Yes. Put it on."

Cautiously, Huw picked up the bracer and slipped it on his forearm. A white gold rune flared on the surface, then faded to a mere etching. "How'd you do that?"

"The magic isn't really in the bracer. The armor is only a focus. The real magic lies in the wearer, in life. Sitting on a bench or the shelf, it's just armor. Magic fire can burn right through it. When someone puts it on, it aligns the field of their life force and shapes it into a protective shield." Amren grinned. "Your forearm is now warded against domini fire."

For three weeks, Amren labored on the plate armor. He'd asked Eimon to bring him Belimawr's measurements so he could fit it to the king. The work consumed him. He ate little and slept less. What time he did scrounge outside the forge, he spent with Esyllt. He was grateful for Rhiain and the affection she showed his daughter. She was no substitute for Cat, but Esyllt had taken to her, and they seemed to be building a strong friendship.

Huw watched Amren as much as Moren would let him and helped where he could—cutting plate, punching and riveting, polishing, engraving, and embossing. When at last it was finished, Amren asked Eimon to inform the king that he wished to present him with a gift. Belimawr sent back that Amren should appear at court first thing the next morning.

That night, the excitement of having finished the armor and worry over whether it would be adequate kept him from sleeping much. In the morning, he skipped breakfast and went straight to the shop to find his armor already loaded in the back of Moren's wagon, wrapped in oilcloth and carefully crated. Huw and Moren stood waiting. They insisted on accompanying him to Belimawr's court where they also helped him assemble the armor on a wheeled stand in the anteroom so that it could be rolled out before the king. Amren was just finishing a final polish when the door to the anteroom opened and Eimon stuck his head in.

"His Majesty is ready for you, Mastersmiths."

Amren knelt to pick up the cart's pull-handle.

"Wait, wait, wait!" Moren said. He rummaged in one of the crates that had held the armor and pulled out a tumble of black cloth, which he draped over the armor. "Kings like drama. And let Huw manage the cart, Master Amren. You stand beside your work and look like a mastersmith."

As they entered the main hall, Amren saw that this wasn't going to be a presentation to just the king. The king's marshal and a handful of lords had assembled to see what he had created, or, perhaps, failed to create. Belimawr lounged on his throne. To his right, and slightly behind him, stood a beardless knight whose head and neck were covered with a white scarf bound by a black cord. His tabard bore a familiar blazon—the lion of Iserterre, but with wings.

"So, Mastersmith Amren!" Belimawr roared. "You have something to show me!"

"I do, sire." Amren glanced at Moren, who nodded, then reached up and threw off the cloth. Whispers and mummers rippled over those gathered.

The armor shone white in the sunlight slanting down from the high windows. A lion rampant, worked in bronze, gleamed on the breastplate, and bronze scrollwork accented the arms and legs. The fan-plates on the knees and elbows were shaped like paws and the helm bore the countenance of a snarling lion's head. Feathered wings were embossed on the pauldrons but shallowly enough that they would not catch the tip of a lance or a sword.

The hall fell silent as Belimawr descended from the dais to study the armor. "This is very fine workmanship," he said, "exceedingly fine, actually, but I have several suits of armor. How will this help me against the Sovereignty?"

Amren smiled. "Can your armor turn aside domini fire?"

Belimawr's eyes widened. "You beat magic that strong into thin plate?" He looked at Moren. "Is this true? Did you see him do it?"

Moren shrugged. "It is a masterwork, to be sure . . . and he did work runes of power upon the surface, but proof against domini fire?" He spread his hands.

Amren clenched his jaw shut on a protest. He hadn't worked the runes, and runes themselves held no power. They emerged from the steel during the magic weld. No one ever seemed to understand that.

Belimawr leaned in close, studying the armor. "I see no runes."

Huw stepped forward. "It'll work, sire. The magic's in there. Just put it on and you'll see—"

"Shush, Huw!" Moren bellowed. "Bring you along, hoping you'll pick up a little polish and you go and show your rough edge! My pardon, sire."

"Sire," Amren said quietly, "I don't know if we can test it, but I can prove there is magic in the steel." Amren pulled the brooch he had made that first day in Moren's shop. "Your sword, sire?"

Belimawr retrieved Caniad from the throne, drew it, and held it out. The brooch glowed—a soft golden light. Then Amren stepped next to the suit of armor. The brooch shed but a faint glimmer.

"Now, sire," Amren said, "if you would put it on? The real magic takes hold when there is a living person inside the suit."

Belimawr frowned. "What will it do to me?"

"Nothing. It takes nothing from you. Because of the forging process and thin steel, armor holds only weak magic, but as Cat, my wife, always tried to show me, life is its own magic. The dominii distort it somehow. The armor acts as a focus, a harness for the magic that is naturally in and around us, and shapes it into a protective shield against other focused power, other magic, that would disrupt it."

"Hmm . . ." Belimawr reached for a greave. Amren and Moren both stepped forward and assisted the king in donning his armor. As each piece was fastened upon him, a rune flared gold on the surface of the steel and faded to black. When the helm was set in place, a shimmer of light ran down the armor from head to toe. Amren again drew out the brooch. It glowed brightly, much brighter than it had in the presence of the sword.

"Very impressive, Mastersmith." Belimawr said, removing the helm. "Very impressive indeed." He turned and walked back up onto the dais and spoke to the paladin in whispers.

Amren couldn't make out any of the words, but the paladin nodded several times and counted off something on the fingers of one hand during his whispered response.

Belimawr turned back around. "Iserterre's knights are valiant and skilled with the sword, but the dominii sweep the battlefield with their magic, stealing away the advantage of our heart and training. I expect that the Sovereignty will march against us when the snows melt next year. I don't believe we can really put this armor to the test without a domini, but I'm not willing to let them know what we are up to. I believe this armor will give us the edge we need. We will need at least a thousand full suits for the knights and another thousand breastplates for the men-at-arms by late spring. Oh, and as much barding for the horses as you can make."

"A thousand?" both Amren and Moren said together.

"But sire," Amren said, "this one took me three weeks. Granted, it is elaborate, but even a simple one would take me a week!" He had expected to make more, perhaps a dozen or two, but a thousand?

"And we don't have that many magic welders in the city!" Moren added. "Never mind ones that could weld magic to plate like this!"

"You have demonstrated yourself to be a talented and resourceful man, Mastersmith Amren, and you came looking for a way to strike at the Sovereignty . . . well you have found it. And you, Mastersmith Moren, are not only a skilled smith, but a proven motivator. I have faith in you both. One thousand."

Amren nodded. "Yes, sire."

Moren seemed about to protest again but just blew out a breath, instead. "Yes, sire."

The three smiths were silent as they left the king's hall, but Moren grumbled halfway back to the shop. Finally, he sent Huw to place an order with the mill for the plate they would need. When the junior smith was gone, Moren threw his hands in the air. "This is your fault!" he roared at Amren. "There is no way we can fill that kind of order! If it was normal plate, sure, but magic-welded? So far, you're the first person I've seen who can put that kind of magic into plate!"

That was near the heart of the issue, Amren realized. Moren couldn't do it. "I can show you how," he said. "I've never done it myself before now. And the magic in the plate is not very strong, just . . . detailed, requiring a lot of concentration, but anyone who can weld magic should be able to learn it."

"And that's our other problem! Where are we going to get more magic welders? The two of us can't do it!"

Amren scratched his chin. "Well . . . *all* the work doesn't have to be done by magic welders. All the cutting, punching, and assembly can be done by anyone who knows armoring. And I think we could teach Huw magic welding—"

Moren snorted. "That lackwit?"

"He has a passion for the forge and he works hard." Amren decided not to mention his own sense of craft in people, not until he understood it better, himself. "I think he could do it. Perhaps we could find a few others, too. Unless you can think of another way."

Moren stomped the rest of the way back to the shop, where he threw open the door. "Look at you!" he bellowed. "Yer a useless bunch of half-wits! We have fifteen hundred full suits of armor to make, and yer all standing around like stumps waiting for the axe! We need to get started on tracing and cutting, but don't one of you touch a hammer to anything or it will be the last thing you ever do with your hands!" He looked around at the sullen, staring faces. "Do you understand me or do I need to demonstrate?"

"Yes sir!" some yelled in response to the first order. "No sir!" others mumbled in answer to the threat.

Moren gave a satisfied nod. "Then what are you waiting for! Get your stumps moving! Oh . . . Willem, Daned, Luc, Tomos . . . when Huw gets back, you come see me and Master Amren! It's time you learn some real smithing!"

Amren grinned. Apparently, Moren didn't think so little of his students as he let on. "Fifteen hundred full suits?"

"If they think there's that many, they'll work all the harder. I'm a proven motivator, remember?"

Amren waved his hands in a warding gesture. "I'm not arguing. You actually enjoy this, though, don't you?"

"What?!"

"Being charged with doing the impossible."

Moren scowled. "Yer as daft as the king! Don't know what I was thinking . . . lending you that forge. Well, there's no help for it, now." He stomped off through the shop, bellowing orders. Amren followed, grinning in spite of the task before them, but sorry that he had skipped breakfast.

The cool, morning drizzle matched Amren's mood as he plodded toward the shop. Over the last few weeks, he had worked on what he thought were simple projects with Moren and the senior apprentices to get a feel for how they handled the merging of magic and steel. Every night, he went back to Dahme Torguardan's tired and frustrated. His own craft, especially his sense for it in others, had seemed to grow daily with the work. He was still convinced it was somehow connected to the crae'ath, though he had no more insight into how. The apprentices, on the other hand, had a hard time feeling the magic at all. Granted, it wasn't easy, but they weren't really trying, either. They insisted on etching the runes on the steel before reaching for the power within them, letting the characters be a guide through which to apply the magic instead of the other way around. They mistrusted either themselves or the magic or maybe both. If that didn't change . . . well, it had to change.

Even before he reached the smithy, Amren felt the discordant flows of magic, five of them—the uncontrolled threads flailing about like whips until they snarled in a useless knot. He paused in the open doorway a moment and watched. The senior apprentices all toiled away at one end of the shop, strangling magic, while at the other end, Moren showed several of the junior apprentices how to weld two different grades of steel to make a stronger blade. The junior students actually had a decent rhythm going, and they weren't even trying to wield magic.

Amren walked over to the senior apprentices. "Stop . . . stop a moment and watch." He pointed towards the junior apprentices. "Why don't they all just strike the blades in the same place, at the same angle, with the same amount of force as Master Moren?"

"Well," said Daned, one of the older students, "every piece of steel is different and has to be worked a little differently."

"And how does Master Moren, or any of you, know where and how hard to strike?"

Daned scratched his head, then shrugged. "I don't know. You just do. You feel it out."

"Exactly! Now, put aside whatever you were working on." Amren picked up a couple of small polishing hammers and stepped behind an anvil. "Forget about smithing for a moment. Forget about magic. Listen."

Amren listened to the rhythm of the junior students for a moment, then strengthened it with his hammers. "You hear that? There is already a rhythm to this place. I just brought it out. Pick up your hammers and follow along."

The senior students all joined in, playing the major beats that Amren set up. "Listen to the sound your hammer makes on your anvil," he said, "and on different parts of it. Use it. Find a way to fit it to the whole." Soon the smithy rang with an energetic cadence. When they stopped, the shop was silent, and Amren looked up to see everyone at the other end of the room staring at them.

Moren's mouth hung open and his face bore an expression of confused horror. "What, did you give up on their smithing and decide to teach them music?"

"Sort of." Amren turned back to his students. "Forging magic into steel is not that much different than welding two different grades of metal. There's no template, stamp, or marking that can help you. Runes are a result, a memory of craft, not a source. You can follow what someone else does, but you have to feel out your own tools, your own vision of what the steel will become, and your own power.

"Let's try something simple." He found several pieces of round, scrap bar stock, stuck them in the fire, and shifted the lever that engaged the waterwheel-driven bellows. Then he traded the pair of polishing hammers for a light cross peen. "We're going to make S-hooks that glow in the presence of magic, like the brooch I made. Shape the metal like you normally would. I'll start the rhythm; you fill it in as you get a feel for your own piece. If you are inclined, add your voice. It brings more of you to your work." He paused and turned toward the other end of the room. "Moren, I think I could use your help with this."

"Might as well," Moren growled as he stomped across the shop, "these addle-pates can burn good steel with or without me."

After only a few minutes, the irons were glowing orange. Amren retrieved one and began rough shaping it. "Remember, when you feel the tug of the magic, don't force it; just open yourself to it, and work it with the steel."

By the second heating, he had found his rhythm, and he reached for the magic. Around him, the ring of the other hammers supported the rhythm he had started, yet each carried their own variation. The magic was there. He felt it—multiple strands, each with its own unique quality. He started to hum. Moren's voice picked up the melody, then Huw's. After that, Amren was only dimly aware of the wash of song that incorporated voices, hammers, and . . . something else.

Almost unexpectedly, threads of white light darted around Amren's hook and flared brightly. He stopped, hammer raised in his hand. It was finished, and he hadn't struck the blow to close the weld. The glaring light didn't fade, either. In fact, the air in the shop seemed to glow ever so faintly. Slowly, Amren became aware of the other sounds and turned. A small crowd had gathered outside the open doors—other artisans, some passersby, a few soldiers wearing lion blazons. They all tapped their feet, and the armsmen thumped their spears on the ground in time to the hammers. The smiths had raised the magic, but the added rhythm fed it, like a storm gathering strength over water.

One by one, the other smiths each finished their work with a decisive ring of their hammers, and their hooks all glowed just as bright, almost blinding, as they responded to the magic in the air. Only when the last was finished did the light in all of them slowly begin to fade. Again, silence filled the shop.

Moren looked up, saw the onlookers, and dropped his hammer onto his anvil with a clang. "Bah! Now we're going to have to close the doors and work in an oven." He started toward the crowd.

Amren stopped him with a hand on his shoulder. "Actually, I've never felt such a strong flow of craft before, and I think it was because of them. I say let them come."

Amren and Moren stood next to Belimawr atop a low rise on the Iserterrian side of the Kophalen Hills. The king wore the armor Amren had made and held the reins to his newly barded warhorse in one hand. Below them to the west, the Iserterrian battle line was drawn up between the arms of two steeper hills. A chill mist wrapped everything in a thick cloak so that they couldn't see more than a few score yards beyond the front line or even much of the flanking hills. Amren pulled his thin wool cloak around his shoulders. He would have preferred to stay in the camp or, better yet, with Esyllt back in Avidan.

Just before he left, she'd had a nightmare about a shadow that tried to pull him into the ground. She'd been frantic and in tears when he'd said good-bye and had made him promise to forge something to kill the shadow. That had been over three weeks ago, and nearly every night *he* had dreamed about shadows. He, Moren, and the senior apprentices had been sent ahead of the much slower army to set up a temporary forge and keep making armor. Now they were to watch the battle, see how the armor faired, and look for ways to improve it. At Amren's request, all their tools and anvils waited with the senior apprentices in a row of small carts just below the hill's crest. Fortunately, no one had questioned him. He hadn't been able to think of a good reason and wasn't about to tell anyone he was afraid of a little girl's dream.

"Well, Mastersmiths," Belimawr said, "you did it. I'm not sure how, but there they are. Look at them."

Amren looked out over the battlefield. Some two thousand men formed a phalanx between the hills. Behind them waited two hundred knights—the cream of Iserterre known as the King's Companions—and fifty Sons of Dawn, their green cloaks blazoned with white wings. Another five hundred knights waited in the mist somewhere on the hills with a handful of archers. All the knights wore full, magic-welded plate armor, and nearly half the men-at-arms had breastplates. Only fifty of the Companion mounts had a complete set of magic-welded barding, but the rest were at least warded by plates over their heads and chests.

"You do know," Amren said, "that like any armor, it can be worn down. Repeated magical assaults will eventually defeat it. How many Lyfeians did you say there were?"

"About ten thousand. And I know your armor isn't indestructible."

Amren made a quick calculation. Another four hundred mounted men-at-arms were out harrowing the Lyfeians and leading them here, but the whole Iserterrian strength numbered less than four thousand.

"The trick," Belimawr said, "is to not let them know how many we are, to hit them hard, and to rob them of the advantage given to them by domini fire. They will run."

"You make it sound easy enough." In truth, it had seemed that simple when they were forging the armor, safe in Avidan. But out here, on the field waiting for an enemy more than twice their number, Amren wasn't so sure.

"The Lyfeians always march in two main divisions with their officers and best knights between them. The dominii ride there, as well. They never send more than one per division, but two will be more than enough. Additional knights ride in the van. If we can pin down their van and break the first division with attacks on both flanks, we might be able to draw out their center and punch through to reach the dominii. Your armor just has to get us that far, then we can do the rest."

"Where are the army's dominii from?"

"A few are dedicated to militia support, but each kingdom has at least one, maybe several, in residence as well. There will probably be one from Pandour. You're wondering if it might be the one you crossed?"

Amren nodded.

"I don't know who they'll send with the army, but the most prominent domini in Pandour is Searlas—tall, balding fellow . . . a bit of a flair for the dramatic. He's rather disagreeable, but then I haven't met a domini who isn't."

"That's him."

"Well, if everything goes as planned, you won't ever meet again."

The low bellow of a Lyfeian war horn drifted out of the mist. "Time for me to go," Belimawr said and climbed into his saddle. He cantered down the hill and took his place at the head of the Companions.

A rumble of hooves announced the Iserterrian men-at-arms before they materialized from the mist, galloping hard. They streamed through gaps in the phalanx and fanned out to either side to stand as a reserve. The phalanx closed ranks behind them, locking shields and lowering pikes in a solid wall of barbed steel. For a moment, everything was still. Then the mists swirled, and the Lyfeian van thundered out of the clinging fog and into the Iserterrian line.

The air erupted in crashing steel and the screams of men and horses. For a moment, the Lyfeians seemed to think their quarry had simply turned to meet them and pressed their attack. Then arrows began to rain out of the mist. The Lyfeians realized they had been drawn into a trap and sounded warning horns as they tried to fall back, but the first division was already advancing behind them. For a moment, the additional numbers bolstered the faltering van, and they pressed forward against the Iserterrian phalanx.

Belimawr sounded a single blast on his war horn, and a deep boom echoed from the mist-shrouded hilltop on either flank. The shower of arrows ceased, to be replaced by the rolling beat of drums cascading like thunder down the slopes. Amren couldn't see into the mist, but he knew what descended from the hills. The drums were disconcerting, but they concealed a greater threat—wings of Iserterrian knights bore down on the Lyfeian flanks.

The Lyfeian column faltered, as the main division turned to defend their flanks. As soon as the pressure on the Iserterrian front eased, Belimawr sounded two blasts on his horn, and the phalanx parted once again. With a roar of "Iserterre!" Belimawr led the Companions through and into the disorganized Lyfeians.

Beset on three sides and probably uncertain of the opposing numbers, the Lyfeians sought to pull back, but the narrow confines of the valley and the pressure on their flanks hampered their withdrawal. Belimawr drove his wedge farther, out of sight into the mist.

The wind shifted, whipping out of the valley, driving the fog before it, and Amren felt the gentle prickle of magic in the air. As the mist cleared, the full impact of the Iserterrian ambush became apparent. Belimawr and his Companions had divided the Lyfeians' forward division, and the rear had not yet been able to maneuver into the narrow valley. But on a low rise just near the far end of the narrow valley stood a solid ring of ordered resistance, the Lyfeian center with the dominii. As the Companions broke through the first division, bolts of jagged fire ripped through the air from the top of the rise. They struck the king's company full on, but splashed harmlessly aside and dissipated. The Companions charged ahead, and the phalanx surged forward behind them.

Moren whooped, and clapped Amren on the shoulder. "Did you see that! We did it, lad! We did it!"

Amren smiled. With any luck, the dominii would begin to wonder if Lyfaye had abandoned them.

Suddenly, the ground shook and a rumble echoed out of the valley. The hillside to the north of the Companions seemed to heave and shift, then collapsed and rolled down onto the Companions, momentarily obscuring everything in a cloud of dust. Amren couldn't tell for sure, but it looked as though at least half of the Companions had been caught in the slide along with the northern flank of the phalanx, and even some of the Lyfeians. Had the dominii done that? *Could* the dominii do that?

Then the light dimmed as if storm clouds had moved in, but the sky was clear. "Shadow . . ." Amren whispered, and reflexively looked down at the ground. There was nothing there. His eyes began to burn, worse than the last time he was near domini magic, and he blinked back tears. If he could feel it this far away—

Bright lances of light radiated from the low rise where the dominii stood, piercing the evening-like gloom. Wherever the rays touched, fallen soldiers, both Lyfeian and Iserterrian, lurched to their feet, glowing a pale, unearthly white. They shambled forward and dragged down soldiers wearing the lion tabard. The Iserterrian line began to waver and pull apart as men scrambled to get away from the evil rising up in their midst.

Cold dread settled over Amren. He hadn't thought beyond warding against domini fire, didn't even know the dominii were capable of this kind of magic. Of course, if the fire always worked on the battlefield, they would have no need to do more. The armor wasn't going to be enough. Esyllt had told him to forge something. He wished, now, that he had asked what. Forge something. . . . Maybe she hadn't seen a *thing*. Magic wasn't confined to steel and hammers. He knew that. He'd felt it in the air in Moren's smithy. So had everyone else, even those who didn't wield magic.

Amren ran to the cart that held his and Moren's tools. He leapt into it, and caught up the reins. "Follow me!" he called to the other smiths and drove the cart up next to Moren. "I have an idea," he said.

"What do we do?" Huw asked, reining up beside them.

Amren wished he had a clear answer. "Spread out behind the phalanx. Follow my rhythm, only we aren't forging metal this time, just magic. Use the tools to focus your craft on what you feel around you."

Moren climbed into the cart beside him, and Amren snapped the reins. They rolled down the hill and onto the battlefield, but what had been a solid wall of armsmen a few minutes ago had collapsed into chaos. At first, most of the Iserterrians had continued to fight, but anyone who fell, friend or foe, rose up to strike back, making it impossible to hold ground. Small groups of Iserterrians began to flee, streaming between the smiths and back up the hill. Amren held up a hand, bringing their little line of carts to a halt at what he hoped was a safe distance.

Even as he climbed into the back of the cart with Moren and settled behind his anvil, Amren felt the wrongness in the magic that swirled around them. It lent a thickness to the air that made it hard to breathe. He picked up two heavy cross peens, glanced at Moren, and nodded. They brought their hammers down with a single ring.

He closed his eyes and felt the note reverberate through the web of magic that cloaked the valley. Threads of power wrapped around everyone. Some were warm, harmonious strands, full of tonal color . . . natural. Others were cold and discordant, black and white, and seemed to tie back to the dominii. But there was something else, almost a haze of golden melody around him. . . . In that one moment, everything made sense. The crae'ath, the Holy Rite, Cat's death, his growing sense of craft . . . the whole Lyfeian Order was bound together through magic, and that magic touched everything else. Like it or not, he was a part of that order, now. In a way, so was Cat, and she was also a part of him. She hadn't recanted on her oath. She had recast and redirected it. He was bound to the web woven by the crae'ath, but he experienced it through an additional bond that was Cat's final gift.

Another unified ring, this time from all the smiths, and he found what the dominii had done. They had twisted the threads of life itself, feeding their dead from the living. That's what made it hard to breathe. The life was slowly being siphoned out of all of them.

A few more beats and Amren found the rhythm of what was supposed to be. He tapped it out on his anvil. As it became more familiar, his blows strengthened and he envisioned a magic-magic weld in place of a steel-magic weld. The other smiths picked up the rhythm, and the sound of hammers on anvils began to rise above the clash of swords. Amren worked a complementary rhythm and built it around the first, re-tempering the threads the dominii had warped.

The Lyfeian rhythm changed slightly, and several of the black and white threads shifted and refocused. A pack of the warrior dead, maybe a dozen or so Lyfeians and Iserterrians, lumbered out of the fray toward the smiths. The dominii must have sensed what he was trying to do. With no time to sort out the intricacies of the adjusted rhythm, Amren stretched out his craft and with two sharp blows from his hammers severed the weld that controlled the small band of dead warriors. They collapsed in a heap.

Pain stabbed Amren's eyes, and the air burned in his lungs. He coughed and tasted a hint of iron. The rhythm faltered. Black and white timbres darted in everywhere, probing. Then the thread held by Tomos unraveled, and it was all Amren could do to hold the remaining strands of magic in place. Dealing with the handful of dead soldiers had sapped just enough of his strength. Without Tomos, he couldn't finish the weld. Their rhythm wasn't strong enough, and his hammers were getting heavier with each blow. They needed more smiths.

No . . . they just needed the base cadence.

Struggling to hold onto the magic, he looked around and saw the mounted reserve wheeling into a line just off to their right. "Iserterre!" he called out. Several of the soldiers turned. Amren made a pounding gesture against his chest with his hammer. A few of the men seemed to understand his intent and began to tap the rhythm on their shields with swords. Their companions picked it up, and the air tingled.

Amren began to hum, but pain lanced through his head, and he coughed again, spitting blood. He wasn't sure if it was the dominii magic or the way he was using his own. He tried again. This time Moren joined him, and they succeeded in weaving a melody around the rhythm. When the magical ties were set, Amren raised one hammer, counting the beat in the air. When he brought it down, the other smiths followed him and they closed the weld with a final resounding ring that carried to the far end of the valley. A visible wave, like a heat-shimmer off bare rock, rolled down the valley. The dominii's magic collapsed—daylight returned, and the walking dead fell to the ground. A cheer rose from the Iserterrians.

The dominii, however, stood untouched. Strong enough to maintain control of the energies in their immediate vicinity, they had wrapped themselves in a glowing shroud that parted the magical wave, letting it flow around them. Amren couldn't do anything about them from here, but first, he had to make sure that the dominii's magic stayed confined to the hill. He picked up the rhythm again, this time merely hardening what was there already, preventing the dominii from reshaping it again. The other smiths joined in, and even the drums from the left flank seemed to align with the magic in the air. Amren pointed at Moren with his hammer, and the mastersmith nodded as he took over the lead rhythm. Tucking his hammers in his belt, Amren hopped off the cart, then ran to the front where he unhitched one of the draft horses. He led it around to the side of the wagon and used the step-board to climb onto its back. Then he rode to the mounted reserve and searched out their captain.

"I need to get to the front! To the dominii!"

"Yes, sir, Mastersmith." The captain sounded his horn. "First, second, and third companies, on me!" Three score men-at-arms formed up around Amren and the captain, and they plunged into the raging sea of men and swords. They forced their way to the front line, where the remaining

Companions struggled against the guard surrounding the Lyfeian command. Belimawr's banner flew at the most forward position. The Companions were mostly afoot now and fighting hard just to keep from being surrounded. The captain led his men in a charge against the Lyfeians pressing the king's left flank. Amren ducked and held onto his horse's mane as he was carried along with the thundering tide.

A Lyfeian soldier appeared in front of him, thrusting a spear upward. Amren twisted to one side, but his horse screamed and collapsed beneath him, and he found himself tumbling across the ground amidst scattered weapons and broken bodies. He scrambled to his knees just in time to see an axe descending toward him. Too late, he reached around for his hammers. A shadow fell over him, and the axe thunked into a shield above his head. One of the paladins stepped in front of him, tattered green cloak fluttering, and drove his blade between the axe-man's gorget and breastplate where a strap had broken loose. He yanked the sword out, and blood gushed down the Lyfeian's armor as he toppled past Amren to the ground.

Amren staggered to his feet as paladins rushed past him. The Lyfeians were giving ground. The first division had already collapsed, but the command guard did not break formation as they retreated. Amren growled. Retreat was not enough. The dominii had to fall. Not just for Cat, but so everyone knew that it was possible . . . so they knew there was hope in fighting back against the Sovereignty.

He could still feel the strengthening magic wrought by Moren and the smiths. He could also feel the faint twisting as it bent around the dominii. He could not wield a blade, and he may not even be able to strike to kill a Lyfeian, but if the dominii could distort the weave and flow of magic, maybe he could too . . . and he knew steel. He'd seen it disintegrate in a failed magic weld. He hefted his hammers and pushed toward the front, feeling the order in the steel around him.

When a small gap opened between two knights, he reached through and struck—one . . . two—beats of a rhythm counter to the order of steel in the Lyfeian's breastplate. The hammer rang off the armor, and the plate cracked and fell away in a shower of brown rust. A blade darted in behind his hammers and the Lyfeian fell, shock frozen on his face. Another Lyfeian stepped forward. Amren repeated the counter rhythm, one . . . two . . . the soldier's armor disintegrated, and he, too, fell to Iserterrian blades. Belimawr appeared at Amren's side, Caniad flashing in his hand, and a knot of Companions and paladins formed around them, protecting Amren as they carved their way up the low hill. Finally, the Lyfeian lines parted, presenting an opening to the two ivory-robed dominii. One was average height and fairly young with blonde hair, but the other was tall and balding—the same one that had killed Cat—Searlas. Fear flashed through Amren, then anger.

An Iserterrian man-at-arms without magical armor rushed forward and swung his sword at the younger domini, who just stood with his arms outstretched.

"No!" Amren shouted, but it was too late.

The blade skated harmlessly to the side. Searlas raised his hands. White flames engulfed the soldier, and he fell, screaming, to the ground.

Amren leapt forward as he felt the magic build around Searlas again. He relaxed, felt its rhythm. A twisting snake of white fire flashed toward him. He swung his hammer. It met the fire and shattered it into countless motes of white light, but pain wracked Amren's body, and he crumpled to the ground. He tried to climb to his feet but couldn't make his limbs work. He knew he couldn't unmake another fire bolt. Steel-clad arms hauled him upright and pressed his hammers back into his hands.

"Don't give up on me yet, Mastersmith Amren!" Belimawr said. "We're almost there. Today *will* be ours!"

The Companions closed back around Amren as another tongue of flame snaked out. It flashed harmlessly off their armor, and the group pushed forward in a knot. White fire washed over them in waves. Two Companions fell as their armor failed. Amren reached out a hand and, calling the barest hint of craft, touched Belimawr's back plate. It couldn't take much more. None of them could. Then, abruptly, the fire stopped.

The Companions parted and Amren stood before the dominii. A shield of magic, maintained by the young domini, glimmered around the Lyfeian holy men, but both were sweat-soaked and looked exhausted. Blood dripped from Searlas's nose. So, they had limits, too.

"You!" Searlas gasped. "How can it be you?"

Amren ignored him and studied the protective forces surrounding the dominii as he reached for his craft. He struck the weave a casual blow with his hammer and watched the play of energy across the shield. This he could manage. He hefted both hammers and struck the shield repeatedly in rapid succession, focusing the magic like a wedge and driving it between the threads of the shield, then letting it bleed out into the pattern woven by the young domini. A web of brighter light appeared in the shield, like cracks in a blade heated white hot and then cooled too rapidly.

"You can't hurt us!" Searlas screamed. "Lyfaye will hold you to your oath!"

"Catrien!" Amren yelled and brought both hammers down on the magical shield. The barrier sparked and collapsed. The young domini crumpled to the ground, where he lay unmoving. Searlas stood defiant, his ice-blue eyes fixed on Amren. He clearly did not doubt the bond of the crae'ath. Neither did Amren, and he backed away as Companions rushed past him. The domini fell without a word.

The hammers slid out of Amren's hands, and he sank to his knees. Iserterrians streamed around him as the Lyfeians broke and fled the valley, but all he could think about was Cat. Nothing could balance what had happened to her. However many dominii fell, she would still be gone. Close, in a way, and yet gone. The tears came then and with them all the rage and sorrow.

"Master Amren!"

Amren looked up to see Belimawr, lion armor dented and badly scorched, standing over him.

"Master Amren, do you know what you have done? No domini has ever been slain on the field of battle!"

Amren shrugged.

"You have hammered fear into the hearts of the Lyfeians and forged hope for us all, sir smith!" He clapped Amren on the shoulder. "Iserterre will not come under the yoke of the Sovereignty! I have half a mind to give you a grant of land, right here, to build a keep to ward our border."

Amren shook his head. "I'm no lord, sire."

"Perhaps not, but it wasn't rank or lineage I was thinking of. Not only did you make this armor when everyone said it couldn't be done," he rapped an armored knuckle on his breastplate, "but you turned mere smiths into a mighty weapon. You have no combat experience to speak of, yet men followed you into battle. Don't let what you started end here, today. You think about it."

Amren lifted the burgundy silk pouch from around his neck. He gently stroked it with one finger, then knelt and dropped it into the large square cut in the earth. Esyllt stood quietly next to him. He said a brief prayer, then rose and waved his hand. Two score men hauled to on their ropes and a massive stone block rolled forward and slid into the hole on top of the pouch. A rune was burnt into the face of the stone, worked by a master stonecutter under Amren's guidance. It was to be the cornerstone of the keep.

There would never be a balance to Cat's death. The balance was in how she had lived and in how he, who had shared her life, lived his own and raised Esyllt. He still wasn't sure if magic was alive, but he had no doubt that magic and life were intimately woven together.

A man with a white scarf over his head and neck stepped up beside Amren. "The Sons of Dawn would stand with you here, if you would have us."

Amren stared at the stone. "Is it true that you are Sidhehana?"

"Does it matter if I am or if I am not? Would it change who we really are or those who would judge us for it?"

Amren smiled. "I'll be happy to have you."

"I am pleased, Sir Amren. What shall you call your new home?"

What *would* he call it? Amren looked out over the former battlefield for a moment, then along the lush green crests of the Kophalen Hills. He didn't want just another fortress hunched over a border valley, waiting for the next enemy. That was its own sort of prison. After everything he'd been through, everything he'd learned, if that was all he could offer, then he should have surrendered to the crae'ath and the Lyfeians that first day. But he hadn't let Cat's death be the end. He hadn't let Avidan be the end. Belimawr hadn't let the battle be the end. Ends weren't what were needed. His home would be more. It would be a place of endless beginnings, a place of craft. "Hammer Song," he said at last. "I believe I shall call it Hammer Song."

"It suits you, Mastersmith."

The paladin turned and walked down the slope to his mount and swung into the saddle. Amren couldn't help but notice that Esyllt's gaze followed him intently the entire way.

"What do you see, you little imp?"

"I'm going to be a knight, too, Papa," she said.

He laughed. "No, dear one. I do not think that path is for you."

Esyllt bobbed her head and grasped his hand. The faintest tingle of magic ran through his arm. "Oh, but yes Papa!" she said. "I dreameded it."

The Treachery of Stone

William Jones

The master builder stepped from his tent to gaze upon what he knew to be a portent. A sanguine hue stained the firmament to the west where the sun gradually dropped from the sky. Dark roiling clouds pushed from the east in pursuit of the dying day. Angry flashes of light danced amid the approaching clouds, followed moments later by a faint rumbling.

"What is it?" Shuka asked, appearing at the master builder's side. "Does the sky speak to you?"

Mela thought about his apprentice's words. *No. The sky does not speak to me, but it does speak to Babylon. The city-god approaches.*

"We have constructed a marvel here," Mela said. "It is a creation of the art handed down from the first among builders, Master Builder Caina of Ur. He taught the mysteries of building, bringing humanity into cities. Now we add to what he began. This is a monument to him."

For over thirty years Mela had been a master builder, seeing the completion of many temples and palaces. But he'd never undertaken such a task as this. He'd seen many things in his life, but this was the greatest.

A cutting breeze blew across the construction camp where thousands of artisans and laborers lived and worked. Shuka tugged his cloak tight, trying to keep the bite of the wind at bay. Mela stood bare-chested, ignoring the cold. He was tall, his skin a rich olive from working under the sun's burning face finishing projects that had been started years before his birth, each consuming the lives of thousands of men.

Shifting his gaze from the horizon, Mela admired his current work. Finally complete, after four hundred years. He had not started the tower, but he had completed it. It was *his* prize. *The greatest of all things on the Earth*. A ziggurat that pierced the heavens.

But Ur-Nansha would be the one who claimed the glory; the thought chilled Mela more than the wind. The King of Babylon owned the Great

Tower; Mela had only guided its construction. But more of Mela's blood and sweat went into the construction than Ur-Nansha's. Throughout the final months of the tower's completion, this solitary worry had nagged at Mela, consuming his waking thoughts and dreams. Ur-Nansha had not built this tower. It rightfully belonged to Master Builder Mela of Ur.

The gigantic structure soared skyward. To Mela, it was magnificent in every way. A double set of stairs led to the first level, and there Mela had ordered the placement of exotic trees and flowers that rivaled any of the gardens in Babylon. The stairs stretched upward from this first landing, wrapping around the square-shaped Great Tower like a snake, leading ever higher toward the pinnacle, the holy *cella* at the top. In the growing gloom, even Mela's sharp eyes could not see that point. It reached higher than a hawk's wing could carry.

Also lost to the eye were the tower's vivid blue and red plaster-works, alcoves, recesses and bas-relief sculpting that complimented its beauty. All who gazed upon the Great Tower of Babylon were struck with awe. Mela had seen it in the eyes of many travelers, some of whom came to Babylon for no other reason than to view the wonder. From hardened mud-brick, limestone and bitumen, Mela had finished the Great Tower. *My tower.*

No. Ur-Nansha cannot claim this, Mela decided.

"Is there something wrong?" Shuka asked, disturbing Mela from his contemplation. "Do you detect a flaw?"

"Yes," Mela said. "There is a flaw, but not in the structure."

Shuka was young and lacked the wisdom to interpret Mela's meaning. The boy was Mela's slave, payment made by Ur-Elaim of Lagash for repairs made to his royal palace. Shuka was one of Ur-Elaim's many sons—a clever boy who would make a fine builder some day, and who would tend to Mela in his old age. The payment was a good one, unlike Ur-Nansha who only paid in gold.

Mela turned to the boy, whose eyes were wide with puzzlement. "Fetch Nebas. Tell her I require her presence."

The mask of worry deepened upon Shuka's face. Clearly the boy thought Mela had found a great flaw and now wished to consult a prophet, a witch, for advice. Without the slightest hesitation, Shuka bolted toward the sprawling village that had sprouted outside the walled city of Babylon. The boy kicked up dust that quickly vanished in the growing breeze.

Nebas pushed through the entrance of the tent with Shuka trailing behind.

The wind had been steadily increasing. Now gusts caused the top and sides of Mela's large tent to tremble and flutter.

"I am not your slave," Nebas said sharply. "I am not at your call whenever you desire." As she spoke, she pulled back the hood of her cloak, revealing an aquiline face, with smooth dark skin and black eyes. Her gaze always disturbed Mela when she set it upon him. "I have already prophesized your future. There is nothing else I can tell you. What is written is written in stone."

Sitting cross-legged on cushions—uncommon agility for a man of Mela's years—he gestured for Nebas to sit. A low, wooden table squatted in the center of the tent, surrounded by plump pillows. Upon the table rested a large plate of fruit and a jug of wine.

Hesitantly, Nebas lowered herself onto the cushions opposite the master builder. She was youthful and as lithe as a cat. Mela sensed her firm body beneath the cumbersome robe. She had a beauty, but her *art* tempered any desire he might have for her. He distrusted such things. He believed in what he could see and touch. Stone. Wood. He shaped his world, and knew the materials such a task required. This woman spoke with spirits and demons, invisible beings only she could see.

Mela settled his gaze on her. "I need you to call upon the city-god's children."

Nebas offered no reply. In her silence, thunder rumbled in the distance. So great was the sound that even through the cushions Mela felt the earth shudder.

"A dangerous thing you ask," Nebas said. She shifted on the pillows. "It comes at a great price—"

"Your weight in gold."

Her eyes widened, and a narrow smile played across her visage. She nodded. "You barter well, Master Builder. I will do this deed."

"I do not have time to haggle. I need it done quickly. The hour of my destiny approaches and I must be ready."

In the past he'd cared little for prophecy, but now, before undertaking a construction such as this, the words of a seer seemed important. And Nebas had foreseen his success, a grand success unrivaled by any other man. Originally he'd thought her words spoke of his completion of the Great Tower. But now he saw a depth that perhaps even she didn't realize. True, he did succeed in completing the Great Tower, but he now knew he was also destined to become its master; to replace Ur-Nansha when the city-god came forth. He felt this deep in his soul. He was not called to Babylon by coincidence. All great works required planning and foresight.

"You must send fire demons into the palace," Mela said. "I need the guards killed. In the palace there is a tablet I must possess."

The narrow smile widened on Nebas's face. "You read much into my prophecy."

"I know my destiny," Mela said.

"Master," Shuka said, breaking his respectful silence. "Is this wise? Will we not anger the city-god? Is it not Ur-Nansha's place to speak with him?"

"Be quiet," Mela snapped, giving a sharp glance to Shuka. The young boy slinked to a shadowy corner of the tent.

Shadows danced about, cast by the swaying lamp hanging from the tent's sapling framing. Nebas's countenance played in and out of the light, adding to her already unsettling demeanor. "If you need this done, it must begin quickly."

In moments the trio had crept through the shadows and trees lining the northern entrance of Ur-Nansha's palace. The ruddy western sky had faded, replaced by a gauzy veil of night. Lights flashed in the east as the storm drew closer, and Mela knew time grew shorter.

With the aid of occasional gusts of wind, Nebas blew on six strips of tender bark. The dull red tips blossomed to a brilliant yellow under her breath. While urging the tiny flames, she uttered words that held no meaning for Mela. Their very sound sent chills crawling over his body, a coldness stronger than the sharpest breeze.

Once she'd finished uttering the foul incantation, Nebas spoke to Mela. "I must make a mark of protection on you." Using the burning strips of bark, she traced a sigil on both Mela's and Shuka's foreheads. Mela expected the hot twigs to sting his flesh, but there was no pain, only a numbness following the tracing of the sigil.

Once finished, Nebas turned toward the palace entrance and tossed the six smoldering strips into the air. With a sudden flash they ignited, transforming from tiny, glowing embers into man-sized blazes that moved and shifted about with inhuman form. In the same wretched tongue, Nebas called to the living flames. Her words sent them away, scorching the earth as they glided toward the palace entrance.

Mela had been at least ten arm lengths from the fiery creatures, and still their heat licked at his face. His bare skin reddened as though he'd been standing near the open mouth of a brick oven.

The glow of the fire demons illuminated the sky above the palace as they moved about the courtyard. Cries filled the air. Mela hesitated for a moment. He had to trust in Nebas's art, but that trust came hard.

"Go!" she yelled. "Go before they are gone!"

Mela forced himself forward. With each step his courage returned. He saw his destiny before him. This added speed to his gait. On his heels was Shuka. *If anything, the boy is loyal*, Mela thought.

Entering the palace was simple. The fire demons left panic in their wake. The blackened and smoldering remains of palace guards filled the courtyard and the main hallway. The stench of burning flesh overwhelmed Mela. His stomach churned and gorge rose in his throat. Shuka pulled part of his hood over his face to fend off the odor.

To those unfamiliar with such buildings, the palace of Ur-Nansha would have been a maze. Dark, elongated chambers led to square rooms, each with several openings. At intervals, oil lamps hung from the low limestone-plastered ceilings, providing faint guidance.

Mela had been inside the building many times—by invitation of Ur-Nansha. He'd seen the vibrant and masterful work of the artisans on the palace's interior walls. But now that beauty had been lost to the passing of the fire demons.

Mela shifted through the hallways toward the king's private chamber. Occasionally, bluish-violet light flashed down a side passage or beyond an entranceway. Sometimes a shriek followed, other times the crack of mud-brick walls collapsing. The creatures worked swiftly.

"Hold!" came a voice as Mela and Shuka turned a corner.

Before them stood a guard armored in a skirt of leather straps, bare-chested and wielding a spear. Beyond hung the purple curtain that marked the entrance to the king's chamber.

Even in the dull light, Mela read the terror in the guard's eyes. The man had obviously been ordered to stay at the chamber's entrance—probably while Ur-Nansha found safe haven. But from his hesitant movements and wide eyes, Mela knew little courage remained in the man. Each pitiful scream echoing off the walls undoubtedly chipped away at what little loyalty still stood.

Drawing his long knife, Mela growled, "Be gone and you will live."

The guard seemed to consider the offer for a brief moment, but a greater fear, the fear of Ur-Nansha and treachery to the city-god, reinforced his courage. The guard lowered his spear, advancing.

Although Mela had been in many brawls in his youth, he'd always managed to avoid military service to any king. His role as a builder had purchased that liberty. And as certain as he was of his destiny, he still wondered about his chances of success against a soldier.

But the question was answered quickly.

Before the guard had taken a second step, a fist-sized stone swished past Mela's brow, hitting the guard's forehead. With a thick *thump* the rock bounced off the man's head, sending him to his knees, then face down on the floor, unconscious.

With the speed of a mouse, Shuka jumped forward, retrieving his stone, apparently ready for a second attack. But the guard remained motionless.

Mela smiled at the boy. "You shame me. While I proffer the weapon of a solider, you wield the weapon of a builder."

Shuka bowed slightly, the bloodied stone still in hand. "I am apprentice to Master Builder Mela of Ur. I have been taught well."

"And you have learned much," Mela said. "Quick, let us hurry. I fear neither of us have enough weapons to battle a larger number of adversaries."

The royal chamber's stone walls were decorated with tremendous circular plates of gold and bronze, emblazoned with images and etchings that Mela did not understand. A vast sea of pillows covered the floor, each ornate and trimmed with fine weaves, and as fat as a well-fed bird. Mela ignored these treasures, seeking another prize.

It didn't take long to find. Resting upon a large altar, flat on its surface, was the tablet the master builder sought. With the words engraved upon it, Mela would possess the secret of speaking to the city-god. Here was an ancient knowledge handed down from the first king of Babylon for this very day. The day the Great Tower was ready.

As Mela hefted the tablet, he thought about his fate. The young kings of Babylon had ordered the construction of the Great Tower, believing it would be a king who would someday talk with the city-god. Mela laughed inwardly, delighting in their error. There would be a new King of Babylon. One worthy of the city's marvel. Like the gods themselves, Mela was a builder, a creator of places, of things. Soon he would be the builder and ruler of a great kingdom. He knew the secrets of the builders, the secrets unknown to the kings of all the cities. His knowledge gave him a vision that even the prophetess could not see. When men worked together under the guidance of a builder, a creator, there was no limit to what could be done.

The Great Tower of Babylon was only a trifle compared to what awaited the world under the guidance of a master builder. He would be the first of a new line of kings.

No sooner had Mela hoisted the tablet into his arms than did the burning heat come.

Shuka gasped. "Look!" the boy cried, pointing to a fire demon drifting toward the chamber entrance.

By the time Mela saw the demon, the purple drape hanging in the doorway was already consumed in flames. Only straggling remnants dangled from the top of the doorway, dropping in clumps to the floor.

Mela felt the creature's feverish fire. Blisters formed on his flesh; his hair began to singe. Shuka turned away, forcing his eyes to the floor, unable to gaze upon the burning demon.

One after another, pillows started to smolder, then erupted into reddish-yellow flames. An acrid smoke quickly filled the room. The fire demon gave no indication of leaving. It drifted back and forth in the doorway as though it were waiting. With its hellish fire, Mela also sensed foulness. This being did not belong in this world. A tinge of regret touched Mela's heart. *It must be done. I know my destiny comes at a cost.*

"Face it!" Mela ordered Shuka. "Turn and face the demon!"

The boy slumped to his knees, sobbing. "I cannot," he said. "I beg you not to make me."

The blue and violet flames of the fire demon danced about, lashing at the stone and the room's burning remnants. Like fierce blazing tongues, the flames lapped at everything as though tasting each material. Everything kissed by the flames quickly erupted into a blaze or melted away.

Sinuous strands of smoke streamed from Shuka's robe. Mela knew the boy's clothing was about to ignite. The master builder considered leaving him, but there was no other way out of the chamber.

"Turn to face the demon!" Mela said again. "It must see the mark Nebas placed on your forehead."

Mela hoped this is what the demon wanted.

Still sobbing, Shuka gradually turned, facing the creature. His head moved in starts as though it were a large block of stone slowly being pulled about.

Heat worked its way through the tablet in Mela's arms. The golden trinkets yet untouched by the flames started to sweat.

Finally, Shuka brought his gaze upon the child of the city-god. The boy still sniffled, but managed to hold his ground when looking upon the abomination.

Again the fire demon danced about, up and down, side-to-side, its violet-blue flames greedily touching the walls and floor and ceiling. For an instant it shifted toward Shuka, as though to consume the boy.

Shuka flinched, readying to flee, though there was no place to run.

"It is all right," Mela said. "If it meant to kill us, it would have done so already. It is only looking for your mark." Mela hoped the mark had not been washed away by sweat.

The boy's eyes were wide with terror, his face glistening, wet strands of hair clinging to his cheeks.

Flares of violet and green danced amid the demon's fiery form. The searing heat decreased, and then the creature soared away as though it had been blown down the corridor by the great breath of a god.

"Come," Mela said. "Nebas's protection has worked, but for how long, I do not know. Let us waste no time."

The two hurried from the room, tracing their path through corridors until they arrived at the palace courtyard, returning to the open night. Through the darkness they headed toward the construction camp outside the city walls. Brilliant flashes of light filled the sky, followed by the mighty grumblings of the gathering storm.

"There is not much time," Mela said, engrossed by the writings upon the stone tablet. "I must prepare. The city-god approaches."

Nebas had been waiting in the tent when Mela and Shuka returned. Mela wasn't sure if her presence was due to a fear of the city-god's children, or confidence that the pair would return. Her compact form reclined on a large pillow. Mela sensed an air of pride about her. Smugness for her successful summoning. Proof of the power of her art.

I will give proof, he thought. *Proof of a greater art.*

"You risk much," she said, as though she had read his mind. "You have killed Ur-Nansha's guards, destroyed his palace, stolen the tablet of the kings, and now you intend to usurp his rule by using the tower to contact the city-god." A husky laugh slipped from her mouth. "You put much faith in my words, Master Builder."

"It is not your prophecy alone that I act upon," Mela said. "It is the word of the ancient prophets of Babylon as well. They predicted this day. They foresaw the Great Tower being completed by this night. They provided the sacred words to speak with the city-god, proclaiming there was only one man who could undertake the task. . . ."

Mela studied the tablet as he spoke, as though quoting from it. "You have foretold my success, and the coming of the storm that is nearly upon us." He fixed his eyes upon the smug woman. "It is not the weight of your words, but the balance between your words and those of the ancient prophets. Only *one* man can undertake this task. I have the tablet. The sacred words." Mela mirrored Nebas's smug posture now. "I am the one."

Nebas watched in silence for several moments, not offering a challenge to his reasoning. She simply gazed at him with her dark eyes as though drinking of his depth, of his soul, of his ability. Measuring him the way a master builder might measure a wall.

The storm rumbled. A deep violet hue stained the sky. The city-god drew near.

"Master," Shuka spoke from the entrance of the tent, where he'd been eyeing the brewing tempest. "Can this city-god be trusted? I've heard many tales about their treachery and deceit. I have little faith to place in them."

The young boy imitated Mela in this. *Good*, Mela thought. *Even without a birth heir, I still will have a legacy. Shuka will carry my teachings into the future. He will show the world what I have done, and give them my knowledge. Master Builder Mela of Ur shall not just build in his day, but in the future as well.*

"I do not go trusting," Mela said. "I go invoking the power of ancient words. Secrets only known by few. I go to prove myself worthy of a pact! Thousands from distant lands have swarmed like ants to see what I have completed. Even now they crawl over it in amazement, sensing its greatness, unable to see it in its entirety. Even the city-god comes to it. I trust in myself, not in gods."

The answer didn't appear to satisfy the young boy. Mela knew that with such a life as his came skepticism, and the work of human treachery taught many lessons.

"You are the greatest of the builders." Shuka stepped forward. "Does this not satisfy you? Do you not take pride in your accomplishments?"

"Accomplishments are fleeting," Nebas said. "They dull with time, they fade like men. And men like Mela always need another accomplishment. A great undertaking that cannot be undone. Do not fool yourself, young one. The path you follow is one of pride and envy. These things are not easily satisfied in any man. This is all the more true in builders."

"I go because it has been fated," Mela said. "My fate cannot be undone."

"In that you are correct," Nebas said. "But fate is illusory, not always appearing in its true form. It is as slippery as a fish in the water."

"Enough!" Mela roared. "Enough of your petty words. I know what I must do because I must do it."

Nebas did not stir under Mela's hard glare. Sprawled upon the pillows, she gestured toward the tent's entrance and said, "Your fate awaits you, Master Builder."

Tens of thousands of spectators had been gathering at the foot of the Great Tower during the final months of its construction. Many were from distant lands, and all had come to see the wonder of Babylon. The monument of the Master Builder Mela of Ur.

Ur-Nansha had not been seen since the appearance of the city-god's children. Mela decided that the king had either fled the city in terror or had been killed by one of the demons. Both paths left him free to meet his fate.

Now that the city guards were gone—Mela suspected they'd fled as well—crowds had begun to line the stairs of the tower. Each stair folded around the square shape of the ziggurat, brimming with onlookers.

Witnesses to a great moment, Mela thought.

As the master builder ascended the stairs, he took pride in the crafting of the walls. They possessed a perfect symmetry. Each had been sized and angled so as to appear in proportion from the ground. *A stone worker's illusion, but one necessary to lend beauty to a structure. With deceit there is often beauty*, Mela concluded.

The intensity of the storm grew as Mela climbed upward, pushing through the throng of people. Bluish-purple flashes now replaced the stark white ones previously prowling the sky. Clouds the color of rotting flesh stirred and swelled overhead. Low-rolling thunder growled, shaking the tower.

Mela pressed onward, scaling the dizzying heights with a quickened pace. The stone stairs twisted their way about the ziggurat, leading ever upward, until the summit pierced the storm clouds. The gathered numbers lessened as Mela continued his trek. He cut through the huddled groups, hearing countless tongues speak amongst themselves, each word foreign and unintelligible. *All of the world has come to see my marvel.*

Although the years of overseeing the construction of the tower had given him endurance lacked by most men his age, the climb outlasted Mela. To keep from dropping in utter exhaustion, he paused to regain his strength.

Soon Shuka came crawling up the stairs. The boy was puffing from the arduous task. Nonetheless, he was determined to reach the summit with his master.

Winded, Mela braced against the waist-high wall that acted as a barrier for the outer side of the stairs. A black and violet mantle had settled over the land. From so high a place, the distant ground below was dotted with a scattered collection of people who were only visible when the angry sky flashed with fire.

"Look!" Shuka's arm stretched downward, pointing at the base of the tower. "Those are torches. It is Ur-Nansha's army approaching." With each utterance, the boy gulped in air to force out the next word.

Shuka was right. The king had not fled. Ur-Nansha probably did not need the tablet with the sacred words. Undoubtedly he had memorized them just as Mela had. Locking away words in the mind was one of the many skills of a master builder. *But why approach with his army*? Mela wondered. *Was Ur-Nansha surrounding himself for protection from the fire demons*?

Then as the specks below began to form ranks, Mela realized the truth. Ur-Nansha had brought the army to wage war against the city-god. *The fool! He plans to mount the tower to do battle.*

As some of the troops formed perfect double lines and others formed squares, a single column detached, snaking up the tower stairs.

"They are too late," Mela said with satisfaction. "I will reach the *cella* first."

Mela ran onward, the muscles in his legs burning with each step.

"Come no further," Mela said. "The remainder is for me alone. Ur-Nansha only brings danger with him. Return to my tent, wait there for my arrival."

As he spoke, tiny droplets of fire rained from the sky. The burning rain bounced on the stone, dancing about in violet and blue shades, colliding with spectators, setting them aflame. Others fell on the tents below, igniting the cloth into furious blazes. Cries and wails filled the burning air.

"Hurry!" Mela bellowed. "Retrieve my belongings from the tent before it is consumed. Ur-Nansha's treachery already brings disaster!"

Shuka fled down the stairs, dodging through the panicking masses.

Moving swiftly, Mela took the stairs two at a time. As he dashed upward, he caught glimpses of burning arrows flying upward. He laughed at the arrogance of Ur-Nansha. He was not the first of men, he was the first of *fools*.

The raining fire smacked against Mela's bare chest and shoulders, biting his flesh. This added to his energy, increasing his speed until he was bounding at a full run, risking stumbling on each stair underfoot.

As he approached the summit, a tremendous shoot of flame burst from the sky, surging downward. With it came a roar and a furious gust of scalding wind. He did not need to look. Mela knew the blast was large enough to encompass the whole of Ur-Nansha's army at the base of the tower. Too far up to actually hear, Mela imagined the screams of agony and terror that certainly filled the air along with the stench of burning flesh.

Stepping onto the *cella*, a large, stone altar that formed the pinnacle of the tower, Mela felt the potent heat radiating from the clouds. His flesh reddened. Pinches of fire nipped at his face as he squinted upward. It was as though he were gazing at a giant fire demon—one far more fearsome than the fiends Nebas had called forth.

Each swallow of air scorched his lungs. He knew if he didn't begin the ritual soon, he would not survive to complete it. His mind numb with weariness and pain, Mela commenced the chant, speaking the ancient words that would bind the city-god to his will.

Each syllable brought a reply of thunder and a flash of fire. The sky above Mela had transformed into a monstrous conflagration. With no more than the first few words uttered, Mela sensed the presence of another. It was nothing more than a feeling in his mind. A mote in an ocean. Not the feeling of another person watching him; rather, the sensation of something dreadful contemplating him. He continued the chant; the sacred language sounded small coming from him.

He fought to speak above the fury of the wind and the roar of thunder.

Suddenly, his mind exploded with the countless thoughts of other beings. Other minds. Human minds. Fear swelled inside him, but he refused to surrender. The thoughts grew stronger, raging in his head, the intensity overwhelming. Soon he no longer knew his own thoughts from the rest. But then came recognition. He heard the anguished pleas, hideous and tortured petitions for death. He felt them swarm in his skull as though they were in the very air. The souls of humans being drawn upward from their mortal bodies to be consumed. The city-god was feeding upon the people on the Great Tower.

Overhead the sky continued to roil and writhe in purples and blues. Bursts of yellow flames parted and folded together like a grotesque mouth smacking its lips—a mockery of a human face. An endless cacophony of thunder rumbled across the land.

Struggling to break free, to untangle his thoughts from the countless others, Mela felt something directly touch his mind. It was a fearsome thing, nameless, and more terrifying than the thoughts of a thousand dying minds. There were no words or understanding in the touch. All that Mela felt was emotion. *Satisfaction.* A thirst quenched; a hunger sated. At that moment, Mela understood the prophecies. He understood his destiny. He comprehended the purpose of the first master builder, Caina, and he began to weep at the treachery.

The Great Tower was to be built, not to speak with the city-god, but to *feed* the city-god. The knowledge passed down from the first master builder to each apprentice was to serve this end. And the greatest treachery was the building of the Great Tower. Like moths to a flame, the tower attracted humans by the thousands from across the earth. The Great Tower served up a bounteous feast for the city-god. Mela had played a part in it. But he realized there were others. Nebas, and those with the secret knowledge—such people served the city-god. Ur-Nansha was not the only fool in this; he was only one of many.

In his final moments, as the *thing* pulled at his soul, Mela realized it wasn't a god. It was a monster, a great foul demon that thrived on human life. Mela wasn't a master builder; he was a tender of crops. He watered and weeded so this *thing* could harvest. The city-god needed crops grown in a single place. Cities were rich fields of humanity, much easier to harvest than wandering bands of humans who lived in tribes. It was the work of the builders who had created the cities, bringing people to a single place, a fertile field for future harvest.

A profound woe wrenched Mela as he realized what seeds had been planted. The knowledge of building great cities would go on, and once again, long after human memory had forgotten this day, another master builder would complete a similar creation. It may be thousands of years away, but the *thing* in the heavens was patient. The day would come. There would be another great feast.

And in his mind, he could hear himself still chanting. The words gained momentum, each echoing through the hot air.

"No!" Mela cried, halting the chant. "I will not take part in this!"

A dreadful silence shrouded the *cella*. The feeling of satisfaction swelled from within the twisting clouds of smoke and fire.

Before Mela uttered another word, before he could flee, flames jetted downward. The tower quaked. Stone erupted as the structure began to collapse. The mudbrick beneath Mela crumbled, turning to ash, opening a great maw in the *cella's* floor. As Mela plummeted to what he knew was certain death, he felt a tugging, a pulling at his mind. The greedy creature in the sky left no morsel behind. A split-second before Mela collided with the deadly stones below, the creature rent his soul from his flesh. In that moment, Mela's thoughts blurred and intermingled with countless others. There was no longer a sense of individuality, only a great mass of pain and sorrow.

With his last effort, Mela searched the minds, looking for Shuka's, hoping for the boy's death. But in the countless souls Mela touched, none belonged to his apprentice.

Quickly his mind faded into the mire of thousands of other minds, each understanding their fate, and each pleading for release. In that moment, Mela of Ur, and all his knowledge, and all his secrets, and all the warnings he had for humanity were consumed by the city-god. All that remained of the Great Tower was a heap of shattered stone.

A handful of scattered spectators fled before the feeding began, seeds of the future. The city-god's hunger was satisfied. Now all that remained was the waiting for the next feast.

In the Light of Dying Fires

Gerard Houarner

She didn't ride up in her court finery, inviting fire from Lord Merexem's ballista atop the wall. The archers studying trained hawks riding air currents to range their arrows didn't bother testing a flight on what looked like another messenger, hooded cloak snapping in her wake as her mare galloped through the last of the morning mist to his position, bearing orders, or perhaps a swig of freshly drawn blood from one of the prisoners.

People believed anything.

He could have protected them easily enough if Lady Rosin Ghaeln had come to woo him with her power and beauty, even from the more potent spellcasters sprinkled in with the archers. But that would have invited attention, a more rigorous testing of his defenses, perhaps suspicion about what role he was to play in the coming battle. Fortunes, he'd been told, could turn on the slightest details overlooked.

They were kindred souls. A good match. If they hadn't been so similar, she might have been the one to finally make him forget about Aum and all that he'd left behind. She'd almost been enough to make him believe he'd found a place in which he could truly be reborn. She was nearly enough to make the feeling of displacement fade, to fire up an emotion he hadn't felt since he left Aum: belonging.

Last night, in his tent, she'd come close to bringing him home from exile. Together, they'd nearly taken a chance on their deeper desires extinguishing the fires of destruction and self-destruction they shared.

He didn't need to catch her gaze, peer into the dark, round stars of her eyes to see the pain gnawing at duty, trying to tear the pride of responsibility down. She reined in the mare abruptly and came to a halt paces away from him. Their horses snorted and shook their heads, bowed, and sidestepped toward each other.

Somewhere in the mountains, the screaming had started. Scouts had ridden into pickets. Arrows had been exchanged, charges called, and it was coming down to flesh and steel, the summoning and spilling of blood. The horns would start up, soon.

But the plan was for Lord Merexem's attention to be drawn to what was happening right in front of him. Jeloc, receiving messengers, displaying power in bright, proud plumes obvious to those with magic in their blood, was just more bait.

Her appearance wasn't part of the strategy. He wasn't supposed to be distracted. But, of course, these things happened in war, and in matters of the heart.

Lady Ghalen raised a hand to undo the catch to her hood. Jeloc stopped her with a look, and she pursed her lips in annoyance, nearly ruining the illusion she'd worked so hard to construct. Wisps of black hair, silken and shiny, waved from under the hood as if alive and searching for something to latch on to.

His own mane of grey with white streaks was carefully gathered and capped beneath his helm. After his work was done, in a year after the blood had dried, or perhaps another hundred, he'd shave it all off. Or perhaps it would simply fall out, as a consequence of what was coming. Then he'd move on to a new world and let his hair grow back in, fresh and black, like hers, to celebrate a step taken on the road of retribution.

But he was still in this world, and his work was not yet done. He bowed his head slightly, just enough to convey respect for her rank but not enough to signal an attack from their besieged enemy.

"Do you think you can ever love me?" the lady asked, picking up the thread of their last conversation without hesitation, as if he hadn't called her brothers Teil and Bhan to drag her out of his tent last night because he wasn't sure what road he walked, what home he needed.

He remembered her scent, only faintly sweet, more roots than fruit, strong and sensual and of the earth. The stench of war couldn't overcome the memory.

Her assured tone enticed him: calm, powerful with unspoken passion, like a low, warning rumble that shook the gut and heart and presaged an earthquake. If she lost her flesh and existed only as a spirit, would her love for him be strong enough to sustain her among the living? Was she really Ymel's equal?

"The spells are ready," he said, determined to stay the course. He was confident there was at least one sorcerer serving the other side capable of breaking his whisper spell and making his words clear to Lord Merexem. As if intentions could not be gleaned from the soaring vortex of energies he'd gathered overhead, spinning in a lofty construction of containment spells, invisible to the untrained eye, mysterious and alarming to those who could discern what lurked beneath reality's illusions.

The hawks knew better, and stayed clear.

Jeloc cocked his head toward the nearby mountains. "We're waiting for your brother's horn to blow from the high pass to signal the relief army's arrival. Merexem's forces will charge out of their gates, thinking they've caught us between the hammer and the anvil. Then we'll attack."

"I know the plan. A good part of it is mine."

Her tone was sharp. He frowned.

"I know," he said.

She was right, of course. They both knew the play of feints and diversions to come, the Worm burrowing to the fortress cistern gate, and the inevitable siege engines rolling forward, their construction having reduced a nearby forest to stumps. Their hands were already bloody with the planned sacrifice of clans backing Lord Joru's play for independence. They were the least of what was going to be lost.

The Lady's gaze refused to wither under his testing glare. The hurt, surely from last night's betrayal, was plain in her bearing. "There are listeners on the wall," she said.

"They can't see my lips when I'm looking at you. They can't hear our words through the beating of our hearts."

"Stop." She forced a frown, but a smile still flickered over her lips.

Jeloc's ploy had worked. He'd used his heartbeat as the source of interference in his whisper spell, and drawn hers into the spell's workings when she'd ridden up to him. She'd been touched by the romantic gesture in his sorcery, even if she didn't trust it.

"You're not answering my question," she said, the smile blowing away like smoke.

"No."

"Is it because of her?"

There it was.

Lady Ghalen had caught the quiver of hurt that had pinched his lips, the old wound still not mended after hundreds of years of wandering from world to world. All those centuries since he'd last seen her alive, and still the loss drained the life and hope from his spirit, like a poisoned quiver lodged forever in his flesh. Ymel Shal-Ikah. "Yes," he said, as if he needed to confess.

"But she's dead."

"Yes."

Lady Ghalen hesitated before his resolve. "And so far away."

"Further than you can imagine." That he'd spoken of his true love to her was the surest sign of their intimacy, even compatibility. That he could speak to her about his pain told him there were possibilities for healing in their being together. Lady Ghalen understood. He'd called her by her heart's name, Rosin, after they became lovers. He'd only ever had one name, and she'd never added to it with a private, pet name, the way so many others had tried to do, as if to cage him in their desires and fantasies.

"Then why can't you give yourself to the living, to what's here now?"

"I have. Everything that I am, is yours. For now."

"I thought you chose my father's side in this war because of me, but I was wrong, wasn't I?"

Balancing sorceries was easier than controlling his emotions as she skirted truth. "You are your father's daughter. It's to your blood I've pledged myself."

"Why?"

"Because I believe in your cause."

She glanced at the wall, frowned. The lines that would have come with wisdom revealed themselves on her smooth, glistening brow: disappointment, hurt. Caution. Fear. Like with so many issues, she seemed to know better than to put words to shadows passing over her face: I don't believe you.

Instead, she said: "I'll do my part." She spared herself the moment in which he might change his mind and choose her over a dead woman. Instead, she turned her mount suddenly, kicked with more enthusiasm than necessary, and bolted back to the lines.

Jeloc was fairly certain that it was because of the chill air from the night's camp in these raw hills that she shivered.

Another rider came out from one of the assault formations to meet her. From the wall, a derisive roar greeted the newcomer. She passed him without exchanging a word or sign.

Jeloc reached for the taps he'd spent days chanting into existence in the earth, the fires, the rising sun hidden behind clouds, the flesh and blood of the masses surrounding him. Above him, the tower of sorcery rose through air and cloud. Spells hung like fruit on vines entwined with the tower's structure, ready to be plucked and empowered by a vortex of stored energies with simple trigger words or motions.

He opened the conduits, letting power flow into and fill his tower. The air crackled and lightning flashed in the sky while his spells ripened. Armed.

Watchers would surmise he was reacting to news he'd received.

The appearance of his construction was formidable. Intimidating, even to Merexem's best defenders. But the labyrinth of his magic held secrets, hidden spaces and spells waiting for a fresh influx of energy.

A volley of fire darts flew from the wall, scattering hawks, descending on the new rider. He'd made no effort to hide the runes decorating the plates of his armor, or the small bundles tied to his helmet and the sword hilt at his hip. He pressed on to Jeloc, barely raising a hand to deflect the assault, and stopping even that show of effort as soon as he was under Jeloc's protection.

"Sir, is this the tact you should be taking with her?" Fayer said, staring over his shoulder as Lady Ghalen merged with her father's gathered forces. Scars marred his youthful visage. He'd studied too hard, even before Lord Juro had passed him on to Jeloc. He liked the boy's fire, the rage burning on childhood hurts, and his fine and fanatical focus. If Jeloc hadn't fallen into this world, Fayer might have become an archmage, Lord Joru's favorite, champion of the clans, and Lady Ghalen's lover. Instead, Fayer was Jeloc's apprentice, and Lord Joru's spy. Like on any world, trust extended only so far to strangers. And not without good reason.

"Should I lie?" Jeloc answered question with question, the way of teacher to student.

"I don't," Fayer said. The challenge was clear, the boy's confused loyalties and love for Ghalen clearer.

But another, far more threatening test called for Jeloc's attention.

A prickly, poisonous thread ran through the drumming which rose from behind the stronghold wall. Ragged and loose at first, the frantic pounding resolved into a rapid beat that was an echo of the pulse of Jeloc's heart. The sound gathered all elements, made the ground tremble and the air vibrate, the fires from torches and cook pits flare, the clouds thicken to a roiling inverse sea rumbling with the promise of rain. The drumming drove into him, shook his gut, until it seemed the blood in his ears was about to burst from their vessels and flood his thoughts.

He thought he felt Ghalen's touch in the violent, primal reverberations. Perhaps Lord Merexem's spellcasters had picked echoes of her heartbeat from his defenses, as a taunt. Of course, he saw the hands beating the drums, each weaving their little part of a larger spell designed to reach into him, sap his will, ruin the construction of his own temple of energies and hijack his power.

Jeloc admired the impudence. He'd invited and counted on it. For the benefit of Merexem's spies, Lord Juro had complained of his new sorcerer's fragile arrogance to certain courtiers.

If he'd lived only one lifetime, he might have been intimidated by the breath of a hundred spellcasters bearing down on him to infiltrate his delicate construction and upset his balance. But he'd been old enough to know better when he'd been banished from his birthplace.

He let the spellcasters think they were succeeding, diverting their workings to a sliver of his tower, where they could taste him, feel and smell his exertion, and be certain of their success without actually threatening him. Their work was crucial to the plan. They deserved what was coming.

With another crossroads of the plan passed, Jeloc turned back to the war of hearts at his doorstep. He wasn't surprised to find Fayer looking over his shoulder in the direction Lady Ghalen had taken. "I nurture what she needs to make her play her part, not to win love," Jeloc said. "Does that matter to you?"

Fayer shook his head, like his horse might to chase off flies. "Of course not."

This was the time to twist the knife so clearly stuck in Fayer's heart. "She'll act as she must. Now, more than ever. To spite me, to prove she was worthy of my love, but I wasn't worthy of hers."

"I don't know much about affairs of the heart. As long as she does what she has to do, the rest will take care of itself."

Jeloc smiled. "So you tell yourselves."

Fayer didn't jerk his head, change his tone, or even twitch a finger, when he said, "Do you have any information to the contrary?"

Jeloc was impressed. There might be more subterfuge to the boy than he'd given him credit for. "You should ask your gods."

The boy's horse started, and Fayer turned to stare at the emptiness at their flank. "Here's one coming now. Why don't you?"

Jeloc turned to catch the haze in the air, at the boundary of his protective spells, where another power was emerging.

Then distant horns blew, catching Jeloc by surprise. Teil, sounding the warning that Lord Merexem's relief was in the pass, calling his brother Bhan to arms. Jeloc thought he'd have more time. He hadn't quite finished gathering his power. He looked to the stronghold's gates, but they remained shut.

A fly buzzed his ear, gnawed at the threads of his thoughts. Enough shit lay underfoot from cavalry charging back and forth over the past few days to give birth to a universe of insects.

Joru's war engines unleashed fiery bolts, arcing high over the walls to seed havoc in Merexem's defenses. The battle was lurching into an opening.

"Show me how you work your magic, Master," Fayer said, and for once, Jeloc sensed his apprentice's complete sincerity. "Lord Joru says his sons are putting their lives in your hands. He reminds you that he's already given you the gift of his daughter."

Jeloc didn't bother to remind the boy what Joru hoped to gain by that gift.

Fayer pulled away, rode back to the lines as the siege towers creaked forward. The gathered clan warriors roared their fear and fury.

A scream cut through the air, startling the hawks. Jeloc thought something had happened to the Worm, that perhaps it had been discovered and stricken by counter measures.

"My mate," the old god grumbled, appearing suddenly by Jeloc's side, waving a bandaged hand at the wall. "She's Merexem's slave, and envies my freedom."

Jeloc quelled his shock, but his mount whinnied in surprise. The hawks flapped their wings, seeking the currents to carry them higher. He'd overlooked, for an instant, what was coming. His mother would have laughed, and asked if he was sure he was ready for the scale and stakes of the game he was playing.

The haze had solidified into a tall, emaciated figure nearly lost in the rags of a great coat and the sad, stringy remains of a turban. He was a sliver of god flesh dressed in weathered glories. Eyes shone bright from the thin, sharp-boned face, contradicting the realities of the dirt caked in wrinkles, the lesion oozing pus beneath the jaw-line and the blackened tongue peeking from the spaces made by missing teeth.

Tygal. Warrior and lawgiver. In his glory, a being separated from mortals and his fellow gods by his capacity for mercy, not power. The songs rising from Lord Juro's campfires traced clan ancestries to this reflection of the world's living spirits.

Tygal, reduced to the form of a beggar by the sins and desires of his worshippers. These days, his mercy was seen as weakness, his former strength and courage stolen by new spirits born from the souls of men, his principles gutted and used by men like Joru and Merexem to bend others to their will.

Sustaining himself on the gentle prayers from the old and infirm in the backward corners of the world, Tygal had no choice but to bargain with the likes of Jeloc.

Broken gods still knew secrets and could show the way to great power, if handled wisely. The trick was to know what the other needed most desperately. Lord Merexem had his ways of trapping discarded spirits and fallen gods in his cause. Jeloc preferred his homeland's founding law: anything can be bought. For a price. He was far more comfortable with the arts of brokering a deal than those of war.

The hawks, recovered from their surprise, hovered dangerously close to extinction on the chance of tasting god flesh.

"At least your old mate remembers you," Jeloc said. The god smelled of pepper, and made Jeloc's skin itch.

"Memory has its thorns," Tygal said. "As you should know."

Ballistas launched missiles. Archers moved past Jeloc, firing from behind the shields of their warrior escorts.

"Our arrangement remains?" Tygal asked.

"A conjunction will open the door to Aum in Lord Merexem's fortress."

"You still remember every conjunction of all of Aum's Gates, after so many years away?"

"Nobody remembers them all. That's why each Gate has its own Keeper. And why I still have friends in Aum who can consult them." The god's ignorance irritated Jeloc, but he was flattered by the assumption that he'd have that much knowledge.

Flies whispered their admiration.

The Worm rose up suddenly from the earth at the cistern gate, glowing golden like a pallid sun breaking free from the land, cracking stone in a geyser of sewage and muddy earth. A panicked roar spilled from the ramparts, though the drumbeats remained true and steady, even louder, as if in response to the new assault. Jeloc detected concern in the quiver of concentration among the opposing spellcasters. They'd been surprised. He'd managed to trick them.

He was in control.

The Worm climbed into the air, shedding dust and earth and stone, as well as broad and sticky leaves of its own flesh, before collapsing blind-head first into the crack it had created. Its flesh rippled, boils rose and burst along its length, unleashing torrents of thick, pale, viscous liquid, like white mud, seeded with the black, meaty pearls of the Worm's limited brain. Still, the creature pressed on, following the command Jeloc had labored so hard to implant in its primitive mind. Another tool, shaped for sacrifice.

"And my place in the Necropolis?" Tygal asked

"My associate waits on the other side of the Gate, in Aum, to guide you there. You have the price for the Gate Mothers and their Tongue? And for the cost of your tomb's security? You won't last long, otherwise."

"Enough for them, and for anything else I might need for a while." The god pulled at his pockets, but didn't draw the offerings he carried.

No obvious treasures. But then, wise gods at the height of their power sometimes knew to prepare for their old age, creating bubble worlds parallel to all realities, but cut off from them. There they'd save holdings to carry them through their eventual fall, and even withdraw into them, choosing eternal banishment in a tiny universe of their making over the sadder fates awaiting them.

Tygal seemed like a wise one. But he'd still warned the god. The consequences of short-changing the Gate Mothers would be the least of Tygal's worries if he thought he could escape all that waited in Aum to feed on the shells of gods and demons drifting to their final days in Aum without the means to buy protection. Fading from existence, or eternal banishment in a barren bolt-hole would have been far more peaceful paths to take.

"Stand by my side, then, and be ready," Jeloc said. He didn't have to ask for what was owed.

Tygal surrendered what he'd promised: the bloody, killing parts grown from the spirits of mortals who'd made him, and the bits of wisdom and patience from which new faiths had briefly taken root in the greedy, festering jungles of mortal flesh and blood. Tygal gave up most of his remaining bits of godhood, of transcendent awareness and bonds to the powers that lay between, and beyond, mortal worlds. What good were these old ways of doing and seeing to the Lords Juro or Merexem? Even to Jeloc, they were only a strong and flexible form of energy that would fuel his construction.

More sacrifice. Magic's heart, in the end. And, another surprise for Merexem. War's soul.

The transaction made him feel that he understood Tygal. Lady Ghalen, as well. They were just like him, willing to surrender everything for what they wanted. He'd give anything to become the thing that he loved—a spirit. He would have given anything to be with Ymel.

The transfer of Tygal's godly energies weighed on Jeloc's shoulders. Their wild, alien vitality fed and sparked to life the wounds and desires he'd spent lifetimes subduing. He gasped as the pain of loss flared to life for a moment, as fresh as the day he'd first felt it. Guilt crushed him. Rage burst in a blinding flash. The reins of his control slipped, just for an instant.

But he'd been prepared. The cold heart of discipline took over. Guilt and rage were channeled to their proper uses. His delicate construction grew higher, stronger. The vortex of power crackled with latent possibilities, a storm greater than the gathering winds and clouds could ever muster. He was careful to siphon a taste of Tygal to Merexem's spellcasters, to lead them where he wanted, which was not where he was going. He could almost hear Fayer reassuring Joru that Jeloc was following the plan.

Now he was ready.

"Stay on your guard," Tygal said.

"You, too," Jeloc replied. "Unless you want to join your old mate in Merexem's stable. I'm sure you have a secret or two he'd love to find."

"The only secrets I have left are the ones your kind keep from yourselves."

Jeloc almost laughed at the old god's presumption, associating him with the teeming mortal masses around them.

The Worm's death cries called Jeloc's attention back to the battlefield. It had settled its broken body into the breach it had created, and lay shuddering, bleeding its molten meat into the stronghold. Joru's allied clans advanced, volleys of flaming arrows and shot arcing through the sky from their lines, smashing into the Worm's flesh, setting it on fire and unleashing acidic bile that would further weaken and crack the wall.

The stronghold gates opened, and twin horse columns charged out, pennants fluttering at the ends of heavy lances. One column curled to counter Lord Joru's forces heading for the breach, the other turned to strike at the siege line to Jeloc's left.

Following the cavalry, footmen marched out in formation, shields sparkling with inset jewels that held the fierce fire of stars. Jeloc studied them, and recoiled. The trick lay in the release of that power, not with a spellcaster's command, but with a word from each shield-bearer. Magic for commoners.

Jeloc had never seen the like, hadn't even thought of arming Lord Joru's warriors with sorcerous weapons. The thought of surrendering control over any magic he'd woven was unsettling. What new god had taught Lord Merexem these tricks?

The sound of insects swarming around his ears coalesced into the voice of an audience, perhaps from an Aum playhouse, laughing at the fool on the stage. Who did he think he was, coming to a new world and challenging the powers that had ruled it for longer than he'd been alive? Did he really think he could bring change? Or preserve old orders? Was he truly stupid enough to think he mattered?

No wonder he'd lost his place in the world he'd been born into. No wonder he'd lost his love. He was nothing. An arrogant little princeling, meddling in the affairs of his betters.

The whispers' sting made Jeloc slap a hand over an ear, as if he'd been bitten.

The drums from the walls beat louder, their reverberations driving deeper into the earth, into Jeloc. Thunder answered the drum beats, crackling first, then settling into a rumble. Lightning flashed. Lanced at the earth. Landed among Joru's warriors, licked at Jeloc's tower of sorcery.

Jeloc took a deep breath. Tygal remained silent beside him. The forces aligned to fight were staggering forward into inevitable, inescapable annihilation.

Dust rose from the footsteps of marching warriors, the hooves of charging mounts. Fires burning on both sides of the battlefield turned the storm's gathering gloom into red darkness. Stone cracked and melted. Animals shrieked, men yelled their courage and their terror. The flesh and metal clash of armies meeting rose briefly before settling into a clatter of weapons punctuated by screams. Jeloc's heart beat faster.

Smoke drifted across his position, scratching at eyes and throat, perfumed with the fragrance of ripped bodies, and pepper from a god. He thought he caught a trace of Lady Ghalen's earthy musk—her time was coming. Fayer's knife work, then Jeloc's spells spitting from his throat as fast as Ghalen's blood from hers, and he'd feel the fresh flow of power into his construction.

The rain came down, sudden and drenching. The lightning strikes stopped lashing at his defenses, but continued to rake Lord Juro's positions. Merexem's shield gems began bursting with blinding and bloody effect.

Jeloc held his mount steady. There were spells he could pluck from above to lend the troops support, but that's what Lord Merexem wanted—to draw him early into the conflict. He looked back at Lord Joru's lines, catching adjustments, a redeployment of forces, but nothing critical. He wasn't needed.

He thought he caught a dun-colored mare and a cloaked figure in the advanced lines.

Impossible. Lady Ghalen had to be at the rear by now, preparing for her sacrifice. Lord Joru would have made certain of that.

"Aren't you afraid she'll haunt you, like the other one?" Tygal asked.

Jeloc clung to the question as if it were driftwood in a typhoon. The battle's unfolding scope was greater than any human conflict he'd witnessed in his travels. This wasn't a sorcerer's duel, or a harrying assault on an army. The invisible forces bending reality all around him weren't the machinations of court intrigue, the tidal flow of pledges and betrayals. There was more death and wildness in magic's power in this tiny patch of a world than he'd ever witnessed or felt before, more than he'd ever allowed himself to face.

He stifled, with venomous anger, the tiny part of him that wished he were back in Aum, in the smaller, if no less unpredictable and deadly conflicts.

"My love is bound to the place I came from," Jeloc said, a little too loudly. Putting out the sparks of his undying rage, he continued, "As the woman from here will be bound to this earth, should she resist moving on to her spirit world. She won't have me to haunt for long, because I'll be gone once my business is done."

"You flesh and blood types have all the answers," Tygal said, suddenly infused with the surly cheeriness of a tavern-dweller, as if relief from the burdens of a dying godhood, like a couple of tall cups of strong ale, allowed him a measure of camaraderie with all who had ever worshiped him.

Jeloc mopped rain water from his face. At least Lord Merexem hadn't poisoned the downpour with his sorcery. "I thought the gods had answers."

"You can't believe what everyone says. But the simple faith that I do have answers keeps me going."

Jeloc snorted, relaxed a little. A good apprentice by his side might have performed the same function: wise fool, relieving the master of his burdens. "You're no different from the mortals who worship you."

Tygal watched a detachment of Lord Merexem's shield warriors ride up, dismount. While half stood guard against Juro's counteract, the rest threw their swords and spears down and positioned themselves to focus the power of the stones on a single point in Jeloc's invisible defenses. With an eyebrow slightly raised, he said, "When this is done, I'm going to enjoy my retirement. No more philosophies. No more right and wrong, justice and punishment. Chaos and order."

"The bargain's done," Jeloc said, following the same action with interest, prepared to be surprised. "I appreciate your willingness to make the deal."

The warriors released the power in their shields' gemstones simultaneously, producing a writhing, white flash that quickly exhausted itself against Jeloc's defenses. Though a drain on his reserves, the assault proved pointless. It seemed to him that Merexem was taunting him with the simple trick Jeloc hadn't thought to use.

Jeloc was disappointed the old wizard hadn't thought of a more threatening ploy.

"I understand there's much to entertain our kind in Aum's Necropolis district," Tygal said, watching as Joru's cavalry swept through the spent shield bearers and their protectors, scattering and cutting down the enemy.

"Those who come find amusement. Though not the type they thought would interest them." Jeloc pushed the boundary of his defenses out to consume Lord Joru's fallen warriors, dead and wounded. They shriveled and blackened without flames, and joined the charred remains of hawks on the ground.

The flies laughed.

"No mortals to trick or torture?"

"I thought you would have done your research before we reached our agreement, Tygal. Mortals, enough. And time. But you'll be surprised what else takes up your attention."

"I guess I'll have to wait and see."

"Yes. If you last long enough."

"I only hope you last long enough to get me to my Gate."

Jeloc opened his mouth, pricked by the insult, a taunt ready. But the buzzing in his ear grew louder as the battle closed around them. Merexem's fortress spewed another column of men, this time clad in armor from head to foot. Jeloc took a closer look, warping the walls of his protective spells to magnify his vision.

The men were half as tall as their comrades already in battle, and their armor appeared to be patchwork constructions of broken, rusted and flawed pieces of metal. They moved stiffly, and when they tripped over bodies or wreckage, they had difficulty climbing back on to their feet. When Joru's allied clans rushed to engaged them, the new warriors pressed forward, apparently immune to blows and wounds. It was only when they were hacked to pieces that Jeloc understood they were hollow men, the empty armor of the dead, animated by spirits of Merexem's summoning.

Jeloc nodded his head in acknowledgment: another handy trick, and one that might serve him well if he ever found his way back to Aum.

When.

When he returned.

The heritage of power he'd wasted sang regrets in his veins. The love he'd gambled away choked his heart.

He'd been brash, stupid, arrogant. He'd believed he could challenge the Matriarch's authority, Aum's curse, the wealth the Gates brought to the city. With someone who loved him at his side, how could he not succeed at bringing down the tyranny of an archaic order, destroying the punishing Mist and returning shadowed Aum to the light and to the breath of seasons and the rhythms of a living world.

The rage of that consuming defeat blazed in his soul. The guilt of all he'd cost everyone he ever loved ground down on him with the weight of mountains. And here he was, thinking he could interfere in the order and rhythms of another world. Who did he think he was?

"Steady, boy," Tygal said above the whispers of flies.

Jeloc cursed, in a forgotten tongue from a dead world. If Tygal understood the affront, he didn't let on. What did the old god care, anyway. He didn't remember what it was like to be strong, to dream of using power for more than playing games and answering prayers. He wasn't even really a god, anymore. There was no strength, no pride left in him.

The rain thinned to a cloying mist, not like Aum's Mist which leached through cracks in the city's wall to sting and consume citizens and strangers alike.

That would have been an answer to Merexem's tricks: linking to Aum through a Gate at the wall and drawing through a cloud of killing Mist. Baiting the enemy to the right ground, with a gateway close to conjunction, at the right time, would be everything in the tactic. Jeloc tapped his hand to try to pound the idea into flesh so he wouldn't forget. The battle was scrambling his thoughts, clouding his vision. It was all he could do to remember the plans he'd made, and the parts he had yet to play.

He took a deep breath, and Tygal's advice.

The tower of his sorcery stood without a shudder, his defensive spells remained intact, his bristling armory of offensive weapons were ready. For all of Lord Merexem's clever devices, none had found their way through to him. The spellcasters from the stronghold seemed to weaken as their powers spread to cover the actions of their forces. They remained invested in the structure of his vortex, though their hold was tenuous. He had to keep himself from tossing them away, to stop feigning to struggle with the power he'd harnessed. Lord Merexem still had to believe he was holding Lord Juro's sorcerer in check.

There were still sacrifices to be made.

Noon passed and the battle flowed back and forth before the stronghold walls, centering on the breach created by the Worm, and on a constantly shifting front along Juro's siege lines as Merexem's forces sortied, probing for weakness. His relief columns were advancing, as far as Jeloc could tell from the fires and movements of Lord Juro's troops, but Merexem had not yet made the effort to concentrate his defenses and meet them. Jeloc supposed he still suspected a trick.

Jeloc sank deeper into his own magic, seeking their comfort and power, preparing for his true part in the conflict. And as he did, time shifted, as if he'd dropped out of the world, the universe, and was looking back through a window warped by his passage. He breathed and moved as always, but the greater world's actions flew by with the speed of an angry cloud of hornets driven from their nest. Jeloc laughed, brushed his ear. Though still calm, his horse's restless motions, exaggerated by the shift in perspective, unsettled Jeloc's stomach and head.

He dismounted and sent the horse away. The animal wandered off in quick bursts on a jagged line through the defensive perimeter and into battle.

The drum beats still sounded from Merexem's stronghold, but they did not run fast alongside the world's rhythms. Bound to every ten of his heart beats, Jeloc found them oddly comforting. As for the difference in pace from the rest of what happened outside, he thought the spellcasters too busy to work their tricks against him as they had before battle began. If the charge of power building under his command had not knocked him loose from the flow of events, he might have forgotten completely about the drums.

The flies agreed.

The battle and the day jumped forward, unreal, like a board game played with living pieces.

Juro's siege engines rolled forward, threatening to batter gates, widen cracks and breaks, rain fire and deliver warriors from rolling towers. Their approach provoked the counter-attack Jeloc had anticipated tactically, but not in nature.

A cloud of wraiths spilled from the gates. Nearly human, faceless forms seemingly made of gossamer spider silk, they settled over the machines, gnawed at wood and sinew, until the siege craft collapsed. Jeloc detected the traces of human ghosts, out-world demons, half-human creatures, even gods both older and younger than Tygal, many known only from the campfire tales he'd been listening to since he'd arrived in this land. Set adrift from the world's living flow and forgotten, Lord Merexem had found and collected them, bound them with his mark, learned what he could and kept them in his keep for just such a day.

Not the parry Jeloc and Juro had counted on, but still a drain on Merexem's resources. The wraiths, released from their binding by duty fulfilled, escaped to the clouds, which flashed like signal flares at their departure, and vanished into the welcome peace of obscurity.

Tygal held a hand out, as if signaling for his fleeing mate to come back to him.

An explosion rocked the earth at the base of the wall of spells Jeloc had cast for himself, and another Worm, this one in Merexem's control, reared up, guts and meat erupting from its savaged corpse. The tower of sorcery swayed as residual magics, gods and spirits enslaved to Merexem, spilled out of the Worm and launched themselves at Jeloc.

This is what happened in battle: the unexpected. But with triggers unleashing a torrent of power, he was strong enough to cast back what was thrown at him, all the way to the stronghold's walls, so that blazing Worm bile and broken gods cracked more stone, opened up other breaches. Stray conjurations, riding filaments of his power, caught up Juro's ballista and a few remaining siege engines, threw them like toys high into the air. They soared and finally dove, transforming at the end of their flight into mechanical that hawks descended on another column of Merexem's warriors emerging from the gates.

The flies cheered his triumph, perhaps with a strain of sarcasm, but he clung to the role of weakened sorcerer he'd agreed to play. The role was not so difficult after what the latest assault had cost him.

The battle lumbered on, concentrated at the stronghold breaches and at the gates. Juro's clans pressed the attack, while Merexem's defenses appeared to crumble. For a moment, Jeloc thought the final turnings of the battle plan they'd designed might not be needed. Lord Juro, commanding from further back, relying on signal casters and messengers to receive information and deliver orders, couldn't catch all that Jeloc was seeing as quickly, or with as much confidence.

Questions perforated the armor of his confidence: Was Lady Ghalen's sacrifice needed? Was there time to stop it? The possibility of being stuck on this world for longer than he'd anticipated, and without Lady Ghalen, opened the wound of his love wider than he thought possible.

But in the next moment, as if answering his doubt, Merexem's men emerged suddenly from the earth, from the mouth of the tunnel dug by the Worm beneath Joru's lines.

Jeloc hadn't anticipated that trick, either. Merexem had spent a great deal to cloak what followed the Worm's approach.

The sudden rush of warriors charging out of the ground, swarming like bugs from under an overturned rock, swept away picket walls and defenders, work camps, supply carts and their attendants, the cook tents and latrines and the wounded nursing themselves back into combat. The siege line broke in the chaos as oil-filled trenches burst too late into flames, trapping defenders. Animals bolting out of pens fell to slaughter with camp followers and families. Horns sounded alarms, as futile as an infant's cry in the midst of fierce fighting. From the stronghold, another column of warriors gushed from the gates, rushing to the gaps in Lord Juro's siege lines.

At last. Jeloc watched the disaster unfold with hypnotic, jittery swiftness. Lord Merexem was moving to meet with his relief forces and turn the action to his advantage.

The battle drained away from the stronghold, washed over the surrounding countryside like a wave advancing beyond the sea's reach. Pools of blood and shells of broken bodies remained behind in tidal drifts.

A hundred separate, desperate encounters erupted around flaming wagons and tents, at the crossroads of dirt paths, around supply depots and wells, at the foot of clan banners flapping in the gusting breeze. And in between those clusters of killing, individuals and gangs of warriors roamed, putting the wounded to death, seeking out other groups to fight, looting, and even, to Jeloc's discerning eye, just trying to survive.

From out of the smoking, screeching desolation, a squadron of horsemen rode into the invisible barrier of his defensive spells and incinerated themselves in a quick succession of fiery bursts. He wasn't sure whose side they'd been fighting for.

It was the aroma of roasted flesh that reminded him how much time had really passed, how long since he'd eaten. Unlike the god beside him, his body needed food and water. As evening closed and night rushed in beneath the clouds, the ground around Jeloc settled into an island of peace, except for carrion feeders skulking between the shadows of nearby fires, feeding on the dead.

Jeloc joined the feasting, but dipped into his own satchel of dried meat and fruits rather than take part in the battlefield banquet. He sipped water instead of wine, because he hadn't yet won, and watched the waning traffic of message riders coming to and from Merexem's fortress. The hills behind which Joru had hidden his own clan's best fighters lit up with new fires, signaling another dire turn.

A sparrow sent by Joru, charmed and protected by Jeloc's spells, flew through his defenses bearing a message. He was being called back to protect his Lord. The message, sent in haste, could have been read by discerning spellcasters. He left the message laying out in the open, in case they'd missed it.

The surge he'd been expecting came, slow at first, then in a rush, almost too fast, blinding him with its intensity. He gasped, wheezed for breath, lost himself for a moment. He had a vision of the knife slicing Ghalen's throat, Fayer weeping as he spat out spells, while Joru watched stoically.

"Who's Ylem?" Tygal asked, when Jeloc opened his eyes again.

Jeloc didn't answer.

He assumed Lady Ghalen's love had given the deliverance of new strength its urgency. She'd blessed the sacrifice of her life with the last of her love, so that he might gain the power he needed more quickly. In the end, she'd given herself to the old ways of her clan, surrendering everything that she was to serve the greater cause.

Old ways. Joru had already commissioned a school of bards to compose the story of his daughter's death in the service of freedom for the clans. No doubt, they'd stood witness as Fayer performed the rituals, spoke the prayers, eased Lady Ghalen into her death and called on ancient dominions desperate for an offering of blood and passion. Fayer had done everything required of him; he'd learned that much from Jeloc.

New energy poured into the vortex spinning overhead, though into places spying spellcasters couldn't see. Incantations he'd prepared for this moment ripened with the fresh nourishment. Revived, he looked again to the hills. He was surprised by sorrow.

He looked to Tygal, found him chanting prayers over dead horsemen.

"It's time for us to move."

"Good. I was thinking I'd made a poor bargain."

"There's still time to believe that."

Jeloc let the spells defending him collapse. The world's pace slowed, regained the cadence of life as he knew it. He emerged from the bubble of his magic world and started toward the hills. Tygal cried out, cursed, called him deal-breaker. The vortex moved with Jeloc, a whirling devil of magic slicing through the night, bristling with his armory. Eddies in the clouds marked its passage.

Jeloc stopped, went down on one knee. In his mind, he found the faults and cracks he'd designed into the construction of his tower, held them firmly in his vision. With a sharp turn of the head, the whirlwind calved, sending the smaller portion of his power infected with Merexem's spies on to Lord Juro, while the greater mass, and the weight of all that it contained, remained with him.

The fragment he'd sent off would collapse like a stick house in a stiff wind before it ever reached the latest battlefield. But it had never been intended as part of any rescue. By the time Merexem and his spellcasters discovered the ruse, Jeloc would be in position to end the game.

Jeloc turned back to Merexem's stronghold, crowned by his power, a torch in his hand to light the way. Tygal fell in step beside him, barking his relief. Together they passed over the slain, staining themselves with spilled blood and gore as they slipped and slid but never fell, and went through the undefended gate.

The fortress was well along the road to ruin. Fires burned in many corners. Only human scavengers remained, court officials, servants, families and children left abandoned by the dead, rifling through libraries, storerooms, kitchens, private chambers, workshops and animal pens in the outer courtyards and halls for whatever they could find to help them live another day. Though many stared, some frankly appraising Jeloc's armor and even Tygal's layered destitution, none challenged their progress or their right to hold on to their meager possessions. Jeloc wondered who was left drumming, and why they were still trying to influence him in such a simplistic manner.

Jeloc's defensive spells discharged a thousand bolts with a twitch of his fingers, disabling Merexem's magical countermeasures as they awakened, and killing the few defending warriors running through the survivors to stop him. Even this maneuver missed the drummers, and he vowed to investigate their defenses fully once the war was settled.

Old kings and sorcerers, frozen in white statuary, stared down at Jeloc as if in judgement when he passed into the massive keep. Tygal greeted the monumental beasts guarding the grand halls and stairs within as if they were alive. He asked them about his mate, but they had no answers for him. Dust fell from the rafters and domes. The crashing of walls drowned the echo of their footsteps. Jeloc thought his own tower of sorcery might be causing part of the damage, but as long as the wreckage didn't fall on him, he didn't care. Rats, dogs and serpents joined the human predators stalking the edges of Jeloc's circle of light, but as in the outer stronghold, no one tried to stop them, as if they all could sense the power bristling overhead. Or perhaps, Jeloc thought, the denizens of Merexem's inner court recognized Tygal, being wiser and more experienced, and honored him with their respect in these final moments of their world.

Tygal called out a name Jeloc recognized from several campfire stories, pausing to listen for the faintest trace of an answer, but none came. He appeared as pathetic as when he'd raised his hand after Merexem's released spirits.

The sewers had broken, and the reek of an army's worth of waste mingled with the stench of that same body of warriors now mostly dead and rotting outside the devastated keep. Through the sewer gratings, smoke from the Worm's destruction continued to rise, acrid and burning. Though the lord's defenders were dead, their advance continued to set off Merexem's sorcerous traps and ambushes, keeping Jeloc's tower occupied. Ghalen's sacrifice was proving its value. The energy of her life allowed him to move quickly, attacking strongholds of clustered spells before they could be set off at his approach, rather than advancing cautiously behind a conservative shield just to preserve his strength. The spells he'd picked for the assault, though costly, proved devastating, and he was proud that he did not have to stop once to conjure in response to an unexpected attack.

Auroras shimmered and shadows convulsed in Jeloc's wake. He didn't look back. With a proper trick of vision, he thought he might catch a glimpse of Juro praying that his daughter's sacrifice had given his ally the power to make the quick, killing thrust that would rescue his ambition. In Aum, Jeloc would have savored the fruit of his intended betrayal. But years of exile had cost him the appetite for small pleasures.

Jeloc glanced at twisted scrolls and broken-backed volumes scattered across the floor. The scholar in him winced at wasted knowledge. What spells had casually fallen into the dust? What histories and biographies, with all their secrets, perhaps even clues to the secret of Aum's curse, lay forgotten, already crumbling into oblivion at his feet? He hesitated, thinking as he had done in the past, of using a new world's trove of knowledge to build a treasure of secrets that might give him enough of an advantage in bargaining with his mother to win his release from exile. He'd tried, and failed, before, but the reversals he'd experienced in battle told him there might be something worthwhile in Lord Merexem's keep. Whatever vengeance he'd dreamed of delivering to his mother and Aum suddenly lacked the keenness of compelling urgency. Blood on the boots, he'd noted before, had always proved a curious salve for wounds of rage and grief.

The flies crowded him, diving into his eyes, ears and mouth, flying straight into the flame of his torch and expiring in popping bursts.

Jeloc waved the torch and hurried on.

"Which of these doors is mine?" Tygal asked. He'd studied every one they'd gone by as if etching their location into a hardened slate of memory.

"Given up on her?"

"I never gave her reason to wait," Tygal said, barely loud enough to be heard.

"We haven't reached it, yet," Jeloc answered, at last.

"Really."

"Yes."

Skulking shadows and extra footsteps followed their advance.

"They punish bargain-breakers harshly in Aum, don't they," Tygal said.

"Consider me the proof of Aum's justice."

Tygal grunted, but didn't press any further.

They found Lord Merexem in a small room off of a grand hall. The chamber, illuminated by lanterns, glowed like a lighthouse beacon.

He sat alone, on a plain wooden chair at an ordinary table, contemplating a plate of cold meat and a flagon of wine beyond arm's reach. He might have been a servant, dressed in plain brown leggings and shirt, protected by nothing more than a long leather vest and worn, knee-high boots. Long, curly hair fell to his shoulders, and it was those locks that provided a clue to his identity. When he turned to glance at his guests, raising one eyebrow and nearly smiling, Jeloc recognized the thin, bony nose; wide, slim lips; and the narrow eyes that were said to make him appear drowsy. The smooth-skinned, youthful face appeared unnatural only when placed in the context of a reported century of life.

"Have you come here to bargain?" Merexem asked. "Or to die?" His voice was hoarse, as if he'd spent every minute of the past day chanting and praying and weaving spells.

Jeloc laughed. "Please, this isn't a banquet tale. The poets you commissioned to memorialize your words are gone." He stepped into the room, and the power he held in check made the ceiling tremble.

Tygal remained outside, leaning against the entry frame. His gaze wandered away from the dull interior, settled on a minute study of the lintel.

"I know. They made up what I said, anyway."

Jeloc whipped out a feeble stroke from the whirlwind of his power. A kiss, more than a lash.

Merexem fell back from the table, onto the floor, raising dust. He coughed, wiped blood from the cut on his neck.

"Come to do your lord's bidding?" he asked, looking up at Jeloc.

Merexem's eyes were dead. His lips barely moved, and his expression remained unchanged, even to the detail of a raised eyebrow. The flies urged Jeloc to finish his work. He remembered, that's not what he wanted to do. Not really. There was a final turn to take, the one he'd gone through all this effort to come to.

But Jeloc thought he should see fear in his enemy. He would have been afraid, had their positions been reversed.

"I'm here to do my own bidding," Jeloc said. It was always good to start negotiating from a position of strength.

"Your lord dies," Merexem said, waving a hand absently. "Join me."

"I don't want to die, yet."

"I'm the rightful ruler."

"You conquered these people and they want to set themselves free."

"I harnessed their self-destruction. You've lived among them, you've seen how they are. Wild. Mad. Passionate about their horses and their feuds and the blood they spill. Tradition for them means carrying on the same fight they've fought for a thousand years. They fear knowledge, wisdom, insight. They want only easy answers, and lots of food and drink."

"It's not a bad life." Jeloc drifted to the table, glanced at the meat. It was more than cold. Maggots squirmed between slices. The flies seemed to swarm in his ears.

"They need guidance," Lord Merexem said. "Help. I can give that to them."

"Guiding this lot is not easy work," Tygal said.

Lord Merexem remained fixed on Jeloc as he said, "You know I would be fair."

Jeloc sat in the chair his enemy had occupied. "So you say."

Merexem still stared at where Jeloc had stood, as if time, for him, had also shifted. Or, perhaps his eyes watched some other place. "She's dead," he said. "But you're the one who sacrificed her."

Jeloc wasn't sure who Lord Merexem was talking about. The flies refused to let him focus. He gave up, saying, "I don't care."

"Then why are you here?"

"To do what I must."

"Does that purpose have anything to do with Lord Juro or myself?"

"No."

"I was afraid of that." He didn't look fearful. His expression still hadn't changed.

Jeloc thought of tricks played with ghosts and empty suits of armor.

"Are you a god?" Merexem asked.

"Hardly."

"We'll see."

Merexem sagged, a puppet whose strings had been cut. Jeloc looked to the door but found the way still open. Tygal glanced up and down the hallway, shook his head. Suddenly, the weight of Lord Merexem's keep, of his entire fortress, seemed to bear down on Jeloc. The chair splintered, collapsed under him. His helm crumpled, cut into his neck and cheeks, slipped off as soon as he hit the stone tile floor. He lay pinned to the ground, armor crinkling and breaking apart under the strain of an unseen hand holding him down. He pushed back with a measure of his reserves, clicking his teeth to unleash spells he never thought he'd have to use. The hand relented, giving him enough room to breathe, and by doing so let him know he was at someone's mercy.

This couldn't be happening. He was in control. The battle raged over a hill, far off.

Still, in war, the unexpected was to be expected.

Calling on his great reserve of power, he released a string of flesh-lashing magics at Merexem's body. At the same time, he shot out hunting eye charms to probe for the threads of control that might lead back to the lord's hiding place. The walls and ceilings shook from the release of power.

Someone screamed.

The walls and ceiling stopped moving.

Suddenly, the flies were gone; the drumming, silenced.

And then Jeloc had nothing. The vortex of his power dissipated like a banquet sugar fantasy in water. The delicate tower he'd put together to hold his reserves was as empty as a drought-blasted field. His spells hung like withered fruit ruined by frost. The scream, he realized, had come from one of the stronghold's survivors lurking nearby. His strike at Merexem, much weaker than it should have been, had been deflected.

Ribs cracked. His heart and guts felt like they were going to pop out of his body, and his lungs lay flat and empty. Sweat poured from his body and his skin burned as if he'd been set on fire, though the fires of his cremation hadn't yet been lit. He shit and pissed and wheezed what was left inside him, and waited for the final stroke.

Merexem's body jerked.

Tygal ran in, tried to pick up Jeloc's head, but couldn't. "The door," he said. "Where's the damned door?"

A panel slid open at the rear of the chamber. Pressure eased on Jeloc, but kept him pinned. He gasped for air and succeeded; tried to rub sharply-pained ribs, but couldn't get his arms off the ground. He managed to turn his head in time to watch Merexem rise.

A familiar scent carried through the secret doorway. Not too sweet, with earthy roots.

Tygal grunted from somewhere deep beneath his rags. "I recognize this one."

Jeloc felt the turn of the final trick in his gut before he saw their faces.

The echoes of drums tripped with rejoicing. The memory of a fly buzzed in his ears.

Fayer came out first, his helmet, sword and charms missing, an arm bloodied, a fresh gash across his forehead still bleeding into his right eye. He kept his palm on the hilt of the only weapon left to him: a workman's knife stuck into his belt. Lady Ghalen followed, black hair free, protective spells spent, clothes torn. Both of her thighs had been dressed for wounds. She hadn't had an easy time betraying him, and averted her gaze as she passed.

"I thought there might be another way in," Jeloc said, closing his eyes against Ghalen's presence. He only thought his heart had stopped when she appeared. Eyes burning, fighting back tears, he had no problem keeping his voice low and soft, to keep from showing emotion. "That's the door for you, Tygal. The conjunction's due any moment."

Defeat was no excuse to break a deal.

He opened his eyes. Body locked in position against the floor, he saw only Tygal as he stood, suddenly appearing bigger, stronger. For an instant, Jeloc had hope. The god might have held a trick up his sleeve to salvage his power and keep his pride. Perhaps he'd made a play using Joru's ambition, turning Fayer and Lady Ghalen, even Jeloc, into pawns. Maybe the old god knew a thing about mortal hearts.

If Tygal had betrayed him, he still had a chance. Jeloc didn't think the god would kill him. It wouldn't be necessary. An old god reclaiming power and glory was all that was required for legend.

But such turnings were for campfire stories, not the world of flesh, bones, and broken hearts. Jeloc's relief lasted for only an instant. Dread shivered itself down the back of his neck when Lord Merexem motioned for Ghalen and Fayer to stand by him.

"Don't worry, old one," Merexem said, his voice rich but dry, the illusion of youth gone. "You may pass. This world doesn't need your kind, anymore." The Lord looked down on Jeloc, a slight smile on his lips. His eyes shined with intelligence and craft, like a hawk's with prey in its sight. He still didn't look his century's age. "That's why I chose to wait in this room. I have a few sources in Aum, too. Not anything like a son of the city, of course. But enough to warn me you'd shown interest in this particular doorway, which so rarely falls into conjunction with your City of Gates. I thought you might come to it before looking for me, to fulfill your bargain. I hear you take your transactions very seriously."

It wasn't Tygal who'd made a fool of him. "You were never gone," Jeloc said to Merexem.

"Hiding in plain sight. Like you, standing on my doorstep, then pretending to walk away."

Tygal stepped back. "I'd help if I could," he said, with a glance down at Jeloc.

Though imperceptible, Jeloc was certain the god shrugged a shoulder and cocked his head to the side.

"Just one of the simpler of the illusions you believed," Lord Merexem said, studying Jeloc as if searching for yet another vulnerability. "Your cornucopia of power, my slack wit, crumbling defenses, the shaking walls as you came to me. Love. Sacrifice. You should have paid attention to the drumming. And the flies."

The truth of fortune's reversal seeped through Jeloc, colder than the floor at his back, or the chill spreading through the keep now that no one was left to tend to the hearths.

Ghalen moved away from Fayer, into Jeloc's full line of sight. He fought against closing his eyes, to save what he could of his dignity. He tried to discern, from the way she looked at him, if she'd chosen her part in his downfall, or if she'd been forced. She gave him nothing, which told him everything. He didn't want to be weak, not in these last moments. The Matriarch of Aum might one day hear of her son's death. He wanted to prove he was more than she thought he ever was. And there was Ymel to consider. With him gone, she'd have no reason to haunt the old city. He could ease her way by being strong. Perhaps he'd meet her, spirit to spirit, on some higher plane beyond the life of flesh.

Last moments.

How could that be true?

People believed what they needed to, whether truth or lie. He'd turned that to his advantage all of his life.

But people were also capable of anything. He'd forgotten to believe in that certainty.

The drums. He thought he'd contained the spellcasters and their poison, but they were the ones who'd lured him into a trap.

The flies. They'd lied. He'd forgotten everything he knew about lying, because they were only flies.

But he'd forgotten about lies before Lord Merexem ever slipped into his mind. Fayer and Lady Ghalen proved that.

Last moments. He'd never believed he'd see them. Never thought they'd be so cold.

Merexem walked around Jeloc, like a hunter examining an animal caught in his trap. He frowned, as if disappointed in his catch. "You're younger than I thought you'd be."

"I count my passing in centuries," Jeloc said.

"But not in wisdom earned." Lord Merexem exchanged a look with Fayer. "Any feelings for your old master?"

"I've given myself to you," Fayer said.

Of course. Fayer deserved a better teacher. Ghalen, a better man to love.

But Juro earned his share of Jeloc's doom by adopting him over a faithful follower and his own daughter.

"Then you'll be the one to kill him. No magic. No tricks. With your knife."

"That would be a waste of my blood," Jeloc said.

"Really." Lord Merexem knocked the maggot-infested plate of meat onto Jeloc. "Do I hear a proposal for an exchange coming?"

Jeloc blew a maggot from his lip, preparing himself for honesty. "I only have the truth to offer."

"That would be novel."

"I'm an exiled son of Aum."

"I've heard the stories."

"I came here—"

"To interfere in the natural flowering of our world."

"To offer you a partnership."

"You weren't going to kill me for Lord Juro?"

"No." His plan, and its final turn, seemed ludicrous in defeat.

Merexem went down on one knee, peered at Jeloc's face. Ghalen made a sound that made Jeloc's heart twist. He'd given her another justification for betrayal. Fayer drew his knife and took a step forward, appearing eager to finish the job. Merexem held a hand up, and Fayer didn't test its power.

"Really," Lord Merexem said.

"I wanted to help you."

"By destroying my forces."

"You were going to suffer losses, anyway. War always costs."

"Not so much. Fayer, here, and the rest of Juro's little band of tricksters weren't going to challenge me. They could never have tamed a Worm, or engaged so many of my spellcasters."

"I wanted you to respect me. My power."

"You succeeded, up to a point."

"And then offer you a partnership. Each of us an apprentice to the other, rebuilding this land into the image envisaged by the old gods, like Tygal, here. A vision you embraced, Lord Merexem."

"Very noble. I hadn't realized Aum's lost son was such a crusader."

"The land we'd build would be the start of a crusade, yes. I have many years to live. So do you."

"You *had* many years."

"By using Aum's Gates, my allies, the tricks I've learned from smugglers, we could use the Gates to travel to other worlds without alerting the city's authorities, and spread the seeds of our power."

Merexem stood, walked around the table. "You've used the Gates to go from world to world despite your exile."

"Yes. I spin my own illusions."

"An empire of worlds."

"An empire I'd use against Aum, in time."

Lord Merexem kicked the table aside, shook his head. "All this for vengeance?"

"All this for pain."

"You certainly know how to spread your pain. I didn't realize your ambition. And you expected me to join your cause?"

"With my victory, yes."

"Defeat does limit choices, doesn't it."

"But not opportunities," Jeloc said, trying his best to sound sincere while pinned like a bug beneath a boot heel. A maggot squirmed on his cheek, and more had worked their way under his shirt, as if anticipating dead meat. Their ability to move through the pattern of the spell crushing him told Jeloc there were faults in his prison, but not how to exploit them.

The secret doorway shimmered, the dark passageway beyond lightened into a cobblestoned alley, like a scene from a play. A beggar sitting under a boarded-up window across the way looked up, spat, then returned his attention to a bowl behind his drawn-up knees. A Gate Mother, her diminutive body curled and twisted like an archaic rune, waited for a traveler to cross through. Someone whistled a merry tavern tune out of sight, a signal from Jeloc's friend that he was there and waiting.

"You know, I've never been tempted to visit your city," Merexem said, crossing the opened Gate's threshold. "Though I've sent others to try to make my deals. The cost was always too high." He turned, paced back and forth, as if reconsidering his decision.

The beggar looked up, scowled at the lord, then cursed and scrambled to his feet, moved off.

"Go through," Merexem said, waving Tygal on. "Before I forget your legacy. You're a disappointment."

"My mate felt the same way, toward the end," Tygal said, stepping over Jeloc. He struggled against the binding forces, but made it through.

Jeloc felt no lessening of pressure, but silently thanked the god for the gauge of Merexem's hold on him. There was still nothing he could do.

Jeloc wondered if Tygal had a reserve, not of treasure but of strength, stuck away in some parallel dimension. Maybe there was another bargain to be struck, with the old god playing a hand.

It was a dim hope, as faint as the light in his attempt to turn Merexem into an ally while helpless at his feet.

Lord Merexem turned his attention to Jeloc, standing over him, toes to the top of Jeloc's skull. Fayer approached from the other end, kicked Jeloc's foot. Lady Ghalen had switched places with Tygal, and now stood in the room's everyday opening. She'd raised her hood. He wished she'd kept it down, so he could draw comfort from the darkness of her hair.

Looking up at the lord made Jeloc slightly dizzy.

"You expected Lady Ghalen to sacrifice herself for you," Merexem said. "You expected her death to call on powers to fill you, so you'd have the advantage when you made your offer to me. You expected my tricks, and my capitulation." Merexem kicked Jeloc's head, moved off.

Fayer came around. His expression blank, he showed Jeloc the knife in his hand. He licked his lips. Showed his teeth. The apprentice wanted to teach his master about death.

Tygal watched from the Gate.

"Your kind always expects that others will act as you think they must,"

Merexem continued, "and most importantly, that they will give everything up for you. Because—what? They love you? Need you? Because your charm and will and habits of authority can bend their spirit? Do you think you're the only one with dreams? That everyone but you is an idiot?"

Lord Merexem's voice rose with an excess of outrage. Jeloc knew only the fireside tales about the man, not the intimate secrets of his true history, but he suspected flaws caused by humiliation at the hands of whatever passed for nobility among the clans. He knew the type.

He'd forgotten he was also a type for others to appraise. He might have been better off going to Lord Merexem first, and making his intentions clear rather than designing an elaborate charade to first impress and intimidate him. There was too much of Aum in his blood.

So much wisdom gained at death's edge.

"I know your kind, too," Tygal said. He left the Gate, took a few steps after Merexem. "You take old ways, true ways, the primal nature of things, and you turn them into your instruments. It's not your fault. You're human. An unfinished creation. The universe is plagued with so many of you. We gods come and go, rising and falling before your mad spirits, trying to deliver the guidance you crave. But always, it seems, you take what's given, and whatever good it might contain, and corrupt it with the darkness inside you."

"There's light in us," Fayer said, surprising Jeloc.

Both Tygal and Lord Merexem turned to him.

"Yes," Tygal said, stopping in front of the apprentice. "But light is not what is being offered here today."

"You should leave," Merexem told the god.

"I should," Tygal said. "But then, I wouldn't be true to my godhood. And that's all that I have left."

With a short step, Tygal closed the distance between himself and Fayer, who raised the knife. The god blocked the move with forearm to the elbow, then grabbed Fayer's wrist, slid his leg between the mortal's legs, turned his hip.

Fayer flipped, feet kicking into the air, and landed with a crack on the stone floor.

His face was an arm's length away from Jeloc's, who watched his apprentice die as Tygal turned the knife back, and into the exposed throat. The spray of blood momentarily blinded Jeloc.

"It's amazing what you can learn to do if you stop acting like you're better than everyone around you," Tygal said.

The pressure on Jeloc lessened enough for him to wipe the blood from his face. Lord Merexem needed the strength to deal with Tygal, who he forced back to the open Gate with a portion of the strength in the spell he was using against Jeloc.

Tygal grunted with the effort to resist. His ragged turban fell off in the struggle and unraveled on the floor.

"I betrayed my father for this," Lady Ghalen said softly from the doorway.

Her tone was not regretful. She was stating a fact.

She held a knife in her hand. Not a sturdy, straightforward working blade with a thick handle, like Fayer's weapon, but a jeweled creation that curled with extravagant emotion and looked like it had forgotten its purpose. A gift, no doubt, from an admiring nobleman.

Merexem ignored her. Jeloc tried to rise, but settled for reaching out a hand to receive the knife, hoping for the jeweled handle first.

Ghalen went on talking from beneath her hood with a thin voice, not frail, but taut, strong, like the rods armorers used to make fine chain mail. "He's probably dead now. And my brothers, too. My family. Friends. Clan. Just so I can have this moment. With you."

Jeloc couldn't see her eyes, but felt the weight of her gaze on him, far heavier than Merexem's spell.

"I wanted you to witness what I'm doing for you. For whatever reason you need me to do this. Because of what we could have been, for each other."

Hope returned to Jeloc, but it was dark and thick, tainted by blood.

"Don't bother," Tygal shouted, bracing himself against the wall with little result.

Lord Merexem grunted.

Jeloc wasn't sure if the sound was laughter, or a cry of effort.

"Understand what I'm doing," Lady Ghalen said. "Everything has a cost."

She plunged the knife into the hood, angled to strike at her own throat.

Merexem turned.

The lady fell against the doorway, slid to the floor, her body blocking the entry. Blood soaked everything she wore, even strands of her black hair now matted to her chest. Her face remained hidden.

There were words to be spoken. Callings. The spells Fayer should have woven from her life. Jeloc screamed them out while blood still flowed from her wound.

Lord Merexem came for Jeloc. For an instant the stronghold's crushing weight crashed on to Jeloc's chest. Long enough to take his breath away, but not long enough to kill.

Tygal advanced on Lord Merexem, who had to turn to face him.

Jeloc gasped for air, spoke an ancient spell, the kind requiring the rawness of a human voice to empower them. Names forged before Tygal's emergence tore at Jeloc's throat, fighting as hard against crossing over into the world as the old god was resisting his escape to Aum.

With time and proper rituals, as Jeloc had planned, the forces would have fallen into alignment with much less of a struggle. Jeloc had left that kind of time back in the land of his enchantment.

Ghalen's blood proved to be the final inducement. The bargain was done, the sacrifice accepted. Jeloc's tower re-assembled, creaking, unsteady, but eager to be filled once more with magic. The power he felt was true, born of blood, not a sorceror's trick.

For that moment, the old ways held sway.

Jeloc pushed aside Merexem's holding spell. The walls groaned. Down the hallway, something snapped and rubble came crashing down. A flurry of small, poisonous enchantments jumped at him. He barely shrugged, and Merexem was spent. Jeloc stood, went to Ghalen. He drew the knife out, but didn't pull the hood back. The handle felt cold against his skin. Her scent still hung about, sweetening death-choked air. When he turned around, Tygal was holding Merexem.

"You must go," Jeloc said. He pointed to the flickering image in the doorway. If the old god moved now, he'd get through before the Gate closed.

But Tygal held on to Lord Merexem, choking his throat so no more lies, truths, or pleas for mercy or deals could cross his lips. The conjunction slipped away. The Gate vanished. The last thing Jeloc saw of his home city was the Gate Mother peering through the opening as if searching for a lost child.

"There'll be other conjunctions," he said to Tygal, who grinned and stared at the man in his grip. "I'll honor our bargain, in thanks for your help."

Tygal laughed. Hard and loud. Merexem's face reddened as he flailed against the armor of the god's layers of rags. "That old bargain's done and delivered," Tygal said. "We'll settle accounts when you've finished the work you started."

Jeloc opened his mouth to protest. But that would have been the old way. Death had taught him something new.

Threes were sacred, a holy number of balance and completion, no matter the world. Two cut throats demanded a third. Jeloc opened Lord

Merexem's, letting blood drown whatever new bargain, or old one, the sorcerer might have had ready to offer.

Tygal let go. The lord joined the rest of the dead on the floor in a tableau of betrayed and betrayers. The living, still standing, had that much in common with the dead. Jeloc dropped the knife, satisfied with the work.

He let his sorcerous tower collapse, casting off dead spells like autumn leaves, releasing the rest of what Lady Ghalen had died to give him. He didn't want the power anymore.

"Joru might have been able to use some of that," Tygal said, brushing himself off. He gathered his turban, shaking out maggots and a slice or two of meat from its tangled mass.

"I think he, or whatever's left of his clans, and Merexem's captains will stop before they kill each other."

"A truce."

"Something like that."

"You're not putting a hand in the deal?"

Jeloc didn't bother answering. He stepped over Ghalen, thankful her ghost had not risen to implore him to join her. She'd fulfilled her purpose at the moment of her death and moved on, without looking back. He'd given her nothing to hold on to.

He left the keep. Tygal didn't join him until he'd reached the outer courtyards. The god, his turban back on his head, carried a sword in one hand, a torch in another. "We have dealings," Tygal said. "I don't want anything to happen to you until they're settled."

They left the stronghold without being stopped. There were no more messengers riding in seeking Lord Merexem's commands. The servants and slaves had finally escaped with what they could carry. Warriors and spellcasters, he was sure, were as weary by now of all the blood as any farmer whose fields had been overrun and livestock taken, as any villager whose trade had been subsumed by the necessities of war.

The drums remained silent. Flies feasted on the dead.

Across the countryside, in the hills, reflected on the clouds, the light of dying fires illuminated armies of the dead and dying.

The shape of Lady Ghalen's face stayed with him as he walked, though he had difficulty recalling her exact features. She'd had black hair. The memory was tainted by blood. Her scent eluded him in the midst of rotting corpses.

There were responsibilities he'd not yet accepted. For all his wandering, he still wasn't wise enough to return to Aum, not prepared for all the ways he could betray, and be betrayed, again. For certain, he wasn't as clever or noble as he'd thought himself to be. The realities on which he'd built his delusions were well beyond his reach.

He was nothing more than a pack horse carrying a cargo of stale rage and over-ripe guilt.

But he was alive. The peace of exhaustion flowed under cover of night; a quiet, gentle tide that could not deny the devastation, only offer the hope of rebirth. He took a deep breath. Burdens shifted, but didn't fall away. He breathed again, grateful for the chance to do so.

Jeloc paused at the place where he'd made his stand at the battle's opening. He picked up a bag of provisions, found a blanket roll protected by an oil skin cover.

He wished he'd found a brush. His long hair, now white, he noticed, in the blaze of Tygal's torch, was tangled and filthy with blood and debris. He searched through the knotted clumps for stray maggots.

"Did you love her?" Tygal asked.

"Yes," Jeloc answered, without thinking.

"Why didn't you say so?"

"Because I needed her sacrifice. And she needed to prove herself to me. It seemed the simplest way to satisfy everyone."s

"But won't you miss her?"

"I'm not sure what I'd do with the love of a living woman." His honesty rang in his ears, as clear and startling as thunder from a clear sky.

"You should try it, sometime."

"Dozens of worlds ago, hundreds, maybe thousands yet to come, it always ends the same. They die. And then so do I. And then I move on to another world."

"You look hale enough."

Jeloc considered, and saw the truth in what Tygal had said. He'd nearly died, but was closer to life than he'd been during his exile. He still breathed. There was hope, if not for vengeance and retribution, then for something else he might find along the journey.

"Will you be moving on to Aum?" Jeloc asked. The god had seemed eager a moment ago to put old business to rest before something else happened.

"Not now," Tygal said. "Not yet. There might be opportunities in this venerable land, now that some of the wildness has been cleared away. What about you? Is it back to Aum, or another world?"

"Not Aum. Not for a while."

Memories dimmed like coals covered in ash.

"At the moment," Jeloc said, sinking both hands into his hair, "I just wish I could get rid of this hair."

Tygal held his sword before the torch and smiled. "If you promise to be very still, that's one prayer this dead god can still answer. And another deal you owe me."

The Perils of Twilight

Peter Andrew Smith

A sudden jolt of the chariot sent Ameni's injured shoulder into spasms and brought the dusty path back into focus. He turned his head with difficulty and squinted in the poor light to assess the ragged line behind him. The haggard horses and battered soldiers looked ready to collapse. They could not continue this way. He stared up at the sky.

"How long until dawn?"

Djati shrugged. "The sun comes slowly to chase away darkness here. But light or dark, there needs to be a time of rest. The horses are going to drop soon if we push them any further."

Ameni cursed under his breath. Since the battle three days ago they had been running back to the border, always keeping one step ahead of the trailing horde. If the nomads caught them before they reached the open lands and the protection of fresh chariots, they would easily be slaughtered. If they did not stop soon, the horses would begin to collapse from exhaustion and they would be overtaken.

Ameni looked up at the cloud-covered sky that was reluctantly brightening. "A glimpse of the god's eye would show us that we have not been abandoned."

"The gods did not abandon us. That was for—"

"Remember your place and keep your tongue silent," Ameni said. "Some things are not to be spoken even in the darkness of this land." Ameni's noble family had faithfully served the House of Pharaoh for generations. The gods banish his spirit forever into darkness if he doubted Pharaoh. He locked eyes with his subordinate.

Djati bowed his head. "The Niece of Pharaoh also needs to rest, Commander of Armies. Her wounds from the battle don't show, but she is still injured. She is like her father, may he shine forever in the sky. She would die before she failed in her duty."

Ameni reluctantly lifted his hand and the column of chariots slowly ground to a halt. "We will not stop long. Make sure the wounded are tended first."

Djati stepped from the chariot and moved along the ragged line. Around him, those who were able watered the horses and replaced bandages on the wounded.

"They are not far behind, Servant of Pharaoh," a high-pitched voice said.

Ameni looked over at Nithotep. She was encrusted with dirt and blood like the rest of them, but her sky-blue eyes marked her as a child of the gods. She handed him a full wineskin, and he drank deeply from it.

"I know, Niece of Pharaoh. But there is greater risk if we push beyond our strength to continue." His voice dropped to a whisper. "Can you tell how far behind us they are?"

She closed her eyes and chanted softly in the tongue of the gods. Ameni tensed as the air became thick around him. Nithotep's eyes shone with a touch of the sun as she opened them.

"I can't tell. The battle with the Cursed-One has left my head throbbing in pain."

Ameni sat on a downed tree and motioned for her to sit next to him. "You have done more for us than any court wizard ever could. You faced an invincible foe and survived. Your father, may he shine forever in the sky, is surely proud of you."

She smiled and he realized at that moment that she was only a child. A girl who should have been coyly teasing suitors instead of slowly dying in this forsaken land.

"You served with him, didn't you?" she asked.

"I was but a boy, no older than you. I drove a chariot when your grandfather, may his light also shine forever above us, was pharaoh and gathered a great army to drive out the nomads. When your father became pharaoh, he allowed my family to continue to serve him and the Eternal Kingdom."

"I did not know my grandfather, but your service was always spoken of with pride at the palace."

"You honor me and my humble house," Ameni said, his gaze downcast. Nithotep's father had been a man who shared glory with those who served the kingdom with honor. He had never been afraid to reward a man's bravery or success.

"Tell me, Servant of the House of Pharaoh, why were we sent here on this hopeless task?"

Ameni's eyes shot up to meet hers.

"The court wizard who journeyed with us was unable to withstand the Cursed-One's magic," Nithotep said. "He died during the opening thrust of the attack."

"Battles do not always happen as planned." Ameni focused on taking another drink from the skin.

"Ameni, look at me."

His eyes obeyed.

"Answer me honestly, Commander of Armies. I am the daughter of my father, who shines in the sky, to whom you swore your life when he was pharaoh. Were we sent here without any hope but to die?" Her shining blue eyes peered into his soul and he knew he could not lie.

"Yes," he whispered. "There was no expectation for us to return."

"Why?"

"For the Eternal Kingdom. We were sent to make sure the Cursed-One died before she could unite the nomad tribes. Divided, the nomads are sand to be ground under our chariot wheels. Working together they are a sandstorm poised to bury us."

"But for Pharaoh to send such a small group . . ."

"Niece of Pharaoh," Ameni said, "do not ask me to question the wisdom of the living embodiment of the gods."

Nithotep lowered her head slightly. "But why me? I am no soldier or even an experienced driver. . . ."

The tone of command was gone and once again the voice was that of a child caught up in things she did not understand. A girl used to the sheltered life of the royal palace and unfamiliar with the ongoing battles in Pharaoh's court.

Ameni looked at her and his heart split. He was a loyal servant of Pharaoh and where he was ordered to go, he went. But this little girl, not much older than his youngest daughter, deserved to know. It was the very least he could do for the chance, however slim, that she had given them to return home. Ameni looked around to make sure no one was within earshot.

"Because you are the only child of your father, whose name is still spoken with reverence."

Ameni had not been surprised when he saw Nithotep's name on the list of the soldiers and chariot drivers he was to lead against the Cursed-One. To have Nithotep die in battle would make her another symbol of service to the Eternal Kingdom instead of a living reminder of the previous pharaoh.

"Ameni, if I ask you something would it stay just between us?"

"Daughter of your father, I hope this entire conversation might stay between us. There are some who would consider it treasonous."

Her eyes widened slightly at his words. "Yes. That would be best."

"What was your question?"

"I can't remember much that happened in the battle," she said, shaking slightly. "I remember the court wizard's death. I remember summoning the touch of the Sun to drive away the darkness of the Cursed-One. Then her screams filled my head and I felt her tearing at my very spirit." Her trembling became more pronounced. "And then it was over."

Ameni took another drink of wine and then offered her the skin.

"When the court wizard fell under the Cursed-One's magic, I feared we would be swallowed up by failure and death in this forsaken land. When you summoned the arrows of light that drove back the darkness, it was as if the gods themselves had stepped down from the sky to save us." Ameni bowed his head toward her. "None of us knew you were gifted in such a way."

"My mother, may she rest in the presence of my father forever, begged him to let me study at the temple. He relented only after she agreed that the subject would never be spoken again in the land."

"May all the gods favor such a wise and blessed woman as your mother for her persistence and your father for his wisdom." Although Ameni did not believe in his heart that a pharaoh ascended to live in the sun after his death, he felt someone divine was looking out for them. If Pharaoh knew of his niece's abilities, she would probably have been pledged to a remote temple and Ameni and his soldiers would have perished three days ago.

"Your magic kept the Cursed-One from spreading her darkness over us. There was nowhere for us to run so we fought. When we saw the Cursed-One with an arrow in her neck . . ." Ameni shrugged. "I think the nomads believed she could never die. They boasted she was the relentless darkness of the night itself. When she fell, their will was broken."

"Then why do they follow us? Why do they hunt us?"

"Whichever tribe ends up killing us will gain great honor." He stopped, unsure whether to continue or not, but he believed that every soldier had the right to know their upcoming battle. "You defeated the Cursed-One. Any shaman who hopes to rule in her place will have to kill you."

"So there is no chance of them giving up?"

He shook his head. "Not until we get to the border and back to the kingdom. They no longer fight as a single army so the forts and fresh chariots stand a decent chance of pushing them back."

Djati stood at a respectful distance and Ameni waved him forward.

"The soldiers and horses have had water," Djati said. "With your permission I will send some rear scouts to see how far the horde is behind us."

Ameni considered the few scouts he had left. "No. We know they are chasing us. We should be focused on getting to the Eternal Kingdom. Better to send scouts ahead and see if one of them can find a patrol and raise the alarm on the border."

The scouts were out of sight before Djati took his place beside Ameni in the lead chariot. As Ameni began leading the ragged column toward the Eternal Kingdom of the Sun, he realized where he had last heard the commanding tone in Nithotep's voice. Her father had used it to order Ameni to split their column of chariots in a move which had let them triumph over an invading nomad army. An order which had left Nithotep an orphan.

The chariots resumed a slow pace as days of fatigue overcame the short rest. Ameni looked at the stunted trees behind the last chariot in the column. This cursed land of hills and scrub hid their movement from a distance but also concealed the nomads. They could be anywhere behind them.

Ameni's shoulder ached from the axe his shield had only partially deflected. All down the row of chariots, fresh blood showed through bandages on both horses and men. If the horde were to overtake them now there would be little they could do but die quickly.

When Ameni heard the sounds of hooves and shouts in the distance, he realized there was a reason the horde had not attacked them from behind. The nomads had taken advantage of the terrain to slip ahead of them. He drew his sword as the underbrush began to shake before the approaching enemy.

Ameni let out a battle cry as the nomads crashed through the scrub and into the chariots. The conflict was a wild melee of slaughter with no order to the nomad attack. Blind rage drove them forward like the biting sand. Ameni saw a glint of metal and raised his shield in time to deflect a thrown axe. His arm went numb and his shield slipped to the ground. He ignored it and thrust his sword into the skull of another nomad. The sounds of men and horses dying surrounded him on every side. His soldiers fought bravely but were slowly being buried under the onslaught.

Nithotep shouted something in the tongue of the gods. A flash lit up the sky as a bit of the sun flared through the clouds and the startled nomads pulled back. With his eyes still dazed, Ameni yelled for the men to fall back and regroup as Djati echoed the cry beside him. Soon all those who were able took up positions in front of Nithotep's chariot. The nomads formed up in a wavering line.

Ameni considered the strength of his army. He had barely a third of his chariots left and only thirty wounded and exhausted soldiers remained. He knew from the heaving flanks of the horses that running was not possible. All that was keeping them alive now was the nomads' fear of Nithotep's magic. Seconds expanded into minutes and an eerie silence fell over the battlefield.

Djati held the chariot's horses as still as he could. "They have more than enough men to overwhelm us. What are they doing?"

"They are waiting." Ameni readied his bow.

"What for?"

The line of nomads split in two. A large man dressed in strips of leather with swirling black tattoos across his skin stomped to the front and began gesturing.

"For him," Ameni said, releasing his arrow.

A rain of arrows followed from the chariots but each one splintered in mid-flight or was hauled to the ground by a wisp of black smoke before reaching the nomads. The shaman laughed loudly and a dark haze rose from the ground and began drifting toward the chariots. Nithotep shouted in response and light flared from the sky, burning away the mist. The shaman gestured and screamed but the darkness did not reappear. He then barked out a nomad word Ameni knew all too well.

"Arrows!" he yelled. "Shield the Niece of Pharaoh."

Even as the words left his lips, Ameni saw an arrow strike home. Nithotep tumbled from her chariot. A mighty roar rose from the nomads and they surged forward. As the sting of axes and arrows descended on his soldiers, Ameni knew there was nothing left to do but die.

"How dare you?" The shout cut through the noise of the battle. A great mass of flame launched from behind the chariots and struck the first wave of nomads. The air filled with the smell of burning flesh and the cries of men and horses.

"You presume to challenge me?" Nithotep rose to stand beside her chariot, an arrow buried in her shoulder. She was speckled with ash and her face was red with rage.

The shaman gestured frantically. Black smoke encircled his feet and fire raced up his legs. He screamed as his body turned to ash. The flames leapt from him to every nomad within fifty feet. They scattered, trying in vain

to outrun the fiery death as it surged around them. Within minutes, the inferno consumed the mighty nomad horde leaving behind charred corpses and the sounds of the dying.

Ameni stared out at the destruction. His soldiers and chariots remained in their defensive positions with swords drawn and shields at the ready, but the battle was already finished. Nithotep collapsed and Ameni jumped from his chariot.

She looked grey and worn and her eyes were closed. He cradled her head in his arms. "Nithotep?"

As she stirred, the sky blue eyes of her family shined at him. "Yes, Servant of Pharaoh?"

"We should move in case there are more nomads. Are you able to travel?"

She winced in pain and gingerly touched the arrow shaft in her shoulder. Ameni gestured for a nearby soldier to come and tend to her wound.

Djati stood nearby. "Permission to send a rear scout to see if we are pursued? I doubt it, but I am tired of being caught unaware by nomads."

"Do so," Ameni said. "And spread the word among the men to stay away from the enemy wounded."

"You want witnesses to say how far ahead we are?"

Ameni pointed at the devastation. "I want witnesses to tell of the powerful wizard who travels with us. One whose magic brought this death and horror among them. Fear might keep them away from us and the border."

Djati remained unmoving.

"There is something else?"

"I will walk with you, Servant of Pharaoh, back to your chariot."

His chariot sat not more than twenty feet away.

"Speak if you would," Ameni said as he fell into step with his driver.

"I do not know if it is my place, but my tongue cannot remain silent."

"Then speak."

"When the Niece of Pharaoh fell, I thought we were lost."

"That is not what you wanted to tell me," Ameni said.

"The fire that swept through the nomad horde leapt from the ground and not the sky."

Ameni stared at Djati. "But I saw the flames come from her father, who rests in the sky."

"At the start they did." Djati's face hardened. "I watched her as the hawk watches its prey. After the arrow struck the Niece of Pharaoh the flames came from the ground."

Djati said nothing more until they reached the chariot.

"It may have been the smoke and the confusion of battle, but I swear that her eyes were black as a nomad's when she did all of this." Djati surveyed the carnage. "I have spoken, now I will keep silent."

Ameni stepped into the chariot and considered the charred remains of the nomad army. He looked over at the slight form of Nithotep weeping softly as her shoulder was treated. Ameni shivered despite the heat of the day.

The scouts found the tracks of other nomads in the area and reported the wounded were taken from the battlefield soon after the chariots left. The soldiers tensed for another attack as they travelled, but nothing happened. Ameni caught a glimpse of a nomad in the distance ahead of them, but no one challenged them to battle as they travelled to the border of the Eternal Kingdom. At the return of flat land, the chariots formed a solid line and began to move more rapidly.

Ameni motioned the column to slow as they came within sight of a border fort.

"Why is there no activity from the fort?" Nithotep asked as her chariot pulled next to his. "Has it fallen to an attack?"

"There is some smoke and battle damage, but the walls seem to have held," Ameni said. "Yet no chariots challenge our way and there are no sentries on the walls. The warning trumpet should have sounded by now."

"If the fort is in enemy hands, there is little we can do to retake it," Djati said.

"This is the border of the Eternal Kingdom. No incursion will remain unchallenged while we have breath," Ameni said.

The muscles around Djati's mouth tightened, but he bowed his head slightly.

"Change the line so that the most severely wounded are at the rear," Ameni said.

"I will ride at the front of the line," Nithotep said.

Ameni began to rebuke her but saw the determination in her face. He gestured to his left side. Within minutes, his soldiers reformed and advanced cautiously toward the silent structure.

The blare of a trumpet cut through the tension. The main gate opened and a small group of chariots rolled out to block their path. Ameni signaled for his chariots to stop.

Djati pointed to the archers taking up positions on the walls of the fortification. "Too few to be of much use if we were attacking them."

Ameni agreed. "Perhaps something has happened here."

"Soldiers of Pharaoh, may he rule forever, I greet you," the lead chariot rider said as he drew close. "What news do you bring from beyond the border of the Eternal Kingdom of the Sun?"

"The gods smile on us." Ameni lifted his hands toward the sun. "We return to tell Pharaoh that the Cursed-One is dead and the Eternal Kingdom's border is safe."

The commander offered a skin of wine to Ameni. "Your news is as welcome as the dawn after a long night."

"Have the nomads crossed the border?"

"No, the gods watch over us. The border has remained quiet."

Ameni handed the wineskin to Djati. "We require fresh horses and supplies to bring this news to Pharaoh so that all may know that the pall of the nomad threat has been lifted from our land."

The good cheer evaporated from the face of his counterpart. "I have some provisions which I could give to you." He spread his hands wide. "Other than that . . ."

"And why do you not have what we require?" Nithotep asked in a low voice. "Your horse is old and underfed and your chariot is in need of repair. Is this how you serve the Eternal Kingdom?"

The commander's hand went to his knife. "Keep your tongue silent or I will cut it from your mouth."

"Draw your knife, coward," she hissed. The air became heavy with the brewing storm. "I will send your spirit to the unending torment that it deserves for failing to serve the Eternal Kingdom."

Ameni had been a soldier too long to blame the messenger for delivering disappointing news. "Niece of Pharaoh, we all serve the Eternal Kingdom. Our enemies are not here. Horses cannot eat sand and chariots cannot be repaired with dust."

Nithotep looked away from the commander of the fort.

The commander's hand moved away from his knife and his face paled. "Niece of Pharaoh . . ."

Nithotep pulled the reins and her horse reared up before moving the chariot past the commander toward the fort. Ameni gestured and his soldiers followed into the courtyard, the commander's chariot next to him.

"Is this typical for the border forts now?" Ameni asked, surveying the chipped walls and the scant number of soldiers.

"These are different days," the commander of the fort said as he handed Ameni a small loaf and another skin of wine. "Pharaoh, may he rule forever, has chosen as he has chosen. May the gods protect us as they always have."

The commander bowed his head as Nithotep approached. She ignored him and he backed away from her quickly.

"I see nothing in this place but shadows of what used to be, Commander of Armies," Nithotep said. "Is the sun setting on the Eternal Kingdom?"

"Our victory gives us a new dawn."

"And what will be different?"

"That is for Pharaoh alone to decide."

"Yes, the wisdom of my uncle is already seen throughout the land." Nithotep waved a hand before Ameni could respond. "I am tired. When do we resume our journey?"

"We leave when the god's eye rises in the sky, Niece of Pharaoh," Ameni said as he escorted her to the middle of the courtyard where his men were settling in for the night. "In the morning we will move on to Kasseish. There should be supplies there to get us back to the capital."

"There will be supplies there," Nithotep said as she lay down beside a fire.

Ameni found a place a short distance from her and closed his eyes.

A scream followed by shouts woke Ameni. With his knife in hand he struggled to find a foe to strike. Soldiers ran toward the walls and horses pounded the ground where they had been tied.

Another scream echoed through the fort and Ameni realized it was Nithotep. He knelt beside her and grabbed her arm. Her eyes snapped open and nomad-black eyes glared at him. Ameni's muscles tensed and he raised his knife to strike. Djati stepped forward with a torch and Nithotep blinked and rubbed her head.

"Just a nightmare," she said, smiling weakly at Ameni as her blue eyes reflected the torchlight. "There is no need for your weapon."

Ameni became aware of the murmurs of his men and lowered his knife. He stood to address the group of soldiers gathering around them. "A dream of our past battle. A reliving of our great victory when the nomads fell like wheat before the sickle!"

A loud cheer chased away the shouts lingering in the fort, and soldiers resumed their places around the fortification.

Ameni handed a wineskin to Nithotep and she drank deeply.

"There is something wrong, Commander of Armies?" she asked.

Ameni peered carefully at the blue eyes which she had inherited from her father and grandfather. "No, Niece of Pharaoh, nothing is wrong," he said. "Sleep well."

She settled back down beside the fire, and Ameni began to walk away.

Djati fell into step beside him. "You lie poorly."

"It is nothing," Ameni said.

"You saw for yourself."

"I saw. I know not what it means."

"You fear the girl has been changed by the Cursed-One's magic."

"Yes," Ameni said.

"But she is Nithotep, daughter of the pharaoh you served until his death."

"I know," Ameni said.

"What will you do?"

"I do not know." Ameni slumped against the wall to look at the sleeping Nithotep. When sleep came, he dreamt of cities falling to dust around him as the Cursed-One laughed.

The morning broke grey and uncertain. They stopped along the road and ate the scant provisions collected from the border fort. The soldiers were better rested but an uneasiness hung over their meal. Ameni could not help notice that Nithotep winced in pain as she chewed the hard bread.

"You are unwell, Niece of Pharaoh?"

"My sleep was troubled," she said. "I dreamt of the Cursed-One screaming throughout the night."

"The events of these past days are enough to shake the sternest soldier."

"Even you are troubled?"

He nodded his head slightly.

"My father often said that food and rest will cure even the worst experiences."

Ameni gazed at her bandaged shoulder. "Your pain is more than in your spirit, though, is it not?"

Nithotep winced again and rubbed at her forehead. "My father, may he shine forever with the other gods, often complained of his head after returning from battle." A grin crept over her face. "Of course, there was a night of revelry to explain away the pain."

Ameni smiled easily. "Your father was a soldier like few others." Memories of the pharaoh's chariot being swarmed by nomads drained the smile from his face. "He knew too well the cost of serving the Eternal Kingdom."

"He also knew that one does not ask for recognition or encouragement before acting. For the Eternal Kingdom to thrive, the most unworthy foot soldier to almighty Pharaoh must do what needs to be done."

Nithotep returned to her chariot without another word.

Ameni considered days past and days yet to come as they worked their way down the dusty road to Kasseish. His head pounded with every thought and his muscles grew more tense with each turn of the chariot wheels.

A calm fell over the chariots as they passed the outlying farms of the city. Workers in the fields stopped to watch them slowly snaking their way down the road. Without fresh horses to pull the chariots, the procession was not much faster than a man could run, so it didn't surprise Ameni to see a small crowd waiting for them outside the city gates.

The three stern faces of the men standing in front of the chariots were a sharp contrast to the excitement of the men and women gathered behind them. Ameni guessed the crowd dressed in little more than rags had used the arrival of his soldiers as an excuse to pause in the day's labor.

"Are you the commander of these chariots?" a man dressed in fine leathers asked.

"I am Ameni, servant of the House of Pharaoh and Commander of Armies. We have returned from the borderlands with news of a great victory."

"The news has already passed our way," the man said with a wave of his hand. "Nomad emissaries have gone to beg terms from Pharaoh, whose wisdom brought about this victory. You may continue on your way."

"We need provisions and fresh horses to bring this news to Pharaoh," Ameni said.

The man's face hardened. "You will not be told again. Go on your way."

Ameni tensed and he felt his face growing hot. "What name shall we bring before Pharaoh when we tell of how his soldiers have been mistreated?"

"I am Amithelk," the man said, looking up and down the line of chariots. "Commanders who cannot care for their soldiers are no concern of mine."

The robed man next to Amithelk leaned forward and whispered in his ear. Amithelk shrugged.

"But perhaps I have been too harsh. The priest reminds me there are supplies for you to purchase if you require them."

"What?" Ameni said, reaching for his sword. "You would dare charge the soldiers of the Eternal Kingdom for supplies?"

"You will receive a fair price," Amithelk said as the priest beside him snickered. "And consider carefully what you do, commander of few chariots. I speak in the name of Pharaoh in this city." He raised his arm to show the walls lined with soldiers, their bows at the ready. "And those are my men to command."

Djati muttered in a low growl and Ameni touched his driver's shoulder. This was a battle they could not win.

"This is how a priest of the gods acts in the Eternal Kingdom?" Nithotep asked in a measured tone that sent a chill up Ameni's back.

"I suggest you keep your crazed woman silent, commander of few chariots," the priest said. "Or the price will increase."

Nithotep gestured and a bolt of light broke through the clouds and knocked the priest to the ground. Wisps of smoke rose from the chest of his corpse.

"You would make me, the child of the pharaoh who shines now in the sky, pay for supplies for soldiers of the Eternal Kingdom?" Nithotep's eyes flashed the color of steel.

The air grew thick and Ameni found it harder and harder to breathe.

Nithotep's voice grew louder. "You are no servant of our land, Amithelk. You are a locust." Her hand formed a fist. "Kill him."

Ameni's arm shot up quickly and his men froze in place. But the crowd of workers who had gathered to greet them surged forward and hauled the screaming Amithelk to the ground.

Shouts rose from the walls of the city and a score of arrows descended. Ameni's yell for shields died in his throat as the volley splintered apart in mid-air and fell harmlessly to the ground. Black tendrils of smoke rose from the earth, reaching up the walls of the city. Scattered screams rang out, bodies fell, and then all went silent.

Ameni's sword was partway drawn as he turned to face Nithotep. Her face was filled with the same outrage he had seen on her grandfather's face as he crushed his enemies in battle. Ameni pushed his sword back into its sheath. He heard the sound of weapons being sheathed behind him.

"Will any more treasonous officials hinder our return to the capital?" she asked. "Will there be any difficulty resupplying these soldiers with fresh horses and drivers?" The air crackled with her rage.

Ameni touched her arm and she glared at him. He felt a wash of cold naked fear that he had not felt since his first days as a soldier—the fear of battle, the fear of pain, the fear of death—as those steel blue eyes considered him. He swallowed with difficulty. "Your father often said that to prune a vine is to bring forth a great crop."

Nithotep's face softened with his words and he felt a wash of relief. She bowed her head toward him. "You are a faithful servant of the Eternal Kingdom, Ameni. My father put his trust in you for good reason."

She turned her attention to the lone official still remaining from the welcoming party. "You are now in command of this city. You answer only to the one the gods choose to rule this land. These soldiers will be resupplied and accorded every privilege, for such befits those bearing great news for the Eternal Kingdom of the Sun."

The official fell to his knees before her. "I pledge my life and my house." As he stood, he raised his voice to a shout. "Today the blessed child of the god who shines in the sky has come to our city after winning a great victory over the nomads!"

A cheer rose up from the crowd and was soon echoed from the walls. A rush of activity took place as the city gave way to the line of chariots that processed to the center square. The wine and food were plentiful as they were honored by the city, but Ameni found it difficult to enjoy himself as he watched his soldiers acting as Nithotep's personal guard. He was unsure which one of them would obey if he gave the order to kill her. He was haunted by the thought that some might strike at him instead.

Ameni brushed his horse in the stable before the sun rose to chase away the darkness.

"We are not in the field anymore, Commander of Armies," Djati said from the doorway. "There are servants here to do that."

"I sent them away. My shoulder needs to be exercised if it is ever to heal properly." He paused to stretch. "I did this for her grandfather's horses when I was her age. He was a powerful man who led us out of dark times."

Djati patted the side of the horse. "It is a fine gift."

"Yes, it is."

"She is like her father. She honors those who serve faithfully."

Ameni continued to brush the horse.

"There will be quite a commotion when we reach the capital," Djati said.

"Yes, old friend, there will be quite the celebration."

Djati cleared his throat. "You know that is not what I mean. Word has spread throughout the land. There has been talk among the soldiers who have joined us. Whispers that she embodies the will of the gods and is a sign of a new dawn for the Eternal Kingdom."

"I know." Ameni concentrated on the strokes of his brushing. He finished one side and moved to the other. "When I look into her eyes, I am afraid it is darkness and not daylight before us."

"She has charmed and entranced the leaders of every city we have passed through since we returned home."

"Except those of Kasseish."

Djati bowed his head slightly.

"The others have not seen her anger or her magic," Ameni said. "We have. Your words from the night we crossed the border gnaw at my spirit like a jackal on a bone."

"That she has changed since the battle?"

Ameni nodded. "I fear the battle with the Cursed-One is still being fought within her."

"The Cursed-One died. We both saw that. Do not let shadows of what was darken what is coming. Even with her temper, the kingdom could do worse."

"Do worse? I can see no good from this. The Eternal Kingdom cannot stand if Pharaoh is not obeyed absolutely."

"Can we stand what is happening now? In the days of her grandfather the nomads trembled before us. You of all people know her father's sacrifice to stop them. They grow stronger each generation as we wither."

Ameni closed his eyes. "The Cursed-One is dead. You said so yourself. The nomads again pay tribute. Pharaoh in his wisdom sent us and now the kingdom is safe."

"Do you really believe those words, Ameni? You have seen what I have seen. Those who return with us from the forsaken lands know her power. She has magic within her unlike anything seen since the days of the old legends." Djati lowered his voice. "If the gods place her there, I think those who ride with us would accept her on the throne."

Ameni opened his mouth to rebuke Djati, but the words stuck in his throat. He could not look into the eyes of his friend and say that he was wrong. Ameni looked away.

"They would, servant of the House of Pharaoh," Djati said.

Ameni shrugged. "But who can understand the will of the gods? We are not priests."

"It has been a long time since you were a common soldier. We all assume the gods ride in the chariot of the Commander of the Armies. Was it not the same when you drove her grandfather's chariot?"

"Those were simpler times." Ameni returned to his task. He paused mid-stroke. "Will the soldiers obey as I command?"

"Some will not," Djati said. He touched the hilt of his knife. "But all who continue to stand after you give the order will obey. You have but to command."

Ameni resumed brushing. All that remained was to decide what the order should be.

In the silence of the stable, Ameni prayed to the gods as he had not prayed since he was a little boy, for he had no idea what they required of him. The gloom of the morning brightened, but the sky remained cloudy and unsettled.

When they reached the capital, the streets were lined with adoring people of all classes. Shouts and thrown greenery lined their route to the palace of Pharaoh. Ameni rode in his chariot with Djati driving and Nithotep beside him. The loudest cheers from the crowds came when Nithotep acknowledged the people with a wave.

Ameni offered his arm to Nithotep as she exited the chariot. Djati caught Ameni's eye from behind her and touched his knife quickly. Ameni took a deep breath and escorted the daughter of his former pharaoh into the palace.

Three quick blasts from the long trumpets announced them as they entered the audience chamber. Pharaoh sat on the raised dais in the middle of the room; a court wizard stood on his right and a handful of soldiers circled the steps leading to the throne. A small group of dignitaries and officials waited at a distance.

Nithotep began to move forward, but Ameni held her back. "You must be invited to draw near to Pharaoh." He stared into her eyes, hoping for some sort of sign, but saw nothing in the dim light of the room.

She gently withdrew her arm from his. "You were always a loyal servant of my father. I trust your service to my family will continue."

She stood on her toes and kissed his cheek. Ameni blushed at such an intimate gesture in a formal setting.

She strode toward the throne, and a gasp went up from those assembled. Palace soldiers shifted to block her path. The court wizard raised his staff ever so slightly.

Pharaoh's voice filled the room. "Daughter of my brother, you presume too much to come unbidden into the presence of the earthly manifestation of the gods. Know your place and withdraw. Ask for mercy and perhaps I will forgive you."

"I know my place," Nithotep said and pointed at the throne. A black haze rose up from the ground and began drifting up the dais.

The court wizard's staff glowed in the darkness. "Loyal servants of the Eternal Kingdom, protect your pharaoh."

The palace guards and a few soldiers rushed to surround the throne.

Ameni realized that all the other soldiers in the palace were looking at him. He held up his hand and they remained in place. None of them had been called to draw near by Pharaoh himself. Ameni would not break tradition and risk dishonoring Pharaoh on the words of a wizard.

The wizard stepped forward and his staff lit up the room, keeping the rising haze at a distance. "Your darkness has no power here; this is the Eternal Kingdom of the Sun."

Nithotep's laughter filled the room. "You think my power has no effect in the land which gave me birth?" She waved her hand and the darkness leapt up and extinguished the staff.

"You think that my father, who shines in the sky, would let your hand be raised against me?" She waved again and fire reached out from the torches into the darkness. The court wizard shouted in the tongues of the gods, but the flames licked up and down his body. His screams echoed in the chamber until his remains fell to the floor.

"Get out of the way, servants of the Eternal Kingdom," Nithotep said to the soldiers blocking her path. "I have no quarrel with you."

Two of the soldiers rushed forward and a blinding light flashed around Nithotep. They fell scratching at their eyes. She paused to slit their throats with her knife before calmly walking forward. The other guards fell back from her path.

Pharaoh stood and grasped at the knife he wore. Fire flared from the torches again and he tumbled off the platform to avoid it. Nithotep ascended to the throne and sat down. She turned to gaze at her uncle struggling to his feet.

"Servants of the Eternal Kingdom," Pharaoh shouted, "draw near and obey your oaths." He pointed his knife at Nithotep. "Kill the one who presumes to take the place of Pharaoh."

Ameni strode to the bottom of the platform. He looked over at Pharaoh before whom he had sworn his life. He saw fear and desperation in the eyes of the ruler of the Eternal Kingdom.

Ameni faced Nithotep and saw the black tinge in her eyes. He was certain he could strike a fatal blow before her magic struck him down. He shifted his weight slightly and prepared himself. Movement to the right caught his eye and Ameni paused.

The nomads' emissaries were bowing before Nithotep and offering their lives to her. Ameni watched them lying prostrate before the throne of pharaoh and realized there was only one choice for him to make in order to save his beloved land. The time for uncertainty was over.

He drew his knife slowly and heard the weapons of his soldiers being drawn behind him. His heart pounded as it always did before battle began and fates were determined. Ameni pointed the tip of his blade at the brother of the pharaoh he had served faithfully.

"Kill the pretender."

As divine blood spilled onto the floor of the audience chamber, Ameni knelt before Nithotep and pledged his loyalty to the new pharaoh of the Eternal Kingdom.

The Gifts of Avalae

Ian McHugh

Carnac manDamag, High Thane of the Tharingii Nordain, had elected to walk for a change and to give his saddle-sore backside a rest. He was fast becoming aware of how thoroughly adapted his leg muscles were for riding, particularly with his son's added weight perched atop his shoulders.

Forcing himself to jollity, Carnac inhaled deeply and smacked his lips. "Smell that, Graigor? That's life. That's a clan still fat after winter and rich in beasts and children."

Walking beside him, his wife, Albeth, wrinkled her nose under her broad-brimmed hat. "You old fool. Smells to me like three hundred scores of farting sheep and horses and near as many people in dire need of bathing."

Graigor giggled and tugged the pointed helices of Carnac's ears. "Smells like farts to me, Da."

"Show some respect, you two," Carnac said. He took another deep breath. "Aye and it smells like farts and sour sweat, too."

Behind them, the Tharingii caravan stretched nearly a mile, a straggling serpent of riders, walkers, horses, donkeys, dogs, sheep, oxen, wagons and cannon. The bawdy cacophony of a clan on the move filled the air.

A cry went up from the scouts ahead—the great hall of the Magmardain had been sighted.

"Look Graigor," Carnac said, when they crested the rise. He pointed at the massive timber building on its steep hill, dominating the valley.

The Magmardain—Ledonaii and Cimbrathii—were there already, encamped on either side of the Hall of the Broken Crown. Firedrake flags mirrored each other across the narrow gap between the opposing clans. The Tharingii weren't the first Nordain to arrive. Dantraii ram's head banners flew over a sprawling camp that covered half the valley. Nearer at hand, a smaller, more orderly cluster of wagons and tents stood between the oak leaf standards of Salithii.

Graigor didn't reply, but Albeth laughed and said, "If you feel two bumps against the top of your head, Carnac, it's because his eyes have popped right out of his face."

Galloping hooves drummed up the slope behind them. Carnac spun on his heel, causing Graigor to squeal in delight.

Carnac's brother, Olwain, chased his new wife up the slope towards them, his face lit by a rare smile. Olwain was as alike in appearance to his brother as he was opposite in character; both were already filling out into the powerful, paunchy heaviness common to men of their family. Unlike Carnac, who kept his blond hair and moustaches cropped, Olwain wore his long, in old-fashioned leather-bound plaits. The helices of his ears he had cropped, in the manner of the Nordain warriors of antiquity.

Olwain's wife rode bareback and without reins. Carnac had to admit Glyn was as fine a rider as any Tharingii man, for all that she was forest-born. She was a striking-looking woman too, tall and straight with sallow skin and hair like a crow's wing, although he preferred his own wife's red curls and comfortable curves. And he certainly preferred Albeth's personality.

Should have married Olwain off to a nice Tharingii girl like Albeth, and alliances be damned, he grumbled to himself. *Damn sure father wouldn't have let that old crook Salwyth talk him into the match.*

Glyn raised a hand in greeting as she slowed her horse to a halt beside them. "Good morning, my thane. Albeth, young Graigor."

"Good morning, Glyn," Carnac said, amiable as he always was for Olwain's sake. "Morning, Brother."

Olwain responded with a terse nod. Still brooding, then.

Glyn threw a glance his way before offering: "Caithwen died."

"Ah, that's sad," Carnac said, and meant it. "And a loss for the clan, too. Gifted witches are among the few riches with which we are currently not well endowed." He yelped as a spark leapt from his wife's finger to his buttock. Graigor squealed. "I didn't mean you aren't a gifted witch, woman," he said. "Just that we have few others like you."

Albeth arched her brows. "She was the last alive who remembered the West."

"Was she really so old?" Glyn asked.

"Over a hundred and seventy," Carnac said, lifting his son down from his shoulders. "Old even for a witch."

"What about that old Walathii diviner, Driw?"

"Driw was born in Magmardia, it's true," Carnac said, "but he was still in swaddling when our ancestors crossed the land-bridge with the hordes yapping at their heels."

Glyn persisted. "The Gars still remember."

With Olwain glowering beside her, Carnac wondered if she was trying to reignite their current dispute. "Aye," he said, "but Gars remember cold mountains and halls of stone, not wide rivers and rolling hills and plains of long grass."

"Sounds no different to what we have now," Albeth said.

"I agree," Carnac said. "The Twin Empires be damned, we have all we need right here, if you ask me."

He regretted the words the moment they were out of his mouth. The muscles in Olwain's jaw bunched. Carnac had said something similar to put an end to their debate a few nights before, when he'd been startled by the intensity of Olwain's interest in the lost lands of their ancestors.

Albeth laughed. "And who did?"

Carnac gnashed his teeth at her. He changed the subject, hoping to avert another argument with Olwain. "Hoy, Glyn, what's say we rest Tharingii's wolf by the shade of Salithii's oak?"

Glyn's face lit up. "The Good Mother's blessing on you, Carnac man-Damag!" With a whoop, she urged her horse to a canter.

Olwain turned his scowl on Carnac for a moment, before yanking his mount around to follow.

"And what did you do now?" Albeth asked.

Carnac waved a hand wearily. "The other night he started spouting some crap about 'reclaiming the birthright of the Nordain,' as he put it. How—let me see if I remember it aright—how our ancestors had their own name once—*Haneshmen*—and weren't merely the 'Blessed Servants' to the Magmardain's 'Most Blessed.' Masters of the West, they were, lords of the Empire of Chahanesh, before the corruption of their leaders brought their downfall and conquest by the Magmardain. I told him what I thought of such nonsense."

Albeth poked him in the ribs. "I'll bet you did—and with all the subtlety of a man swatting a fly with a shovel, no doubt."

"Aye, well, now he's got his trousers in a twist." Carnac sighed. "I never heard such foolishness from him until *she* came along."

Albeth looked at him severely. "Now, Carnac, I don't know what you can be holding Glyn responsible for."

Carnac snorted, but let the matter drop.

He left Graigor and the disposition of the Tharingii camp to Albeth and hiked over to see his Salithii counterpart.

Thane Salwyth, a tall, lean man of Carnac's father's generation, greeted him at the edge of the Salithii wagons. Vanity, Carnac knew, caused Salwyth to shave his thinning hair to stubble. The other man's pointed ears were pierced with gold rings from tip to lobe.

"Well met, Salwyth. How fares your clan?"

"Good. Winter was mild our way."

"Ours too," Carnac said. "We should have a deal of trade to discuss, I think."

"Aye." Salwyth's leathered face creased into a smile. "You're looking more like your father each time I see you, laddie."

Carnac looked down at himself critically. "I'm getting fatter, you mean. I told you we had a good winter."

Salwyth chuckled. "And how's my niece?"

"Did she not greet you already?"

"Aye, well, she hollered a 'hallo' as she galloped past with your little brother trailing from her apron strings."

"She's well. And Olwain's besotted with her," Carnac said. Unable to contain himself, he added, "I think he's letting her do his thinking for him, though."

Salwyth arched his brows. "Well, she always was a strong-minded lass," he said. "Might you not be doing Olwain a disservice? A man who prefers to keep his opinions to himself is not necessarily free of opinions."

Carnac grunted, conceding the point.

"Well," Salwyth said, evidently satisfied that the matter was closed. He produced a Gar-made seeing glass and waved it in front of Carnac. "Have a gander at the sentries around the Dantraii camp."

Curious, Carnac extended the glass and looked. Instead of spears, swords or bows, the Dantraii warriors cradled blunt-ended tubes of iron and wood, flared to a paddle-shaped stock at one end, like a crossbow's.

"What are they?" he asked.

"The latest toy from the Gars. A black-powder weapon."

Carnac lowered the glass from his eye. "Some sort of long fire-jar is it? The burrowers have been peddling those for years. Good for naught but frightening horses and exploding in your hands, if you ask me."

"Ah, but this is a different thing." Salwyth took back the glass. "A 'musket' they call it. A hand-cannon, if you can believe that."

"A hand-cannon? And what kind of wee balls do you fire from it? Acorns?"

"Well, it seems even an acorn-sized ball can bring down a man, or a horse for that matter. At fifty paces they go through plate like it was woolen cloth."

"Truly?" Carnac shook his head in wonder. "And what sort of range do they have?"

"Only about a hundred paces. The Gars claim two hundred, but you'd be lucky to hit the side of yonder hall at that range. And they take twice as long to reload as a crossbow."

Carnac barked a laugh. "I reckon I'll be sticking to longbows and real-sized cannon then. You'll get eight hundred yards out of a longbow and half a dozen arrows into the air for every one of their wee acorns."

"Ah, my young thane." Salwyth tapped the seeing glass in an ambivalent gesture. "The advantage of these muskets is you can stick a blade to the end of them and use them as a spear after you've fired them. Conveniently, the Gars also make a long knife for just such a purpose.

"Imagine you're facing a Dantraii host of archers and cannon, cavalry and spearmen—except the spearmen carry loaded muskets. You lob arrows and cannonballs at each other for a while, as usual, and the witches play with their lightnings. They keep their cavalry in reserve and wait while you charge. When you get to fifty paces, they all fire their muskets at once. And, then, *they* charge."

Carnac considered this. At length, he licked his lips and asked, "Are the Gars here already?"

"Aye, they're camped over the back of the hall. And they've got wagon-loads of muskets to trade. Some of my lads are over there now."

Carnac grinned. "I'd better get over there and grab some then, hadn't I?"

Carnac winced at the musket's report. Olwain swore, nearly dropping the weapon, and waggled a finger in his ear. A couple of boys ran out to retrieve the shield he'd been aiming at. The men gathered around, whistling and cursing in wonder when they returned—just as Carnac had when the Gars gave him the same demonstration. Olwain's shot had struck well off center, but had left a splintered, fist-sized hole right through the brass and oak of the shield.

"What'll those damn Gars think of next, eh lads?" Carnac said.

"We could make these for ourselves, Carnac." There was an odd note in Olwain's voice as he cradled the weapon in his hands.

"Nonsense, we haven't the craft or the tools," Carnac said, more sharply than he'd intended. "And, besides, we don't maintain the kind of forges the Gars do."

"Of course we have the craft!" Olwain swept an arm about to encompass the Tharingii camp. "Have we not smiths? Have we not witches? Do we not make our own swords and arrowheads? Stirrups and bits for our horses? Brooches for our cloaks? We make our own cannon balls and our own gunpowder, brother. And forges? Would it be such a hard thing to build and maintain such as we would need?"

The men around them had fallen silent, watching the unexpected confrontation between their thane and his brother.

Olwain forestalled Carnac's reply. "We could make these muskets for ourselves. And we could make our own cannon if we wished. How many muskets will the Gars sell us? Three, four score? We could make one for every man of Tharingii."

"To what purpose, Olwain?" Carnac said.

Olwain's face flushed. To Carnac's surprise, he seemed undaunted. "To be freed of our dependence on what the cursed burrowers will condescend to sell us!"

"We *trade* with the Gars, in case you haven't noticed, brother. We are not beggars. Anyway, where would you get the metal for your forges, if not from the Gars? Will you mine for it yourself?"

Olwain shrugged. "We might buy our metals from them, or we might trade further south for it."

"Aye, and pay Dantraii tithes to do so," Carnac said.

"Or not!" Olwain shook the musket at him. "Dantraii don't hold all the roads south."

Carnac glared. In a low growl, he repeated his earlier question, "To what purpose, Olwain?"

Olwain swallowed, but held his ground. He appealed to the men assembled around them. "My father always said no man will ever wear the Broken Crown again. Broken it is and broken it shall remain. Each year, less and less of the bearskinned are born among the Magmardain. The feud between Cimbrathii and Ledonaii is a relic from Magmardia's fall—irrelevant, but it keeps them too busy to lord over the rest of us."

"True enough," Carnac said, wanting to keep the argument between the two of them. "But what of it?"

Olwain turned back to him. "What if a new crown were forged?"

Carnac felt a chill in his belly. "A new crown?"

"Aye. A new crown for a Nordain brow. A *Hanesh* brow."

"Easy words," Carnac said, "until you're staring up at some bearskinned Magmardain brute over your locked shields. When did you start swallowing that Dantraii crap, Olwain manDamag?"

Olwain snorted. "Ha! If there were a crown, why should it be a Dantraii to wear it?"

Carnac ticked off fingers. "Because Dantraii lands bestride the trade routes to the south. Because they're richer than any other clan and can afford to buy more and better blades, armor, and cannon than any other clan. And because they breed like rabbits and there's more of them than there is of anyone else."

"All true." Olwain relaxed his stance a little. "But if every Tharingii man had a musket and every Tharingii family had a cannon, could even Dantraii stand against us?"

Carnac stared at him in amazement. "And how long, Olwain, before other clans copy us? We have the craft you say, but we have no more craft among us than any other clan. And their witches are just as capable as ours of unraveling runes of warding and blowing up a primed cannon where it stands—or causing a loaded musket to explode in a man's face, no doubt. What kind of destruction would we wreak amongst ourselves then, brother of mine?"

Olwain's lips peeled back in a snarl. "By the time they realized what we had done, a Tharingii would wear a king's crown and ancient Chahanesh would be reborn."

With that, he flung the musket to the ground at Carnac's feet and shoved his way through the ring of startled onlookers.

Carnac let him go. He closed his eyes for a minute and forced his breathing back to its normal rhythm. Then he glanced up at the sky and muttered a brief prayer to the Storm King and the Red Lady, both. He looked around at his clansmen.

"Utter no word of this folly before any man of another clan," he said. "Olwain is acting a fool. The wars of empires in the West brought our ancestors naught but despair. To be sure, we feud from time to time with men of other clans—amongst ourselves sometimes." A few men nudged each other, a couple exchanged sheepish grins. "Often men are injured, sometimes men die. But we do not conquer each other, or our neighbors, nor steal each other's lands. What would our children suffer if we waged war against our own kin? Tharingii cannot stand against all the other clans of Nordain and Magmardain. Not even if we could shoot thunderbolts from our arses." That won him a couple of quiet chuckles.

He gave them a moment before he went on. "If Tharingii launched such a war, we would lose. Chahanesh died long before our ancestors were driven from the West. We have nothing left of it but a name. To try and revive it would see the death of our clan. We would not be forgiven. Those we sought to conquer would pursue us until every man and woman and babe of Tharingii was dead and the Leaping Wolf burned from the face of the world."

Most of the men responded with vigorous nods or words of wholehearted agreement. Carnac was disturbed to see a few, though, who nodded with unseeing eyes, their thoughts turned inwards.

He cursed under his breath, his anger heating anew, and pushed his way out of the circle. He marched through the camp to his family's wagons, where Glyn sat in the shade of an awning with Albeth and her sisters. Without a word, Carnac grabbed Glyn by the arm and hauled her to her feet. Ignoring the outraged cries, he dragged her away from the camp.

Albeth charged after. "Carnac! What the hells has gotten into you?"

Glyn wrenched at his grip and kicked him in the calf. "Let me go!"

He rounded on her. "What madness have you put into my brother's head, woman?"

Released, she frowned at him, apparently perplexed. "What?"

"All this insanity about kings and crowns he's started spouting!" He wagged a finger in her face. "All since you came along!"

"Me? How long has he been your shadow?"

"Eh?" he grunted, blindsided by the question.

"The shadow to your sun, Carnac," she said. "All his life, that's how long. I told him I wanted a husband who was his own man and who spoke his own mind. All I've done is encouraged him to speak up for himself. His ideas are his own."

"Don't lie to me, you forest devil!"

"Carnac!" Albeth protested.

"Olwain's my brother," he said. "I know his mind better than any man—and you've poisoned it!"

"If you think that, Carnac manDamag," Glyn said, jabbing him in the chest, "you don't know him at all." She spun on her heel and strode away.

Albeth opened her mouth to speak, then shook her head and hurried after Glyn. Carnac kicked impotently at a tussock of grass, left with the uncomfortable thought that Glyn's words might be true.

Carnac paused a moment on the threshold of the great hall and allowed his eyes to adjust to the smoky gloom inside. Around him, Albeth, Olwain and the other thanes and witches of the Tharingii clan did the same.

Six furred, bear-headed Magmardain warriors—three Ledonaii and three Cimbrathii—faced each other inside the doorway. Carnac felt uncomfortably small walking between them. Bearskinned Magmardain guards lined the walls of the hall, one between each of the carved tree trunks that held up the high roof. No Nordain guards were allowed to enter the hall.

He surveyed those in attendance as he stepped down onto the sunken, circular floor in the center of the hall. The Tharingii were the last to arrive.

A gong sounded. Carnac and his companions hurried to the cushions set for them, between those of the Salithii and the Gars. The molemen had pulled aside their veils in the dimness of the hall, exposing pallid faces with luminous pink eyes and fleshy tentacles that lined their jowls in place of whiskers. Their enormous, black-clawed hands rested on the ceremonial hammers and picks they cradled in their laps.

Carnac nodded greetings to Salwyth and Ramul Lambai Azgar, the Gar elder he'd traded with for the new muskets. The Gars had three representatives in the council—one for each of the fallen cities of Old Gar—although they had founded only one city east of the land bridge. Aside from the Gars, the council comprised the high thanes of each of the Nordain clans, six in all, and the two rival Magmardain princes. As with Carnac, they'd all brought with them a gaggle of elders and advisers.

It was Ledonaii's turn to host this year. White-haired Pagan magLedon stood before his throne and thumped the butt of his staff three times on the floor. Four yards to his left, a distance greater than the reach of a Magmardain arm and longsword, Culyan magCimbran sat in an identical throne and tried to look as though Pagan were acting as his herald.

The old prince filled his still-powerful chest and launched into his welcoming speech. "My brothers—"

Albeth harrumphed loudly. She was far from the only woman present. Pagan ignored her. "My *brothers* and friends, Thanes of Nordain, Lords of Gulgaroth, we welcome you on behalf of the king who was and will be again. It is the one-hundred and forty-eighth year since the fall of Magmardia and the Three Cities. This year, my brothers, the last among us who knew the West has died. While our friends the Gars remember, let us—"

A resounding boom rattled the walls of the hall. Dust and bits of thatch fell from the ceiling. An unearthly shriek followed, along with frightened cries from outside. The occupants of the hall reached for their weapons and rushed for the doors. Pagan of Ledonaii was one of the first out, his body changing as he went, so that he emerged into the daylight as a white-furred bear. Carnac and Olwain were hot on his heels, among the Cimbrathii and Ledonaii guards.

"Mother Mercy, what are these?" Olwain whispered as they stumbled to a halt.

Three monstrous, winged beasts had alighted before the hall. Carnac was glad to have Albeth arrive at his shoulder, the green glow of a killing spell wrapping the fingers of her left hand.

Center and fore, an emerald serpent balanced on raptor talons that could have crushed a man. A gigantic white lion with a scorpion tail and an equally outsized, horned and cloven-footed horse loomed by the serpent's flanks. Slender beings in fantastical armor of gleaming gold and bronze sat astride the shoulders of each beast.

Pagan magLedon pushed between his warriors. "I am Pagan manKurgan magLedon, Prince of Ledonaii," he said, his words slurring over his bear's teeth and tongue, "and you are on Magmardain land. Name yourselves."

The foremost rider bowed and replied in a musical voice. "Greetings, Lords of Old Magmardia. I am Malakhieh. And we are the Avalae, Gods of Avaleinaea. We have come to offer friendship and wondrous gifts—"

"Liar!" a deep voice bellowed. "False god!"

The guards beside Carnac gave way and the old Gar, Ramul Lambai, strode forward, five feet tall and near as great in girth. In his anger, he'd forgotten to affix his veil and his eyes were slitted against the light. His fleshy whiskers writhed in agitation. Ramul planted himself in front of the winged serpent, his runestaff in one outsized fist and an iron mallet in the other. The monster hissed.

The Gar drew in the dirt with great sweeps of his staff, then slammed the point of the staff into the image's center. The lines blazed and Carnac saw it was the Garish rune for iron.

Ramul marched towards the riders, a tiny figure before their steeds. Yet the monsters shied from his advance. He raised his hammer above his head.

"Be gone, deceivers." His voice boomed. "Or taste black iron."

"My lords, do not listen to this burrower," Malakhieh cried, his voice suddenly shrill. "He wishes only to ensure your dependence—"

"Be gone!" Ramul flung his hammer at the serpent.

The monsters sprang into the air with powerful beats of their wings. As they fled, Ramul raised a shovel-like hand. His hammer looped back towards him and smacked into his palm. He swept his gaze about the surrounding Nordain and Magmardain clansmen.

"Those are not gods," he said. "Their mortal cousins inhabit the forests to the south of Gulgaroth. Those," he pointed skyward, "have sold their souls for life eternal and their blood runs cold in their veins. They are powerful sorcerers and amuse themselves by twisting beasts and men alike into monsters such as those you saw. But they are not gods. They can be killed. Gars have killed them, when they came to us with their false promises. Iron is poison to them. Heed me well, sons of Old Magmardia."

With that, he plucked his staff from the ground. The fires of his rune faded and vanished.

Carnac looked to his wife. She gave him a shaky smile as the glow faded from her fingers. Beside her, Olwain's gaze was fixed on the three specks dwindling into the eastern sky.

Over the following days, the camps were abuzz with speculation as to the origin and purpose of the Avalae. The Gars would not be drawn further on their people's encounter with the foreigners. The normal businesses of feasting, trading and marrying also proceeded apace.

Olwain took no part in these activities, instead announcing that he was going hunting with a party of friends. Some days after returning from his expedition, he stepped under the awning at the front of the thane's tent, where Carnac sat with Graigor while the boy played with his carved warriors and horses. As Olwain helped himself to a cushion, Carnac took his pipe from his mouth and breathed out a long cloud of smoke.

"And how was your hunting?" he asked. "Fruitless, I assume, and you fell off your horse to boot, otherwise you wouldn't have avoided me for three days since you came back."

Olwain didn't smile. "We didn't go hunting. We went to see the Avalae."

In the middle of another drag on his pipe, Carnac exhaled sharply and spat the tabac plug halfway to the next tent. Graigor laughed and sprang to his feet to go and find it. Olwain sat quietly while Carnac spluttered and coughed.

"We went across the river and lit a fire behind the ridge," he said at length. "They came to us."

Carnac wiped his mouth and eyes, then stared at him in disbelief. "Why would you do a damn fool thing like that, Olwain? I *know* you heard what the Gar had to say about these foreigners."

"Aye, I heard the Gar, and I heard what Malakhieh said in response. I heard more since. There was naught the foreigner had to say of our circumstances that I didn't already know for myself." He looked at Carnac with red-rimmed and dilated eyes. "The burrowers hold us in thrall, and the bearskins keep us weak and divided. The Avalae offer us the chance to make our own destiny. The Nordain can be as proud as our ancestors once were. We can be *Haneshmen* again."

Damn me, Carnac thought, pulling back from his brother's fevered stare, *Glyn was telling the truth.* "Can you not hear the poison in those words, brother?" he asked. "These creatures are not gods."

Olwain smiled, slyly. "Don't think me a fool, Carnac. I know that, though it pleases them to style themselves as such. But even the Gar said they're powerful sorcerers. If obtaining their gifts means pandering to their delusions of deity for a while, then so be it."

"Would you forsake our gods, then?"

"*Magmardain* gods," Olwain said, shrugging. "And why not? Didn't our ancestors cast aside their own gods once the Magmardain yoke was on their necks?"

"*What* yoke, Olwain?" Carnac shouted. "We're a free people!"

Olwain reached out suddenly and caught Carnac's wrist. "Come with me, brother, and I'll make you king! Ledonaii and Cimbrathii and Dantraii and all the clans—even the Gars—will bow to you."

"Me? And what of you, Olwain?"

"Me?" He laughed. "Why, I'll be the Prophet of the New Age, as we cast off the borrowed gods who failed us in the West."

Carefully, Carnac pulled his arm free of his brother's grasp.

Olwain's face fell. "So be it." He pushed himself to his feet, seeming to gather himself for a moment before striding away without a backward glance.

Was this madness always in him? Carnac wondered. *How did I never see it?*

"Because you chose not to, Carnac manDamag," he said, standing. "You fat fool."

Graigor looked up at him with wide eyes.

"Go and find your mother. Tell her I've gone to see the other thanes because your uncle Olwain's a mad fool."

The boy nodded and sprinted away.

Carnac hurried to the edge of the camp where the clan's horses were tethered. Several groups of Tharingii men were gathering their herds. Carnac's steps faltered. He felt a cold weight in the pit of his belly.

He called out to the nearest of the departing clansmen. "Hoy, Fingid, where are you moving your horses to?"

The other man glanced briefly his way, jaw set, then turned his back without answering. Carnac's face heated. He started to reach for his belt knife, paused with his fingers touching the hilt.

And what will that achieve, he asked himself, *you and Fingid stabbing each other to death beneath your horses' hooves?* He released the knife and untied his old stallion, Horga, from the line, abandoning dignity to scramble up onto the horse's bare back.

"You've got to lose some weight," he puffed to himself.

Leaving the camp, he was disturbed to see his brother speaking animatedly to a sizeable knot of men and women at the edge of the Tharingii tents.

Olwain, you snake, Carnac thought. *You're no brother of mine, to sit beside me and offer me a crown when you've already spread your poison behind my back.*

Nearby, the Wolf banner of their clan hung limply in the breathless air. *An omen?* Carnac wondered with a chill. He looked more closely at the crowd gathered around Olwain and realized that, while they were all Nordain, none of them were Tharingii.

Damn me, it's even worse than I thought. He nudged Horga into a canter.

He found Salwyth of Salithii shoeing horses with his sons.

"I need help," he said, without preamble.

Salwyth hammered down the end of a nail and straightened. "With Olwain you mean?"

"You know already?"

"Aye, there's more than a few folk been thinking the same fool thoughts as him. I caught wind yesterday of certain whisperings among my own folk, although no one's found the courage to say anything openly to me."

Carnac clapped his hands to his temples. "If you knew yesterday, why'd you say nothing to me?"

Salwyth met his glare coolly. "Because the Magmardain and the other thanes were of the opinion that you might be of a mind with your brother. I told them you were ignorant, not an idiot. I said you'd come to me as soon as you found out." He flashed a humorless smile. "I'm relieved you proved me right, laddie."

"And when was this decided?" Carnac said, too outraged to care how shrill he sounded. "Without me there to defend myself and Tharingii honor?"

"Last night, although there was precious little else on which the council was of a single mind."

Carnac snorted. Even in a crisis, *that* was far from unusual.

Salwyth handed his hammer to his eldest son in exchange for his scabbarded sword. All the sons bore arms, Carnac noted. "There's sorcery afoot here," Salwyth said. "Matters are moving apace faster than if this were mundane treachery. Come on."

He leapt lightly onto the back of one of his newly shod animals.

Carnac watched him sourly. "*Got* to lose some weight."

They galloped up the slope to the great hall. Magmardain men, women and children watched their hectic passage. Carnac noted how many of the men wore armor and had arms in hand.

He dropped heavily from Horga's back when they reached the hall. Trusting the old horse to stay where he was put, Carnac strode to the weathered bronze bell that hung beside the doors. He took the heavy wooden mallet from its hook and swung it, double-handed, at the bell. The din of its tolling almost deafened him. He struck it four more times and went to wait with Salwyth before the doors.

The older man unfolded his arms to point down the valley. The group around Olwain had broken up and were scattering back to the various Nordain encampments. At the same time, a handful of wagons, each with its attendant string of livestock, emerged from the Tharingii camp and rolled down towards the river.

"Damn," was all Carnac could think to say.

The Gars arrived first: three squat, veiled figures emerging from the shadows within the hall and striding over to stand beside them. Carnac recognized Ramul Lambai by the runestaff he carried. Otherwise, the Gars were indistinguishable. They didn't respond to his nod of greeting.

He was disheartened but unsurprised when the Magmardain princes arrived together, striding up from the Cimbrathii camp amid a large party of bearskinned warriors. They quickly surrounded Carnac, Salwyth and the Gars.

Pagan magLedon wore his bear's shape. His blunt muzzle turned to Salwyth. Carnac noted the curt nod of approval he gave the Salithii thane.

Culyan magCimbran glared down at him from barely a hand's breadth away. "Your brother is a menace, manDamag." His face lengthened towards Carnac's, cheeks rippling and sprouting fur. It was said that the bearskin blood had grown so weak in the house of magCimbran that its princes could no longer fully shift. At that moment, Carnac felt disinclined to find out.

"Aye, he is. But what would you have me do with him?"

"Confine him, silence him," Culyan said.

Carnac stood back and folded his arms across his chest. "I'm Thane of my people. They heed my words because I make sense. If they choose not to listen to me, that's their lookout. I'm no prince to go putting folk in chains or lopping off their heads, just because they're acting like fools."

Culyan snarled. "Then I'll do it!"

"You interfere in another clan's business and you'll have a war on your hands, magCimbran." The words belonged to Thane Manyn of Dantraii. He and the other Nordain thanes pushed their horses through the encircling Magmardain guards. Manyn walked his mount right up to the Cimbrathii. The helices of his ears were cropped in the same old-style fashion as Olwain's. His clansmen insisted that he'd done it to himself, taking nothing to dull the pain.

"Enough!" Pagan magLedon snapped, his teeth gnashing audibly. "This is every clan's business. It is not Tharingii's fault. Our people have dreamed of retaking the West since long before Olwain manDamag gave their fantasies voice. Not one of us did enough to quell that folly."

Culyan batted the muzzle of Thane Manyn's horse away from his face. The animal whickered. "Only Nordain hearts have been poisoned. No Magmardain have heeded the foreigner's words."

"*Our* people," Pagan said firmly, facing his half-shifted counterpart.

And that, Carnac thought, *would be the difference between a Ledonaii yoke and a Cimbrathii one, should we ever consent to wear such a thing.*

Ramul Lambai spoke into the silence that followed. "The ensorscellment in the Avalae's words works quickly in the hearts of those who are prone to such fantasies."

Suspecting he already knew the answer, Carnac asked, "Might we still reason with them?"

"We might," the Gar said. "Though most likely it is too late."

"What happened, when the Avalae came to Gulgaroth?" Salwyth said.

All eyes fell on the dark-veiled Gar. Ramul hesitated, then growled deep in his throat. "You would no longer recognize, as Gars, those who heeded the false gods. We have sealed them in the deepest chambers below the city where we hope they will devour each other."

Carnac shuddered at the implications of that: the Gars hadn't been strong enough to destroy those of their kin who had been turned by the Avalae.

"Will you tell Olwain and his followers of this horror?" Pagan asked.

Ramul nodded. "Aye, I will. But do not fill your hearts with hope."

Pagan called for mounts to be brought.

As they galloped toward the river at the best pace the ponies of the Gars could sustain, more wagons carrying families, with their horses and livestock in tow, broke from the camps of the other Nordain clans and headed down to rendezvous with Olwain's Tharingii followers.

Carnac spied Glyn waiting at the edge of the Tharingii camp, seated astride her filly. He called out to Salwyth and they veered aside to meet her. The rest of the riders slowed and turned behind them. Albeth and Graigor stood at the fore of a worried crowd of clansfolk.

"Olwain is taking them to Avaleinaea," Glyn said.

"I tried to talk to him, Carnac." Albeth clenched a fist helplessly. "I may as well have been reasoning with a stone. There's an enchantment on him that I can't even grapple with, let alone unravel. This sorcery is like a rope woven with smoke."

"There is a terrible price to pay for the gifts of Avalae," Ramul Lambai said, reining his pony in beside them. "If they accept them, they will no longer be human."

"Olwain and the others have chosen not to believe it," Glyn said.

"There's little choice in it, I fear," Salwyth said.

Carnac slid from Horga's back and took a few steps towards his sister-in-law. "Glyn, I've wronged you. There is a place for you in my household. Will you stay?"

Her jaw worked silently before she was able to say, "I'll go with my husband. Perhaps I can still make him see sense before it's too late."

"It's already too late . . ." he said, but she spun her horse and put her heels to its ribs.

Albeth ran a few steps after her and raised a hand, a faint glow at her fingertips. "Return to your kin if you are able, sister," she called.

Carnac felt small fingers grip his.

"Father, where are they going?"

He looked down at his son. "To Avaleinaea, where the false gods live."

"Does Uncle Olwain not believe in the true gods any longer?"

"No son, not anymore."

"They're not going anywhere," Culyan magCimbran growled. "That looks to be all of them." He signaled to the bearskin rider beside him, who raised a war horn to his muzzle and blew three sharp notes. Magmardain horsemen appeared on the rise beyond the ford, where Olwain's followers were making their crossing.

Thane Manyn rounded on him. "What is the meaning of this, magCimbran?"

Pagan magLedon answered. "Be still, Manyn. This matter must be dealt with." He put his heels to his horse. The Gars and the rest of the Magmardain followed, pursuing Glyn down the slope with the angry and bewildered Nordain thanes hot on their heels.

"Dealt with?" Carnac pushed Graigor towards Albeth's arms and scrabbled back up on his horse.

He caught up with the rest as they arrived at the ford, urging Horga through to the front of the pack, where the other thanes and the Magmardain princes confronted Olwain. His brother faced them from across the water, ahorse and with shield set and sword in hand. Carnac scanned the caravan, but could catch no sight of Glyn amongst the wagons.

The company of archers, musketeers and mounted men backing Olwain outnumbered the bearskinned warriors who confronted them, as did those who had put themselves between the wagons and the warriors on the rise above. But they were Nordain against Magmardain who, bearskinned or not, were bigger, stronger and held the superior position.

"Let us pass," Olwain said. "Or we'll fight our way free."

"Don't be a fool, Olwain," Carnac cried. "If it comes to fighting you'll all be slaughtered."

"I've naught to say to you, brother."

"Then listen and answer to *me,*" said the white bear, Pagan magLedon. "If we let you go free, what will you do?"

"We will go to Avaleinaea, and make our lives anew."

Culyan magCimbran spat on the ground. "Liar! You'll return armed with foul magics to conquer us all."

Olwain started to deny the accusation. Feeling sick to the stomach as he did so, Carnac spoke over him, "You deceive no-one, Olwain."

"Your own brother damns you!" Culyan cried triumphantly.

"Curse you for a fool, manDamag," Manyn of Dantraii said, and rode to put himself between the two parties. "What will you do, magCimbran, slaughter them, babes and all?"

"There's no other way," Ramul Lambai said. "They have a contagion of the mind beyond the ken of your folk and mine. What cannot be cured must be cleansed."

"*Cleansed*, you say?" Salwyth rounded on the Gar. "Even the babies? What of Glyn? Can she be the only one following her idiot husband out of duty alone?"

"I'll not allow it," Thane Manyn said. "No matter what the treachery in their hearts."

Culyan magCimbran snarled. "You can't stop it."

"Then you'll have war, magCimbran" Salwyth said, putting himself beside Manyn. The thanes of Ylaii, Istanii and Walathii followed his example.

Horga pranced on the spot, sensing Carnac's indecision. Across the river, a hateful smirk twisted his brother's face. *This is exactly what you want, you faithless bastard,* Carnac thought. *But I'll not have our father's name stained with the blood of innocents.*

"Can *you* give such an order?" he asked the Magmardain princes. He wheeled Horga to address their clansmen. "Can *you* carry it out?"

He thought he saw doubt furrow the Ledonaii prince's pale-furred brow. From the lowering of his muzzle, Carnac guessed that Pagan magLedon felt as sickened as any man there.

Culyan magCimbran snarled. "If you won't, Ledonaii, I will!"

He raised his fist.

"Culyan, no!" Pagan said. "*Please.*"

The fist remained in the air. The Cimbrathii prince stared at his Ledonaii counterpart, shocked more than anything, Carnac suspected, that his rival had begged him.

Pagan shifted back to human form.

Culyan's fist opened; he lowered his arm. "Aye."

Culyan put his heels to his stallion's ribs. The smaller mounts of the Nordain thanes skittered aside as the great warhorse surged past. Olwain's mare shied, but held her ground at her master's command as the warhorse reared before her.

"Leave," Culyan said. "And never return to these lands. Should we ever encounter you or yours again, we *will* hunt you down to the last screaming babe. We will feed your hearts to dogs and burn you, heartless, so that in death you will never know peace. May the Red Lady spurn you and spit on your faithless souls."

Carnac felt the hairs rise all over his body at the ferocity of the curse. A ripple passed, without a breath of wind to drive it, through the grass around their horses' hooves. The Weigher of Souls was listening.

White-faced and silent, Olwain and his followers turned their mounts and returned to their wagons.

"I fear you will pay a high price for your mercy, my lords," Ramul Lambai said.

"Aye," Pagan magLedon said. "Such is the way of things."

Sitting motionless, wearing their shining helms and armor, the Avalae looked like brass statues in the firelight. Their monstrous steeds were wreathed in flickering shadow behind them, their red eyes glittering. Around the opposite edge of the circle of light, Olwain's followers shifted uneasily. If Olwain was intimidated, Glyn thought, he didn't show it.

Malakhieh lifted his helmet. Glyn realized with a start that the foreigner was actually a woman.

Lavender hair tumbled about her flawless, ivory face. Her lips were rich red and her eyes a sparkling sapphire under upswept brows. The pupils were not round but horizontally slit.

Malakhieh's companions removed their helms as well, and Glyn saw these were indeed males, though they shaved their whiskers closely. One wore corn-colored hair in an elaborate braid, the other was completely bald. Small, round ears were set high and flat on the sides of their heads.

"What would you ask of us, Olwain manDamag?" Malakhieh said.

Olwain reached behind himself and picked up a musket, which he laid across his knees. Malakhieh's only reaction was a slight widening of her eyes, but her companions both recoiled visibly.

"More of these," Olwain said. "Or, if not muskets, then the iron to make them."

The Avalae licked her lips. "You dream too small, son of the West. We have long abandoned the use of such crude matter as iron," she said. "Ask a different favor, mortal."

Glyn saw a smile flicker behind her husband's moustache. So, the question had been a test. His intellect had not gone the way of his reason. Malakhieh saw the smile too, the curl of her lip said she was not well pleased.

Olwain pretended not to notice. "No matter. For me and mine, then, I ask for the strength of our horses." He caressed the Leaping Wolf brooch that pinned his cloak. "We would be as wolves among the flocks of those who spurned us."

The red lips parted cruelly. "And what do you offer in return?"

"What price do you set?"

"Your allegiance, in our hour of need."

The words hung between them for a moment before Olwain nodded. "So be it."

Glyn knew his acquiescence for a lie. Seeing the Avalae's smile widen, she realized with a chill that Malakhieh knew it too. No matter Olwain's intentions, the promise would bind him.

Glyn reached toward her husband. "Olwain . . ."

"Be still!"

Malakhieh laughed. "The terms are accepted."

Glyn dreamed of running.

She hunched forward, stretched out her legs and galloped, her hooves drumming against the hard ground.

She awoke with a start.

A horse stood over her. She lifted her gaze higher, and screamed. A man's outsized, naked torso rose from the animal's shoulders where its neck and head should have been. Olwain's face peered down at her, his eyes red with unspent tears. The bottom half of his face protruded strangely.

His lips peeled back, revealing massive fangs. "Oh, Glyn. What have we done?"

Horrified, Glyn looked down at herself. Her hips grew out of a horse's chest—her own filly's. Clumsily, she pushed herself up off her side and, with a lurch, came to her hoofed feet.

Olwain caught her shoulders. With a cry of revulsion, she tore herself away from him, kicking out at his chest and legs with her front hooves. Olwain shied away, his face twisting with hurt. She fled.

"Glyn!" he bellowed.

She galloped through the camp as men, women and children awoke to discover their new bodies. Cries of shock and terror filled the air. A shadow passed over her and Glyn was buffeted by a great blast of air. She skidded onto her haunches as the winged lion thumped to the ground in front of her. She found her feet again and launched herself aside. Malakhieh's second follower swooped in front of her on his flying horse, forcing her to turn again. She turned back, towards Olwain, and found Malakhieh's green serpent blocking her path.

A mewl of terror escaped her as Glyn wheeled frantically, searching for an escape.

"Kill her," Malakieh said. "Show them what we think of such ingratitude."

With a growl that rattled Glyn's ribs, the white lion padded forward. She could see its rider's sneer beneath his helm.

"No!" Olwain cried. "I'll not have her harmed!"

"*Silence!*" Malakhieh said. Olwain and the others scrabbled at their throats in panic, their voices abruptly cut off. Air hissed audibly between Malakhieh's teeth. "Now, bow to your makers."

All around, creatures that had yesterday been free Nordain clansfolk crumpled to their knees. Glyn felt a terrible pressure against her shoulders and spine but remained upright. Her four legs trembled with the effort.

Beside Malakhieh's beast, Olwain slumped with the horse's part of his body fallen on its side. His head sagged between his shoulders as he held his human torso off the ground with his arms.

"Please," he managed to gasp. "Spare her."

Above him, the bronze-helmed head tipped in his direction. Malakhieh regarded him for a time, then chuckled. "Very well," she said. "We are merciful gods. Release her. Let the savages see what we have made."

Behind Glyn, the lion roared. She fled.

No one followed her, either to join her escape or to pursue.

She galloped blindly, but Albeth's spell guided her. Carnac's parting words were in her heart, and her course steered inevitably back to Tharingii rather than to her blood-kin.

The clan was on the move, heading home. Outriders caught sight of her coming. She heard their cries of horror before they put their war horns to their lips. The sight and scent of the riding men awoke a terrible appetite within her.

With a wail of anguish, she accelerated, leaving them behind.

Carnac was waiting with a party of warriors when she came in sight of the caravan. Glyn saw their muskets and bows come up as soon as she was near enough for them to see her clearly. Her mouth watered and her stomach knotted as the wind brought their smell to her.

Meat!

The hunger fought with Albeth's spell. She slowed to a trot, then a walk, and finally collapsed to her knees twenty paces in front of them. She buried her face in her hands.

Running footsteps approached. A cloak draped her naked torso. Strong arms held her against a studded leather vest.

"Lords above and below, what have they done to you?"

Carnac's closeness all but brought her undone. She shoved him off. "Get away from me!"

His broad face scrunched in hurt and confusion.

Gasping with the effort of restraining her monstrous urges, she said, "To be wolves among your flock, Carnac. That's the gift your brother asked them for."

His bewildered expression only deepened.

"To *feed* as wolves among the flock," she said.

Carnac leapt to his feet as Albeth emerged from the tent, looking completely spent. "Well?"

She brushed a stray lock of hair from her eyes and drank deeply from the gourd in her other hand before answering. Other witches exited behind her, looking just as wrung out.

"Naught," Albeth said. "The Avalae spell slides away from our thoughts like the wind through open fingers. And our closeness only distresses her. Did you send riders after the Gars?"

He nodded. "Aye, of course I did. And to the other clans. What help the molemen can be I don't know, when they couldn't save their own kin."

His wife shrugged. "They've had a longer study of Avalae spellcraft than we have. That she's fighting the curse herself gives me hope. How long, do you think?"

Carnac cast an eye at the sun, standing directly overhead. "Not until dark, or even the morning, at the pace Gars travel."

"We'll need to circle the wagons tonight."

"Ah, you be leaving the warcraft to me, woman," he said, drawing her into his arms. "And I'll not criticize your spellweaving."

Ramul Lambai arrived barely an hour later, borne upon the saddle of one of the Tharingii riders sent to find him. Carnac caught him as the moleman dropped gracelessly to the ground. The Gar allowed himself to be steadied on his feet while he caught his flapping veil. He squinted up at Carnac.

"That's the last time I consent to be carried aboard one of your great smelly beasts, Tharingii," he said. "It gives me little enough pleasure to learn that I was right."

"Aye, and me even less," Carnac said. "But could you have slain the children of your own blood?"

The moleman's fleshy whiskers curled in agitation before he affixed his veil. "No. That was our downfall as well."

The rest of the Gars arrived and the Tharingii caravan drew up into a vast wagon fort before Ramul Lambai re-emerged from Glyn's guarded tent. He left his veil aside in the failing light, his pink eyes open wide and faintly glowing.

"She'll live," he said, as Carnac sprang once more to his feet. "And it'll be your wife's healing magic that'll bring her back to health." He exhaled heavily, the breath whistling past his thick whiskers. "The horse is a ruin. You'll have to get someone to drag the carcass away."

"What of Olwain and the rest?" Carnac asked. "Is there hope for them?"

Ramul Lambai shook his head. "I'm sorry. It was Albeth's guiding spell underneath the Avalae curse that allowed us to slice the strands of their spellworking. Without that, your brother and all else who followed him are lost."

Carnac gazed eastward, where stars were already beginning to light the deepening blue of the sky. He was surprised to find that his eyes were dry. "Why would they do this?" he said, half to himself.

"The Avalae?" Ramul Lambai said. "Because they fear us—what our peoples once were and could be again. They wish to weaken us by seeding their cankers in our midst."

"Then I pray that my snake of a brother has taken his fools' caravan to Avaleinaea, so the Avalae can reap their own bitter harvest."

He didn't need to see the second shake of the Gar's head to know that he was wishing in vain.

Carnac awoke with a start sometime in the early hours of the night. For a moment he lay on his back, disorientated and wondering why Albeth wasn't beside him. He shifted in discomfort, unable to fathom why he should've gone to bed with his armor on. Then the alarm sounded again, a discordant blast of a sentry's horn.

Carnac leapt from his blankets, grabbing his sword and wrenching it free of its scabbard.

The whites of Graigor's eyes glittered in the shadows across the tent.

"Hide yourself, son, and stay quiet," Carnac said, strapping his shield to his arm.

"I want mama!"

"She's with Aunt Glyn. Be brave, Graigor. Make me proud."

Jamming his helmet onto his head, Carnac ducked outside. His bare forearms goose-pimpled in the cool air. Shouts and horns sounded from all sides of the camp. A quick glance at the moon told him he'd had his head down a bare half hour since he came off watch.

A cannon discharged on the camp's nearest perimeter.

"To the wagons!" he cried. His kinsmen burst from their own tents, armed and in various states of armor or undress. He led them at a sprint to the edge of the camp, gathering more along the way. He sent those with bows and muskets to distribute themselves along the makeshift fortifications, the rest to assemble in groups behind the archers and gunners. In the heart of the camp, more men would be mounting their horses, ready to act as a reserve in case the outer defenses were breached.

He ran to the closest cannon, manned efficiently by the brothers manVarda. Up on the wagon boards, another manVarda brother lobbed an arrow into the darkness. Carnac glimpsed galloping forms in the moonlight.

An answering arrow wobbled out of the night and clattered in the spokes of a wagon wheel.

Mangel manVarda grunted. "Fools are trying to shoot longbows on the hoof."

"Not so daft, perhaps," Carnac said, hitching himself up on the wagon's tail-step to get a better view. "Since they have no horse's head to get in the way of their draw."

Mangel stared at him a moment, then spat a curse and turned his attention back to his gun.

A barrage of musket fire erupted to Carnac's left. The Gars had positioned themselves in a double line across several wagon beds. The blades on the ends of their musket barrels glinted as the ranks swapped places. At the near end of the company, Ramul Lambai drew back his arm and, with a sharp cry, flung his hammer into the night. A heartbeat later a great thump sounded across the field, as though one of the gods had just dropped a mountain from the sky. Screams followed that sounded neither quite like man nor horse.

A warhorn sounded. Two sharp blasts and one long. A pause, and then it repeated. More horns took up the cry.

"Breach!" Carnac bellowed. "To me!" He leapt from the wagon and ran in the direction that the first horn had sounded.

The night was lit a sickly green, accompanied by the skin-crawling shriek of a killing spell. Albeth and the other witches were giving an account of themselves.

A burning figure crashed over the tent directly in front of Carnac, not quite the right shape for a man on horseback. Battling horsemen and man-horses followed it. Carnac hurled himself into the fray, holding his shield high as he slashed at the hamstrings of one of Olwain's followers. With a cry, the creature toppled. Carnac danced back and then in to hack at its bestial face until half the head came away and he was sure the thing was dead.

He looked up just in time to avoid being run over by a retreating Tharingii rider. Another heavy body cannoned into his back. He rolled aside, losing his shield and came back to his feet. A riderless horse danced about its master's body. Carnac ran for it and flung himself up onto the animal's back.

He raised his sword. "Tharingii! To me!"

Albeth wandered through the battered Tharingii camp. Her knees threatened to give way beneath her, her strength expended in her battle magics. Cries of grief cut the darkness, and not just for the fallen. Olwain's followers had retreated shortly after they breached the wagon circle, but they had not left empty handed.

She found the manVarda brothers gathered forlornly at the slashed and fallen ruins of their tents. She saw immediately that, while all the brothers were present, there were fewer wives and children with them than there should have been.

"Mangel," she said to the eldest. "Who have you lost?"

The older man didn't turn to face her. "Darryc's wife and son. Both of Pedrac's boys. My Lilla." His shoulder started to shake. His daughter, a handful of years older than Graigor, who's mother had died birthing her.

Albeth felt her chin tremble and clamped her jaw tight. "Have you seen my Graigor?"

His sudden stillness, followed by the slump of his head, was answer enough.

She nodded silently, unable to trust her voice a third time. She doubted that he saw the gesture. She moved on.

Carnac looked away, unable to stomach the sight. The corpse on the spit was charred and butchered, too small for an adult. There was not enough left to say whose child it had been. It was unlikely that they would be able to identify any of the bodies, beyond whether they belonged to man, woman or child, and that there were enough to account for all who'd been stolen.

His fists clenched so tightly around the hilt of his sword that they ached. He leaned on the blade like an old man clutching his cane.

A hand came to rest on his shoulder. Carnac looked up at Pagan MagLedon. The old prince's face was creased with sympathy.

Ledonaii had been the first to respond to Carnac's messengers, arriving while Tharingii were still counting the cost of the raid. Together, they had set out in pursuit.

Two days later, they'd come across the raiders' camp, surprising them at dawn. What they'd found had been a horror—Olwain's followers gorged to the point of stupidity, lolling among the carnage of a feast of human flesh. The battle had been brief and one-sided, the monsters fighting only to get away. Some had.

Across the battlefield, men of Tharingii and Ledonaii worked with hatchets and knives on the monsters they had brought down, adding personal elaborations to Culyan magCimbran's curse—often while their victims were still alive—before they fed the remains to the dogs and the fires.

The prone figure at Carnac's feet shifted awkwardly, a broken foreleg flopping, the canonbone cleanly snapped. Carnac looked down at the monster that had been his brother. Olwain's human torso expanded and contracted bizarrely as he panted for air, his distorted face further twisted by pain.

"Oh, Olwain," Carnac murmured, as he hadn't done since they were boys.

"The hunger," Olwain gasped. "It consumes us."

Carnac's eyes filled with tears. He took up the weight of his sword. Pagan stepped clear.

"Damn you, brother," Carnac said. His voice broke. "My *son*!"

Olwain roared like a beast, raising clawed hands to fend off the blade. His bellows became wails as Carnac hacked at his wrists. Carnac swung and slashed in a frenzy, needing the noise to stop. A hand came away. The sword struck the monster's skull. Hoofed feet thrashed. Carnac brought the edge of the blade down another time, and again, then stabbed the point down through the battered head and into the earth beneath. He staggered back.

Pagan magLedon approached again. He offered Carnac a knife, hilt first. Carnac stared at it stupidly for a moment, then accepted the blade. He knelt down beside the tapered barrel of the monster's horse body, sliced along the base of the ribs, through the diaphragm and cut inside the chest cavity until he could pull out the heart.

He stood, the bloody organ in his hand. He dropped it to the ground and crushed it under his boot.

Ramul Lambai squatted a respectful distance away, like a crow among the carnage in his dark robes and veils.

"Master Gar," Carnac said. The steadiness of his voice surprised him. "Do you know the way to Avaleinaea?"

Eye of the Destroyer

Aliette de Bodard

At the end of the monsoon season, four messengers came to my house to take my wife away. Three priests, one for each god of the Triad: Creator, Protector and Destroyer. And a Gifted hermit, for the untamed wisdom of the forest.

I stood on the porch, shock-still. Deri had been playing in the shadow of a nearby bo tree with our two-year-old child, Karale. As soon as she heard them, she came by my side, wrapping the end of her sari around her head to ward off the sun. She did not even spare a glance for me. She was too intent on the visitors.

The white-haired hermit spoke first. Her face looked ageless, and her skin held the pallor of things that lived forever in shadow. "My name is Emodhe. I was Gifted by the Triad three days ago, and they gave me a warning. The King of Demons has broken his chains."

The enemy of the gods, free to summon his armies. I shivered. It was written, of course, that the gods would never be able to contain him forever, that he would rise again and again. Our last war against him we had won because. . . .

"No," I said. Everyone's eyes turned to me, and I realized how childish I sounded. "I will not let you take her."

The priest of the Destroyer—bare-headed, with the third eye of the god painted in red paste on his forehead—turned towards me. "The Destroyer has chosen your wife to bestow on her some of his powers, to allow mankind to defeat the demons once again. Did you think that choice would rest on your shoulders, Angave?"

His contemptuous gaze mocked me, but I did not back away. "It need not be her."

"No," Emodhe said. She sounded almost apologetic. In time, she would have much more arrogance than this, but with her mere innocence she had destroyed enough—for she, no doubt, was the one who had seen my wife as leader of the armies, and who had passed this on to the priests. "Already the Shifting Kingdoms have raised an army against the menace. All it lacks is someone to lead it. But you are right. If your wife refuses, the Destroyer will find someone else. The gods always find a way."

In the silence that followed, Deri asked, "Can I think before I decide?"

"There is not much time," the priest of the Creator said, "but you may. You have until the sun reaches its apex." He was the eldest among them, assured and composed, with his grey hair tied behind him in a ponytail, and a yellow thread wrapped around his chest. When he gestured to the others, he radiated authority, and they moved away from the house to sit in the shade. I looked up, saw that the sun was already high in the sky.

Emodhe was the last to leave. She stared at me, and in her green eyes I saw a hint of pity, and of something else, an inhuman detachment that I would never be able to embrace. Then she shook her head and joined her companions.

"You cannot mean to go," I said to Deri.

She was toying, nervously, with the five gold bracelets that had been my wedding gift to her; the snakes of lapis-lazuli on the clasp glinted in the sunlight. I knew she was upset.

She said at last, "Angave—"

"You cannot."

"Why? I was chosen. Do you think you can go against that?"

"I can try."

She shook her head.

"It's not a gift," I said. "The gods are not a sari you can wrap around yourself and discard afterwards. You do not understand the true nature of the Triad."

"And do you?"

"I am an Eye of the Destroyer. I know that it is hard to come back once the god seizes you." In vigil after vigil in the temple, I had kept Deri in my mind, so that I would not leave the world forever behind. True communion with the Triad is the striving of our lives, and Eyes, whatever god they serve, experience it with every flood of visions. Some are not strong enough to stop from the ultimate gift. Some are found dead in the morning, or not found at all. An anchor to the mortal world is needed to make us come back.

"I am strong," Deri said. "I was trained to be High Priestess of the Destroyer once. I will come back."

"But I do not know why you would choose to leave."

"Oh, Angave," she said, turning to look at the priests. "If you do not understand, then there is no way I can explain it to you."

"Try," I said, gently.

She brought her hands to her neck, readjusted her sari to keep it from slipping from her head. The henna patterns on the back of her hands read: loyalty, duty. She frightened me. Her words were a stranger's.

"I want to matter," she said at last. "To make my own way."

"You matter."

She laughed, but said nothing.

"I want to understand," I said, "why you would leave me and Karale. You have a duty here."

"I have a duty outside. You see only the good of your family. I see that if Emodhe is right, then we are all in danger. I see that I cannot afford to let this chance pass."

I knew I would not sway her, but still I tried. "It is not a chance."

"What do you fear, Angave?" she said, raising her eyes to meet mine. Her voice was soft.

"That you will change."

"All of us change, every day. 'The Destroyer is at work in every breath and every move,'" she quoted from the Third Book. "'Things must die so they can change.'"

"I still fear change. You will not come back to me as the one I have always known. You may not come back at all."

She looked thoughtful for a while. The air was stifling. "I can offer you nothing," she said at last. "I will come back. I am your wife, and I bore and raised your child. Such bonds are not so easily severed."

"Promise me something."

Her eyes were unreadable.

"Keep the bracelets I gave you," I said. "If you cannot hold the thought of me in your mind to come back, then perhaps they will be your anchor to cast the god aside."

"I will try. But I cannot make promises I am not sure to keep."

"I understand."

She raised her face to mine, ran her fingertips on my lips. It was the most she could do before strangers. "Thank you."

She left escorted by the priests. She did not look back, not once, but my eyes did not leave her until she turned the bend in the path that led to the village—I lost her, then, and had to turn away.

I picked up Karale, and took him home. That night I baked flatbreads on the hearthstones for both of us, and we ate them with chickpeas and cardamom, and not until we were finished did I see that I had set aside a third bread and a third serving of food. Karale, being too young to understand such things, said nothing.

I threw the bread away and went to sleep. The visions came, the ones from the god, and there was no Deri to hold them at bay. I had no reason to go back.

Come, the gods said, laughing—all the minor deities that the common people worship in their hearths, each of them a reflection of the Triad that gave birth to it, and each of them with the inscrutable eyes of those whose thoughts move beyond the mortal world. Come, said Ryasa, goddess of fire, guest to every house, and devourer of sacrifices. Come. See her.

I went. I soared with them into the sky, casting my flesh aside, and I saw.

The sanctum is empty. They left her here, in the middle of the room, alone. Her bracelets have been taken from her. She protested, told them that her husband had insisted, all in vain.

This is necessary, they said. The Destroyer will not come unless you hold a true vigil. And she said yes, she had to, but she feels naked, and she wishes her husband were there to comfort her, even if he no longer knows her.

Above her, in the stifling darkness, the statue of the Destroyer smiles. Its throat shines a faint blue, in memory of the poison that He drank from the sea at the beginning of the world. Coconut butter and incense burn on a pedestal before the statue.

She looks into His eyes. What does one say to a god? To the only god who can descend on earth and take a human form? To the god who is strongest among the Triad now, because it is war and war is His province?

I hate you, she thinks. Every night you take my husband away from me, and every night less and less of him comes back. I hate you, and I will not let you take me as you are taking him.

But the eyes, the knowing eyes, will not leave her, and they hold no contempt and no hatred.

The eyes of the statue. There is the shadow of a third eye on the forehead, for the Destroyer is the only one among the Triad who can see the future. The eye is closed, a bare suggestion of a lid carved on the stone above the other eyes. But it is moving, flowing upwards like an inverted waterfall.

She stands, transfixed. The eye opens. She feels something alien rise within her, something that fills her with a terrible longing. She needs to—

She reaches out, touches the statue. It is warm under her fingertips and throbs like a living thing.

The eye turns, focuses on her. It is green, the color of the light under the canopy of the forest. Green, like the leaves of some huge tree that reaches into the sky, upwards, until there is nothing left but the light of the city of the gods.

The eye sees her, and she is lost.

I woke up sweating. "Deri," I called, desperately, but there was no one. Only Karale's soft snoring on the other mat. Deri, I thought, and there was only the silence of our house, the growing emptiness in my chest. I had lost her.

In silence I got up and brewed some tea. I sat for a while on the porch, cradling the copper bowl between my hands, breathing the smell of cardamom and cinnamon. My head ached. I had never had such visions in my dreams. It took a fast and a vigil to truly become the Eye of the god.

Outside, it was dawn. The path leading to the village shimmered with dust, and everything was leeched of colors.

I do not know what made me turn away and look to my left. Some sixth sense, perhaps, but when I do not see the visions of the god I am as blind as any mortal. Call it luck, then.

There was a middle-aged woman there, with black hair and dark skin, and almond eyes of a startling shade of blue. She sat on the grass, carelessly, but her eyes watched me.

"Priest," she said.

Living near the Shifting Cities, on the boundaries of the primal forest, one learns to beware of things. So close to the trees the eyes are easily deceived, and one has to learn to look.

Her shape shimmered, and between the flashes of the woman was a suggestion of a huge figure with teeth and claws.

I bowed, with both hands joined in greeting. "My lady."

She laughed, shaking her head with an amused light in her eyes. "You humans are always so formal."

You humans. I held in my mind the beginning of a mantra against intrusions in the house. "What do you want?" I asked. *In the name of fire, which barred Lysae's way to the mortal world, I forbid you entry to this dwelling. In the name of rain. . . .*

"To talk." She glanced at the sky, and I remembered that demons were not meant to walk in daylight.

"You are far from home," I said.

"The King has risen, priest, and he calls us all to his former prison. His strength sustains the strongest of us. Soon, the sun will hide its face from us, and we will be free to walk the paths of the world."

Deri. I thought of her, alone against such power, and shook my head. She was not alone. She had the might of the Triad behind her.

The rakshasa before me was silent for a while, staring at me. In the depths of her eyes I saw nothing but a deadly hunger, the one that drove them to prey on unwary travelers in the forest. It was vast and relentless, as deep as the caverns under Mount Seilesa, under which the gods had trapped the King.

Old, I thought. "What do you want?" I asked again, shivering.

She rose, came closer to me. She smelled musty, of things hidden below the ground, of fallen leaves, and of flowers blooming in the green shadows below the trees. And of blood. "I came to kill her, but I am too late."

"My wife?"

"Yes," she said. "What a delight it would have been, to consume the memories of one chosen by the gods. One seen by the Eyes of the Triad."

"You will not have her."

She shrugged, ruefully. "It is too late. I thought it might make a difference to the coming struggle if I could remove the gods' interference."

"This house is warded against your kind."

"Wards always have flaws," she said. "And I am old and have feasted on the thoughts of many travelers." Her shape wavered, turned into that of a young man with the emaciated face of ascetics and clothes of bark. "From him, who was to be visited by the god, I learned many things about wards."

She ought to have sickened me by talking so casually of people she had killed—no, worse than killed, for she had their thoughts, their memories, their shapes. But her very indifference to that deadened me. I stood against the wood of my door, and did not move. "There is nothing for you here," I said, thinking of Karale.

"I know. I knew before I came near your house that she was gone. There is no Triad here, priest. No longer do the gods look at this place."

No longer. They had never looked. I was under the gaze of the gods only in the temple, on vigils.

"Their attention is elsewhere," said the rakshasa, straightening to look north, towards Mount Seilesa. "The Destroyer has your wife, like so many others before."

"Before?"

"I am old, priest. I have lost count of those I consumed to hold myself together. I have been drawn countless times from under the canopy to battle with your armies. I have seen many chosen of the gods." She smiled, and there was a little sadness in that smile. "You have lost her, you know. Forever and ever, until the Destroyer dances to end the world."

"She will come back," I said. "She has something to remember me by."

"It will have been taken from her. And the Destroyer does not let go that easily. He never lets go."

"She will come back." The copper bowl of tea between my fingers was tepid.

"Her will to return is gone," the rakshasa said. "I know such things."

I said nothing. She had half-turned away from me and was preparing to leave. The tea was still between us, and I had no wish to drink it. I hesitated. Still, she had been honest with me, and something about her drew me—a sense of something vast and inhuman, and yet as lost and as bewildered as I felt within.

"Wait," I said.

She turned, stared at me with no expression.

"It is a long road to Mount Seilesa." I held out the bowl to her. Odors of cardamom and cinnamon hung in the air between both of us as she walked towards me, and took it.

She drained the tea in a single gulp. "I do not feel thirst as humans do, priest. But I thank you for the kindness." She licked her lips. I thought I saw white fangs in her mouth. "I do not think we will meet again in this world."

I did not move from the porch. "No," I said.

"Fare thee well, then." And she, too, was gone.

Armies are gathering. In the darkness she sees only the banners of the human kingdoms: tigers for Ingara, entwined cobras for Sasti, and many more, unfurling in the wind with the sound of boat-sails.

She stands beneath the largest banner, the one that bears the flame, the sword, and the flute. The symbols of the Triad. She hears the whinnies of horses as they strain against their harnesses, the quiet sounds of charioteers soothing their beasts. But what she hears most are the prayers of the archers as they string their bows. They flow over her, strengthen her.

The armies of the demons she cannot see with her human eyes, but there are other ways to see. She knows that the oldest demons have been called forth. She can feel their hatred for what she is. And, far beyond them, in the caves beneath Mount Seilesa, the King awaits her, to fight her yet another time.

She rubs her arm absent-mindedly, and sees that her skin is lighter there. Bracelets. She once wore bracelets. She thinks of twin snakes, with maws of lapis-lazuli. A gift.

Angave.

She remembers her husband, and it is a bittersweet thing: the love she first felt for him, the way she abandoned everything for him. And, later, the way her prison slowly constricted around her, until she felt nothing but regrets for what could have been.

She had been the niece of the High Priestess of the Destroyer at Lakshma when she and Angave had first met—and destined to follow her. To wield real power, in a land where women are still inferior to men.

But, although priests may marry, the High Priestess must remain celibate, for her only devotion is to the god and to the people. For Angave, she gave up everything.

For what? she asks herself, not without bitterness. To stay at home and watch her husband every night, consumed by his visions, become more and more distant from her. She had nothing to offer him that could match being an Eye of the Destroyer.

She gave everything up for a dream, a promise that was not kept.

And now she has a chance to wield the power she was born to. To erase the past.

She rubs her arm again, hoping to be rid of the mark.

Two days after the visit of the rakshasa, I took up my vigil at the temple. With my wife gone, there was no one to take care of Karale, so I brought him with me into the sanctum. He went to sleep without a noise, without looking at me. I knew that he missed his mother.

My nights had been filled with visions of Deri, and in each of them she was lost to me, and each time I found it harder to come back. My vigil was no different: I heard Deri harangue the troops, saw the respectful way they stood back for her.

Deri, I thought. Give it up. But I knew the rakshasa was right: there was no coming back. My wife had tasted power, and through power did the god hold her.

I woke with a start. It was late, and the temple was deserted. Karale still slept curled at the feet of the friezes depicting the feats of the Destroyer. The god had left me, Deri had left me, and all I had was the certainty that nothing would ever make sense again.

I waited for the feeling to diminish. When I could move again, I opened the thick book of visions on the altar and took up the kanta, the writing needle, to engrave on the palm-leaves everything the god had shown me. My hands shook. I tore the leaf with my last sentence, and knew that, even with the copyist's application of coal powder on every letter, the final words would still not be legible.

I heard the door open and close behind me. I did not move. Some other priest, I thought, come to make an offering to the god.

But it was Emodhe. Her face under the light of the lamps was unreadable. She carried hibiscus flowers and coconut paste, which she set before the statue with quiet reverence.

"I would have thought you no longer needed those," I said. "Since you already commune with the gods." I knew what I was doing: I was trying to wound her as deeply as she had wounded me.

If she guessed that, she did not say a word of it. She turned to look at me. Her face would have been held beautiful by many a man: huge green eyes, with pronounced cheekbones, and an aquiline nose which only emphasized her delicate mouth. It moved me not at all. I knew that she had renounced the world to seek wisdom, and that human feelings, compassion, love, were all beyond her.

"I thought I would find you here," Emodhe said at last. She slid gracefully into a cross-legged position mere steps from the altar.

I shrugged. "I am an Eye of the Destroyer. There is a vigil to be taken."

She sighed. "Duty. You feel bound to this temple, don't you?"

"It is my place."

Emodhe walked to the altar. She took the book from its resting place, and flipped to the end to read the last pages. "The Eyes of the Destroyer are on Mount Seilesa tonight, as on all other nights," she said.

"On Deri."

"Of course." Her gaze remained, obstinately, on the book in her hands.

"You lied to me," I said.

"I never lie."

"You said that the gods would find another way if she refused. There was no other way."

"I—who told you that?"

"I had a rakshasa at my door. She wanted to kill Deri. If she had not mattered that much, why would the demon have come?"

"I did not lie," Emodhe said. "But you must know that the Eyes of the gods were on that house, whether or not Deri accepted, and that the rakshasa would have felt that."

"You took her from me."

"She made her own choices," Emodhe said. She still had the book open on her knees, and one hand stroked the last leaf, the one I had written on. "We all do, in the end."

"I do not need a lesson in wisdom. The rakshasa also said Deri wasn't coming back. Is that true?"

Emodhe was silent while I recounted what the rakshasa had told me. At last she said, "I have learned much from the gods, and from the forest. You must understand that many men before Deri were chosen to be the avatars of the Destroyer. The forest remembers them all. And it remembers that the gods are harsh masters. Still, those who are chosen do come back, from time to time. If they have the will."

"She has no will," I said. "Have you not read the book?"

"I do not need to read the book," Emodhe said. "She looked to me like a trapped thing that had too long awaited its freedom. Now that she has it, why should she come back?"

"She was free," I said. "It was by her choice that she stayed with me."

"Sometimes, we make choices and regret them. I do not judge you. I am telling you what I saw, being young enough in the way of hermits to remember how things go in the mortal world."

I thought of Deri, my wife, putting her hands to her neck to prevent her sari from slipping. I remembered the day I had came home to find her nursing Karale, tears streaming down her face. What happened? I had asked. She had turned her face away from me and would not answer. Nothing, she had said when I had pressed her. Nothing.

I had been blind. "I should never have let her go."

Emodhe did not speak. She was looking at me with pity in her eyes, and it galled me. She was a hermit: what could she know of love, or of wives who became as strangers?

The rakshasa had been right: Deri was moving away from me. With every battle against the demons, every day that she woke up knowing her full powers, knowing that she was free, I was losing more and more of her.

I should never have let her go.

Emodhe still sat cross-legged with the impassive expression of a god, a painted statue like the one overshadowing her.

"Will you ask the priests to take care of my son?"

"Why?"

"I am going," I said, rising.

"You cannot leave your duties."

"I know where my duty lies. I am going after my wife, to remind her of what being human means."

"Will you allow the gods to lose?"

"The gods never lose."

Emodhe said nothing. At last, she closed the book with a noise of finality. "Sit here." Her voice echoed with power. I could not deny her, and she knew it.

I sat before her.

"I will not allow you to rush in the midst of a battlefield looking for your wife. There will be enough bloodshed without adding yours, Angave."

"I don't care."

"I know that, you fool." She said it with a trace of affection, as if my behavior was intrinsically amusing. "I suppose I was responsible for most of this, coming to you the way I did."

My silence was answer enough.

Emodhe sighed. "I do not think you can make much of a difference either way, Angave. It is a full eight-day walk to Mount Seilesa, and the war will be over, or in its last throes, when you reach it—if you do reach it."

She looked up, into the eyes of the statue, and said, "Lord, you who destroy all things so that they can be reborn, I ask for a favor for this man, your faithful servant." She cocked her head, waiting for an answer.

There was none. Emodhe looked mildly thoughtful, as if she had not expected one. She reached out to the altar, put the book back on it, and took the coconut paste she had offered to the Destroyer. She dipped her hand in it.

"Bend your head," she said.

I obeyed. I felt the tip of her finger on my forehead. The smell of coconut and flames filled my nostrils. She was drawing a circle on my brow.

"There," she said, withdrawing her hand. She had said or done nothing more, but a hermit's power, unlike that of a priest, needed no mantras or prayers to manifest. "I have given you protection."

"Against what?"

"I have removed you from the gaze of the gods."

"The gods do not look at me when I do not take a vigil."

"They always look," Emodhe said. "They look harder in some places, that is all. A word of warning, Angave: you will not be seen by humans or by demons. None will be able to harm you. But if you do anything of significance, anything that affects someone else, the spell will be broken. And it will not hold against your wife, who is god-touched."

I stifled a bitter laugh. "I had guessed as much. Thank you." Those were hard words to say.

She shrugged. "Do not thank me, Angave. It may be of no use at all. May the Triad walk before you."

It was a farewell, a dismissal, also. I rose, joined both hands against my chest, and gave her the standard answer, though she had no need of it. "And may its shadow cover you."

Late in the afternoon, as the sun comes down, they have their second battle against demons. A charioteer all in red drives her on the field of slaughter, and everywhere she sees blades flash in the last light of the sun, and the smell of blood rises to her nostrils.

She hears the screams of those who die. Archers shoot volleys of arrows, and demons fall, but the darkness does not abate. Of the King there is no sign, but a faint, malevolent presence at the rear of the army. He awaits her; he will not show himself to anyone but her.

Not now. She is not strong enough.

Later, as they count their dead and light the first funeral pyres, she stares at her arm again, at the lighter patch of skin.

It is hard to focus on it. I am human, she thinks. I had—have a husband, and a child. I have to come back.

To a cage, says an older voice, one that is still hers. You are not bound anymore, Deri.

And then the god rises again, and the thoughts are drowned beneath those of the city of heaven.

I left the temple at dawn. By the crushed leaves and fallen trees, it was easy to follow the trail of the army. I made good time, for no one ever saw me, or asked me where I was headed.

I saw other traces of their passage: the wounded from skirmishes, making their slow way home, the remnants of funeral pyres scattered in the wake of the battles. They smelled of cold cinders, and reminded me too much of the ashes scattered on wedding days, those that symbolized the grievances husband and wife agreed to cast aside.

At night I slept under the canopy of banyan trees and dreamt of Deri. I sent myself to sleep with thoughts of what I would say to her once I found her, deluding myself that it would be easy to tear her from the Destroyer's grasp.

I knew it would not.

The last battle takes place in full daylight. The army of demons, shedding bodies like a dying tree sheds its leaves, retreats until there is nothing but Mount Seilesa at its back. And still the King does not come forth.

She stands at the edge of what is left of her troops, rubbing the mark on her arm, and motions for her charioteer to move them forward, into the press of bodies. The battered banners above her still shine like a beacon.

The sky is dark with arrows, with thrown spears, and the earth drinks the blood of the combatants as it drinks the rain. Slowly she raises her spear, and feels the blood-frenzy come over her until all mortal words are forgotten. A haze of red covers the battlefield.

I am coming, she screams to the wind.

Come, then, says the wind, and it has the voice of the King.

She knows she is now stronger than he.

So she goes forward, in her chariot with the red driver, scything through the dead and the dying, to meet him at last.

On the eve of the seventh day I reached the edge of the battlefield. A desolate silence had spread over the remnants of the two armies.

The slopes of Mount Seilesa rose before me, towering in the dying light; the sky was painted the color of blood, and the smell of open wounds clogged my nostrils, so strong that it brought the taste of rotten flesh to my tongue.

Demons prowled the edges of the battlefield. But Emodhe's spell still held, for they withdrew, leaving me alone in a land ravaged by the fight, and barely recognizable as the lush plains that lay at the feet of Mount Seilesa.

Deri. . . .

It was not my wife that I saw there. It was a familiar face, as familiar as my own, but not Deri's.

A middle-aged woman, with black hair and dark skin, lying among the fallen. Her blue eyes stared straight at me.

I stopped, knelt by her side, and took her hand before remembering what maintained Emodhe's spell. I realized then that she could not have seen me, and that I had mistaken the look in her eyes.

Too late.

She could see me now. Emodhe's protection ebbed away, leaving a tingling sensation on my skin.

"Priest," the rakshasa said, and smiled. There was pain in every feature of her face. "I had not thought to find you here."

I unstoppered my flask, gave her a sip of water.

"Thank you," she said. "It seems you spend your time offering me things to drink." She still managed to sound amused by that.

"You should not have come here," I said, looking at the corpses strewn around us, at the darkness that crept across the sky and left us all in shadow.

She shrugged. The movement seemed to widen the wound in her abdomen. "What choice was there, priest? The King called, and we came. Always he promises us the same thing: that we will walk in daylight and will have no need to consume human flesh to hold ourselves together."

"You knew it was a lie."

"I am old and have seen many things, priest. Perhaps one day he will win."

"He cannot. The gods will always intervene."

She grimaced. Her face froze, for a moment, into that of an old man. "That they do. Your wife came to lead the armies of the Kingdoms, and we were lost. Who can resist the Destroyer incarnate?" She paused, looked at me. There was sly amusement in her eyes. "You have come for her?"

"I have come to bring her back."

"You are too late," she said. "I tried to warn you. You should have listened, but you would not trust me."

"Would you blame me for that?" I felt drained of urgency. For days I had been thinking only of Deri, of her eyes and face, of her touch. It had been my anchor to the real world, to keep away the visions that flooded me. And now there was nothing left. Emodhe's spell was gone, leaving me adrift.

"No, I do not blame you." She gripped my hand with a strength greater than that of a human. "Your wife's thoughts are those of the Triad, and her mind has beheld the city of the gods. Such people are hard to bring back. I will give you a gift, priest. If you dare to use it."

"Why?"

"In memory of what we said to one another, a long time ago. For the kindness of your gifts, if not their uses." She was starting to lose her shape:

her body shifted between the myriad images of all the people she had consumed. "And I am dying because of the Triad. If I can throw this in the face of the gods, why should I not?"

She held my hands, and I could not break free, and her eyes were on me. I remembered the vision of Deri I had had, of what had happened when the third eye of the Destroyer had opened.

Like the rest of the rakshasa, the eyes would not stay fixed in a single aspect, moving from the trusting ones of a child to those of older men and women. I watched the shift, the desperate convulsions of shape in the hope that she could find one to evade death, but there was none, she was mortal, in the end, felled by a treacherous human blow.

At this thought, I knew that she was inside me, crawling her way into me like a snake into its nest. I tried to remember a mantra for the protection of the mind, but the words had deserted me, and all I heard was the dry laughter of demons. I was caught, fooled by a dying rakshasa. I—

And then she died. The hands on mine went limp, and the eyes stared sightlessly into my face. I thought that in death she would revert to her natural aspect, but her corpse was that of the woman I had always seen. I wondered whether she had a natural shape.

I felt, at the back of my mind, the tremendous pressure of myriad memories that were not mine. All the thoughts of those she had once consumed, all the images they had seen, the lives they had lived.

A gift, she said, a fading voice in my mind. *Fare thee well, priest.*

And then she was gone, and I stood over her corpse, which was no different from the hundreds scattered on the battlefield. Darkness was coming fast. I said a quick prayer to the Triad over the rakshasa, for I was still a priest of the Destroyer, and then rose and went towards Mount Seilesa. Without conscious thought, I knew where my wife was.

A chariot waited at the foot of the mountain, its driver slumped on the ground. Dried blood covered his red cloak. The horses lay nearby, a tangle of legs, flesh and glistening muscles reeking of blood and spilled entrails.

My wife stood before the entrance to a cave sealed with a boulder on which shone the triple sigil of the Triad. Rage still emanated from inside the cave.

"Deri!" I called.

She raised her gaze. The eyes that turned towards me held nothing human. Blood had invaded the cornea, and the battle-frenzy had scourged every trace of pity from her face.

"Deri!"

She leapt towards me with her spear raised.

It was sheer luck that she missed me. The dying light of the day revealed the shadow of two more arms hanging in the air around her. A ghostly necklace of skulls clinked as she moved. "Come back," I said.

She held her bloody spear as if it were part of her. Tendrils came from the cave, curled around her for a while, and then withdrew.

"I remember you," she said. Her voice quivered with power.

"I am Angave, of the Destroyer's hearth," I said, as if speaking to a young child. "You are my lawful wife. I have come to bring you home."

Her face twisted out of shape. "Home?" She shook her head. "It was never home to me, Angave. Only a prison."

I swallowed. I knew that she was faster than I, that the god was strong within her, and that I had nothing. Faint memories which could prove a deadly gift, a shattered spell, a blind love. Not enough. "I am sorry. I know that nothing I say can atone for the way I behaved. I did not see. I thought that love would be enough to keep us whole."

Deri leapt at me again. This time she caught me in the plexus; I fell, the breath drained from me. The point of the spear rested on my throat. It seemed to me that the bloody metal was beating the same rhythm as my heart.

"Love is never enough. But there is no reason to be sorry," she said. "Soon it will not matter."

"I was wrong to ignore your feelings, but I meant well."

"It does not suffice." I could not tell whether the voice was hers or that of the god. "Your acts speak for you. It is all I ever saw."

"What of Karale?"

Her face wavered. For a moment the eyes were hers again. "I am the Arm of the Destroyer. I know no human bonds. I have earned my freedom." And she raised the spear to strike.

I lifted my arms to ward it, and felt the memories of the rakshasa rise in me. Memories of soldiers who had suffered spear-thrusts, who knew the futility of my gesture.

Memories. As if in a vision I saw the spear begin its descent, and Emodhe's spell had been stripped from me, I was defenseless against it. I had nothing but—

Memories. I hung onto the haft of the spear with one hand, and with the other I gripped one of Deri's ankles as hard as I could. And all the while the memories, wakened by the proximity of death, rose in me like a tide, threatening to overwhelm me.

"Deri." I groped in the dark, as for a vision. I felt her mind the way I had felt it in my dreams, heard her thoughts, which were no longer those of my wife. I felt the memories in my mind slip away from me. Calling her back. An anchor to tear her from her communion with the god.

Memories of women holding children by the hands. Of old men, sick and dying. Of soldiers going forth to battle, and hermits turning their back on the world, yet remaining bound to it. Of myself and Deri in the first days of our marriage, when the future sparkled before us like water in a pool, and of Karale's birth. But those were only a small part of it. I saw everything that she saw, and felt her thoughts peel away from the city of heaven, layer by layer.

And then the memories faded from both of our minds, and there was nothing left but us.

The spear fell. It buried itself in my shoulder instead of my throat. An excruciating pain arced through my whole body, and I screamed. I could not help myself.

Deri did not move. "Angave?" she asked in a small voice.

"Deri."

Her eyes still held the shadow of something far more than mortal. "I dreamt that—"

"I know what you dreamt," I said. "Deri, I am sorry. I did not see it. I thought you were happy with the way things were. It will change, I promise."

She said nothing. She disengaged the spear from my body, staring at the bleeding wound with bewildered eyes.

"Come," I said, gently. "Let us go home."

I have my wife and she sleeps by my side, and our child grows daily and is a joy to behold. But sometimes, thinking back over the war, I know that I was right when I told her she would change. She has realized that all bonds can be dissolved. She has learned that her power lies beyond the hearth, and that she has not even a wife's love to tie her to me. She is no longer mine.

I am an Eye of the Destroyer, but I need no vision to tell me what the god has wrought inside our hearth. The Destroyer makes endings so that new beginnings may come. But I fear that when the end comes for us, it will be bitter, and that whatever is built over the ruins, it shall bring me no joy.

Greatshadow

James Maxey

For twenty odd years, Bigsby the Dwarf ran a seafood shop near the docks of Commonground. The city was a lawless place, haven of pirates, abode of goblins, home to thieves and thugs; fortunately, even scoundrels needed to eat. Bigsby hadn't grown wealthy serving such a clientele. Still, he scraped by, and over the years had accumulated a treasure of interesting stories to share with friends over a pint of ale.

By reputation, Bigsby was a mirthful sort, good company in a bad city. Lately though, Bigsby was rarely seen at his favorite bars. He spent his evenings at the shop, sullenly chopping at blocks of ice. His lantern burned late into the night. His face took on a pale tone, his eyes lined with red.

One evening, after he'd shuttered the windows and started to work on the ice, Bigsby heard a knock. He stopped chopping.

"It can't be him," he muttered.

The knock came again, more firmly.

"Go away," he shouted. "We're closed!"

He looked at the flat surface of the ice. With his ice-pick, he began to doodle on the surface, scratching out a map of the islands from memory, contemplating the distance between Commonground and his former home. Even with good winds, it took three days to sail from the Silver City. If the visitors he was expecting left on the Feast's Eve, two days ago, they couldn't have arrived yet.

Again, the knocks came, swiftly followed by a thump, then a crash, as the door came off its hinges.

A giant of a man stood in the doorway. The intruder was heavily muscled and horribly scarred, with a face that looked sewn together with bits from several different people.

Bigsby opened his mouth. A squeak issued forth.

He cleared his throat.

"F-Fish?" he said. "Are y-you here for . . ."

"I'm here for you, traitor."

Someone else had answered. Bigsby glanced away from the monster. In the doorway stood another man, hardly any taller than himself. This stranger was hunched over beneath his tattered cloak, his body bent until his head was even with his waist. The hunched man leaned on a gnarled wooden staff. Rags tightly entwined his body, concealing every inch of skin. His eyes glowed like embers beneath the dingy hood.

"D-did you say . . . t-trader?" Bigsby wiped away the sweat stinging his eyes. "That I am. A humble trader in—"

The hooded stranger chuckled. "You have no secrets, dear Bigsby. I call you traitor with precision. You were a traitor twenty years ago when you cruelly poisoned Lord Brightmoon. Now you contemplate the betrayal of a friend. I know of the letter."

Bigsby hadn't heard the name Brightmoon in years. He'd all but forgotten the enormous price placed on his head. Countless souls in Commonground would betray him for the money, if they knew the truth.

Bigsby narrowed his eyes. He'd killed before. It was time to kill again. With desperate speed, he flung the ice-pick at the giant man's throat as he dove from his chair. He yanked at the drawer that held his knives. It fell to the floor in a clatter. He grabbed his sharpest, longest blade and spun to face his attackers.

He was met with a bemused chuckle from the hooded hunchback. The ice-pick was buried to the hilt in the tall man's throat, but the brute seemed unaware of this.

"You don't know who you face," the crooked man said.

"Then enlighten me, stranger." Bigsby snarled, holding his blade so that lantern light gleamed from its well-honed edge.

"Hmm." The hunchback nodded. "Stranger. That will do. My silent friend goes by Patch."

Bigsby stared at Patch and at the hilt of the ice-pick. The man wasn't even bleeding.

Stranger stepped forward. With a terrible groan he reached his spindly arm high and grabbed the ice-pick, freeing it with a grunt. He laid the weapon on the block of ice.

"I'm not here for the reward," Stranger said.

"You'd be disappointed," Bigsby said. "I've never poisoned anyone."

"But you did receive a letter, yes? From a man named Jack Blade. You're meeting him tomorrow. He's requested you lead him and his companions to the lair of the dragon, Greatshadow."

"Don't be absurd," Bigsby said. "I-I wouldn't know how to find Greatshadow. Why would anyone think that?"

"Because you drunkenly boasted of it one night. You said you'd stumbled upon the place and found it filled with riches. You wisely fled, of course."

"Ah," Bigsby said. "Perhaps I said such a thing, once, years ago, while drunk. It isn't true."

"Just another lie in a life of lies, then? But I see you speak the truth. You don't know how to find the dragon. But you won't admit this to Jack Blade. Instead, you plan to lead him on a wild goose chase into the Blackwater Swamp."

Bigsby felt limp hearing these words. When Stranger had spouted the truth about his distant past, Bigsby assumed the man had done some careful sleuthing. When Stranger had spoken about Jack's letter, he guessed it had been intercepted and read. But to know about his plans to lead the others into the swamp . . . he'd shared this with no one. Stranger was obviously a wizard. Bigsby swallowed hard.

"It's true," he said. "But this isn't betrayal. I've heard rumors that Greatshadow lives in the swamp. We might find him."

"You might meet your death by quicksand. But you'll never find Greatshadow in the swamp. The dragon lives in the mountain wastelands. The path to his abode is within my very blood. I shall lead you."

"Oh," Bigsby said, biting his nails. "Good."

"You'd as soon face the swamps," Stranger said.

"I saw Greatshadow once," Bigsby whispered. "Ten years ago, when the Armada of the Silver Kingdom sailed into this bay. I was watching from the window when night seemed to suddenly fall as the dragon's shadow passed. Then, the darkness vanished when Greatshadow breathed flames. It was horrible. The whole of the ocean was ablaze. Not a ship survived. Charred, bloated bodies washed ashore for days. I'm not eager to face the beast in his lair."

"My poor Bigsby," Stranger said. "What you are eager to do no longer matters. You'll do as I tell you, or I will reveal the price on your head to every soul in this accursed city."

Bigsby stared at his knife. He'd survived some terrible scraps over the years, but what chance did he have against a wizard? He let the knife fall from his grasp.

"Curse you," he mumbled. "I'll do as you say."

"It's not such a bad thing," Stranger said. "I promise you Bigsby, this is no journey of self destruction. Greatshadow will meet his end. When he does, you may leave with all the treasure you can carry. Even with your small stature, that's immeasurable wealth. The dragon has more diamonds than the mer-king has pearls."

Bigsby rubbed his chin. Certainly, a trip to Greatshadow's lair was suicide. But, just in case, he would wear pants with really big pockets.

"Let us hasten," Stranger said. "You aren't the only ally I seek tonight."

Bigsby followed the wizard through the busted doorway. Patch picked up the door and leaned it into place. Bigsby shook his head with a sigh. The broken door was the least of his worries, but he dreaded the thought of haggling with Jardon the carpenter to get it repaired. The little goblin charged as if each nail were made of gold.

Stranger led the way to Blackstone's Barge. The squat ship glowed upon the dark water with the light of a hundred lanterns. The shouts and squeals of drunken men and women filled the air as the trio crossed the swaying plank. Stranger pushed open the door. Thick smoke rolled forth.

Inside, Bigsby hung close to Patch. He normally dreaded crossing a crowded room. Bigsby had been tripped over by more than a few drunken fools with foul tempers. But, drunk or sober, people got out of Patch's way.

In the far corner of the room was a rough-hewn wooden booth. Bigsby knew the woman sitting there by reputation. Everyone called her Infidel. She was a muscular woman, with dark eyes beneath a stern brow. Her red hair was cropped close to her scalp, and black tattoos covered the length of her arms. A scar ran down her left cheek, from eye to lip.

She sat alone, carving letters into the thick oak table with a dagger as she sipped a large flagon of mead. Bigsby was a good judge of body language. This woman wasn't in the mood for company.

"Infidel," Stranger said. "It's my honor to meet you."

She glared at him.

"What the devil are you?" she asked, raising an eyebrow.

"A humble traveler, in need of your assistance."

"Right. Seriously, what are you beneath those rags? You sure as hell ain't human. You're not a goblin, neither."

"Madam, I suffer many deformities. How unkind of you to draw attention to them."

"Bullshit," Infidel said, reaching toward Stranger's hood.

Patch caught her wrist. It looked almost accidental, as if Patch had been moving his arm in her direction on a whim and happened to meet her hand. With his fingers closed, her arm was immobile. She strained to pull free, but Patch didn't budge.

"Let's forget about my face, *Isadora*," Stranger said.

Infidel responded by using her free hand to drive the dagger deep into Patch's elbow. With a twist of the blade, Patch's hand sprung open. In an instant, Infidel flew from the booth and tackled Stranger, the dagger pressed to his throat. His hood slipped back, revealing a burlap sack enshrouding a misshapen head.

"Where did you learn that name?" Infidel growled.

Before Stranger could respond, Patch leaned over and grabbed the woman by her ears. She shrieked as he lifted her from the floor. If Patch felt any pain from the injury to his elbow, it failed to show on his impassive face.

"A bargain, Infidel," Stranger said calmly. "I don't speak that name again. You don't look beneath my hood."

Infidel responded by chopping down with the dagger, burying it deep into Patch's thigh. She pulled it free and struck again, and again. Patch didn't even flinch.

Stranger chuckled.

"There's another name you'll be interested in hearing," he said. "Tristrum Castlebridge."

Infidel raised an eyebrow as she thrust the dagger toward Stranger, who stood just beyond its tip. "You're one of *his* men?"

"Hardly," Stranger said. "We plot his demise."

"You certainly know the words a woman wants to hear," she said, a sudden smile upon her lips. "Drop me."

Patch let loose of her ears and she landed on her feet.

"Goddammit," she grumbled, rubbing her ears. "Where'd you pick up the big guy?"

"Patch is an old friend," Stranger said. "Several, actually."

She pulled the bent remains of a gold ring from a particularly bloody spot on her upper ear.

"You owe me a new earring," she said.

"Treasures aplenty await you," Stranger said.

"Sure. Whatever. What's with the dwarf?"

Bigsby bowed politely. "Bigsby's the name. I'm—"

"You're the fish guy."

Bigsby was surprised she'd ever noticed him.

"If it makes you feel any better, I didn't fare any better against Patch than you did."

"That's freaking great. Wait until word gets out I'm no better than a dwarf fishmonger in a brawl."

"Killing Tristrum Castlebridge will more than assure your reputation," Stranger said.

Infidel cracked her knuckles. "Let's talk more about this killing thing."

She looked around the silent room. Everyone—man, woman, and goblin—stared at them.

"Hey!" she shouted. "Mind your business! Me and my buddies are plotting a murder!"

A few of the larger men laughed, while most of the goblins in the room turned a paler blue than usual. All turned away, and soon the room was awash in voices.

"Have a seat," she said.

Stranger twisted his bent body at awkward angles, grunting as he slipped along the bench. Bigsby climbed in beside him.

"You both look like you could use a little ear-hanging from the big guy," Infidel said. "Put a few inches on you, Shorty. Maybe take the kinks out of your back, Rag-face." She raised her arms above her head and stretched, her sinews popping. "Does wonders for the spine."

"Tomorrow, a ship will arrive," Stranger said.

"Ships arrive every day," Infidel said.

"This one carries a band of adventurers."

"Tristrum's one of them?"

"He leads them," Stranger said.

"He's the bossy sort."

"They've come to kill Greatshadow."

Infidel perked up. "And we tag along to watch them die? Could be fun."

"I think they will succeed," Stranger said.

"Shyeah. Right."

"Tristrum carries Frostbite."

Infidel raised an eyebrow.

Bigsby wondered what was significant about some knight missing a few toes.

"Frostbite's been missing for years," Infidel said. "How'd Tristrum get it?"

"Unimportant. The sword will protect him from Greatshadow's flames. The dragon's skin will have no resistance to its cold bite. A single cut will freeze the dragon's blood."

"So Tristrum might actually beat Greatshadow."

"He'll claim this land in the name of the Silver Kingdom," Stranger said. "I would rather this island remain under . . . local control. So after Tristrum and his friends exhaust themselves besting the dragon—"

"We take them out," Infidel said. "Gotcha."

"Excuse me," Bigsby said. "But if this Tristrum fellow is tough enough to best Greatshadow, what makes you think we're tough enough to fight him?"

"We?" Infidel rolled her eyes. "Don't flatter yourself. Frostbite's a good sword, yeah, but it doesn't worry me. What do you bring to the party, fishmonger?"

"Bigsby has a friend among Tristrum's party."

"Jack Blade," Bigsby said. "He was kind to me when I lived in the Silver City. He helped me escape."

"Escape what?"

Bigsby clenched his fists. *Stupid!* Twenty years of caution thrown to the wolves.

"Taxes," Bigsby said. He grinned sheepishly.

"Yeah," Infidel said. "Taxes are a bitch."

The ship sailed into the harbor the following evening, under a Northsea flag.

"That's not a Northsea ship," Infidel said, as she, Bigsby, Stranger and Patch watched from a hill above the harbor. "Who's he fooling?"

"The dragon, possibly," Stranger said. "Ships of the Silver Armada don't have a lucky history in this port."

"It has three lanterns hanging from starboard," Bigsby said. "That's the signal."

"We'd better get a move on, then," Infidel said. "Slow as you three move, they'll be old and gray before we get down there. That'll scare Greatshadow. A bunch of toothless old men limping into his lair, waving their canes."

Bigsby thought a bunch of toothless old men would probably fare as well as anyone. He chased after Infidel as she loped down the hill. Despite her cruel humor, Bigsby felt safer near her than he did in the presence of Patch and Stranger.

Bigsby was out of breath by the time they made it to the docks. He looked behind him. Stranger and Patch were nowhere to be seen.

"Infidel," he called out.

She stopped and looked toward him. "Yeah?"

"Stranger," Bigsby said between gasps. "You trust him?"

"This some joke?"

Bigsby shook his head. "I have a rowboat. We could escape in it before Stranger finds us."

"Sounds like a plan. Go for it. But I'm sticking around. There's killing to be done."

She headed toward the ship. Bigsby looked back. Stranger stood at the far end of the docks. There was still time to run. But once he made it to the boat, where would he go? He'd lived in Commonground most of his adult life. Plus, there was still Jack to consider. Bigsby couldn't care less if Stranger and Infidel murdered Tristrum, but Jack had once been his friend. It seemed only fair to warn him. Of course, if he did, Stranger would know it. The bastard could read minds.

"Don't forget that," Stranger called out, a dozen yards away.

Bigsby shook his head. Could things get any worse?

"Oh look," Stranger said, drawing beside Bigsby, his eyes fixed on the deck of the ship. "They have a Truthspeaker among them."

"Great." Bigsby stared at the black-robed figure on the deck. "They're even worse than mind-readers."

"Don't forget *that*, either," Stranger said.

Fortunately, the Truthspeaker remained on the deck of the ship as Jack Blade bounded from the gangplank to the dock. He raced forward and grabbed Bigsby by the shoulders, lifting him in the air with his embrace. "Old friend!" he said.

"Ixnay on the endfray," Bigsby whispered. "People don't know I used to live in the Silver City."

"Understood." Jack set Bigsby back on his feet. "My, the years have been, uh, years since I've seen you. Put on a little weight, I see."

"The years have been kind to you," Bigsby said. And they had. Jack hadn't aged at all. He still had the same long flowing tresses, and still dressed with a youthful flair, wearing a fancy silk cloak over his immaculate black leather armor. Bigsby could see his face reflected in Jack's polished thigh-high boots. "Wearing clothes like that around here's asking for trouble," Bigsby said.

"Let trouble come," Jack said. "It's important to look good in public."

Infidel stood nearby, leaning against a piling. She looked Blade over with a sneer. "You look like you're on your way to a ball instead of a dragon hunt."

Jack smiled. "Bigsby. You've brought friends."

"Um. Yeah. This is, uh, In—"

"Ingred," Infidel said.

"Charmed," Jack said, with a bow.

"And this," Bigsby said, "is Patch."

Jack looked at the hulking figure, and managed a smile. "A pleasure."

"Finally," Bigsby said, motioning toward the robed hunchback, "this is, uh, Stranger."

Jack's smile wavered a little as he studied Stranger's ragged form.

"I'm not a leper, if that's what you're thinking," Stranger said.

"Jack!" A voice thundered down from the deck. A silver-haired man clanked down the gangplank, his armor gleaming red in the fading sunlight. Without introduction, Bigsby knew this to be the famed knight Tristrum Castlebridge. It was clear from the steely gleam in his eyes, the noble thrust of his chin, and the frost-encrusted scabbard that hung from his waist. Plus the name "Castlebridge" was stitched in gold thread around the hem of his flowing purple cloak.

"Is this the fellow you spoke of?" Tristrum asked.

"May I introduce you to Bigsby, the Fish Baron of Commonground."

Infidel snickered.

Tristrum cast his gaze upon her. She stared back. He looked down at Bigsby. "Is she with you?"

"Yes," Bigsby said. "I thought an extra blade might come in handy."

"It confirms all I've heard about Commonground," Tristrum said, "that the best man you could find for the job is a woman."

Bigsby dared a glance toward Infidel. She didn't have her hand upon her sword.

"I also brought Patch." Bigsby gestured toward the monster behind him.

"Beefy fellow, aren't you?" Tristrum said.

Patch stared silently, as flies crawled about his face.

The hunchback stepped forward. "And I am Stranger."

"I see," Tristrum said.

"Bigsby has told me of your desire to rid the land of Greatshadow," Stranger said. "I share your desire. I know I am nothing but a withered old man, but I beg you to allow me to accompany you. I speak the language of every tribe upon this island, even the Dragontongue."

"Hmm," Tristrum said. "That could be useful."

"Tristrum!"

It was a deep, booming voice that called out the knight's name. It was like the voice of thunder, the voice of the heavens. Down the gangplank strode a man in a black cotton robe, a thick, gilt-edged book held in his right hand, a jagged, yet well-honed scythe in his left.

"Thomas," Tristrum said. "Good of you to join us. This is Jack's friend Bigs—"

"Can you think of any reason for me to know the names of this lot?"

Tristrum flinched at the question.

"You there." Thomas the Truthspeaker extended a long, bony finger toward Bigsby.

The dwarf looked into the man's dark eyes, like pools of ink with little pearls gleaming in them. He felt faint.

"Yes, sir?" he asked.

"Why do you offer your services to us? Answer truthfully!"

Bigsby tried to lie. *Because I humbly wish to be of service to your noble cause.* His heart skipped a beat. *Because I can think of no greater duty . . .* he couldn't complete the thought. It felt as if the Truthspeaker's bony fingers had reached into his chest and gripped his heart.

"Because we seek to enrich ourselves with the dragon's treasure when you perish!" Bigsby blurted out.

Tristrum chuckled. "You have too little faith in us, dwarf. It is the dragon who shall perish, not us."

The Truthspeaker smiled. The expression didn't suit him. "Let us have an understanding, dwarf. We will tolerate your heathen presence, as well as this band of rabble you've gathered, because we need your knowledge. In return, we shall provide you a modest share of the dragon's wealth. There is no need for you to like us, and no need for us to like you."

"Wow," Infidel said. "It's like I think it and you say it."

"In our kingdom," the Truthspeaker said, "women speak only when spoken to."

"Not your kingdom," Infidel said.

"Since you choose to dress like a man, you can help unload the ship." Thomas pointed toward Patch. "You also."

Stranger nodded. Patch lumbered forward. Infidel stood silent for a moment, her hand edging closer to her sword. Then, with a shrug, she headed up the gangplank.

The caravan of adventurers left at dawn, while the cutthroats of Commonground were still sleeping off the previous night's revelries. This was Bigsby's favorite time of day. Usually by now he'd been working for a few hours, and would take a moment at daybreak to step outside his shop and watch the sun come up at the mouth of the bay. He would smoke his pipe and listen to the gulls and be filled with a tremendous sense that all was right with his world. He wondered if he would ever feel that way again.

Commonground was a long city, but a narrow one. It stretched for miles along the hilly shores of the bay, but once one ventured over those hills, even the half-hearted pretense of civilization was left behind. Commonground was located on the southeastern shore of a large island marked on most maps as the Isle of Fear. Bigsby had never much worried about what lay beyond the hills. Now, he was being forced to think about it by another one of Jack's companions, a man named Magidance, who'd made his appearance only moments before they'd departed.

". . . wildcats, wolves, and wyverns," Magidance said, finishing the list of various threats that lay before them. It had been several minutes since he started with "Ants: giant, man-eating."

The band of dragon hunters marched at a vigorous pace. Bigsby struggled to keep stride with Infidel, but kept slipping behind, to find himself once more within earshot of Magidance at the rear of the party.

"Seventy-three species capable of killing a man," Magidance said.

"If you're so worried, why are you here?" Bigsby asked.

Magidance shrugged. "I may have been drinking a little when Jack talked me into this."

Bigsby couldn't guess why Jack had recruited such a sickly looking fellow. Magidance was a pale, scrawny man, with bags under his eyes and thinning hair. He was armed only with a dagger, and Bigsby wondered if even the dagger was too much for him to handle.

The rest of Jack's companions looked brawnier, consisting of a half dozen men-at-arms with well-kept weapons, and another ten burly men who carried the gear.

"Shame we can't have horses." Magidance sighed. "How long did you say this would take? Are we close?"

"We haven't traveled an hour!" Bigsby said.

"Horses *are* particularly favored by dragons," Magidance said. "Domestic animals are plump and slow compared with a dragon's normal fare. That's the real reason people haven't settled here. Dragon's don't give a damn about people as food, but civilization is built on livestock. I'll bet there are no cheese shops in Commonground."

"The goblins make a kind of cheese from the milk of cave goats," Bigsby said. "It's seasoned with the husks of firespiders."

"Sounds intriguing. I suppose I'd try it. I'll put anything in my mouth at least once. When I was up north, I had some fantastic cheese in a village of the snowmen. It was made from whale's milk of all things, and was half-transparent, like ice riddled with air. Master Solodon wouldn't touch the stuff. Said it smelled like rotten teeth. It did, I suppose. But it was salty on the tongue, like anchovies."

"Solo . . . did you say Solodon?" Bigsby asked.

"As in 'the Great and Wondrous Master of Mysteries Solodon,'" Magidance said. "Formerly master of me, as well. I apprenticed with him."

"You? You're a wizard?"

"Not according to Thomas the Truthspeaker. He says I'm a thrice-damned liar who shouldn't be suffered to live. Fortunately, he gave Tristrum his word he wouldn't kill me."

"Why does he think you're a liar? Aren't you a real wizard?"

"Magic is nothing but a lie you tell the universe," Magidance said. "The trick is to make the universe believe it. Truthspeakers and wizards are eternal enemies. But dragon hunts make for strange alliances."

"Thomas seems like a very mean man," Bigsby said. By now he and Magidance had fallen far enough behind that they could speak freely, though not so far back that they couldn't dash for the safety of the group should a strange growl come from the bushes.

"Thomas is a very righteous man," Magidance said. "As was Solodon. Only someone with weak morals could see them as mean."

Bigsby frowned. He'd expected a sympathetic ear, not a scolding.

"Perhaps it's true," Magidance said with a shrug. "There may be a hell, and it may be my fate. Better than sharing heaven with that bastard, eh?"

A scream came from the trail ahead.

Bigsby ran toward the safety of the larger party. One of the porters thrashed about on the ground, as Infidel dove into the tall grass.

"Snakebite!" someone shouted.

Magidance ran past Bigsby, trailing a stream of obscenities.

"Got it!" Infidel yelled. She stood. On the end of her dagger writhed a yard-long white snake with black stripes.

"I didn't hear 'zebra snakes' in your list," Jack said to Magidance.

Magidance fell to his knees beside the snakebite victim. He produced a small sack from his cape. The bitten man thrashed about, screaming between gasps.

"Hold him!" Magidance shouted.

Jack and two other men grabbed the victim's flailing limbs, pinning them.

Magidance pulled the tiny, toothful jawbone of a snake from his pouch. He pressed this into the man's flesh above the wound, then below, all the while humming rhythmically. He then blew a pinch of white powder into the man's eyes. The man cried in pain, then fell still and silent.

"Not even noon and we've lost a man," Tristrum grumbled.

"He'll live," Magidance said. "I've cured worse."

"Will he be able to travel?" Thomas asked.

"Not soon. He'll sleep the rest of the day. Tomorrow, he'll be too weak to walk. But in a week, he should be good as new. If we take him back to the ship—"

"No," Tristrum said. "We'll set up a tent here. Leave him food and water. We journey on."

"Leave him? Alone?"

"He won't stand a chance out here," Bigsby said. "There are monsters about. Man-eaters!"

"All the more reason for haste," Tristrum said. "It would slow us to carry him."

"Sir," Magidance said. "Perhaps we could—"

"Enough!" Thomas said, in a tone that silenced even Tristrum. He knelt beside the peaceful form of the victim. "This isn't open to debate. I've known this man since he was a boy. His name is Pious, and he is a good and faithful servant. He deserves the best possible fate."

Thomas cradled Pious in his arms. Pious was young, barely old enough to shave. His face was angelic in slumber.

"Wake," Thomas said.

Pious stirred, his eyelids fluttering open.

"You've lived well." Thomas placed a kiss upon the young man's brow. "You are welcomed home."

As he said this, a breeze stirred the tall grass and wispy clouds dimmed the sun. A chill ran down Bigsby's spine. Pious closed his eyes. His chest fell still. Thomas looked up with a dreamy smile.

Magidance swayed as if about to faint. "You . . . you killed him."

"I *saved* him," Thomas said.

Magidance started to speak, then stopped. He trembled, his hands in tight fists, before stomping away, red-faced. As he passed Bigsby he mumbled, in conclusion to his list, "Zealots."

In the following days, the pretense that Bigsby was guiding the party grew thin. Whenever directions were asked, Stranger would be the one to jump in with an answer. Bigsby never even approached the front with Stranger, Tristrum, and Thomas. Instead, he stayed as far away from them as possible, at the rear of the party, usually in the company of Magidance, and now Infidel, who seemed to enjoy Magidance's dry humor. If she did enjoy it, she was in luck, for he seldom shut up.

Magidance carried a folded leather map that he made notes on as they traveled.

"Most maps refer to this as the Isle of Fear, though some still call it the Isle of Fire. The coast is mapped reasonably well, but the interior is all guesswork. I did find a five-hundred-year old atlas that called this place Myhryrha, which is an oldtongue word for *wine*. It showed several fair-sized cities on this island. That's the real reason I agreed to come. The thought of finding the ruins of a lost civilization. That's the sort of stuff that gets your name remembered through the ages."

"I've heard goblins speak of hidden cities," Bigsby said.

"Hell, I've been to three of them," Infidel said. "Me and Boggy McBee used to do a little tomb raiding. I gave it up, though. Too much digging, not enough gold."

The talk of lost cities caught Bigsby's imagination. Every shadow in the forest, every strangely shaped rock, hinted that they passed through ancient ruins. The land gave his imagination plenty to work with. This was rocky ground, with huge stones the size of houses all around. Ahead, low mountains loomed, their round peaks gleaming domes of white stone.

On the evening of their ninth day of travel, as they journeyed around the base of a stony mountain, the air filled with an incredible stench. Stranger led them to the source of the smell. It was an enormous turd, the size of a small horse, black with flies.

"We're near," Stranger said.

Magidance stepped closer to the dragon dropping, carrying a small glass dish.

"My God," he said, brushing away flies and scooping some of the brown-green excrement onto the glass. "On the mage markets, dragon's dung sells for its weight in gold. It's useful for an invisibility spell. This alone covers the cost of our trip."

"We've not come this distance to content ourselves with dung," Tristrum said.

"We should leave," Stranger said. "The goblins who live nearby will be drawn to the smell. They use the dung for—Aanh!"

Stranger fell forward, a small, rough-hewn arrow jutting from his crooked back.

Suddenly, the air was filled with high-pitched trills and the whistling of hundreds of arrows. All around Bigsby, men began to fall. Fortunately, Tristrum stood between him and the brunt of the attack. The arrows bounced harmlessly from Tristrum's gleaming armor. Magidance took shelter behind Patch, who stood stoically as arrows sank into his broad chest. Magidance shouted words in a language Bigsby had never heard. A strong wind swept up behind them, blowing the poorly made arrows back in the direction they had come. Tristrum ran forward, sword drawn.

The dirty blue faces of dozens of goblins rose from behind nearby rocks and bushes. Bows were thrown to the ground and jagged blades drawn as the goblins readied for hand-to-hand combat.

Tristrum, Jack, and Infidel were upon them in seconds, their swords biting into goblin bone with each hack. Thomas joined in, swinging his scythe in a wide arc, liberating heads from torsos.

In less than a minute the battle ended, with a score of goblins dead on the ground and the rest vanished into the sheltering brush.

Jack knelt over one of the bodies left behind.

"Look at this," he said, holding up a small shield covered in a scaly skin.

"Dragon hide," Magidance said. "Where would—"

"The dragon keeps a harem of young females," Stranger said, through teeth gritted with pain. Patch stood by him now, helping him to his feet. The bloody arrow yanked from Stranger's back was still in Patch's hand. "Greatshadow kills his mates after they first give birth, before they grow old and powerful enough to challenge him. He tosses their bodies, and the helpless male chicks, into a deep gorge not far from here. Female chicks are allowed to live, for his future pleasure. The goblins must raid the gorge for the bodies."

"Then we're near," Tristrum said.

"With a brisk march, we could be at his lair in less than an hour," Stranger said.

Tristrum shielded his eyes as he looked toward the sun. "I'm not sure we—"

He never got to complete his thought, as Infidel suddenly shouted, "Stay away from him!"

All eyes turned to see the female warrior with dagger drawn, standing between Thomas and one of the porters, who lay bleeding on the ground.

"I'll not stand by and witness another act of mercy on your part," Infidel said, her eyes narrow slits.

"You will not stand at all." Thomas stretched his arm toward her and commanded in a rumbling voice, "On your knees!"

Infidel's body swayed drunkenly. Her knees bent, her legs trembled, but she did not kneel.

"Your resistance prolongs the inevitable," Thomas said.

Infidel staggered forward, her dagger rising toward the holy man's throat.

"Halt!" Thomas thundered.

Infidel jerked like a dog reaching the end of its leash. Sweat poured down her face.

"You cannot win this fight," Thomas said. "I see into your very soul."

Infidel growled, as she moved her limbs in spastic jerks. A trickle of blood flowed from her mouth.

"Your bravado masks the heart of a frightened girl," Thomas said, his voice calm. "I see a great shame within you. You've even contemplated taking a dagger to your own throat. No doubt, that would be for the best."

Infidel grunted as her dagger moved toward her neck.

"No!" Bigsby cried out. He ran forward, his knife drawn, and plunged his blade into the Truthspeaker's thigh.

Thomas fell backwards, knocking Bigsby to the ground.

Infidel crumpled to the ground, suddenly limp.

Bigsby struggled from beneath Thomas, only to find a hand on the back of his neck. He was lifted from the ground, dangling in the grip of Tristrum.

"Traitorous wretch." Tristrum snarled. "You cannot strike a holy man in my presence and live!"

Thomas struggled back to his feet with the help of one of the men-at-arms. He faced Bigsby. His eyes once more looked like inky pools of night.

"I can see into you now," Thomas said. "Your cowardly attack has revealed your true nature. There is a terrible sin in your past. Confess!"

"Ahhhn!" Bigsby bit his lip to silence himself, but it was to no avail. His mouth moved against his will.

"It's true! Ahhhhhhh! Oh, God. I poisoned Lord Brightmoon! Nnnnah!"

"Truly?" Tristrum tossed Bigsby to the ground. "Then I won't break your neck after all. It would be rude to deprive Brightmoon's son of the pleasure."

Tristrum looked toward one of the henchmen. "Tie him up. And the woman."

But when they looked to where Infidel had fallen, she was gone.

"How shocking to learn the truth about one's companions," Stranger said with a sigh.

Jack Blade turned his face away as Thomas glanced in his direction.

"It's been a long day," Tristrum said, looking toward the darkening sky. "We make camp here. The goblins should be too frightened to return, and the stench of his own dung should keep the dragon from catching our scent. We'll leave for our assault come daylight, with every able-bodied man. And Thomas?"

"Yes?"

"Allow Magidance to tend to the wounded. Your wound as well."

"As you wish," Thomas said with a nod and a scowl.

That night, Bigsby sweltered in the heat of his tent. The stench of the nearby dung stung his eyes until tears rolled down his cheeks. He couldn't wipe them away. His hands were bound behind his back with a stout rope. Deep down, he knew he deserved this fate. After all these years, his secret was out. His future led to the gallows.

From outside the tent, there was a faint groan, fading away into a gurgle. The flap of the tent pushed open, allowing cool air to flow over Bigsby.

"Stay quiet," Infidel whispered. She crawled to his side and cut the ropes that bound him.

He rolled onto his back, rubbing his wrists. Infidel was already slipping from the tent. Bigsby hurried after her.

Outside, he couldn't see her. At his feet lay one of Tristrum's men, his throat slit.

Infidel's hand fell upon his shoulder. She dragged him into the bushes. They traveled for several minutes across the rocky ground before Infidel motioned for him to stop.

"I won't lie to you," she said. "We're probably going to die."

"I'm a dead man anyway, if I fall into their hands."

"I have to go back," Infidel said. "Steal what I can. We won't make it far with only the clothes on our backs."

Bigsby nodded. Then he asked, "Why did you save me?"

"Did you really kill Lord Brightmoon?"

"Yes," Bigsby said quietly. "My father was his cook. Lord Brightmoon was a cruel man. He would have my father beaten for the smallest trifles. 'This soup scalded my tongue! Have the chef beaten. This ham is too salty! Have the chef lashed.'"

Bigsby looked down at his hands. "My father was younger than I am now, but his hair was gray, and his face lined with wrinkles. Lord Brightmoon was killing him one day at a time. When I began my apprenticeship, I returned the favor and poisoned the bastard."

Bigsby began to weep.

Infidel lowered her head.

"My father paid the price for my sin," Bigsby said. "When I fled, I left a note confessing . . . no, *boasting* of my crime. I later learned they executed my father anyway. I . . . maybe I do deserve to hang."

"No," Infidel said. "I witnessed Tristrum's reaction to the news. He was gleeful, laughing. Lord Brightmoon's death brought Tristrum closer to the throne. But the hypocrite was all tears and sobs at the funeral. God, even then he was a bastard."

Bigsby wiped his cheeks. "You knew Tristrum?"

"Worse," Infidel said. "I loved him."

Bigsby sniffled, and stared at the muscular, tattooed woman before him. He didn't know what to say.

"I was born into wealth," Infidel said. "My father was an advisor in Tristrum's court. I was a stupid little girl who imagined that when I grew up, I would win Tristrum's heart."

Infidel sighed.

"When I was thirteen, Tristrum returned from battle. After the death of Brightmoon, there had been a minor uprising in the southern provinces. Tristrum had been gone for a year, helping to suppress the uprising.

"I was warned," Infidel said. "Some of the older girls told me that when Tristrum returned from battle he carried a terrible temper, that he could fly into brutal rages.

"I was pleased by this. If the other women avoided Tristrum, I would have a chance. I'd let him see that I was different, that I would love him even in his darkest moments."

Infidel rose from the rock she was sitting on. She stalked to a nearby tree, and sunk her dagger into it with an overhand thrust.

"I waited in his chambers, only to talk. And the bastard attacked me," she said, her face turned from Bigsby. "He beat me with his fists, kicked me when I fell, and laughed at my tears. The servants pulled me from the room more dead than alive. When my father learned of the attack, he was furious. Not at Tristrum, but at me. He said I deserved it for startling Tristrum in the privacy of his quarters. He banished me to a nunnery."

She looked at Bigsby, shrugging. "It didn't take. I ran away. I've spent the rest of my life on the road."

"I'm sorry," Bigsby said.

"Don't be. I understand Tristrum now. I've been awakened to the deep satisfaction of violence. That rush of power that comes when the sword leaves my scabbard. That electric thrill when I see my opponent's blood. It's better than sex. Tristrum made me who I am. I can't wait to thank him properly."

Bigsby didn't know what to say to this.

"A touching tale," said a voice from the darkness.

Two shadows moved toward them, resolving into Stranger and Patch. Patch tossed two packs onto the ground.

"You'll never make it back to Commonground without supplies," Stranger said. "Not that reaching Commonground will do you much good. You'll both be fugitives, and where will you go when even Commonground can't hide you?"

"We'll survive," Infidel said.

"You can do more than survive," Stranger said. "You can triumph. You can perform the duties you agreed to, and kill Tristrum once he kills the dragon."

"I used to stay up nights dreaming about killing Tristrum. But now . . . ?" Infidel's fingers closed on a phantom neck before her. "Now I just want to throttle that damn Truthspeaker."

"I don't want to kill anybody," Bigsby said. "I just want my life back."

"If none of Tristrum's party survives, your secret is safe," Stranger said.

"But Jack . . . and Magidance . . . "

"They stood by you earlier, eh?" Stranger said.

"I'm in." Infidel pulled her dagger from the tree.

"I guess I have no choice," Bigsby said.

"Follow me," Stranger said.

They marched through the darkness for an hour. Stranger led them to a small cave and told them to rest while they could.

"From here, you can watch the entrance to Greatshadow's lair. Once Tristrum's party enters, you must follow swiftly. Have no fear of being seen. Tristrum and his men will be too focused on what's before them to worry about what's behind them."

"Patch and I will be with Tristrum. After the battle, his men should be no match for Patch. Tristrum himself may be another matter. But I have faith in you, Infidel."

"What about Thomas and Magidance?" Infidel asked. "How do we counter their magic?"

"Should they survive Greatshadow, I will handle them," Stranger said.

"What about me?" Bigsby asked. "I'm no match for any of them."

"You did well enough striking Thomas from behind," Stranger said.

Bigsby was wide-awake when dawn came. Infidel had slept a little, coming fully awake as light seeped into the cave. Across a rocky valley they could see a huge gash in the mountain's face. Bones lay in great heaps at the entrance.

Before the mists of morning burned away, Tristrum and his men appeared. Tristrum led the way, followed by five men-at-arms bearing spears and shields. Thomas, Stranger, and Magidance followed with Patch shuffling behind.

Searching the shadows, Bigsby spotted Jack Blade, well in front of the others, creeping among the bone mounds at the lair's mouth.

Stranger cast a single glance their way, and nodded. Infidel slipped from the small cave and crouched behind a boulder. Bigsby followed.

A moment later, Infidel peeked around the rock.

"They're almost there," she whispered. "Can't see Jack. Must be inside. C'mon."

Infidel scrambled across the rocky ground, keeping low. Bigsby breathed deep to gather his courage and chased after her. Quicker than he would have liked, they reached the bone field. Up close, the jagged rock revealed itself to be covered with intricately carved demons. Stairs were cut into the rock, leading into darkness.

"I've seen carvings like this before, when we robbed the tomb of Kuranath," Infidel said. "This place was a temple."

Without waiting for Bigsby's reply, she raced up the steps, staying close to the wall. She motioned for him to follow.

As he reached the top step, Bigsby caught his breath. For as far as he could see, the floor was made of seamless, gleaming silver. The room was enormous, hundreds of yards deep with a ceiling that vanished into shadows high overhead. From cracks in the rock, shafts of light pierced the darkness.

In the distance, the room held more stairs, rising into an immense, shadowy chamber. Tristrum and his men gathered at the foot of the steps. Jack was near the top step, moving cautiously.

Infidel grabbed Bigsby and dragged him into a niche in the wall. She held a finger to her lips.

Jack crept forward into the shadows.

Then a scream, abruptly halted, echoed through the chamber. Tristrum and his men readied their weapons. Jack's head came bouncing down the stairs.

From the shadows emerged a strange creature, almost human, but taller than Patch. It had four arms, each carrying a sword of flame. It wore a full suit of armor that glowed red, as if fresh from the forge.

"Run!" Magidance shouted, spinning around to follow his own advice.

Tristrum's men hurled their spears. One missed, clattering on the gleaming steps. The other four spears crumbled to ash as they touched the glowing armor.

"Halt!" Thomas cried, motioning toward Magidance. The wizard's legs stiffened and he tumbled, skidding across the polished floor.

"Fool!" Magidance screamed. "That's a *godslayer*! A soldier of the wars between the real and the unreal! We cannot best it."

Tristrum's men looked like they had doubts as well. They drew swords, but crept backwards as the godslayer stepped toward them.

Thomas alone held his ground.

"I fear thee not, Devil!"

The godslayer raised a sword overhead, preparing to strike the Truthspeaker, who strode boldly forward.

"You are an abomination!" Thomas cried, holding his holy book before him.

The godslayer staggered backwards, as if struck a powerful blow.

"An obscenity!"

Again, the godslayer was pushed back. It lost it's footing, and fell to one knee.

"Accursed soul!" Thomas raised his scythe over his head. His body glowed with brilliant blue light. He brought the scythe down with all his might, into the center of the godslayer's breastplate.

A crack of thunder shook the chamber. The godslayer's armor and weapons shattered, falling in jagged shards. Naked now, the godslayer was revealed as a bronzed-skinned, well-muscled youth, with golden hair and a serene smile. Bigsby couldn't help but notice the creature also had the longest penis he'd ever seen.

The tip of Thomas's scythe rested against the creature's chest, but had not scratched it. With a grunt, Thomas raised his scythe to strike again.

Still smiling serenely, the godslayer grabbed the fallen spear from the steps. With a single motion, he brought the tip of the spear up to the Truthspeaker's belly. Thomas cried out as the spear pierced him, his scythe clattering to the ground.

"Now!" Tristrum cried.

His five men charged, swords raised against the godslayer. The smiling devil kicked out at the first to reach him, catching him firmly in the chest. The man's sword flew from his grasp as he fell. With a graceful sweep of his lower left arm, the godslayer plucked the sword from the air and used it to sever the head of the second man-at-arms. As the man toppled, his sword, too, was captured. In a blur of motion, the four-armed youth waded forward, killing two more men before Bigsby could blink, and arming himself with their swords. The final man gave a panicked cry and lunged forward, his sword thrust with both hands toward the godslayer's chest. The godslayer danced aside, slow by a second. The man's sword drew a thin red gash across the devil's ribs. The godslayer repaid the scratch with a dozen savage blows that tore the man to bits.

Bigsby's limbs felt like lead. He watched helplessly as the godslayer descended the steps.

Only Tristrum, Stranger, and Patch remained standing. Magidance tried desperately to regain his footing, slipping and sliding across the gleaming floor in his panic.

Tristrum pulled Frostbite from its scabbard. Impossibly, a gentle snow began to fall inside the chamber. Bigsby's breath suddenly came out in clouds.

"I see you can bleed," Tristrum said, addressing the godslayer while tightening his grip on his shield.

The four-armed devil leapt forward in a whirl of blades. Tristrum grunted as two of the blades fell against his shield, while another slipped harmlessly across his breastplate. He used Frostbite to parry the final sword. The parried blade iced over. The godslayer struck again, and again Tristrum blocked the blows. This time, the impact of the godslayer's attack caused the blade touched by Frostbite to shatter.

The godslayer's brow furrowed as he glanced at the bladeless hilt held in his upper right hand.

Tristrum attacked, driving Frostbite's tip into the creature's chest. The godslayer drew a sharp breath of pain, and raised his lower right arm, bringing his blade up under Tristrum's armpit, slipping it between the joints in his armor.

Tristrum cried out and fell back, his sword-arm useless at his side. Frostbite hung for a second in the godslayer's chest, then slipped out and clattered noisily at his feet. A crust of red ice quickly sealed over the wound.

Stranger motioned toward Patch.

"Goddammit," Infidel grumbled, rushing from the shadows.

The godslayer struck at Tristrum, more savagely than before. Tristrum's shield splintered, and one of the beast's blades cut a deep gash into Tristrum's neck. Tristrum staggered backwards, his hand over the wound. He turned to flee, but the godslayer kicked out, tripping him.

The godslayer readied to deliver the killing blow. Before he could strike, Patch reached him, landing a solid punch to his nose.

The creature looked bewildered, as if he hadn't noticed the huge man. Patch struck him once more, causing a trickle of blood to run from his nose.

The godslayer struck with his remaining blades, piercing the patchwork man, then twisting the swords with a growl.

Patch's torso came free of his legs. He fell forward, locking his hands around the godslayer's neck as his legs stumbled away.

The godslayer began to spin around, hacking at Patch's arms. On his third rotation, Patch's torso and left arm flew free, leaving only his right hand around the godslayer's neck.

By then Infidel reached the godslayer.

She used her momentum to slide forward, between the godslayer's legs. As she passed, she grabbed his manhood with both hands. She stood suddenly, yanking with all her might, and the four-armed devil fell forward.

Infidel released her grip on the godslayer's member and drew a sword in one hand, a dagger in the other. As the godslayer hit the ground, she struck, drawing each blade across the creature's hamstrings. The godslayer rolled to his back, his legs useless as he raised himself on two arms. He still carried a sword in each of his free hands, and used these to strike at Infidel, the blades flashing in silvery arcs.

Infidel easily avoided the blows, then leapt forward, dropping her dagger, thrusting her sword with both hands into the godslayer's throat. She used her momentum to vault over the creature, as the tip of her blade dug ever deeper, nearly twisting his neck from his body.

The godslayer fell limp, a bubble of red blood rising from his lips. Infidel kicked at his head, then kicked again, and again. The head tore free, rolling across the floor to where Magidance had fallen, but the mage was now nowhere to be seen.

Infidel snickered, wiping her mouth. "Heh heh heh."

She walked to Tristrum. He was alive, still conscious, but his life seeped between his fingers with each heartbeat.

Infidel knelt over him.

"Hey," she said, touching his cheek. "The name Isadora mean anything to you?"

Tristrum stared at her, his eyes wide with confusion.

"No?" she said. "Hell, why should it?"

Then Tristrum stiffened. He whispered, "The girl . . ."

"I've hated you for so long," she said, her voice trembling. "So do I kill you now? Or do I sit and watch the life drain from you? What will give me the most satisfaction?"

She never made the decision. A roar rumbled through the chamber. Infidel vanished in a rolling wall of flame. Bigsby felt himself pushed from his feet by an unseen hand. The weight of a man fell upon him, as fire roared above his head. Strangely, he felt no heat. Indeed, he felt as if he'd been plunged into ice water.

"Remain silent," Magidance whispered, unseen. The weight rolled from Bigsby's chest.

As the flames receded, Bigsby could see the smoldering remains of Infidel, her bones still kneeling over the blackened corpse of Tristrum. Stranger alone survived, standing calmly as his robes burned.

From the chamber beyond came Greatshadow.

Bigsby wet himself.

The dragon was impossibly large, having to crouch in order to slither into the enormous room. Greatshadow's skin was black with soot. The stench of sulfur filled the air. The dragon spoke, in a language Bigsby had never heard, yet understood instantly.

"Bold fool," Greatshadow growled, drawing his head near Stranger. "Do you know what you've cost me? Centuries. Three centuries of incantations are needed to enslave a godslayer. I'm pleased you survived. Your crime deserves a long, painful punishment."

Stranger pulled away the last of his charred rags and padding. He stood revealed, a dragon seven feet long from snout to tail, with a red scaly hide and a pair of wings upon his back, one twisted at an unnatural angle.

"You made my life a long, painful punishment," Stranger said. "From the day you plucked me from my mother's womb and threw me still wet into the gorge."

"Bigsby," Magidance whispered. Bigsby glanced over his shoulder to see the wizard, Frostbite in his grasp. "We can still snatch victory from the jaws of defeat. This land shall belong to the Silver Kingdom. Our fate rests in your hands."

Magidance held the enchanted blade toward him.

"Take this. While Stranger distracts Greatshadow, you must strike swiftly."

"But—"

"There is no time for debate," Magidance said. "I have transferred my invisibility and can hide you as you approach. You must do this, Bigsby."

"But—"

"Hurry. At this distance, dragons read thoughts. Shielding our minds weakens me with each second. Hurry!"

Bigsby took the sword. Instantly, he realized Magidance was right. The sword filled him with power, gave him strength and courage. *A single blow*, it whispered to him, *and I will rob Greatshadow of his fire.*

Bigsby stalked forward, the sword gripped in both hands.

"You amuse me, little Brokenwing," Greatshadow said. He pushed Stranger to the ground and pinned him with a single claw. Stranger kicked and bit, to no avail.

Bigsby reached Greatshadow. The dragon crouched in such a way that Bigsby could strike at the beast's throat just above the chest.

The sword whispered to him, filling him with cold resolve. *Let me freeze his blood,* the sword mind-whispered. *Let us liberate the land from his fiery rule.*

Bigsby looked at Infidel's crouching corpse. Dark fumes billowed in her rib cage, swirling like a heart of smoke. Briefly, a thought flickered through his mind that this had been a death she would have approved of, a better fate than dying on the gallows in some distant land for the crime of striking a holy man.

Bigsby suddenly realized the magnitude of the action he was about to commit. He dropped the sword, and cried out, "Greatshadow!"

Across the room, Magidance toppled to the ground, unable to shield Bigsby further.

The enormous dragon snaked its head around. Now that he no longer held Frostbite, Bigsby could feel the furnace-like heat of Greatshadow's breath.

Greatshadow stared right through him.

"Hmmm," Greatshadow said. "Perhaps that blade could have killed me. You believed it would, at least."

"Take it," Bigsby said. "Destroy it. It's the only threat you face. All I ask is that you allow us to leave."

"You are in no position to ask anything of me," the dragon said.

"No," Bigsby said.

"But you don't have enough meat on you to be worth eating," said Greatshadow. "Go. Take this failure with you."

He rolled Stranger over on his belly, and twisted the disfigured wing, breaking the bones with a sickening snap. Stranger squealed. Greatshadow flicked his claw, sending the small dragon skidding.

"Little Brokenwing," Greatshadow growled. "A life of pain awaits you, if you flee this island. But should you choose to remain here beyond the dawn of the third day, I will find you, and grant you swift death."

Bigsby ran to help Stranger stand.

"Yes, Father," the young dragon said between gasps of pain as he rose.

Bigsby helped support Stranger as they limped from the ancient temple. On the steps, drenched in sweat, Magidance waited.

"Well, that was just great." He spat in Bigsby's direction. "We were so close, and you chickened out."

"I found my courage," Bigsby said. "I won't ask you to understand my reasons. Now, will you help me? We have three days to get Stranger off this island."

"Not Stranger," the small dragon said. "He gave me my name. I am Brokenwing."

Magidance looked the dragon over.

"Hmm," he said, gently touching the damaged wing.

Brokenwing winced.

"I think I can set this to heal properly," Magidance said. "And I know places to hide you until you grow stronger."

"You would help me?" Brokenwing asked.

"How many chances will I get to study a live dragon up close? We'll never make it back to Commonground in three days, though."

"We can make it to the Red River by nightfall," Brokenwing said. "We can build a raft and let it carry us to the sea."

"What about the men we left in camp?"

"They're too far away to reach and still make it. They're on their own," Brokenwing said.

Magidance scratched his chin. "Ah, what the hell. It's not like any of them owe me money."

Night found them on the Red River, afloat on a crude raft. The moon turned the water to a silvery sheet as smooth and gleaming as the floor of Greatshadow's lair. Bigsby was skeptical that the raft would survive the night, given the haste with which they'd assembled it. But, even with his concerns, he couldn't keep his eyes open. He stretched out beside Brokenwing, who was already sleeping, as Magidance stood over them, using a long stout pole to move the raft around obstacles.

"So, try me," Magidance said. "I'm dying to hear."

"What?" Bigsby asked, drowsily.

"Your reasons. Why didn't you kill him?"

"Greatshadow keeps this land wild. When he falls, this place will be overrun with farms and churches and men like Tristrum."

Magidance nodded. "That *was* the plan."

"It wasn't my plan," Bigsby said. "I like this place as it is, untamed and untamable. I think the world still needs a place where the wicked can hide from the righteous."

Magidance raised an eyebrow. "Damn," he said. "That's not a bad reason at all."

Magic's Choice

R. W. Day

Conn first saw the lady when he was five years old, on the day they came to break his arm. He was seated at his writing table, as close to the fire as it was possible to get, for it was dark winter and perilously cold. His hands clenched around the stylus as he laboriously practiced carving letters into the wax of his practice tablet when he realized that Brother Bernard was gone. An unfamiliar brother leaned against the wall, blue hood pulled so far forward that Conn could not see his face. He put the stylus down, scraped back the chair against the harsh stone floor, but before he could even voice a question, four burly demi-brothers took hold of him. One on each limb, they carried him through the labyrinth of corridors that made up the Schola di San Iuxta Major.

Panic rose like pond water in a hard rain, but he fought it down, for struggle was futile. Conn allowed himself to be taken without protest, silently mouthing the Rules of Submission as Brother Bernard had taught him, though with his eyes improperly open, for even through the fear, Conn was curious about the rest of the schola, the parts forbidden to him. Through tunnels and along corridors, rising and falling on spiral stairs, they bore him far from the rooms and small gardens he called home, up and up into a high tower room with walls hung with tapestries depicting ancient battles. A high altar to Bonassus covered with the rotting remains of fruit offerings stood waiting under a narrow slit of a window set high in the tower wall.

They bound Conn to an oak table in the center of the room, and when the demi-brothers backed away, Conn saw her. He'd never before seen a lady, for the schola was a world of men, even down to the cooks and launderers, so Conn stared with frank curiosity as she sat calmly on a great bench off to the side of the altar. She was not what he had been led to expect from the old tales and ballads.

Those ladies were young and lovely, dressed in gowns with full skirts and flowing sleeves, but this one was old, older even than Brother Bernard, and she wore armor. Her iron-grey hair was pulled back into a tight knot with frizzy tendrils escaping on the sides. Her face was severe, almost dour, but something in her expression as she stood and approached him reminded Conn of the look that Brother Bernard gave when Conn had mastered the Five Rules or identified a particularly challenging herb. Approval.

"He's not afraid. Surrounded by strangers, ripped from his only known home and he's curious, not afraid." The lady stepped back, and her expression changed to distaste, as though she'd walked in something nasty in the cattleyard. Two men, one tall, one shorter, both garbed in iron-grey woolen cloaks stepped out of the shadows to surround him. Conn's stomach clenched as he recognized them from his readings as greycloaks, wielders of magic.

"His fear or lack thereof is irrelevant, Excellency," the taller one said. This one was missing an eye, and the bare socket seemed to be searching Conn out, peering into his soul; a shiver passed over him.

"Three inches up the right forearm, straight, not spiral," the other greycloak said in a detached, almost bored voice. The demi-brothers swarmed back over him, holding him down, which Conn thought unnecessary considering the ties, until the strange brother grasped hold of his right arm and his world exploded in pain.

It took two months before his arm completely healed, and he would bear the mark of the break for the rest of his life. That was how it began.

The child Malen stirred restlessly in her sleep, wrapping the worn furs tightly around her as the wind blew through chinks in the hut and snow piled unmercifully on the thatched roof. Her body, small even for her four years, twitched and jerked like a puppet on a string as the dream took her into pain that was not her own. Shrieks drawn from her throat ripped her into wakefulness. She wanted her mother, but feared to set her father off again. He was always berating her mother for bearing a useless daughter, a fey child who dreamed futile dreams like she was some kind of greycloak, not a strong son to farm by his side. Even if she were to call, her mother would not come, would not dare cross her father.

So Malen quieted on her own, breathing slowly and regularly so as to deceive her parents into thinking she slept. Though her eyes were open and fixed on the carefully banked fire, she did not see the fire, nor the rough hut, heard neither the snores of her father nor the snuffling of the sheep and cow from their corner. She saw instead a thin-faced boy with hair the color of ripe chestnuts, heard his piercing screams of rage and pain.

Conn saw the lady again when he was eight, and this time, when the demis came for him, he abandoned any pretense of submission and fought as hard as he could, kicking and biting and hitting, but it did no good. The cut they sliced on his left thigh was deep, deep and long enough to require a hospitaller brother to have to stitch it up while the lady watched, her lined face impassive.

"Thirteen stitches, evenly spaced," the half-blind greycloak said to the hospitaller.

Conn held every muscle tight, trying not to cry, trying to be brave as the needle pierced his skin and the thread tore through him, imagining himself as Andreu the Great when he'd been tortured by Nuria. But Andreu had been a grown man of five and thirty and the son of a king, and Conn was eight and the son of nobody, so the tears leaked from his eyes as rain leaked from the roof of the cow stable in spring. After it was over and he was back in his own rooms, he asked Brother Bernard one of the forbidden questions.

"Why? Why do they do this to me?"

Brother Bernard was stooped over the hearth, stirring a potion in a small cauldron suspended over the fire. Even through the thick woad-dyed wool of his robe, Conn could see the brother's back stiffen, his shoulders set.

"And don't lie."

Brother Bernard straightened, holding a clay vessel with steam rising from it. "Drink this. It will make you feel better."

Conn took it, letting the warmth of the liquid filter through the clay into his hands, sipping at the honey-sweet medicine.

Brother Bernard sat beside Conn's bed on a three-legged stool, stroking his hair as the boy sank back into the straw mattress. "I never lie to you. I speak only truth, or keep silent. I can't give you the answers you want; I'm bound by my vows to be in submission to those in authority over me. You should bind yourself to the Rules as well. Submission may be the only thing that brings you a modicum of peace in this life, my boy."

Brother Bernard had not been looking at Conn as he'd spoken, had instead been staring down at his fingers which were working the patterns of prayer almost subconsciously. The Rules of Submission governed every aspect of the schola, but Conn was not to be a brother—he couldn't, he hadn't the lineage. He had no lineage, no name even, for Conn was not a name, just a word. *Unknown*. His breath caught sharply. "If you could tell me, if you weren't bound by the Rules, would you?"

Now Bernard met his eyes. "That's a very perspicacious question. No, I would not, for the knowledge would bring you neither peace nor certainty. Trust in those set above you, submit to authority and when these things," and he gestured to Conn's leg which still throbbed like the beat of the great drum that tolled the hours of meditation, "when these things happen to you, try to consider it just a dream."

The medicine must have contained something to make him sleep, for at the word "dream," as though by the magic of a greycloak, he plunged into sleep and a dream so vivid, surely it was real.

A girl on a mountaintop, running, bare feet against grass, and Conn felt every blade slapping against her legs, heard the songs of strange mountain birds, smelled air thin and fresh, so different from his lowland home. Strange thoughts and feelings darted through his mind like nothing he'd ever known in his life.

The feeling, he realized, as he moved from dream-state to waking, was freedom.

As the days passed with mind-stilting sameness, Conn did come to think of the tortures the greycloaks and the lady had wrought upon him as a dream, or rather a nightmare. He pushed it aside, embracing the dream of someday breaking free from the schola and living in the outside world. From his reading and his few conversations with the younger demis with whom he often worked, he knew that some children as young as eight or nine were apprenticed or fostered out to learn trades, or trained to fight so that they might one day serve in the King of Marjehar's army.

But by ten, Conn was still studying and reading, still copying texts in a careful hand for a library he had never been permitted to enter, still tending to the cows, weeding the herb beds, harvesting summer vegetables in the small gardens, but never working with the demis in the main fields close to the village, never even seeing the village itself.

By eleven, when boys chosen for the schola would make first vows, living communally in the high-towered dormitories, Conn still had never seen another child save in dreams, the dreams of the mountain girl which continued to come with regularity, offering him a glimpse of a life he could otherwise barely imagine. He learned to welcome sleep, to seek the dreams as the only release from a life that, despite Brother Bernard's best efforts, felt like a too-tight tunic that made it hard to breathe.

So all through his twelfth and thirteenth years, Conn dreamed the life of the girl. In the dreams, he splashed barefoot across clear streams full of flat stones, water rushing over his ankles. He climbed trees, the pungent smell of pinesap overwhelming him, needles scratching his arms raw as he carefully selected his footing. In the dreams too, he worked as he never worked in life, scratching out rough furrows with an iron hoe, planting and nurturing and harvesting wheat. And in some of the best of the dreams, he was aware that the body he occupied was not male but female, and with some small degree of lucid dreaming, he'd raise his hands to cup budding breasts, then suddenly come awake, very much a thirteen-year-old boy.

It was high summer when the dreams came to an end.

He had been set to cleaning out the loft above the cow stable, so that Demi Goren could haul it away and make room for the hay harvest soon to be gathered. In the very back of the loft, far under the eaves where the hay had rotted down to a glutinous, stinking mess, Conn's shovel hit something hard.

He dropped the tool and dug through the muck to find a small bundle, wrapped in cracked leather that broke apart when Conn unfolded it. Within the leather rested a small book, crudely stitched up the spine with gut, pages yellow, but on the first page, unmistakably, his own name.

I, Conn, start this book on this first day past the Equinox, because I wish to know who I am.

His name, words he could well have written, but not in his hand. This writing was old, in a style he'd seen many times in manuscripts of a hundred years ago. They'd taught a more formal hand then.

Brother Bernard, he knew, would not answer his questions, would confiscate the journal as soon as he saw it, so Conn slipped the book into the pocket of his robe and descended the ladder. "Demi Goren?"

The hunchbacked old man, who was stroking the flank of an old cow, looked up quizzically.

"Am I the first boy called Conn who has lived here?"

"Take your questions to Brother Bernard, lad." The demis rarely spoke; in that, they were like the silent brothers who gave over their voices to Bonassus in exchange for wisdom. But Conn was not to be put off and continued to ask and ask, his voice growing higher and more frantic as he waved the journal about, trying to show the old man what he'd found while the old demi stubbornly kept to the Rule, never losing patience. Conn was practically shouting when Brother Bernard hurried into the barn.

He'd whisked the journal from Conn's hand without a word, then dragged the boy by the arm back to his room. For the first time, Brother

Bernard seemed truly angry, though the man fought to hide it, anger being a venial violation of the Rules.

"The demi-brothers are not put here to amuse you or entertain you or answer your impertinent questions."

"I deserve to know who I am! That book," he pointed to the journal, "was written by someone called Conn. How many more Conns have there been? What do you keep me here for? I want to know about the world, about work, about women—"

"All you need to know about the world beyond these walls is in the texts I set for you. The outside world is cruel, and women are the cruelest part of it and have no place in the life of a sworn brother—"

"I'm not going to be a brother, I can't be a brother," Conn shouted. "I'm not good enough to be a brother, or a soldier. I'm not even worthy of being apprenticed in trade, or even to muck out the horse stables or clean out the library. Why do you keep me here? If women are so evil, then, do you want to make me your catamite?" Conn didn't know exactly what the word meant, but he knew it was bad. He'd heard some of the young brothers use it about two of their number who'd been caught, doing something nobody would talk about.

Brother Bernard's hand flashed out, catching Conn across the mouth. He tasted blood as the brother's ring of dedication sliced his lip. Conn shook, not from the pain, but from shock, for apart from those two times with the greycloaks, he had never bled, never experienced real pain, had in fact been prohibited from any activity which might lead to injury, wrapped in wool like a piece of fine Dalmutian tableware.

Brother Bernard's face turned deathly pale and all anger drained from his eyes. "Forgive me," he whispered. "Oh, please forgive me."

Without waiting for Conn to forgive or not—if it was even Conn he'd been talking to—Bernard tended to the cut, wiping the blood from Conn's mouth with a damp cloth. "It's slight. Oh, thank Bonassus."

"It hurts." His mouth felt swollen, his teeth loose.

"Yes, keep the cool cloth against it and it will pass. Conn, I apologize. I should know better than to let the words of a thirteen-year-old child stir me so. I am confining myself to my room to copy and recite the Rules, and you should do likewise." He sighed, touching Conn's hair. "I understand that this life is hard. There's meaning behind your suffering, I swear it, and a destiny of sorts, but you must be patient. Embrace the Second Law, '*the path to true submission lies through patience, fortitude the jewel in the crown of obedience.*' Copy it and its exegesis, and pray for enlightenment."

So Conn copied and read and prayed, but his small windowless room grew increasingly close and stuffy with the remains of the breakfast fire slowly smoking. The exegesis on the Second Rule was written by the dullest brothers in the history of the schola, so as the candle burned down the hours, Conn's fingers loosened around the quill, his eyes closed and he dreamed one of the girl-dreams where he sat.

But it was somehow more intense, sharper than normal. The mountain air felt cool to Conn, but warm to the girl whose mind he shared. She was lying beside a field of corn, heavy stalks bowing beneath the weight of the grain. She was supposed to be harvesting, but her basket lay abandoned at her side, half full, and she sipped from a skin of something cold and delicious, water with some tart flavor added.

The snorting of horses and the sound of hooves churning up the ground brought the girl to her feet. The sight of the man who dismounted and approached the girl jerked Conn out of her consciousness and took him back to a high tower room and a knife and a needle. *Run!* he tried to warn her, for the man was a greycloak.

But no, the cloak this man wore had subtle variations in color and weave, was crudely fashioned the way a true greycloak's would never be. And he was speaking low, reassuring words about her parents and a great house in Porta Guernau. Then without word or warning, hands tore at the girl, men's heavy bodies forced her down into sweet grass; an iron gouge descended, then white-hot agony pierced their shared eye. Conn's heart exploded in a frantic tattoo and screams ripped from his throat as he fell forward, ink spilling over text and tablet and table, black-pooled blood congealing on the floor.

He awoke in his bed, covered by a light summer blanket. Brother Bernard sat at his side, the marks of worry on his face.

"I dreamed," Conn said, and his throat hurt to speak or swallow. "A girl, I've dreamed her before. She was free, so free, and they hurt her." It was not enough, no words could truly express what the unknown dream girl had meant to him, nor the pain, which far exceeded anything the greycloaks had inflicted.

"You see," Bernard whispered. "Freedom leads to pain. Forget freedom—it's an illusion, a deception. Submit. Obey. Do not question your fate or seek answers in dreams like a greycloak. Trust me, Conn."

"Why should I?" His voice was crow-harsh, though all his anger had drained away.

"Because I love you, my son." Brother Bernard rose and left without speaking further, leaving those words lying in Conn's stomach like lead, the first time in all his life that he'd heard them.

Ermessen was weary down to the bone, and this journey was only making her old bones ache even more. Her age was starting to catch up with her. After forty years in armor, forty years living from camp to camp, fighting battles first for her brother and now her nephew, she'd about come to her limit. But she couldn't give up, couldn't stop. Not yet.

"Excellency, we're within ten minutes' ride of the schola." Berenger reined in his horse. He was such a handsome man, golden hair barely holding a hint of grey, body with no trace of excess weight, so splendid in his polished armor. The perfect knight from the moment the first wooden sword was placed in his tiny hand. Born to command, whereas she had been forced to fight for every honor, to be just as strong and twice as fast as any man.

"I've made this ride more times than I care to recall, Berenger. I know to the second how far we are from the schola." The boy would be fourteen, almost fifteen now. What was he like, what kind of man was he becoming? She would speak to Bernard alone, for his letters had revealed nothing of consequence, and she needed more than bland and innocuous accounts of days spent at study. Thoughts, heretical and treasonous thoughts, had plagued her of late.

"It pains you, this task?"

She turned, startled that he'd seen it. "Of course. I'm a soldier, not a sadist."

They slowed their horses, and behind them the great train of horsemen and the wagons slowed as well. "Nor am I. But it's the law, the only way our kind can rule over their kind," he nodded backwards to the wagons where the greycloaks rode, "without continual war and bloodshed."

Ermessen laughed. "In what lands do you dwell? I've been at war all my life, first in Ardreba, then pacifying, well, attempting to pacify Mendiko Battar—"

"Mendi Province."

"Mendi Province, if you will, then. War is a constant, bloodshed a way of life, and that is exactly what the magi want."

"How do you mean, Excellency?"

"If we're continually at war, we have no time to think about how much power they've accumulated, despite their relatively small numbers. The Mage-Kings were created to control the magi. Look around you, Berenger. You've lived at court your entire life. Look at my nephew, look at his heir. Imagine Prince Gombal ruling over the magi. Who will rule, and who will be the ruled, I ask you?"

She spurred her horse forward, for she'd said too much. Berenger was in oath-submission to King Arnaud and his heir, as was Ermessen herself. But as a daughter of kings, descendant of Andreu the Great and Gombal the Conqueror, she was bound by older oaths and promises, and perhaps this boy in the schola would be the means by which she could keep them.

"The very image," she whispered as she stood above the sleeping boy. No, boy no longer, for the first signs of manhood shadowed his upper lip, his round face taking on mature planes and angles.

"As it must be." The magi's voice was too loud and Conn stirred. Ermessen did not know this one; he was young, not yet thirty, and when she'd offered her hand, he had taken it with his left, for his right was nothing save for a stump. Accustomed to honest battle wounds, the mutilations of the greycloaks disturbed and offended her.

"Magister, you will address me with the proper forms," she said coldly.

"Yes, Excellency." He carefully lowered his eyes, but Ermessen didn't need to see them to read his hatred. She led him through the low door, out into the corridor where Brother Bernard waited, his eyes fixed nervously on the hulking blacksmith they'd brought from the village.

"Is this truly necessary?" Brother Bernard grabbed hold of Ermessen's shoulder in a forward manner that should have earned a reprimand, but she knew he was moved by love and concern. Much could be forgiven in the name of love. But before she could reply, a cold voice blew down the long hall.

"Of course. You know the law, Brother. Perhaps your proximity to the child has softened you. Ermessen, we might wish to consider relieving the brother of his responsibility." On the second Mendian campaign, Ermessen and five of her knights had been trapped on a plateau in the midst of the Dawn Range. The wind from the north, flooding down from the heights of Mount Hasi had near frozen them to death. The voice of Ferrer, High Magi, was like that wind.

"I'm sure Brother Bernard understands the necessity of what we do." She reached into the pocket of her jerkin, pushed a vial into Brother Bernard's hand. "Give him this in wine, it will dull the pain some."

Abbot Calvet shoved past the magi, desperately trying, she thought, to assert his authority. "We have no wine here, General. The boy is strong. He has been trained in the paths of submission, and he will not require the Draught of Abyss."

Obedience and submission or no, Ermessen noticed that Brother Bernard did not surrender the vial. Ignoring the abbot, she snapped her finger, and Taron, one of her newer squires, a likely lad with hair the color of fire, was immediately at her side. "In my left saddlebag there's a small skin of Ardreban White. Fetch it and bring it to Brother Bernard at once. Gentlemen, I believe the tower room awaits us."

Giving them no alternative, she swept out, carrying blacksmith and brothers and magi and knights in her wake, leaving Brother Bernard to do what he could to prepare the boy. Somehow, in the past few minutes, she had made a choice, a watershed had been reached, a bridge crossed. Abbot Calvet had said it. *The boy is strong.* He would have to be. Half a millennia of tradition walked with her up the spiral stairs to the Chamber of the Sacrifice; five hundred years of pain, soul-destroying murder and a dynasty built on blood. Her dynasty, and her blood when it came down to it, so it was for Ermessen to end it, with this Conn's help, if Disme Battle-brand willed it.

Brother Bernard brought the boy in unconscious, counter to all tradition—and counter to tradition and Abbot Calvet's orders, he stayed in the tower. He would do penance for his disobedience when this was done, but from the moment the message came, spelling out what would have to be done, he had determined on this course and he'd hold to it come storm or snow or sunshine. For too many years he'd straddled the fence, one foot firmly on the path of submission, one standing with the Lady Ermessen, but now his path was clear. What they did here, with Conn, with those who had come before him, it violated every precept of the schola's oath, which affirmed life and its value. He'd first come to doubt what his superiors called divine purpose twenty years ago when, still a young brother, he'd been forced to witness the accession of Arnaud III.

Lady Ermessen had seen him there, had taken note of the distaste and horror on his face, and she'd sought him out, encouraged him to question these traditions. In the intervening years, Bernard had studied, searching for answers deep within the library, and what he'd found disturbed him nearly as much as the fate of the boys. He'd been taught from the day he was eleven that the Rules of Submission were set down by Bonassus, dictated through Brother Iuxta Mayor, before the walls of the schola bearing his name were even glints in a mason's eye.

But almost two years ago, Bernard had been in the Records Hall attempting to decipher a crumbling scroll, an innocuous document relating the history of Gombal the Conqueror. He found a smaller document tucked within it, older by far, but better preserved, and it spoke of a time before the Rules. Of the institution of the Rule as a means of controlling the scholas so that they might serve the Mage-Kings. So that *he* and such as he might play their parts in the Sacrifice of the Succession. Not two thousand years old, but a mere five hundred, and not holy writ at all. His foundation crumbled, leaving him with one certainty. Conn. And now, with Lady Ermessen here, Bernard knew it was time to tell the boy the truth. Let him choose a path for himself, not submit blindly to what was chosen for him.

The smith's raucous laughter as he told some off-color joke about the size of his hammer brought Bernard back to the moment. He brushed the sleeping boy's hair, whispering an unheard apology. Then he backed away. He should leave, should not be here in the first place, but he glanced at Lady Ermessen, not his abbot, for permission, and she granted it with a nod.

She snarled at the greycloak, Ferrer. "Get this over with."

"Yes, quite. Smith, you'll need to remove the right lower molar and the tooth next furthest out."

"Pay first," the man said, and the other greycloak pushed a bag of gold into his hand. Satisfied, the smith bent to his work. Seeing the wicked pliers, Bernard turned away and stifled his ears, unable to watch, unwilling to hear the cries that even the draught could not silence. He watched Lady Ermessen instead, whose eyes were fixed unflinching upon Conn, as the smith did his work. But Bernard noticed, as he turned away, that her wind-roughened cheeks were wet with tears.

Conn woke from troubled dreams, dream-memories of the lady and the greycloaks, of the girl and of pain, hers and his own, to find that his jaw ached with an intensity he'd never imagined. It hit him as though he'd slammed against a wall, sending him retching over the side of his bed into a bucket that someone had placed there. Blood mixed with vomit, and his tongue probed the inside of his mouth, finding gaps where once there had been teeth.

"Why?" he whispered, wrenching the light blanket into knots as he fought the pain. "Why?" For he knew that parts of the ragged dream were memories, and they'd been at him again.

"Do you really want to know?" The lady sat on Brother Bernard's stool, legs encased in worn leather boots crossed in front of her, arms folded over her chest.

"Yes." It hurt to talk, hurt to move his jaw, but it was worth it if someone would finally give him answers.

She stood. "I am Ermessen Andrianeu, Conn. I lead the armies of King Arnaud III, and I am his aunt. If you want answers, I'll give them to you, but not here. Are you able to stand?"

Conn struggled to his feet. Yes, he could stand. To get answers, he could run or fly if it came to it. He followed the lady out into the corridor, which was lined with armored men. She paused in front of one, a short, bearded man wearing a fierce expression. "No one comes down this corridor till I say, do you understand me? Not Abbot Calvet, not either of the greycloaks, nobody."

"As you command, Excellency."

The lady led him to the end of the corridor and out the door into the small garden, now harvested and ready for fall, through the postern gate which Conn had never touched, for it was forbidden to him, and out into the orchard. Conn stared into the field of gnarled apple trees and beyond to the forest, and beyond that where distant hills rose up to become mountains. Never in his waking life had he seen beyond walls. He forgot even the pain of his missing teeth.

"Sit." The lady sat on a bench under a huge old tree. Apples had fallen around it, some half rotted, and the smell was divine, was freedom. She picked a ripe apple from the tree and started cutting into it with a wicked-looking knife. "I'd offer you an apple, but I doubt you could stand to chew it just now. I want to tell you a story, Conn, if you have the patience to listen."

Patience. Brother Bernard had spent years drilling patience into him, though not so much over the last two years. It suddenly came over him that the old brother had not quoted the Rules at him for a good long time. "Yes. I can listen."

"Once upon a time," she said with a wry smile. "That's how stories are supposed to start, as I understand. You will have to forgive my ignorance, as I have no children. Once upon a time about five hundred years ago, there was a king of Dalmu called Andreu. At that time, Marjehar was ruled by a magi called Nuria."

"I know this story," Conn said. "Nuria was so evil that even the other greycloaks hated her, so they invited the King of Dalmu to come and reign in her place."

"You've studied history," the lady said. "That's good, it will help. Though the truth is somewhat different from how they sing it in the ballads, that is essentially correct. The other greycloaks—you do know that that term is offensive to them?"

"Yes," Conn said, uncertain of whether she was reprimanding him, and not caring.

"Good." She smiled grimly. "In any case, Nuria commanded a large force; she had many knights in fealty to her, many men at arms under her command in addition of course to her formidable magical power." She paused and bit into the apple. "Conn, what do you know about the greycloaks?"

"They work magic. They come and hurt me. Along with you."

"Well struck. I regret my role in any pain you have experienced and hope you will understand once I have finished why it was necessary. If you see a greycloak, and I have seen dozens of them, you'll notice that they're never whole. Always lame or missing a limb or an eye, or dumb because their tongue's been hacked out, or half-deaf because their ears are gone. Brother Bernard could likely explain the theory of it; it relates somehow to the schola's teaching that by forgoing a sense, the others become stronger, deepening awareness and opening paths to magic, but what the brothers do temporarily, the greycloaks make permanent."

"I don't understand. I know there are brothers who vow silence or who will not walk or who go blindfolded. Brother Bernard says it's got to do with meditation and being closer to the gods."

"Yes. Meditation is a form of magic. Anyone can work magic, Conn, if they're willing to pay the price. You will not know this, being raised in isolation, but village girls work love spells by cutting off their hair, or perform minor curses by opening light cuts in their palms. Those are small magics; they come and go, and the working of them exhausts the maker so that few do much of that sort of thing. But the high magic requires a deeper sacrifice, so to become a greycloak—"

"They mutilate themselves." A sudden thought occurred to him. "Or others?"

"Yes. And no. You cannot gain power through the sacrifice of another. It must be of yourself, your own body, your own soul. The things done to you have not been to gift magic upon anyone. At least not as such. Let me finish." She glanced back at the postern gate and up to the sun, which was sinking into the western hills. "We've not much time. Magic has limits, it isn't the all powerful force you might think, so very few people will undertake to gouge out their own eyes or cut off their own hands—the commitment must be absolute, the desire pure. Andreu was able to defeat Nuria through a series of what the histories call clever maneuvers, but what we'd likely see as cheating today. He did not fight fair, because a man cannot defeat a mage in a fair fight. Andreu killed Nuria and was crowned king, but the dilemma was that a non-magical king could not hope to rule over magic folk."

"So did Andreu maim himself?"

She shook her head. "No. Ancient tradition of both Dalmu and Marjehar dictates that a king must be whole. No mutilated man may ascend to the throne. By maiming himself, Andreu might have secured the loyalty and cooperation of the greycloaks, but he'd have lost the respect of his nobility and people, and no amount of magic could make up for that."

The orchard suddenly came to life as heavy drumbeats resounded, sending flights of birds winging off towards the hills. General Ermessen cursed. "The brothers will be going to prayers, and after that, we must leave. Listen closely. Andreu was safe, he'd earned his throne and had the cooperation of the remaining greycloaks, but he worried for his heirs. What followed was either a remarkable coincidence or the work of the gods, take your pick. Andreu's queen bore him twin sons. Two boys, as alike as two drops of rain, sharing one soul between them as twins do. The greycloaks immediately saw the possibilities. When Andreu's chosen heir, who became Gombal the Conqueror, came to his throne, he was commanded by the greycloaks to kill his brother, to slay the other half of himself, and desiring power above all things, he obeyed. The theory was that such a sacrifice would be sufficient to imbue Gombal with magic, and it worked."

The birds were settling in the trees again, some lighting onto the orchard floor to peck at the insects there. Conn stood, moving closer to watch their tiny movements. "But how could they know that every queen would have twins . . . oh. Magic."

"Yes. Spells are worked and every heir to Andreu's throne since has been one of a set of twins. One boy is chosen as heir, one as sacrifice. Because for most, it is pain beyond belief to sacrifice a beloved brother, the boys are raised apart. They are absolute images of each other."

"But as they grow up, wouldn't things happen to change the likeness, you know, scars and . . ." Suspicion, like a seed, opened and grew within his belly.

The lady stood, turning away from Conn. "When he was five years old, my grand-nephew who will one day be Gombal VII, broke his right arm falling from his pony. When he was eight, a sword cut on his thigh left him with a wound that took thirteen stitches to close. Two weeks ago, at practice in the jousting yard, the quintain slammed into his face and knocked out two of his teeth." She turned to face him. "Do you understand now?"

It clicked, falling into place like tumblers in a lock. As though the wind had been knocked out of him, Conn staggered backwards onto the bench, the pain tearing into his jaw anew, pain that had been inflicted to ensure he stayed the image of a brother he had never known he had. "No, oh, no. There has to be a way out of this! I'll cut myself, hurt myself in some way to break the image."

"The brothers will not allow that. Surely you've noticed you are carefully kept from all harm?"

"I don't want to die," he whispered.

"Nor do I want you to. I didn't tell you all this to dishearten you, Conn. I've watched two others of your name slaughtered in that tower room, once when my brother took the throne and again for my nephew. I've no mind to see it again, and with your help, I won't. Will you work with me to stop this evil tradition and bring an end to the Mage-Kings?"

"I will." There was no question, not really. "Tell me what to do."

The closing drum echoed, and in the distance, Conn heard the jingle of horses being saddled, men's voices raised. Lady Ermessen—his aunt, he had an aunt, a family of sorts—heard them too. "It's time for me to leave. I will send someone to teach you the art of the sword. You're old for a beginner, but if you have the will, you can learn. Trust only Brother Bernard; he's my man and will guide you well. The king is young, there's no reason why he shouldn't reign for another twenty years or more, so we have time to prepare."

The short fierce man came striding across the long grass towards them. "Excellency, the abbot became enraged when we forbid him the boy's rooms. He's gone for Magister Ferrer and Duke Berenger."

"Go ready my horse, we leave immediately." She took Conn's shoulders in her strong grip. "I know you're sick of hearing of obedience, but now it's more essential than ever. Let no one save Bernard know what you know, co-operate with the abbot in all things, do not draw attention to yourself. I will be in touch as I can, but I have work to do as well, an army to raise. The grey-cloaks may have magic, but they are few, and we are many. Don't lose heart."

"I won't." He stood tall, trying to put on the bearing of a prince, warping his face into a mask of arrogance such as he imagined a prince might wear. It felt wrong; regardless of who his father was, he was still just Conn. Funny, he'd always thought knowing who he was would matter, but it didn't really. He smiled shyly at her. "Thank you for your honesty, Aunt. If I can presume to call you that."

She smiled back at him. "It's amazing, one minute you are the image of Gombal, and the next so utterly unlike him as it is possible to be. Between us, Conn King's Son, we might just remake our world."

"Your move." Ermessen leaned back from the carved ivory game pieces as Berenger studied the board. He'd grown old of late, looking almost as old as she, though she had twenty years on him easily. "So how fared our prince on his first campaign?"

"Oh, you know how it is with the Mendians, a few minor skirmishes and a lot of sniping. Got so we couldn't make camp anywhere that wasn't densely forested or we'd wake to find twenty men riddled with arrows." He'd sidestepped her question.

"They're ferocious warriors, no question." Perrando, the swordsmaster she'd sent to Conn was Mendian, though she could hardly say that to Berenger. "But my grand-nephew spoke of a great battle, at the Ford of Karaan?"

"Oh, that. We surprised a party of peasants, two of them had swords they'd scavenged from somewhere and His Highness took it upon himself to relieve them of their burdens." Berenger moved his knight.

"And their lives?" Her king was threatened. How appropriate.

"As you say." Berenger stood abruptly, walked across to the wide tower window. Carrying the king piece with her, Ermessen joined him, watching the street scene: knights in half-armor celebrating their return, merchants hawking their wares to basket-laden women, children running, heedless of the heat. It was deathly hot; the air shimmered with the force of it. "He killed them all, Ermessen. Men, women, children, killed without hesitation, without remorse, as though running his sword through straw practice dummies. Last night at table he boasted of slaying twenty enemies. All but two of those were innocents."

"He's still young," she said, choosing her words carefully. "Perhaps he can be guided?"

"Perhaps." She heard the doubt in him.

"Or perhaps not. You know, old friend, there is an alternative, another young man of royal blood." Ermessen had not become the only woman ever to command the armies of Marjehar-Dalmu by being overly cautious.

"Surely you don't mean the twin? How can you think such a thing? Leaving aside the religious and magical implications, the boy's been raised in a schola. I doubt he's turned his hand to anything more strenuous than weeding herbs. A king must be a leader of men, Excellency."

"It was just a passing thought." Ermessen replaced the game piece, though it was an exercise in futility; Berenger had already won. But perhaps the seeds planted today would bear fruit when the time came to make her move, when Arnaud died, Disme willing, years later.

From the west gate, a ruckus began to build, shouts and cries, the clashing of chainmail and plate armor, and far, far above them, the low blast of the Horn of Mourning. Her heart stopped and she saw the color drain from Berenger's face. That horn was blown only when one of the Andrianeu passed. Most of the lesser members of the family were at their estates far from Porta Guernau, Ermessen herself was very much alive, so that narrowed the list of possibilities to two. "Where is my grand-nephew, Berenger?" she asked, voice shaking.

"Sleeping." He met her eyes; fear reflecting fear. "Sleeping off his overindulgence."

"And my nephew?"

"I believe His Majesty went bird hunting in the marshes."

The sounds below intensified as frantic footfalls erupted up the stairs. A young knight, his helm in his hand and tears streaming down his face, fell to one knee in front of her. "Excellency, I regret to inform you that the king is dead."

There was no time to assemble more than a tiny party, hastily armed and riding whatever horses could be commandeered. A delay might have drawn attention, and attention was the last thing Ermessen wanted. She had maybe a day's head start before Berenger and Prince Gombal started for San Iuxta, less, if Berenger perceived her statements about the 'alternative' as a threat to Gombal. She had to reach Conn first and pray he was ready.

Damn and blast her idiotic nephew, managing to break his neck hunting. Of all the undignified ways for a king to die! She'd hoped for ten years or more to prepare Conn. Perrando and Bernard sent good word of him; he would never be an expert swordsman, he'd started far too late for that, but he could, according to Perrando, hold his own. Bernard reported that he had a strong understanding of history and tactics, but it would all be for naught if Gombal slaughtered him out of hand. Abbot Calvet would have received word of the death of the king; the birds had been sent at the moment the horn had blown, he'd be watching Conn day and night, might already have moved him to the Tower of Sacrifice. If that were the case, they were finished for certain.

She'd dispatched her own messages, sent her own birds winging eastward to her lands, to alert those in fealty to her that the time to fulfill their oaths had come. But a quick calculation told her that if Berenger rallied his own sworn men to join the royal armies, her men would be overwhelmed. Unless the promised help from Mendi arrived. So much depended on fragile birds' wings.

The moons soared above her as Ermessen drove her horse on, through the marshes and north, following the course of the great river, on and on into the night, pushing aside fears and doubts and the aching pangs of age, hoping there would be an army for Conn to lead, and praying also that there would still be a Conn to lead it.

All afternoon, birds had darkened the summer sky, their numbers so great they blotted out the sun at times. Conn sat in the small garden, muscles aching from a particularly challenging set of drills Perrando had put him through, wondering what it all meant. He'd taken to spending a few hours in the garden each day, regardless of weather; after hours of shield-drill or learning the histories of ancient Dalmutian kings and battle tactics from hundreds of years ago, the act of sorting weed from herb was grounding. And sometimes, when the air was right and the schola quiet, he could lie upon the grass and imagine himself on that mountaintop with the girl.

He'd felt freer since General Ermessen told him the truth—it had been a great weight lifted from his shoulders, and fortunately, since that time, Prince Gombal must have avoided injury, for there had been no further visits from the greycloaks, no trips to the west tower. No visits either from his great-aunt, but she had sent word to him through Brother Bernard and Perrando, and Conn knew he wasn't abandoned. He had been worried about how Perrando would explain his presence around the schola, but apparently the swordsman was as skilled with a set of carving knives as he was with a sword. With Brother Bernard's help, Perrando passed himself off as a traveling craftsman, and in the hours when he was not training Conn, he carved decorative panels in the schola's refectory.

The training was exhausting. Conn had become reasonably adept with the sword, able to block most of Perrando's blows, though he wished sometimes he could practice against others. They'd even managed to teach him to ride, sneaking him from his rooms at night. Though he wasn't good at it and would likely always be more comfortable walking, he knew that when it came to it, he'd ride into battle on his own accord.

It grew late; surely past time for evening prayers, but there had been no drum. Nothing but birds, and air that felt increasingly heavy. He heard no voices from beyond the walls, none of the sounds made by eleven-year-old boys, even novice brothers, at play on a summer day.

And the birds, message laden, dispersing to the far corners of the land, what did they mean?

"Conn."

Brother Bernard stood utterly still in his robes, a large, wrapped package in his hand. There was something in his tone that made Conn sure he wished to take this news standing, so he pulled himself up from the grass, brushed off his robes and waited. Bernard's face, lined with age and pockmarked now from an illness that struck the schola two years previous, was grave. "I've just come from Abbot Calvet. Earlier today he received word from Porta Guernau. King Arnaud was thrown from his horse while hunting. He is dead."

Conn's heart began pounding in his chest. His father, his unknown father was dead. All their plans, all his training culminated in this one moment. He started to speak, but his mouth had gone dry and words fled from him.

"I am ordered to take you, by force if necessary, to the west tower to await the coming of Crown Prince Gombal."

"Perrando?"

"He has gone to the orchard with two horses, ready to take you from this place. If you leave by the postern gate, you should have a good chance. They'll search the schola first, then the grounds. No one will believe you capable of running away. I've done my part to ensure the opinion of you amongst my fellows remains low. A shy, bookish youth, incapable of initiative." Brother Bernard smiled wryly.

"But they'll question you," Conn said, a lump building in his throat. "You'll be in trouble for helping me."

Brother Bernard's smile did not fade. "A small price to pay. I am not an expressive man, Conn. It's not in my nature to be effusive with my praise or affection, but these years with you have been a great pleasure."

Conn swallowed hard, forcing away the tears that threatened to unman him. "I . . . I know I haven't always been the most obedient—"

"We will have no more talk of obedience. Now is the time for you to lead, not follow." Bernard glanced behind him. "And in that vein, I offer you this gift." He unwrapped the bundle, revealing a beautiful sword. Even at the distance, Conn could tell the quality of the blade was unsurpassed, and the hilt, though plain and unornamented, held a look of great authority. "This is the sword of Andreu the Great. It's rested for five hundred years in the Chamber of Silence. It has rested long enough. Take it."

Conn hesitated, but Bernard pressed the bundle into his hands, giving an awkward one-armed farewell embrace. "Go with the gods, my son."

Perrando waited, two sets of reins in his hands, two horses pawing impatiently at the ground. "There was a plan in place. The general is riding north, we're to meet her at the southern tip of the Grove of Harri." Perrando boosted Conn into the saddle, then mounted his own horse and started down the slope to the edge of the woods where the shadows would hide their passage. Conn turned back to look upon the schola, its four towers stabbing the sky, bleached stone walls hiding the rooms and corridors which he'd heard of, studied plans and drawings for, but never traversed. His world had been circumscribed by the role he'd been forced to play. Victim. Sacrifice. But no more. The darkening sky seemed huge with possibilities, it dwarfed him, and for a long moment, Conn froze there as the horse moved restlessly, waiting for the command to follow Perrando's mount.

"Goodbye," Conn whispered to the only home he'd ever known, and turned his horse to the south.

Two days' hard ride had them almost to the Salbatore River, and every muscle in Conn's body ached to the point of collapse. His short sojourns on horseback had in no way prepared him for this, and nothing could have prepared him for the sight of the river. He'd read descriptions of it, knew it began as a tiny trickle high on Mt. Hasi, could trace it on any map as it descended onto the lowland plains to empty into the sea at Porta Guernau. But a line on a map was a far cry from this frenzy of water, flowing fast as it came out of the mountains, gradually slowing to a languid channel in the lowlands. Upstream it narrowed so you could toss a rock across, here it was so wide that a man's voice would be swallowed up in the water if he tried to call to another man on the opposite shore. The Grandmother of Rivers, the Mendians called it.

Perrando had driven them unmercifully, forgoing the easy route for more complex paths to throw off pursuit, and now he made the decision that Conn would not be able to ford the river, even at its narrowest. So they descended further south till they found a small ferry, run by an old farmer to pick up some small coin from those with reason to avoid the well-traveled bridges further south. Perrando paid the ferryman his asking price without haggling and they led their horses onto the swaying wooden platform.

The wooden ferry creaked and rocked as the weathered farmer worked his pole deep into the river bed, pushing them towards the opposite bank.

"Is it deep here?" Conn asked.

"Fair to middling." The man glanced up at Conn, then quickly away.

"Come help me with these saddlebags," Perrando said in a gruff voice. The saddlebags seemed fine to Conn, but he went obediently to bend over the leather satchels. Perrando grasped his arm with an iron grip. "Don't draw attention to yourself, boy. You're the image of the prince, remember? *He's* not spent the last twenty years walled up in a schola, he gets out and people see him. The last thing we want is that fellow to remember your face—he'd sell his own children into slavery if there's profit in it."

Conn looked back at the man who seemed to be ignoring them, rhythmically poling them across the river. Despite intensive lessons with Bernard about intrigue and tactics, the histories of kings and magi who'd fought and clawed their way to power over the bodies of their rivals, Conn did not easily think that way. "Should we pay him more to keep him quiet?"

"Good Bonassus, no! Then he'll know for certain there's something amiss. Just stay quiet and follow my lead. We'll be across soon and on our way to the grove. With luck, Her Excellency's already there waiting for us."

And with no luck, it would be Prince Gombal and his forces; Conn knew that only too well. Gombal had greycloaks on his side. Surely they had spells for tracking people. Perhaps they were watching him even now, through the eyes of the birds which flew over the river, perching on the poles of the ferry and the dock they approached. He'd heard greycloaks could do that and more. He'd read tales of the battles of Gombal the Conqueror who'd gone into Mendiko Battar and laid waste to the countryside with a force of only twenty men and three greycloaks. They'd ignited the forests, and the land was only now beginning to recover from the damage, though hundreds of years had passed. No wonder the Mendians hated magic.

The ferry bumped hard against the dock; Conn and Perrando wasted no time in putting distance between them and the ferryman. They did not speak through the rest of that day, and in the evening, when a misting rain began to fall, they came upon the Grove of Harran. Of all the wonders Conn had seen since leaving the schola this was the greatest. Trees more than ten times the height of a man rose up before him, so close together that from a distance, they seemed to form a solid wall. As they approached, the wall resolved into hundreds of trunks as thick as barrels from the schola's cellars.

Once sacred to the Mendian goddess Sorgin, the great wood was said to look just as it had when the Conqueror invaded. His greycloaks had refused to burn it, and the great trees had grown taller and thicker since. The sky disappeared behind the massive canopy and light penetrated only in thin shafts that managed to evade the tree cover.

"We walk from here," Perrando said. "The horses will require to be led. Mendians don't ride, as a general rule, you know."

"No, I didn't. Does it have to do with them not using magic?" He swung off the horse gratefully, taking the reins and encouraging the animal forward.

"In a sense. Horses, like magic, come from Marjehar, and all things Marjeharan are suspect among my people."

It seemed impossible that Perrando could know where he was going in the intense dark of the forest, but he seemed to, so Conn set his steps to match the stocky swordsman. "But if you'd use magic, if you had greycloaks of your own, then you might be able to drive the Marjeharans out."

Perrando snorted. "We'll drive them out sure enough without dishonorable magic. General Ermessen won't have greycloaks in her force. The rightness of her cause and the strength of her arm will prevail. You'll see. Besides, it's forbidden for a son or daughter of Mendia to harm themselves in any way. Our gods would reject anyone who spurns their gifts of life and health and strength."

"But isn't magic another type of strength?"

"It's false." Perrando slowed to lead his horse around a marshy patch of ground. "It's built on lies. I love my people, but they're as bad as the greycloaks with all their talk of fate. Those schola brothers have the right of it. Power is about will, and the truly strong of will aren't those who lop off their arms or gouge out their eyes drunk as lords or in a fit of passion. Those brothers with the blindfolds, they could choose otherwise at any time, but they don't. That's will. That's strength. Choosing who you are, not accepting whatever fate, or your own foolish pride, makes you."

Conn considered that. "That's what I'm doing, isn't it?"

"Yes. You're freeing yourself."

"And when I'm king, I'll free Mendi Province." It was the first time he'd let himself say those words—*when I am king*. It sounded strange, awkward. King Conn I. Or would he have to take a proper royal name? Ermessen would know. He'd been so deep in thought he almost walked into the back of Perrando's horse. A light glimmered ahead of them in the undergrowth.

Perrando put up his hand. "Hold here." His sword slithered from its worn sheath with only the slightest of sounds. He looped his horse's reins around a branch and disappeared into the darkness.

Conn counted the seconds as his heart beat so loudly that it surely was audible to the whole forest. If Perrando got lost or was killed, he'd be alone. He *was* alone, for the first time in his entire life. There had always been someone within ten feet of him—the schola was like an anthill, and just as crowded. But here—

"It's all right, come on." Perrando returned for his horse. "It's Her Excellency."

Conn followed quickly, eager to see Ermessen again. But as the light of the fire illuminated the clearing, he could hardly recognize the lady. Her hair was drenched with sweat, armor covered in mud. The small troop of men accompanying her looked little better, but Conn's heart leapt to see them. Ermessen stood as he entered the small clearing. "You've changed, grown to a man." She clasped him on each shoulder and he realized that where at fifteen she had been taller than he, now he had several inches of height on her.

"You haven't changed," he said.

She laughed. "You lie like a courtier already. Come and sit beside the fire; you must be exhausted. Was there trouble on the road?"

"Possibly," Perrando said from where he was tending to the horses. "A ferryman might have recognized Conn, though if he did, I suppose he'd have taken him for Gombal."

"It's not unknown for the prince to travel the countryside incognito, or pretending to be incognito," one of the men lounging by the fireside said. "He thinks it clever to seduce women, then proclaim his identity as though a revelation from the gods. Likely they know from the start who he is, of course."

"Well, it can't be helped," Ermessen said. "Tomorrow we join with the rest of my forces, and Bonassus willing, the Mendians. Without their help, we've little chance." She handed Conn a skin of wine. "Go easy with that. Drink enough to help you sleep, but not so much as to leave your head swollen in the morning. Listen, Conn, if things should go awry, either tomorrow or later on—"

"I'm sure it won't. Everything will go as planned." He didn't know whether he was trying to convince her or himself.

"Don't be ridiculous, your studies of history should have taught you that battles never go as planned. Accurate battle planning is as improbable as peace between man and wife. We can only hope things go wrong in our favor. Now if they don't, if I fall, and Perrando and the rest, get yourself up into Mendi, to Mt. Hasi. Among the people on the northernmost slope there's help for you of a sort. A refuge, if nothing else."

"If you fall, I'll fall at your side," Conn said, not able to imagine himself wholly alone. He'd rather be dead. The fire popped and Ermessen tossed another log into the orange-yellow flames.

"You bloody well won't. You'll run when I tell you, Conn. Don't forget they've got to take you alive. Nobody but Gombal can kill you, and my grand-nephew, my *other* grand-nephew," she corrected herself with a soft smile, "is not known for his courage on the field. They'll keep him far back from any fighting, believe me, if for no other reason than to keep him whole till he's crowned. If you stay with us, you'll be captured and all will be lost. If I tell you to run, if Perrando or any of the men here tells you to run, you run. Do you promise?"

Conn nodded. The wine tasted sour, but it warmed him, spreading liquid heat through his lungs and stomach and down into his legs. "But it won't come to that."

"Here's hoping." Ermessen stood and stretched. "My gods, I'm old for this. There's one other thing you should do before tomorrow. You know that Conn isn't the name of a king."

"It isn't a name at all," Conn said. "But it's all I've got."

"I want you to take another name, a king's name. We're turning the monarchy upside down, lad. The Mage-Kings aren't popular, haven't been for a great many years, but people will want some continuity with the past."

"You give me a name." Nobody named themselves, after all. Among the Mendians, mothers gave milk names, and fathers youth names, and then warriors had the names they earned for themselves. Marjeharans were named by their fathers. His father was dead, and hadn't ever regarded him as anything more than a convenience, a path for the promised son to take his power. Brother Bernard had been the closest he'd had to a father, and Ermessen the closest to a mother.

She regarded him for a long moment. "Hmm. The most common royal name is Gombal, which I'd not recommend for obvious reasons. Prophecy says there will never be a second Andreu till the end of the world has come, so I'd avoid that as well."

Conn thought back through his studies of history. "What about Rickard?" King Rickard II had been a great scholar king, eschewing the use of magic and lessening the influence of the greycloaks.

Ermessen nodded her approval. "An honorable choice."

"I would be honored to bear it. Though I'll always think of myself as Conn, I expect."

Ermessen took a rolled blanket from a saddlebag perched atop a fallen tree and laid it out near the fire. "Sleep then, Prince Rickard, known as Conn. We've watches set and the night is far advanced. Tomorrow, gods willing, you take your kingdom."

Conn sank into the soft bed of dead leaves that Ermessen had selected for his bedroll, grateful for the comfort, though in truth, he could easily have slept on rocks or broken glass as tired as he was. *Today a nameless orphan, tomorrow a king. Such a funny, funny world.* He wondered where Brother Bernard was, hoped he'd not been troubled overmuch by the Abbot. The first thing he'd do when he was king would be to send for Bernard. He'd be chief councilor. And Ermessen could lead the armies, and Perrando could be her second. And he'd marry a girl from Mendi, from the mountaintops. From his dreams. The soft sounds of the soldiers and the horses, snuffling and snoring, became a strange music that soothed Conn into a deep and dreamless sleep.

Ermessen looked across the field, heart sinking. The forces arrayed against them were formidable—almost the entire royal army and a goodly number of Berenger's sworn men, and likely more on the way. Five hundred knights, she estimated. And she had less than half of that, with no sign of the promised help from Mendi.

"Should we try to put them off?" Danel, her aide, sounded nervous.

"There's no point to it. Every delay will give the rest of the king's armies more time to assemble. I should know, I'm ostensibly their general." Fighting her own force, men she'd trained, men she'd fought beside, bled with. She'd known in her mind it would come to this, but not in her heart. "And anyway they've no reason to agree to delay."

"Excellency, three of the enemy have broken off and are riding forward under a banner of truce."

Berenger would observe all the forms. "Danel, Oswald, with me." She swung onto her waiting stallion; Danel grabbed the standard bearing her personal arms, a silver lioness couchant on a green field, while Oswald took up the kingdom banner of Marjehar, an eagle of gold on a crimson field. She would remind Berenger that she too fought for a royal heir.

"Wait! What's happening?" Conn pushed through the line of armored men.

"We will negotiate the terms of the battle; it's how this is done."

"As . . ." The boy shook slightly. "As king, shouldn't I be there?"

"No, absolutely not." Her horse was restless beneath her thighs. The beast was not her usual warhorse; she hoped this wasn't a sign of bad behavior to come. "Do nothing that will draw attention to yourself or put you in a position to be snatched by Gombal's greycloaks. If you're one of a pack of soldiers, they'll have a harder time tracking you. Perrando, keep him off the front lines."

"Yes, Excellency." The swordsman bowed and took Conn gently by the arm. Ermessen spurred her horse forward with the bannermen taking positions behind her, and together they rode out to meet Berenger.

Gombal was not with him, which was not surprising. Berenger would not put the prince at risk of magic, though he had to know her forces had no greycloaks. Not so with the royal army. Ferrer, cloak flying behind him, his missing hand tucked into the front of his robe, kept his mount slightly to the front of the party. Typical. Ermessen ignored him, focusing solely on Berenger.

"Well met, Your Grace." The old words of parley came so easy, and for the first time she realized what a sad lie they were.

"Well met, Excellency. Though in truth, I'd rather have my heart ripped from my body than to see this day dawn."

"Likewise. But you and I both know that Gombal is as fit to be king as I'm fit to be one of Disme's virgins, and besides, a throne cemented with kin's blood is ill-constructed."

"It is our way." He had been matching her gaze for gaze, but now looked away, and Ermessen noticed he did not defend Gombal's fitness. He was too honest a man for that.

"Ways change, times change."

"Oh, enough of this." Magister Ferrer's impatience was clear even to his mount which jerked and danced like a performing circus horse. "Give us the boy and you'll be allowed to go into exile. Deny us, and we'll take him by force and slaughter you and yours to the last man."

She ignored him. It was poorly done of Berenger to bring him. The greycloaks were supposed to serve the army, not attempt to rule it. Berenger grimaced. "I apologize. Not being a knight, Magister Ferrer does not understand how this is done. But he has given you our opening position. Ermessen," he used her name, something rare indeed, "please. Surely this untried, unknown boy is not worth your life, or the lives of those sworn to you."

She looked down at her gloved hands, lightly holding the reins. Those hands had granted life and death, had created and destroyed, all in the service of Marjehar. Fifty odd years since she'd knelt before the great altar in the presence of the king—her grandsire—and sworn the oath of a squire, the first woman in ten generations to do so. She'd promised to uphold not any individual king, but the land of Marjehar-Dalmu and the royal line. Conn—Rickard, she forced herself to name him—was as much a part of that line as Gombal. "There are fitting reasons to die, Berenger. Or to kill. This, I believe, is one of them." She wheeled her horse close to Berenger, so Ferrer could not hear unless he was listening with magic. "Search your own heart, my friend, as we battle today. Truth is the preeminent of the Five Knightly Virtues, you know, and being true to oneself is the jewel in knighthood's crown."

He bowed his head. "We will not use magic on this field of battle, I swear it."

She had reached him—normally that was something the opponent had to request. Ferrer sputtered with protest, but Berenger stared him down. "We do not need it, our numbers alone will carry the day, and I will not use unfair advantage against our own kind. Your further presence here is not required, Magister. I suggest you withdraw your magi to the high ground where you can wait out the battle in safety."

Ermessen watched as he rode away. "As much as this pains me to say, we will not target the greycloaks with our archers."

"Might solve quite a few difficulties if you did, but I thank you. We will give quarter when asked it and will take prisoners."

"We will do the same."

"Done, then. Is one hour sufficient preparation time?"

"Why wait? Thirty minutes. Let's have this done." She'd long grown beyond taking any great joy in battle, but this was untenable. "Berenger, please . . ."

He caught up the pendant he wore that signified him as second general. "I swore an oath. Regardless of how I feel about the current occupant of the throne, I swore, Ermessen. I can't be false to that." He turned his horse and rode away, his bannerman following.

She had tried, but really, she'd known from the beginning that there was no chance of success. The battle today was inevitable from the moment she stood before Conn in the schola and named him king's son and royal.

"Do we have any chance, Excellency?" Danel asked as they watched Gombal's lines open to receive Berenger and his man. There were so many of them, the line extended near to the edges of the wood.

"There's always hope, Danel. Commend your spirit to whatever god you serve and wield your sword with honor."

She dug her heels into the flanks of the horse, letting it have its head, and with one last fierce surge of joy, said goodbye to her life.

Chaos, blood, smoke, the clashing of sword on sword, clatter of sword on wooden shield, and the shrieks of the wounded—it was like nothing Conn had anticipated, completely unlike the manuscripts depicting ancient battles as serene and dignified, quiet. *On this field were slain six hundred knights,* the chronicle recorded of the Battle of Byrne. Was it like this, this same madness?

Kept to the back of the force, helmet obscuring his peripheral vision and amplifying his harsh breathing, Conn struggled to see the progress of the fighting, but Perrando was ever beside him, pulling him further and further back towards the foothills of the Dawn Range. A horse waited, tethered to a tree two hundred paces or so away, and he knew it was for him. So that he could run.

The sword of Andreu lay heavy in his hand, but he'd yet to swing it against the foe. Instead, he watched banners rise and fall, charting the progress of the fight through the wordless language of heraldry, studied diligently at Perrando's command so that he would instantly know friend from foe.

Ermessen's banner still flew, though it had fallen several times as its bearer had been killed. But the other banners, those of her sworn men, those were dropping at an alarming rate, and the fighting was moving closer and closer to his position. A knight Conn did not recognize was battling three others—he dropped his sword in sign of submission, and the largest of his opponents shoved his sword into the eye-slot of the helm and the man fell.

"So much for giving quarter," Perrando muttered. "The ravens will feast well tonight." He drew his sword. "When I say, take horse and fly, lad. This is about to become a slaughter."

To Conn, it was a slaughter already. He pulled his helmet off, breathing free air. Neither side was using archers anymore, the combat was too close.

"Fool! They'll have lookouts posted, just waiting to catch sight of you!" Perrando said. "Go, go! Any who survive will meet you on Mt. Hasi, now go!" He shoved Conn towards the waiting horse and turned to engage the enemy. Stumbling backwards, Conn saw Ermessen falter under Duke Berenger's assault. A spear from behind took Perrando through his boiled-leather cuirass. *Oh gods, why didn't he wear plate, the Mendian idiot?* Tears stung Conn's eyes. He'd reached the horse and swung himself into the saddle, still watching. Ermessen dropped her sword; she must not have seen that they were slaughtering prisoners.

"No!" he cried out. "No!"

But perhaps he'd been wrong, for Berenger was making the signs of assent, and Ermessen removed her helmet. Conn imagined her giving her surrender, Berenger speaking the formal words granting protection as his prisoner. But another man wearing the device of the prince's personal guard swung his sword, taking Ermessen unsuspecting across the throat. Blood spattered in a great shower, even from this distance Conn could see it. Berenger's sword struck and the man toppled over.

Every instinct in him screamed, *Turn back, help them,* but he knew it was too late. There was no more time, they'd be after him, and his only advantage was the horse. Conn spurred the animal up the hill, feeling its great muscles working, such a magnificent warhorse, and he remembered where he'd seen it before. It was Ermessen's. The lump in his throat swelled so he thought it would burst. Mt. Hasi loomed in the northern sky, unmistakable, a giant among the dwarfish foothills. It was his only hope of survival.

He kicked the horse into a gallop, making for the grove where they'd passed the night. Within that tangle of trees, he'd be able to hide. Conn risked a glance behind him. The last of Ermessen's now-leaderless forces had somehow managed to regroup and had placed themselves between Conn and his pursuers. Ahead of him lay the grove's darkness and safety. The clash of swords and the screams of the dying faded as he cleared the first rows of trees and pressed on, putting good distance between himself and any pursuit. As the forest thickened, his horse slowed to a walk and then stopped altogether. Remembering with sorrow how he and Perrando had led their horses through the grove, Conn dismounted. He'd push through the grove to the other side, then make his way up to Mt. Hasi. He would survive.

He'd not gone more than fifty paces before the horse stopped in its tracks, turning its head to look back towards the battlefield. Conn did the same, though of course neither he nor the horse could see what they'd left behind. The vision of the slaughter lived in his memory. It came to him then, that life was more than bare survival, and the lady who gave him this chance at freedom deserved better than to lie rotting on a field or to be manhandled by enemies. He'd wait till the sun set, then return to the field, disguised as best he could, and bury her if he could manage it. Then, and only then, would he follow her orders and seek whatever force waited at the mountain.

The moon was a slender crescent, providing scant light as he crept along the treeline, listening to the low moans of the wounded, the calling of night birds. What before had been a field of late summer grass, ample grazing for the livestock of nearby villages, was now transformed into a sea of mud, dirt and blood forming a bier for the bodies of men and horses. There was movement and the distant light of campfires on the far side of the field where Gombal's forces gathered, but nothing stirred where Ermessen and Perrando had fallen.

Conn had never before looked upon a dead body. That was a part of his education neither Perrando nor Brother Bernard had undertaken. When brothers died, they were cremated; their ashes scattered and dispersed in the gardens, symbolizing their spiritual union with the gods, the end of their need for physical form. Before the cremation, they were laid in state, he'd been told. Neat, orderly, dressed in fine robes.

There was nothing neat or orderly about these dead. Abandoned where they'd fallen, some in hideous poses of pain. And the stench: blood and iron and the beginnings of putrescence, like meat on the edge of turning. In the darkness, the corpses were silhouetted against the moonlight, a shadow garden of death.

He found Ermessen easily for she wore no helm, and Perrando nearby, and a number of dead knights wearing Gombal's and Berenger's devices. He'd just about worked up the nerve to reach down and roll Ermessen over onto her back when he heard voices. Conn froze. If he ran, he'd be seen for certain. Only one chance. He dropped to the ground beside her body, relaxing all his muscles the way the brothers did in meditation, face to the ground, his breathing as shallow and quiet as possible. Conn became a corpse.

". . . headed into the hills at last sighting. I suppose he's gone into Mendi. Ermessen always had good contacts amongst the Mendians." He recognized Duke Berenger's low voice.

"That bitch. I never trusted her, never. Father was a fool to let her have control over the twin. Women can never be trusted to act with honor." Conn's heart skipped a beat. Prince Gombal, for certain, and his voice sounded so like Conn's own, it was like hearing himself in an echo.

"My Prince, the Lady Ermessen served your family well for over forty years. She taught me all I know about war, and about being a knight. She was—"

"She *was* a traitor." Gombal sounded on the edge of hysteria. "And I want her head struck off and put on a pike on the city walls of Porta Guernau, right alongside that traitor brother."

Oh sweet Dione's tears, does he mean Brother Bernard? Conn's eyes grew moist, and he forced down sobs. If he was found here, then all the sacrifices Bernard and Ermessen had made would be in vain.

"Highness, it is traditional to give honorable burial to one's foes." Berenger spoke patiently, as though explaining the obvious to a rather stupid child. "We grant it to them, and they to us. It is part of the code of knighthood, you know." Conn heard the creaking of armor.

"I am king. You will address me as Majesty, and I don't give a damn what's traditional. I want her head, and by Disme, I'll have it. And these others, leave them to rot on the field. Let the ravens take them."

"My Pr . . . Your Majesty, surely you can see the wrong in that. These men were just fulfilling their oaths. They had no choice." Berenger seemed to have knelt down next to Ermessen's body. He was within three or four paces of Conn.

Still, still. Quiet as a rabbit avoiding a hawk.

"There is always a choice, Berenger. They're traitors. They chose to be traitors. I choose to let them rot. We are not pawns of fate, like the Mendians believe. All children of the gods have choices, General."

A hand on his shoulder. Conn exhaled slightly, allowing his limbs to flop as Berenger turned him. It was over. He wasn't wearing a helmet, just a quilted arming cap that would do nothing to hide his face. He opened his eyes and looked up into the inscrutable face of the duke.

"Yes," Berenger said, rising, brushing his hands against his cuisses, staring straight down at Conn. "Yes, my king. We do indeed have choices."

Berenger's gaze caught Conn's and held it as he slid his blade from the scabbard. Unwilling to watch what he knew was coming, Conn shut his eyes, steeling himself for the blow. It did not come. Instead, he heard a whispered prayer and the crunching of bone. "Your prize. Majesty." Berenger's voice held disdain, and Conn risked a glance, saw the duke holding Ermessen's severed head. He closed his eyes again, whispered his own prayer. Footsteps retreated across the field, leaving Conn wondering if he'd just made an ally.

The mountain air was as he'd remembered it from his dreams, colder and clearer than at the schola, fresher by far than what he'd left behind at the battlefield. Conn rode hard for three days, always moving upwards, always keeping the peak of Mt. Hasi in view. There were trails through the Dawn Range, and he'd used them. A few times he thought he'd heard the sounds of pursuit, but it had come to nothing and the chance of getting lost or of the horse taking injury if he abandoned the trails outweighed the fear of discovery.

The Dawn Range peaks were well worn down by time and covered with a scattering of pines; Mt. Hasi was the same, only on a grander scale. Here the river Salbatore had its origin, here, legend said, the Mendian Goddess Amma mated with the sun god, Di, four times a year, giving birth to the seasons. And here, Ermessen had told him, he would find friends, though he had to wonder what friends these Mendians would be. If they had come as promised, the outcome of the battle might have been quite different.

But how will I find them? The mountain was vast, the northern slopes so heavily forested he could barely see beyond a hundred paces down the twisting path. He'd passed several small villages as he ascended towards the summit, and had bartered for food, though he'd been careful not to stay in any village too long. These people were poor, and no doubt Gombal had offered a substantial reward for his capture.

On this journey, Conn had come to a decision. No matter how this fell out, whether he found allies or not, whether he was ever able to return to Marjehar and fight for a throne he wasn't even sure he wanted, he would not allow himself to be taken alive. Before leaving the battlefield, he'd taken a bronze dagger from Perrando's body. Small, but enough to do the job. Gombal would not ride to power on his blood, no matter what else transpired. Somehow, he'd find the strength to be sure of that.

A gurgling mountain stream ran alongside the path. Conn stopped to let his horse drink. The water sounded disturbingly like the noise Ermessen had made when that man had slashed her throat. *No.* He forced that thought away. He would think not of past or future, but of the moment, letting the beauty of the day push the horror from his mind. It was late summer, leaves just on the edge of turning, the fragrant air holding a bare hint of autumn's chill. Birdsong had been his constant accompaniment as he'd risen higher and higher on the mountain.

A branch cracked; the forest went totally still. He put a hand on the hilt of his sword, slowly turning in the direction of the noise.

A man stood under the shade of a massive old pine, holding a longbow drawn taut, arrow trembling as he held it in check. Other men and women stood beside him, but Conn had no thought for any of them, not even for the bowman who threatened his life. Another woman, close to his own age, waited beside the tree, elfin thin and graceful in her rags, her eyes vacant sockets. And the face was one he knew, familiar from the dreams of his youth. She was real. Conn sunk to his knees, trembling.

"Shoot him, Berdoi," said a young man with a strange scar down the side of his head. "He's Marjeharan, you can tell by that fancy sword." Conn realized his ear had been clumsily lopped off.

Berdoi seemed doubtful. "He could be the one we were told to expect. And not all Marjeharans are evil, Eguerr. The Lady Ermessen has been a good friend to us, and so have many of the brothers."

"Doesn't matter," Eguerr said, and Conn noted how careful his speech was, as though he had scant idea of how it sounded to others. "One or two good apples can't make up for a barrel of rot."

A middle-aged woman came forward to take hold of Conn's chin and lift his face. She had a scar where her nose had once been. What had happened to these people? Never had he seen so much mutilation, save for. . . . He'd always been told there were no Mendian magi, was that wrong?

Berdoi lowered his weapon, relaxing the tension on the string, but keeping the arrow nocked. "What do you say, Malen?"

The blind girl regarded Conn through sightless eyes. "I say that kings ought not kneel save before the gods. Stand up."

"How did you know . . . how can you see. . . ." He struggled for words. "I've seen you. I know you."

"And I know you. I used to dream of you before the bad men came. I didn't know it then, but those dreams were sent to me by Amma, teaching me to use my inward eye so that when my outer eyes were taken, I'd still have sight."

"You can see me," Conn whispered. Here was magic indeed.

"So he's the one?" Berdoi lowered his bow and let the arrow fall.

"I'm Conn. I mean Rickard." The name still sounded foreign. "General Ermessen sent me here—"

"Where is she?" Berdoi asked, suspiciously.

"She's—"

Malen shook her head. "I told you she'd fallen with all her host. I saw it. We must return to the village. They're seeking you with magic, and we can't protect you here." She turned away and with miraculous certainty of foot, began to follow a narrow path up the side of the mountain. The other woman took Conn's horse, and Berdoi turned to follow, awkwardly, the walk of a man with something gravely wrong with his leg. His tunic parted mid stride, and Conn saw that he had no left foot, just a stump encased in dirty rags.

"Wait," Conn called. "What is wrong with you people? Are you greycloaks? Is that how you can see without eyes, or protect me from magic?"

Berdoi stopped and laughed, but there was no mirth in him. "Greycloaks? Do I look like a powerful and wealthy magi, kinglet?"

Conn took in the tattered tunic, many times patched, the sunken eyes and wasted face, the obvious signs of famine and poverty. "No, sir."

"Sir, he calls me." Berdoi laughed shortly. "They teach them manners in the lowlands, don't they? We're what you get when ignorant fools try to become magi." He turned back and stumped up the path, and Conn followed, sweat pouring down his face as the unfamiliar exertion strained his muscles.

"I don't understand."

"You know how greycloaks are made, yes?"

"Yes." They crossed over a low stream on a path of rocks and skirted around a waterfall so beautiful it took Conn's breath away. He wondered if Malen could see that too.

"Then work it out. You're going to be king, or so they tell me, you ought to be able to add two and two." Berdoi picked up his speed, moving amazingly well considering his limp, and Conn struggled to keep pace. Finally, Malen slowed in front of them, and they came down a slight rise into a valley nestled amongst the trees. A few huts, a largish hall, all constructed of wattle and daub, with poorly thatched roofs that seemed inadequate to keep rain and snow at bay. The noseless woman led Conn's horse away, and as if at a signal, people began to appear.

From out of the houses and the hall, from behind trees and from within the forest, straightening from garden patches and small fields, leaving aside the spinning of wool and the sharpening of knives, they came to stare at the newcomer, and Conn stood and let them stare without protest. He supposed that a king had to be used to such things, after all. He tried not to stare back, but it was almost impossible, for every single man, woman and child down to the tiny toddler trailing after the skirts of a woman near as old as Ermessen, was mutilated in some way. Arms, hands, feet, eyes, fingers. Those who seemed whole undoubtedly had hidden deficits.

"Do you understand now?" Malen asked, and he did, but it made no sense.

"You can't, you can't gain power through sacrifice of others!" That was a cornerstone of magical philosophy.

"No, you can't. But that doesn't stop people from trying, and where better to draw your sacrificial victims than amongst the rebellious Mendians?" Malen said in a bitter voice. "He came when I was twelve, said he wished to hire me to be a maid in his great Marjeharan house. My parents were poor farmers, and my mother wanted more for me than she'd had. So they took his coin, and he took me away. Then he took my eyes and left me for dead on the mountainside."

Berdoi's hands closed on his bow as though it were a lifeline. "I was fourteen, and they didn't even bother with coin, just snatched my brother and me from our wheatfield. My brother died when infection took hold of his leg. I survived. I still wonder which of us was the lucky one."

The older woman brushed her remaining hand over the head of the toddler. "I was twenty, a wife and soon to be a mother when my husband's father took my arm. I lost the baby, which grieved me greatly then, but I see now it was a mercy of Amma."

"As long as there is magic in this world," Malen said, "as long as it is accepted and praised and cherished, as long as those who possess it are masters, there will be those who will be willing to kill and maim to acquire it. Ermessen promised us that if we helped you, if we worked to bring down the Mage-Kings, you would do away with the greycloaks and break their power."

Conn began to shake with cold despite the heat of the day. "I don't know how . . . I mean, they have magic. I don't know how to fight that."

"He's exhausted," the old lady said. "Give him some soup and a bed, let him rest. This place is protected, not by man's magic, but by the power of Amma, and you can rest easy here."

He let someone put a bowl in his hand and ate perfunctorily, not tasting the food except to note that it was warm, which was good as he was suddenly cold, so very cold, chilled through with the thought of what he'd seen, what he'd done, and most of all, what was left for him to do. How could he win a war when the other side had magic and would use it to their advantage? How could he bring an end to the greycloaks? It was too much, just too much. He was twenty years old, hardly more than a boy.

He let himself be led into a hut that smelled of damp sheep, and then stretched out on a pile of skins. Hands pulled his boots off, and he tried to protest; he wasn't to be waited on, but it felt good to relax, good to trust again.

The door was nothing but a skin nailed to the opening of the hut; it was pushed aside, and Malen entered. Adjusting her skirts, she sat cross-legged beside him. "You mustn't be afraid of their magic. It has limits, you know, and they are very few in number now."

"You're magical too, aren't you? You have the Sight." He'd heard of such things, rare talent that some greycloaks, particularly those who blinded themselves totally, were granted.

"It's not magic. It's a gift from Amma. I have always been able to See; formerly only in dreams, but now awake as well. And I have seen . . ."

"What? Have you seen the outcome of the war? What should I do?"

She sighed. "Is he very like you, your twin?"

"Yes. Our hair is kept somewhat differently, but aside from that, looking at him is as gazing into a mirror."

"Hair . . . no. There were helmets. Listen, young king. Of one thing I am certain. Your brother will go to any length to be sure that he and no other kills you. No soldier, no greycloak, no archer can be allowed to end your life. We are a small, poorly trained force, though the main Mendian army, such as it is, is yours as well."

"That was the force Ermessen was waiting for," Conn said bitterly. "If they'd come, she might still be alive."

"No. If they had gone, they would also be dead. They held back because I asked it of them. And now they will follow you into battle because I say. I am trusted because I See, because I'm chosen of the gods, and whatever influence I have is yours. But if there is war, well, you've seen the chaos of battle. If you fight, how could your brother ensure your survival? One stray sword blow or an arrow sent off course and his hopes are destroyed. And magic doesn't kill as you might think. It's very hard for the greycloaks to pick individual targets. The usual strategy, I am told, is to destroy large masses of men, send lightnings or boulders or trees falling or to open up the earth to swallow the enemy."

Conn sat up, noting how lovely she was, even with the awful scars. "I understand. If I die at anyone's hand but Gombal's, he can never be Mage-King. But how does that help me?"

She stood up. "I had a dream, Conn King's Son. In my dream, two men of identical visage fought before two armies, and on the outcome of that battle hinged the fate of the world."

Single combat. Of course; Gombal would have to accept, it would be his chance to kill Conn, and surely his brother would think little of his martial prowess, having spent his entire life with peaceful brothers. To be honest, Conn had doubts himself if he had a chance of winning. He was almost afraid to ask, but had to know whether there was any hope or not. "Who won?"

She sighed. "It could be you, it could be him. All I saw was a face in a helm, visor back, dead eyes staring up into a rainy sky."

Conn leaned back against the skins as she bid him goodnight, but he stayed awake long after, staring up at a spiderweb anchored across the rough ceiling, at once terrified and implacably calm. If Malen had seen the battle, then it was fact, it had happened. It *would* happen, and one way or another, this would all end.

The prince was asleep when the messenger arrived, which was a good thing. Berenger was able to receive the message and send the poor fellow on his way without any unpleasantness. Prince Gombal would have insisted that the man be tortured into revealing the location of the twin, though from the gnarled and battered look of him, physical pain would likely be small coercion.

But even if the prince had demanded it, Berenger would have refused. Honoring flags of truce and the sanctity of messengers and heralds was part of the code under which he lived, and he didn't intend to sacrifice those standards for anyone, not even a king. Gombal's behavior on this campaign had grown increasingly erratic and unpredictable. One moment he'd be embracing some common soldier as his best friend and in the next lopping his head off for some imagined slight. Only his small coterie of friends and the magi were exempt; the latter out of affection, the former undoubtedly from fear. It was typical of the ignorant to fear the greycloaks, but he, Berenger, had no fear of them at all, understanding the limitations of magic as he did.

They need us as much as we need them. More, actually, considering we don't really need them at all. Magister Ferrer had proven singularly useless in tracking the twin. It was as though Mt. Hasi had simply swallowed him up. And now this message. This offer. It was well done of the lad to put himself at risk like this. He had to know that Gombal had years of training at arms, while he himself had whatever Ermessen had managed to procure for him within the walls of the schola. The boy had courage, he'd seen that after the battle at the Grove. And loyalty, and a care for the men who would suffer and die in a mass battle. Gombal offered up his soldiers as though they were tin men on a child's play battlefield.

"Did I hear a rider?" Magister Ferrer stepped out of his pavilion, finer even than Prince Gombal's, which was larger than most commoner's houses and well appointed with red Dalmutian carpets and carved oak furnishings.

"Yes. A messenger from the boy, he's calling himself Prince Rickard now. He's offered single combat, the victor to determine the outcome of the war."

A smile crossed Ferrer's foxlike face and he stroked his pointed beard. "We will, of course, accept. His Majesty has held a sword since he was five years old—it will be child's play."

"The Prince will object. The terms under which the combat is offered includes amnesty for all those who fought against him and honorable burial for General Ermessen."

"Terms, my dear duke, are mere words on a page to a king. Gombal will see that. I will make him see." Ferrer's smile sent a shudder through Berenger. "He will kill the usurper and claim his power, then my magi will destroy every last one of the rebels."

"I need to see to my horse." Berenger turned away, unable to dissemble any further. *Words on a page.* There was no honor here. None.

On the highlands of Mt. Hasi it had felt like early fall, but here, in the southlands, it was still high summer, and though Conn had grown used to the weight of armor, it would never feel to him as a second skin the way it seemed to more experienced warriors. Today, under the prickling noon heat, it was near unbearable. Because Gombal had agreed without argument to all his terms, had even restored the body of Brother Bernard to the schola as an act of goodwill, Conn had allowed his brother to select the place for their combat. They were met on a wide field that had once been a river bed, with high cliffs above them where Conn could dimly make out the shapes of the greycloaks, watching. The armies of both sides arrayed behind their respective champions, waiting in a silence that was a living, breathing thing.

Banners snapped in a wind that seemed to come from nowhere and clouds skittered across the sky, darkening the sun, but bringing no relief from the suffocating heat. He glanced up to the cliffside. The terms were clear, no magical intervention. Across the field, Gombal was approaching, wearing a breastplate so highly polished that the clouds were a mercy, for the sun reflecting from it would have been blinding.

Conn turned back to look at his own force, mostly Mendian, along with what remained of Ermessen's knights and a surprising number of commoners who had appeared from nowhere, armed mostly with scythes and pitchforks. The Mage-Kings, apparently, were less than popular with the people they ruled. In contrast, Gombal's army stood in intimidating rows, the knights mounted, swords in hand, shields at the ready. By the terms of their pact, those swords should not be wielded. No blood would spill on this ground today save his own, one way or another.

"Go on," Malen said, raising her hand to stroke his cheek. "Don't think too much, just fight."

"I guess whatever's meant to be will happen," Conn said, picking up his helm. "Funny how those Rules of Submission keep rolling around my head."

"No. Not submission, not fate. Despite the teachings of my people, nothing is cast in stone. Not even the things I see are fated—they're just possible outcomes. You choose. Now go. I'll be waiting." And she kissed him, her lips finding his with the same amazing accuracy with which she performed any task.

It was the first time Malen had shown him any affection beyond what she displayed to others, though over the past weeks Conn had come to care deeply for her, and it warmed him in a way that was far more pleasant than the summer's heat. And far more distracting. He banished the thought of her, pulled the helm down over his head, blotting out sound and restricting sight, and started forward.

Malen allowed her mind to flow free, seeing the battlefield as from the eye of a raven encircling it. Already the birds were gathering; they seemed to instinctively associate mass numbers of knights with feast, but this fight should prove poor fare indeed. She watched, as if in a dream, as Conn and Gombal circled, heard their breathing, harsh and fast as they closed, swords swinging, shields rising and falling to block, both young, both strong, relentless arms raining blows on opponents. Conn had nobility of purpose, Gombal a lifetime of training, and both were fighting for their lives.

She gasped as Gombal landed a blow on Conn's leg that caught where the armor gapped and first blood was spilled. Then Conn, using his sword as a hammer, battered and bruised Gombal's shield arm till the sickening crack of bone snapping sent Gombal reeling back, and Malen felt the pain in him.

She was not the only one who saw it, felt it. Above them, on the cliffside, the greycloaks stirred and the wind stirred with them, the air grew thick with the promise of lightning and the rumble of thunder rolled over the valley. Whether it was their magic imbuing Gombal with strength or sheer desperation, the prince abandoned his shield, ignored his pain and redoubled his attack, dodging and weaving, using every trick of footwork that a legion of teachers had drilled into him, putting Conn on the defensive.

Beside her, screams ripped from unsuspecting throats; the lightning had come, blasting amidst the line of Conn's troops, sending ten and twenty men to their deaths at once. Word given or no, the greycloaks had entered the battle.

Every muscle screaming in protest, Conn forced himself to lift the shield, to swing the sword, to focus on the center of his opponent's body as he'd been taught, to anticipate where Gombal would strike next. When the screams began, he looked back just long enough for his brother to land another blow, this one on his sword arm. The impact sent him reeling, numbing his arm, and he felt blood trickling inside his armor, which was, when it came down to it, mostly hardened leather with only elbows, knees and helm of steel.

"You gave your word!" His voice was muffled by the helm, which was growing increasingly close.

"My word? My word to a traitor, a usurper? You stand there with a stolen king's sword, but it won't save you, *brother.* You will die and your forces with you to the last man. My kingdom will know peace." There was ragged pain in Gombal's voice too, and his left arm hung a-kilter; they were both tiring.

"The peace of the grave for you," Conn said, but Gombal's sword came down and caught his left shoulder, knocking the shield from his hand. Behind him thunder crashed, followed by screams as magic took its toll. A light rain began to fall over the fields, slicking the grass beneath his boots.

"Only one Mage-King, brother, only one!" Gombal backed away, preparing for a new offensive, and suddenly, as though a great lamp had been lit illuminating the darkness, Conn saw the way out. The traditions of the royal house led to nothing but death. If there was to be sacrifice, let it be his. His choice was clear.

"Yes, my brother," he whispered, steeling himself for the blow. "Only one." And his sword came down, not to strike Gombal, but his own shield hand, tearing through flesh and bone and ligament in a roaring fire of pain that sent him staggering back. And yet, through the pain came something else, something new. An awareness that had not been present before.

He could *see* his blood vessels, see each miniscule particle of the blood surging from his body, and by reaching out his mind, he could stop the flow, could knit healing skin over bare bone, could turn off his pain as though snuffing out a candle. The ground, too, was suddenly more than ground, it was a living entity, with water deep below it, the river which had once flowed in this place, now hidden deep away, but not beyond his reach. At his thought, the ground moved aside, cutting a chasm behind Gombal, isolating him from his men.

Gombal. The prince was up, his visor pushed back, staring around him in utter disbelief. The greycloaks were enraged; Conn could feel them reaching into the sky, preparing to draw power from the sun itself as they stood upon their refuge of rocky cliff. Rock. Rock solid, rock steady, but rock was not solid, not really. It was full of tiny cracks and crevasses, faults that were and faults that could be, and as Conn's awareness traveled into the heart of the stone, forcing cracks wider, the high cliff began to shake and slide.

Far across the field, Gombal's knights looked up at the sound, then spurred their horses forward as the cliff came tumbling down, burying the greycloaks in a pile of rock and rubble. Instantly, the lightning ceased, the thunder stilled, though the rain kept falling, harder now. Conn pulled his own helmet off awkwardly with one hand, looking not at Gombal still standing there, sword in hand, but at the dust settling across the field where the cliff once was. He heard the cheers of his own force, and restless muttering from Gombal's troops. In the center of the line, one knight broke loose and began to cross the field in a slow canter. His muscular warhorse took the chasm separating the force from the prince with ease.

"Kill me," Gombal said. "You've got a king's sword and a king's power, now kill me and finish it. If you can." His sword was up, his face implacable.

"No. I won't kill you, brother. There must be a way we can live together in some kind of peace."

Out of the corner of his eye, Conn saw a man dismounting, and his heart sank. General Berenger. He knew he could use magic against him, but that was not how he wanted to live, to rule. He took this power to save his friends and followers, but he would never use it again, not even to save his own life.

"No peace between us," Gombal said, and raised his sword to charge.

Conn lifted the sword of Andreu to block a blow that never landed. Gombal jerked backwards, a knife flashed out and a waterfall of blood arched up from his throat. His body fell to the ground in a heap of armor and blood, and General Berenger dropped to his knees before Conn, helm cast aside, golden head bowed.

"Majesty, I am your man if you'll have me."

"General, I would be honored." He reached out and helped the man to his feet. This was how peace would be built. On forgiveness and friendship, not on magic. Never again would any man or woman pay magic's price. On that, Conn was resolved.

Nicole Cardiff has been reading fantasy and science fiction novels almost since she can remember. A native of Florida, she received her BFA from the Savannah College of Art and Design in illustration in 2005, and began her freelance illustration career shortly after graduating. She was one of the few students to do all-digital work at the time, and now does a range of professional work from collectible card games to covers, and has a long list of game credits to her name. Primarily working for Wizards of the Coast and Sony Online, she loves illustrating stories of all kinds. She is currently based out of Burbank, CA with her fiancé, and she still reads every chance she gets.

You can find more of her work at www.artofnicolecardiff.com.

David B. Coe is the author of eleven fantasy novels and the occasional short story. His LonTobyn Chronicle received the IAFA Crawford Fantasy Award for best work by a new author, and the five volumes of Winds of the Forelands have received critical acclaim. His latest novel, *The Dark-Eyes' War*, a February 2010 release from Tor Books, is the third and final volume in his Blood of the Southlands trilogy, which began with *The Sorcerers' Plague* and *The Horsemen's Gambit*. David is currently working on several new projects. His novels have been translated into more than half a dozen languages.

David is also part of the Magical Words group blog (www.magicalwords.net), a site devoted to discussions of the craft and business of writing fantasy. He has a Ph.D. in environmental history. Visit him at www.DavidBCoe.com.

Jay Lake lives in Portland, Oregon, where he works on numerous writing and editing projects. His 2010 books are *Pinion* from Tor Books, *The Baby Killers* from PS Publishing, and *The Sky That Wraps* from Subterranean Press. His short fiction appears regularly in literary and genre markets worldwide. Jay is a winner of the John W. Campbell Award for Best New Writer, and a multiple nominee for the Hugo and World Fantasy Awards.

Gerard Houarner fell to Earth in the fifties and is a product of the NYC school system and the City College of New York, where he studied writing under Joseph Heller and Joel Oppenheimer and crashed hallucinogenic William Burroughs seminars back in the day. He went on to earn a couple of Masters degrees in psychology from Columbia University so he could earn a living. That living has taken him to Hells Kitchen, the Lower East Side at the beginning of the AIDS epidemic, and in the Bronx at the start of the crack epidemic. His latest collection, *A Blood of Killers*, is available now, as is his latest novel, *Road from Hell.* Still out there and receiving positive reviews is *The Oz Suite*, a mini-collection of dark interpretations of Oz stories and myths. For more information and the latest news, visit www.gerardhouarner.com.

K. L. Van der Veer lives in Connecticut. For him, fantasy isn't just another genre, it is the mythos of the modern world. He believes that through the magic and adventure of stories, authors become guides on a journey to unlock the mysteries of an inner realm guarded by fearsome specters of our own making. His interest in fantasy has led him to join Fantasy and Legends Organization, where he works to bring the light of imagination to bear on our perceptions of reality. His fantasist philosophy: Everyone who revels in the forest has elf-nature. Everyone who would right an injustice has paladin-nature. To dream and imagine is to awaken the miraculous power of creation within us. It is the grail, and if we would bring that magic to life, we must drink of our creative spirit and greet each dawn with the words, "Today, I will change the world . . ."

William Jones has received Bram Stoker Award, International Horror Guild Award, and Origins Award nominations for his works. He is the editor of several fiction anthologies, including *The Anthology of Dark Wisdom: The Best of Dark Fiction*, *Frontier Cthulhu: Ancient Horrors in the New World*, *High Seas Cthulhu*, and the Horrors Beyond series. His book, *The Strange Cases of Rudolph Pearson* was selected by editor Ellen Datlow as a "seminal" work for readers of Lovecraftian horror. He also has written a number role-playing game supplements, and his writings have been translated into several languages. His most recent novel is *Pallid Light: The Waking Dead.* When not writing, he rambles on his website: williamsramblings.blogspot.com. He lives in Michigan.

Visit William Jones on the Internet at www.williamjoneswriter.com and through his Twitter account: rudolphpearson.

Peter Andrew Smith lives and writes fiction in a small town on the East Coast of Canada. He shares his life with his patient wife Meredith and two small dogs who are constantly watching the property line to ensure there are no mystical or mundane invasions. Peter's recent and older publications are listed on his website at www.peterandrewsmith.com.

Ian McHugh is a 2006 graduate of the Clarion West writers' workshop and the 2008 grand prize winner in the Writers of the Future contest. He has sold stories to markets including *Asimov's*, *Beneath Ceaseless Skies*, *Greatest Uncommon Denominator*, *Andromeda Spaceways Inflight Magazine*, *Pseudopod* and the anthologies *Clockwork Phoenix 2* and *Twenty Epics*. For a full list of Ian's past and forthcoming publications, and to read and hear his stories available free online, visit ianmchugh.wordpress.com.

Aliette de Bodard lives in Paris, where she holds a job as a computer engineer. Her short fiction has appeared or is forthcoming in *Realms of Fantasy*, *Interzone*, and *Orson Scott Card's Intergalactic Medicine Show*. She is a Campbell Award finalist for 2009. Visit www.aliettedebodard.com for more information.

James Maxey is the author of the Dragon Age trilogy, consisting of the novels *Bitterwood*, *Dragonforge*, and *Dragonseed*. His short fiction has appeared in *Asimov's*, *Orson Scott Card's Intergalactic Medicine Show*, and numerous anthologies. More information about his writing can be found at dragonprophet.blogspot.com.

R. W. Day has been writing since she figured out which end of her crayon was up. She's sold a dozen or so stories to various markets, including *Cabinet des Fees*, *The Town Drunk*, and *Fictitious Force*. Her first novel, *A Strong and Sudden Thaw*, was shortlisted for the 2006 Lambda Award for SF/Fantasy/Horror and has recently been re-released in a new edition from Lethe Press. She lives in Portsmouth, Virginia and works for a local law library. Find out more at rwday.wordpress.com.

W. H. Horner is publisher and editor-in-chief of Fantasist Enterprises, an independent publishing house specializing in fantasy and horror short fiction anthologies, novels, art, and music. His passion is publishing works that bridge the gap between cookie-cutter genre fiction and high literary art, as well as exploring the places in between genre specifications. He holds a BA in English and a MA in Writing Popular Fiction. William is an adjunct faculty mentor with Seton Hill University's MFA in Writing Popular Fiction program. He is also the founder and director of the First Writes, a writing group that meets in Wilmington, Delaware. For more information about William and his freelance editorial and design services, please visit www.whhorner.com, and to learn more about his projects with Fantasist Enterprises, please go to www.fantasistent.com.

Fleeing from what should have been a perfect crime, four crooks in a black Mustang race into the Pennsylvania highlands. On the backseat, a briefcase full of cash. On their tail, a tattooed madman who wants them dead.

The driver calls himself Axle. A local boy, he knows the landscape, the coal-hauling roads and steep trails that lead to the perfect hideout: the crater of an abandoned mine. But Axle fears the crater. Terrible things happened there. Things that he has spent years trying to forget.

Enter Kwetis, the nightflyer, a specter from Axle's ancestral past. Part memory, part nightmare, Kwetis has planned a heist of his own. And soon Axle, his partners in crime, and their pursuer will learn that their arrival at the mine was foretold long ago . . . and that each of them is a piece of a plan devised by the spirits of the Earth.

A finalist for the 2009 Eric Hoffer Award.

Nominated for the 2009 Black Quill Award for Best Small-Press Chill.

Appeared on the Preliminary Ballot for the 2008 Bram Stoker Award for Superior Achievement in a First Novel.

Trade Paperback • 260 Pages • 8 Illustrations • $15.00
ISBN 13: 978-1-934571-00-2 • ISBN 10: 1-934571-00-8

www.VeinsTheNovel.com | www.FantasistEnt.com

Fasten your seatbelts and prepare to take your reading experience to a whole new level. With *Veins: The Soundtrack*, author and musician Lawrence C. Connolly provides a series of instrumental soundscapes inspired by themes and scenes from his critically acclaimed supernatural thriller *Veins*. Performing with his band, Connolly delivers a mix of trance, rock, and ambient compositions designed to complement the novel.

The CD also includes two music and spoken-word bonus tracks, each showcasing a complete story from *Visions*, "Aberrations" and "Echoes."

Packaged with Star E. Olson's distinctive cover art and including a synopsis and full production credits, *Veins: The Soundtrack* is a must for every dark fantasy reader.

Read the book. Hear the soundtrack. Enter a world where fantasy lives.

6 Tracks & 2 Bonus Tracks • Total Run Time: 38:13 • $10.00
UPC: 700261267371 • ID#: FE-934571-00-2

Polish your cutlass and prepare your spells for what awaits on a journey across leagues of unimaginable adventure. Ride the waves to mystery and magic.

Featuring 28 stories of mermaids, pirates, and magic beyond your wildest dreams, including tales by Danielle Ackley-McPhail and Patrick Thomas, and an introduction by Lawrence C. Connolly, *Sails & Sorcery* is beautifully illustrated by Julie Dillon.

Trade Paperback • 456 Pages
28 Stories • 42 Illustrations • $23.00
ISBN 13: 978-0-9713608-9-1 • ISBN 10: 0-9713608-9-8

www.FEBooks.net

Magic surrounds us. The Enlightenment did not kill it with science, nor did the Industrial Revolution extinguish it with mechanation. Elves may feel cramped in the big city, but they get by. The wild lands disappear, but werewolves still find time to hunt, though with care.

Explore 26 worlds of mystery, wonder, danger, and horror in *Modern Magic*. You may find them to be not unlike the world in which you live.

Trade Paperback • 280 Pages
26 Stories • 35 Illustrations • $17.00
ISBN 13: 978-0-9713608-4-6 • ISBN 10: 0-9713608-4-7

The Fantastical Visions series features selections of stories that explore the sub-genres of fantasy.

Young men and women struggle to find their places in worlds harsh and beautiful. Lives are changed as people grapple with relationships and the consequences of their decisions. Greed and cunning are sometimes punished, and sometimes rewarded. Sometimes it is better to give than to receive, and sometimes a gift can be a curse.

Eighteen works of modern myth explore the many facets of the human condition, taking the reader on an emotional journey through fantastic landscapes.

Trade Paperback • 308 Pages
18 Stories • 27 Illustrations •$17.00
ISBN 13: 978-0-9713608-7-7
ISBN 10: 0-9713608-7-1

Featuring the art of Stephanie Pui-Mun Law

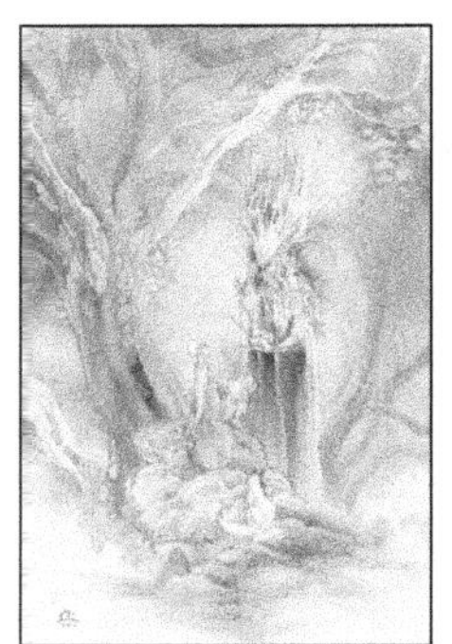

www.ingramcontent.com/pod-product-compliance
Lightning Source LLC
LaVergne TN
LVHW010054110826
845155LV00028B/334

* 9 7 8 1 9 3 4 5 7 1 0 2 6 *